Praise for Lulu Taylor

'Absorbing, compelling and completely unputdownable,
every Lulu Taylor novel grips you to the very end'
Lisa Jewell

'I love Lulu Taylor's enchanting novels – captivating stories
that keep me hooked until the final page!'
Veronica Henry

'I raced through this gripping tale about secrets
and lies and long-buried emotions bubbling
explosively to the surface'
Daily Mail

'Wonderfully written . . . this indulgent
read is totally irresistible'
Closer

'This is a fantastic, all-consuming read'
Heat

'Utterly compelling. A really excellent winter's story'
Lucy Diamond

A Legacy of Secrets

Lulu Taylor is the author of fifteen novels including six *Sunday Times* bestsellers. Her first novel, *Heiresses*, was nominated for the RNA Readers' Choice award and *The Last Song of Winter* won the RNA's Historical Romantic Novel Award. Lulu lives in Dorset where she continues to find inspiration for her stories of families, secrets and the mysteries of the past.

A Legacy of Secrets

LULU TAYLOR

PAN BOOKS

First published 2025 by Pan Books
an imprint of Pan Macmillan
The Smithson, 6 Briset Street, London EC1M 5NR
EU representative: Macmillan Publishers Ireland Ltd, 1st Floor,
The Liffey Trust Centre, 117–126 Sheriff Street Upper,
Dublin 1 D01 YC43
Associated companies throughout the world

ISBN 978-1-0350-8620-7

1 3 5 7 9 8 6 4 2

A CIP catalogue record for this book is available from the British Library.

Typeset in 10.5/15pt Sabon LT Std by Six Red Marbles UK, Thetford, Norfolk
Printed and bound in the UK using 100% Renewable Electricity by CPI Group (UK) Ltd

MIX
Paper | Supporting
responsible forestry
FSC
www.fsc.org   FSC® C116313

Visit **www.panmacmillan.com** to read more about
all our books and to buy them.

To my daughter, Tabby

Prologue
June 1952

Caundle Court was dressed for a party and, against the summer night sky, it looked quite magical. The windows were ablaze with light from glittering chandeliers. Small square golden lanterns glowed from the gate along the drive that curved past a field of cattle on one side and the old cricket pitch and rackety pavilion on the other. At its end was Caundle, once a priory and now a grand residence, noted for the many chimneys in decorative dark red brick laid in intricate lattice shapes, and the great mullioned windows at the front softened by the blooms of lilac wisteria that dropped around them. The house looked splendid in its party finery, but the cloak of night hid how much of it was distinctly shabby.

The fact of this ramshackle quality was something that kept village gossips very busy.

'How can such a rich family keep their house in such a state?' women would ask one another in the post office in Caundle Parva, or over crumpets in the tea room. 'It's out of character for *her*, isn't it?'

After all, Gloria Templeton, the chatelaine of Caundle

Court, was a member of the absurdly rich and glamorous Carrington family. But the thing was, you could be a rich Carrington or a poor Carrington – relatively – depending on the side of the family to which you belonged.

The bankers were dripping in gold. The landed farmer Carringtons were still fabulously well off but not so much as the banking Carringtons. Gloria Templeton was on the banking side, so they could not understand why it was not a matter of pride for her to keep the house looking magnificent.

'Ever since the major's plane went down – so very unlucky, poor man, so missed – she's hardly ever been here,' the local ladies would say a little indignantly.

Everyone agreed it was a shame that the big house was left so unattended when it ought to be playing a proper role in village life. The word was that Mrs Templeton had a very fine house in London, and even entertained the royal family. So why let poor Caundle fall into such a state?

The villagers were hopeful that things were about to change. And plenty of Carrington money had been spent tonight in honour of the birthday party celebrating the coming-of-age of the heir to the house, Brinsley Templeton. He would take possession of the place now that he'd attained his majority, and perhaps he would restore it to a glory it once knew, in the days of the major's parents and those of the ancestors whose marble tombs adorned the church.

Everyone seems to have forgotten that it is also my *birthday.*

Felicity Templeton stood in front of the cheval glass in her bedroom, inspecting her reflection. She was wearing a green satin evening dress with a full skirt and slim shoulder straps, and, she thought, it suited her. Her pearls gleamed at her neck and ears.

Eighteen today. A woman. Am I pretty? He *said I am.* He *said I'm beautiful.*

She pushed that thought out of her mind. There was no point in thinking about him. That was all over.

Pretty or not, there was no doubt that she drew the eye with her startling looks: the fine, fly-away dark blonde hair, elfin chin and extremely large, round blue eyes. They were certainly striking but could sometimes look too much, too huge, too round, as though she was a little deformed. At least, that was what her younger sister said. Prudence claimed that it was Felicity's swollen brain that made her eyes so huge. 'Popping from your head like a frog's with the pressure of all those thoughts of yours.'

Felicity would usually try to thwack her for this, but she didn't mind too much the idea that she was bursting with intellect. Her father had called her the Little Thinker.

'Something in those eyes of yours, Flick, tells me you feel things very much,' he'd once said, looking unusually serious. 'Just be careful, my dear. Try not to let yourself be hurt.'

How would one try that? Surely no one chose to be hurt? Besides, it was too late by then anyway. And not long after, Father did the most hurtful thing he could do by dying, after the war had ended when they had all thought he was safe.

Flick thought of her father now, as she pressed her lips together one final time. Red lipstick made them slick, and she had kholed her huge eyes and made her lashes stand stiff and straight with black mascara. *Do I look like a clown, or a beauty? It's so hard to tell. Mother must think she looks wonderful, and what a fright she is. Perhaps I look like neither.* She sighed. *What would Father make of all this fuss?*

She recalled lots of parties when he was alive so perhaps he would have enjoyed this evening. And he would certainly have made sure that everyone remembered it was also Flick's birthday just as much as Brinsley's.

There had been a gift for her that morning, wrapped in silver tissue and waiting by her plate at the breakfast table. Urged by her mother, Flick had opened it to find a long black jewel case, and in it a three-stranded pearl necklace with a pair of matching pearl drop earrings, each with a diamond as the stud. They were beautiful and appropriate for an eighteenth birthday, and Flick was pleased to get them and thanked her mother.

'I'll wear them tonight,' she promised.

But Gloria's attention was all on Brinsley, her pride and joy, whose pile of gifts included inherited items – cufflinks, a signet ring, dress studs – as well as a very fine watch that was quite new.

'It could be worse,' Prue muttered to her. 'And it's a very pretty necklace, though I can't see you wearing it much.'

But it *was* worse. One of Brinsley's packages included the key to a fine new Austin motorcar that sat on the driveway outside.

'What do you think, Brinny? Do you like it?' demanded

Gloria, as they all stood at the window of the breakfast room, admiring it. She clasped her son to her very large bosom and hugged him tightly.

'Yes, of course, Mother, thank you.' But even placid Brinsley looked exasperated. He had never wanted a car and had no idea how to drive one. He had always been ferried everywhere on account of his ankles, and seemed to expect that would simply continue. After all, there were motors and drivers available to him. Flick would have loved such a present, much more than a necklace, and at once wondered if there was some way she could trade with Brinsley so she took possession of his smart car.

But perhaps I don't need to. After all, I am supposed to be coming into my inheritance, according to Mother.

Gloria had long dangled the promise of future riches in front of the children, and the time had come when the twins were supposed to receive at least some of their inheritance. But Gloria had now gone quiet on the subject.

The bedroom door opened and Prue put her head around it. 'Come on, Flick, it's all kicking off and you know she wants you on parade. You're needed on the meet and greet, so get a move on!'

The noise from downstairs floated through the open door: the buzz of voices and the sound of the string quartet playing in the hall.

'All right, I'm coming.'

Prue disappeared, and Flick took a deep breath. The party was just something to get through. At least it would keep her mind off things. And then, very soon, it would be back to

Oxford and relative freedom. Away from the suffocating presence of her mother, at least.

The sooner, the better.

Flick came slowly down the main stairs of Caundle Court, moving carefully in her unfamiliar satin pumps. A great crystal chandelier hung in the hall, suspended from the intricate plasterwork ceiling, its twelve curved arms glittering like a spider's web on a frosty morning. Flick's satin dress shimmered as she reached the black-and-white marbled floor of the hall. At the bottom of the stairs was a copy of Canova's famous sculpture of *The Three Graces*, brought back by some Templeton ancestor in the nineteenth century as a memento of his travels. The sculpture had been sent over from Italy, packed for protection in the dense leafy branches of the Mediterranean ilex, but even so, Euphrosyne had lost a little finger on the journey, and her sister Thalia had cracked a heel. Only Aglaea remained untouched.

In front of the sculpture was the string quartet, valiantly playing Mozart against the growing murmur of the crowd.

I hope the Graces are enjoying this, Flick thought. *After all, they are supposed to preside over parties for the gods.*

She felt proud of this educated thought, and then deflated that there was no one to share it with, or to care one way or the other.

'There you are!' cried her mother as she spotted Flick. 'Come here at once, the Harrison-Gowers have just arrived. Isn't it too lovely?'

Flick went over obediently, nodding to accept the birthday

wishes from guests as she went. She had picked up the faint-est whiff of condescension from her mother, who famously thought most of the local families to be bumpkins. One of her favourite things was to mutter 'Infra dig!' with a satisfied sigh on hearing the names of her neighbours. They were below her dignity.

And how she can think that, looking the way she does, Flick thought, going to stand by her mother. Gloria was swathed in a gown of canary-yellow chiffon trimmed with frothy fronds of yellow swansdown around her shoulders. Bright yellow ostrich feathers nodded in her intricately curled red-brown hair. And if that was not enough, a huge necklace of diamonds and yellow sapphires sparkled around her neck, with more jewels dangling from her ears.

Prue came gliding up from a knot of guests to take her place beside Flick. 'Does she think she's a chicken?' she whispered to her sister.

Flick giggled. 'A chicken or a dandelion.'

They were used to their mother's ways. Everything she wore verged on fancy dress. She yearned to be the centre of attention at all times and used any method she could to make sure of it, not least the vast amounts of make-up she wore. Gloria had been a beauty once, or so she said, and her por-traits seemed to show a fierce, pale-skinned, red-haired prettiness. That was all lost now beneath layers of founda-tion, powder and rouge, the blue eyeshadow and the bright red lipstick she favoured. She was tall too, and wore the highest heels she could manage, so that she towered over nearly everyone.

Beside her, the three children looked washed out and certainly overshadowed.

Flick caught her brother's eye but it was hard to read his expression behind his spectacles. She smiled at him and saw the ghost of a smile back. She always felt she had failed as a twin. She ought to know Brinsley better than anyone in the world and yet she felt he was still a stranger to her.

Gloria leaned down to whisper to Flick: 'Stand up straight, darling! You look like a miserable hunchback.' She sighed happily. 'Oh, I feel wonderful. It ought to be a party for me really, don't you think?'

'Yes, Mother,' Flick said obediently.

Gloria scanned the room again and gasped. 'Now there is the Morfield boy. Henry. Such a lovely young man. I'm told their house in Cornwall is very fine indeed! I'm sure he wants to talk to you, Felicity.' Gloria put a hand to her daughter's back and pushed her. 'Go and say hello.'

'I thought you wanted me here . . .'

'I don't now. Go and talk to him. He'll be excellent practice. I'm worried you haven't got a clue how to flirt.'

Flick looked across the room at Henry Morfield. He was quite good-looking with a clever, sophisticated air. At least he wasn't like so many of the others: pink-faced and nervous, in conversation with other gawky young men just like them. They looked smart in their white tie but so young, and they talked only of hunting, horses and dogs. Tedious beyond belief.

'Go on!' hissed Gloria, and she delivered a sharp push to Flick's lower back that sent her off across the marble floor.

She had no desire to talk to Henry Morfield, no matter how good-looking or how fine his house, because she was in love with someone else and so there was no point. But she knew better than to disobey Gloria so she walked slowly towards him, wondering what to say. Passing the library door, she was startled to be grabbed by the arm and pulled inside.

'You can thank me later,' said a sardonic voice, and the light flicked on to show her very handsome cousin Edmund grinning at her. He looked typically elegant in a perfectly cut tailcoat and white tie, though he'd added a flourish of his own with a green-and-purple silk paisley scarf. His dark blond hair dropped winningly over one eye, making him look even more rakish than usual. 'Want a drink? We've got some vodka.'

Diana stepped out of the shadows holding a bottle and a couple of glasses.

'You're here!' Flick exclaimed, rushing to hug her friend as best she could around the bottle. 'Thank you for coming.'

'I wouldn't miss it.' Diana smiled. 'I've been spending the last few days at Carrington Towers with this reprobate.'

'Carrington Towers.' Edmund rolled his eyes. 'My parents would have fifty screaming fits if they heard you calling their precious house that.'

Diana gave him a mischievous look. 'I know.'

'You look ravishing,' Flick said, admiring the red silk dress that hugged all of Diana's very fine curves. While Flick was flat-chested and slim, Diana had a ripe bosom and bottom and a wasp waist between, a figure she showed off to its fullest advantage at all times. She had dark brown hair, almond-shaped brown eyes and a small mole on her cheek that looked like the most perfectly placed beauty spot. No wonder Edmund had not been able to resist her for long.

Diana dangled the glasses at her impishly. 'So . . . fancy a drink then?'

'Would I? Yes please.'

Diana poured out some generous measures. 'No ice, sorry, darling. No lemon. Nothing to put in it either.'

'It's just a sharpener,' Flick said, taking a glass. The vodka burned her throat as it went down. She hoped it would do its work quickly and give her the confidence she wanted so badly. 'Mother's supplied plenty of champagne.'

Edmund sat on the edge of the billiard table. 'It's filthy stuff. What's she thinking of?'

'That's just for the guests,' Flick said. 'Her Pol Roger is kept in a secret hiding place and refilled just for her.'

Edmund laughed. 'What a character she is. She's rich as Croesus. She could fill the fountains with Pol and not even notice the expense. And I'm quite offended she's not using the family vintage.'

'You know what she's like,' Flick said, taking another sip of the vodka.

Edmund nodded. 'Of course.'

Diana gave her a sympathetic look. 'I expect you can't wait to get back to Oxford.'

'Well . . .' Flick gave her a sad look. 'I don't know whether it's better to be miserable here, or miserable there.'

Diana laughed. 'Miserable *there*, darling! Every time!'

The library door opened and Prue appeared. 'There you are, Flick!'

'Yes. Don't you get bored being sent to look for me all the time?'

'I certainly do. But Mother is getting edgy about where you are.'

Flick put down her vodka. She could always come back to it later. She smoothed her dress and sighed. 'Once more unto the breach. I'll see you all later. Mother wants me to practise flirting, so off I go.'

'You'll be wonderful!' Diana called after her as she headed back into the party.

Henry Morfield was nowhere to be seen when Flick emerged, much to her relief. But when he did reappear, he seemed hell-bent on talking to her – no doubt encouraged by Gloria – so Flick ended up dodging him all night, even slipping into the dining room and adjusting the place names so that he was not on her left as her mother had planned.

Gloria must have noticed the switch when they all sat down, but it seemed she was too taken up with the aged earl on her left and Brinsley on her right to make a fuss, to Flick's relief. Flick talked to the vicar instead, enjoying watching him get slowly tipsier on her right, and to Edmund, whose name place she'd changed with Henry's, on her left.

She was mentioned – just – in her mother's fulsome tribute to Brinsley, and included in the birthday toast, but the focus of the evening was on her brother. Ironically, he loathed such attention, squinting away behind his spectacles. He had the same large blue eyes as his sister, but was much more myopic.

When the dinner at last was over, the dancing began. The party was in full flow, with everyone replete from the excellent food and relaxed from the fine selection of wine. Edmund and Diana took to the floor almost at once. *What a beautiful couple they make*, Flick thought. And no one was left under any illusion of how powerful their connection was. They danced so intently with one another, it was almost embarrassing to watch.

Her heart was swamped with loss. She'd had a taste of passion like that, and lost it. It was awful. It wasn't fair. Her broken heart would never mend, she was sure of it, and she would never, ever love anyone else.

Full of misery and longing, Flick darted into the darkened library, retrieved her glass of vodka, and let herself out of the French windows onto the terrace. She made her way along the gravel pathway between the formal knot garden all the way to the clover-shaped fountain at the very end which played gently in the cool night air.

Flick sat on the edge of the fountain, feeling the chill rising from the water, the stone cold through her silk dress. She pulled a silver case and matchbox from her pocket, extracted a cigarette from the case and lit it. Exhaling a stream of smoke, she gazed up at the stars.

I miss him. I miss him like crazy.

Crazy was the word. He *was* crazy – intense, melodramatic, capable of ridiculous cruelty and sublime passion. He seemed to have the key to life, and to understand how things worked on some extra-sensory level. His world was powerful and mad. He was disorganised, chaotic, rebellious, rude and yet utterly seductive. And he made *her* crazy. She barely knew who she was when she was with him. Perhaps that was part of the appeal.

But it was over. He had told her so that last night in Oxford, walking away in his dark greatcoat, leaving her weeping with only the tiniest crumb to pin her hopes on.

I just have to get on with it, she thought bleakly. *Even though my life is as good as over.*

The sound of footsteps on the gravel made her look up. Henry Morfield was walking down the gravelled path towards her, a cigarette held elegantly between his fingers. 'So there you are.'

He found me after all. I can hardly dash off now. I'll just have to grin and bear it.

She smiled as brightly as she could manage. 'So I am. I suppose my mother told you to come and find me.'

'I know she's keen for us to chat. But I am too. And I've been trying to pin you down all evening. You're very elusive.' He came up to her, his face still half hidden in the shadows, and sat down near her on the fountain's edge.

'I'm just getting some air,' she said lightly. 'It's so hot in there.'

'Oh yes, very,' he said easily. 'Don't you like to dance?'

'I do. But not tonight. It's too crowded.'

'It certainly is. But a lovely party.'

'Yes, lovely.'

13

Henry looked at her quizzically. 'Is something wrong? I sense you're not at all interested in talking to me.'

Flick pointed her cigarette at the fountain behind them. 'Do you see this fountain is clover-shaped? Like a shamrock. It ought to be good luck, don't you think? But it isn't. It's very bad luck. Once, after a party, they found a man floating in here, dead. In his evening clothes. He'd got completely blotto and must've fallen in and drowned. And while he floated there, the party went on, oblivious. Can you imagine?'

'That's very horrible. But I'm puzzled as to its relevance to us talking.'

Flick tossed the glowing end of her cigarette into the fountain where it was instantly extinguished. 'I know you want to talk to me. Get to know me. Perhaps even woo me a little. I'm sure I'm considered a decent catch with my money.'

'That is the last thing on my mind,' Henry said with a touch of embarrassment.

'Of course you're going to say that, and I'm sure it's very tasteless of me to mention it. But, honestly, I'm going to do you a favour. You don't want to get involved with my family. We're bad luck. It all seems so wonderful, but I promise, there's some sort of curse on this family. We're unlucky. If you marry me, I can guarantee that terrible things will happen. You'll be much better off with a sweet, ordinary girl who just wants to get married and live a life doing the ordinary things that you like, and who wants to raise an ordinary family. It's not like that with us. Can't you tell?'

'I'm afraid not. I'm not sure I'd be so happy with an

ordinary girl. You're interesting. Terribly pretty. Bright and amusing. Kind, too, I should think.'

'You're wrong,' she said obstinately. 'I'm not very nice at all. I'm selfish. Stubborn. Cross a lot of the time. I want so much more than I've got. Greedy, you see? I'd make your life a misery. Drive us both to drink.'

Henry laughed. 'If you want to put me off, you're not doing a very good job. You sound much more attractive now. Who could resist all this? A family curse, a headstrong beauty and plenty to drink as well.'

She half laughed too at his response. She couldn't help liking him despite herself. 'It's not just that. I love someone else.'

'Ah.' Henry shrugged. 'Now that *is* an obstacle to a budding romance. Who is the lucky fellow?'

'No one you know.'

'An unsuitable match, perhaps? Someone married? Or just unrequited? I'm sorry. That's painful, I'm sure.'

'It is. But I can't talk about it.' Flick sighed and stood up. 'I'm terribly sorry, you seem very nice, but it's just not a possibility between us. I hope you can see that.'

She walked away resolutely, returning the way she had come, back around the fountain and crunching down the gravel path. She fixed her eyes on the glimmer of her satin shoes, her spirits swooping again.

I'm destined to be alone, she thought gloomily. She believed every word she had said to Henry. People were better off without her. And her loneliness was not enough to make her compromise and accept something less than she wanted.

And the blessed party still isn't over.

There was the birthday cake to be cut, and hours to go before everyone left and there was some blessed peace again. And after that . . . well, she would face all that when she had to.

She went to step through the French windows back into the library when she was startled by a sudden hand on her arm, and a presence beside her. Gasping, she looked up at a dark shape silhouetted against the pale light on the terrace.

'Flick . . . I've found you.'

I know that voice. For a second, she was confused. Then, with a rush of joy, she knew exactly who it was, throwing herself into his arms and exclaiming, 'Oh Caius, you're here! I can't believe it. You're here.'

His arms were tight around her and his mouth by her ear. 'I told you I'd come and find you, didn't I?'

'Not exactly,' she said, half laughing and half tearful as he pulled her close. She knew the roughness of his black coat, the smell of tobacco, sweat and damp that permeated it. She loved that smell.

'I couldn't miss your birthday. You know that.'

'But . . . but . . .' Flick was full of happiness and confusion. 'You didn't want me!'

'My little darling, I asked you just to wait. Have you waited?' In the half-light on the terrace, Caius's dark eyes gazed down at her, tender and a little apprehensive. A lock of his dark hair, coal black, fell across one eyebrow just as she remembered.

'Of course! Of course I have.'

'You always knew I'd come to you, didn't you?'

'I didn't know, I wasn't sure.' She laughed with pleasure.

'I couldn't live without you, you know that, don't you?' He bent to kiss her, and she sank into the bliss of it. When they pulled apart at last, she sighed happily.

'Come in! You must come in to the party!'

'Are you sure?' He pulled back so that he could smile down at her.

'Yes!'

'Then it's lucky I borrowed these togs from a friend.' Caius took off his coat and revealed his white tie and tails. He looked unbearably handsome.

Joyful, Flick grabbed him by the hand and led him inside.

The night had transformed for her. Caius was back. Her handsome, talented, amazing lover had come to find her, just when she had given up hope. It had been so long – an agonising, heartbreaking wait – but he had returned on her birthday like a wish come true. He could not live without her, just as she had found life without him a grey trudge of despair. And oh, the joy of his presence: that magnetism of his, and his dark good looks. His clothes might be a touch shabby compared to the other rich young men at the party, but he outshone them by miles.

Edmund and Diana were astonished to see them together as he took her in his arms and whirled her around the dance

17

floor. When she was summoned to Gloria to prepare for the chorus of 'Happy Birthday' and the cutting of the magnificent pink-and-blue birthday cake on its silver stand, she took Caius with her.

'And who is this?' Gloria said coolly as Flick led him to her.

'My friend, Caius Knolle,' Flick said proudly. 'He is a very talented pianist.'

'Oh yes, of course. I know exactly who you are.' Gloria raised a painted eyebrow. 'How . . . interesting. I don't recall inviting you, Mr Knolle.'

Caius fixed her with an intense, dark gaze and smiled his most charming smile. He took her bejewelled hand, bowed over it and kissed it, murmuring, 'Enchanted, madam.' When he looked up at her, he said, 'I couldn't resist coming to see you. Gloria by name, and a vision of glory too.'

Gloria accepted the compliment with pleasure, softening as she shimmered in her canary-yellow splendour. 'Thank you, Mr Knolle. A little forward. But I forgive you. Come, Felicity. It's time to cut the cake.'

Flick didn't care now about being the afterthought. Caius had come back. That was all that mattered. The singing and the cake, the fireworks in the garden, all passed in a blur of excitement and happiness. This was how it was supposed to be.

When Caius kissed her in the darkness of the garden, concealed from the others by a box hedge, she almost melted with delight.

Gazing up at him in the light of the garden lanterns, under

the pops and explosions of the celebratory fireworks, she said, 'But why did you come back?'

'Like I said – because I discovered that I can't live without you. I tried and it was hopeless. Life was miserable. I realised that it's a terrible idea to be apart.'

Flick sighed. 'You can't think how I've missed you! It's been awful.' She felt whole again, as though the universe had been realigned into the right place at last. She clung to him and said impetuously, 'Let's go! Let's run away together. Let's get married.'

He laughed. 'Married? Well . . . I can think of nothing more lovely, darling. But do you realise how much you'll be giving up?' He waved back at the house. 'I can't give you anything like this, you know.'

'I don't care about that!' Flick said passionately.

'And won't your mother object?'

'She might at first. But you won her over beautifully tonight. She won't be able to resist you, just like me.'

'You know . . . you might be right, Pug. I think we'd be happy for ever,' Caius murmured. He kissed her again slowly.

When she surfaced from it, sighing with pleasure, she said, 'Then let's go. Now. I can pack quickly. We can slip away before anyone notices.'

He stared at her intently and said wonderingly, 'I think you actually might mean it. You'd really run away with a poor piano player like me?'

'Of course I would! I want to!' She had never been more certain of anything. 'There's nothing I want more. And I believe we can conquer the world together.'

He took her hand and looked at her intently. 'As long as you're sure.'

'I'm utterly sure.'

'Then I'll go to the car, it's on the drive. I borrowed that from a friend as well. I'll wait for you there.'

'I'll be there in ten minutes,' she said, before turning to hurry inside. On her way through the marble hall, she saw Henry Morfield, standing by *The Three Graces*, watching her as she hurried past and up the stairs to her room, his expression unreadable.

What did he matter now? She'd rather liked him but he was nothing compared to Caius.

She flew to her bedroom, to pull out her suitcase and begin to pack it with whatever she thought she might need. Then, grabbing her shawl, she hauled the case to the door, then paused to look back at her room.

It was so familiar. Here she had wept and dreamed and grown up. Now she was leaving Caundle for the biggest adventure of her life, and who knew when she'd ever be back?

There was no time to say goodbye to the others: to Brinny and Prudence, to Edmund and Diana. She couldn't risk being stopped or Caius changing his mind. They were going to be together for ever.

Flick closed the bedroom door behind her and hurried for the stairs.

Now it begins. Life.

At last.

PART ONE

Chapter One

ETTA

1991

There were certainly some advantages to having a lot of money at one's disposal, Etta thought, as she walked through the front door of what looked like a handsome townhouse on Wimpole Street, one of dozens that lined it. Only a discreet brass plaque gave away its name, and even then, no clue of what it did.

One advantage of money is being able to come to a place like this.

When she had first made enquiries about the test, she'd had a lot of off-putting replies telling her that she would need a legal process and various signed affidavits and all the rest of it. But money could smooth a lot of paths, and that was how she had ended up here, without all the faff that most people had to go through.

This was her second visit, and she had already handed over her credit card details several times. It was a costly business, private medicine. They practically charged you to answer the phone. Every appointment and every element was itemised and billed.

Who cares, it's worth it.

A well-groomed receptionist sat behind a smart desk. She was exactly the kind of girl Etta would expect to find in a place like this: private-school accent, blonde hair in a bob, a string of pearls at her neck, striped shirt and mini-skirt. She took Etta's name and then handed her a clipboard with forms on it.

'I think I filled these in last time I was here,' Etta said, frowning.

'Oh, we ask for them every time,' the receptionist said cheerfully. 'Just in case something changes.'

'Right.' *And a fresh charge each time.* Etta took the pen and board and went to sit on the turquoise sofa in the waiting room. Back she went through the questionnaire. Any health issues? No, no, no, no, no. She ticked all the negative boxes, grateful that she didn't have any of the nasty-sounding conditions they suggested might be a possibility. There were a couple of yeses. She drank a bit more than was strictly advisable. Yes, she was on the pill. What was her blood pressure? Who knew?

The receptionist was taking a call from her mother when Etta handed back the board, saying, 'Yes, Mumsie, you know I'm going to be home at the weekend, I can't miss Guppy's bash . . .'

Etta went back to sit down and wait her turn.

It was strange to think how much hinged on what she was about to do. It was everything and yet it was nothing. It would give her the answer to a mystery that had plagued her for years and yet, nothing at all would change as a result.

At least, I don't think so.

But knowledge could be dangerous as well as powerful. Perhaps it would change everything.

What do I want it to be?

She had asked herself dozens of times what she wanted, and the answer was always the same. It didn't matter because it wasn't about science and physical building blocks. It was about emotions, heart and love.

And that's why I already know the answer.

It wasn't that she needed to know. It was that others did. And she wanted to be able to give those answers, give some resolution and some peace. While there was still time.

She was called into the clinician's room bang on time – another advantage of being able to go private. It was a typical medical room – white walls, boxes of surgical gloves, medical waste bins, a desk and obvious modern technology: an extremely large, bulky computer sat on the desk – but very comfortable.

The young male clinician who sat in front of the desk greeted her as he gestured to her to take a seat.

'So what happens now?' Etta asked, preliminaries over.

'We collect your sample.'

'Will it hurt?'

'Not a bit. It's very straightforward. Just like a blood test. We'll take some blood samples from you.'

'Oh.' Etta raised her eyebrows. 'Is that all?'

The clinician nodded slowly and then said, 'But if you're

game, then I wonder if I could also take a cheek swab from you?'

'A swab?'

'Very simple procedure. I just rub a thing like a giant cotton bud inside your cheek. It picks up cells. We can analyse those cells and extract the information we need. It's not terribly reliable yet, but it's probably the future of this kind of test. If you don't mind, it would be useful to have both samples for the lab to look at.'

Etta shrugged. 'I don't mind at all.'

'Thanks. It will definitely help us develop our processes. Now, before we get started, can I ask you about the other samples?'

'Yes. That's all in hand. I have one sample here with me.'

'Okay, great. With all the necessary identification checks?'

'They're not necessary with this sample.'

'Okay.'

'The second sample will be taken here this week. There's an appointment booked, in any case.'

'Good, good. Again, make sure that all legal identification checks are carried out. It's no good without.'

Etta opened her handbag to take out the envelope she had brought with her. 'And we won't bother with the third sample.'

The clinician raised his eyebrows. 'There's a third?'

'Is that unusual?'

'Well . . . I don't mean to sound as if I'm judging, but it's more usually one, or sometimes two.'

'My family always likes to do things in an extravagant way.'

'The extra sample will add to the cost, I'm afraid . . .'

'That doesn't matter. This sample might be a bit trickier but you did say that you could test things other than blood . . . like hair.'

'We can. It's less accurate, but we can.'

'I think the process of elimination will help us in any case. If it's not one of the other two samples, then it must be this one. I think.'

'Perhaps I can throw another test in for free!' joked the clinician, then he quickly became serious. 'I apologise. I realise it's no joking matter.'

'Please, don't worry. I suppose it is quite a strange situation.' She took a sealed envelope out of her bag and handed it to the clinician. 'Here you are. It was all I could find.'

The clinician looked down at the envelope which Etta had carefully annotated. 'That's very good. Thank you. We'll do our best to get a result out of it, one way or another.' He looked up at her and smiled. 'Now, shall we get on and take your sample? It will only take a moment, and then you can be on your way.'

He was right, it took only a few minutes for the small glass test tubes to be filled with Etta's dark ruby blood. She watched the samples being sealed, and the clinician writing on the little labels in biro.

The cheek swab had been the work of a second or two,

and the giant cotton bud was in its own sealed plastic bag as well, waiting to be put in an envelope.

'They can all go off to the lab,' he said cheerfully, 'and you can leave now, if you like. Have you done all your identity checks?'

'Oh yes, I did that last time.'

'Good. So if you can just check in with Sophie at the desk on your way out. She'll take payment for today.'

'Thank you,' Etta said, pulling her jacket back on. She couldn't even feel the place where the syringe had entered a vein. It was that quick and easy. 'And how long will it take before we get the results?'

'It will be a few weeks at least. We'll let you know.'

Etta felt a stab of anxiety. 'A few weeks?'

'Perhaps longer. It's a delicate and time-consuming process.'

'Is there any chance you can put a rush on this?'

'Is there an urgency? I thought that as this is private rather than court mandated . . .'

'I'm afraid it is rather urgent. You see, my mother isn't well. And I've promised her that I'll be able to tell her the truth sooner rather than later.'

The clinician blinked at her, evidently taken off guard again. 'Oh, I see. That sounds complicated.'

Etta smiled. She picked up her bag and prepared to head back to the reception. She turned to face the clinician one last time. 'I want this to be my gift to her. To be able to prove to her, once and for all, who my father is. I think it will be the thing that brings her peace.'

Chapter Two

FLICK

Autumn 1951

Was anyone ever so desperate to leave home?

Flick stood in her mother's lavish bedroom, staring at a large Louis Vuitton wardrobe trunk designed to transport ball dresses on transatlantic voyages.

'I found it terribly useful on the *Queen Mary*,' Gloria said, opening the trunk to show the two rails and the compartments behind. 'Look, space for shoes! Wonderful drawers for evening bags and furs. You're bound to have limited hanging space in that room in Oxford. You must take it, darling. I insist.'

Her mother was quite a sight in a white satin dressing gown, her hair in a high turban that concealed her hair rollers, and her face thick with cold cream.

Flick sighed. 'I'm not turning up with a giant trunk for my ball dresses. The other girls will hate me.'

Gloria looked doubtful under her cold cream mask. 'I don't see why. They're more likely to be your friends in my opinion. I'm afraid people like us attract friends like flies to a honey pot.' She shrugged. 'Whatever you wish. But you will need at least three ball dresses, won't you? And there are bound to be cocktail parties. Your dear father said it was one long round of parties when he was at Oxford.'

'I'm not *at* Oxford,' Flick said dryly. 'I'm at St Pandionia's School for Young Ladies. Brinny is at Oxford.'

'You'll be at all the parties, and that's nearly the same,' Gloria said brightly.

'Thank you, Mother, but I don't want the trunk. Do you mind if I finish packing?'

Flick went out of her mother's palatial bedroom, rolling her eyes and shaking her head in frustration.

Her mother made no secret of the fact that she believed wholeheartedly that it was entirely natural for Brinsley to be going to Magdalen College to read History, while Flick was bound for a finishing school in North Oxford where she would be taught all sorts of useful skills including planning menus, managing staff and how to get in and out of a motor-car in a pencil skirt and heels. It was ridiculous, considering that Flick was just as bright as Brinsley and devoured history books the way her friends gulped down novels and editions of *Vogue*. But the twins had different destinies, because Brinny was a boy and she, Flick, was a girl.

It was unfair. But as Brinny had said when they talked it over, going to finishing school was at least her way out of home. There would be a life beyond it, and who knew what opportunities it would bring.

And then there was the inheritance.

Gloria had declared that Flick would receive a substantial inheritance on her eighteenth birthday.

'It will help you make the kind of marriage I want for you,' Gloria had said firmly. 'You're lucky you don't have to bother with studying, like some poor bluestocking bound to be a teacher or a governess or something awful like that. And I hope that you won't make my mistake and settle for *this*.' Gloria had flung her arms outwards, as though Caundle Court, with its hundred rooms and acres of grounds, was no more than a hovel. 'Your father was many excellent things, but the truth is that I married down. I don't want that for you, my darling! Life is so much nicer at the very top, I promise you that.'

Flick had wanted to laugh. Her mother was a terrible snob and made no effort to hide it. Flick half suspected that the dishevelled state of the house had been a sort of revenge on Father for not being a richer, more important and titled catch. Gloria had loved him, Flick was sure of that, but she couldn't forgive Philip for being the love of her life and yet not the man of her dreams. Caundle had suffered and the children had suffered as a result. No one would credit the conditions that Brinsley, Flick and Prue had endured growing up, not with the money in their mother's background.

Some of that had been pure neglect. Gloria always found it hard to remember things and people that were not right in front of her.

As Flick walked down the hall, Prue came out of her room. She slumped in the doorway, looking wan and gloomy.

'Cheer up,' Flick said as she went past. 'You're going to be an only child soon.'

'How can you say that?' Prue drifted after her. 'You're going to leave me alone with her! How can you?'

'Survival of the oldest. You'll be perfectly all right.'

Prue followed Flick into her bedroom and threw herself down on the bed, displacing several silk cushions. 'It's the end of my life!' She picked up a lace-edged pillow and put it over her face. From underneath, her muffled voice emerged. 'I want to die!'

Flick laughed, picking up a pile of folded jumpers from the floor and pressing them into her suitcase. Prue had definitely inherited their mother's taste for drama. 'Don't be silly. You might enjoy it.'

Prue took off the pillow and sat up, opening her blue eyes. She was like her older sister, but, Flick thought, much prettier in a conventional way. Her eyes weren't as big and round, and her hair was naturally curly and much more amenable to being rolled into fashionable shapes. Flick's straight hair could be put in rollers, but the curls dropped quickly unless she soaked them in setting fluid, but she hated the hard, crispy hair that resulted even if the curls lasted days.

'I am not going to enjoy it,' Prue said firmly. 'I will either be here on my own – and you know Mother won't stick around for long once you and Brinny have gone – or I'll have to go with her to London.'

'You could stay with a friend? Your chum Joan seems very nice. And her family is sane, I should think.'

Prue sighed. 'Perhaps that's the only way.'

'Or stay with the cousins. There's always Vivienne. She'd love to have you with them.'

Prue nodded. 'Anything would be better.'

'You'll be sent off to ghastly finishing school yourself quite soon. Mother will make you do the awful London rounds. Parties. Balls.'

'I think it sounds quite fun,' Prue said, brightening.

'It's really not. But you might enjoy it more than I did.' Flick lost patience and crammed the rest of her things willy-nilly into her case, threw some shoes in on top, and forced the case closed, clicking the catches into place. 'Right.' She stood up. 'Let's see – books and papers. Cases packed. I think I'm just about ready to go.'

'Oh!' wailed Prue, throwing herself back down again. 'Don't go, don't go!'

Flick went over to her sister, sat down and put a calming hand on her arm. 'Cheer up, Prue. Think of this as the spur you need to change things. And maybe life in London with Mother wouldn't be so bad – all the galleries and museums and things to do and see. And you can always come to Oxford to visit. I shouldn't think I'll have much to do there. We can go to the Botanic Gardens or something.'

'All right.' Prue sniffed and looked up. 'If you're really determined to leave me here, then I suppose I'd better come and wave you off.'

Gloria had arranged for the driver to take them to Oxford, their luggage following behind in another motor driven by the head gardener. She wasn't going to accompany them for the melee of arrival, among goodness knew how many others, but would make a state visit at some later point when she could be the centre of attention.

The farewells were made, kisses given and received, and then Brinsley and Flick climbed into the motorcar. Gloria and Prue waved vigorously from the grand front steps as the motor pulled away across the gravel, heading for the driveway. The twins waved back through the windows and then settled back as the house receded in the distance.

Flick sniffed. Her mother's potent lily of the valley scent had invaded her nostrils and made her nose twitch. 'That's that then. Thank God.'

Brinsley looked over at her. He was very much the male version of her looks, his slightly bulbous blue eyes appearing even larger than his sister's behind the thick spectacles he wore. Flick's elfin looks didn't translate quite so well to a man, at least not to Brinny. He was perfectly nice-looking but somewhat watery and unremarkable. He had suffered from weak ankles all his life, which was perhaps why he hadn't grown as tall as Father. 'You sound as if you're never going back.'

They gazed at one another. They loved each other in a way that they never questioned. It was a bond as natural to them as breathing. But they were not the same at all and were both baffled by the other and what pleased them. Perhaps it was because of spending so much of their lives apart, with Brinsley away at school and Flick at home.

'Of course I'll come back,' Flick replied. 'There'll be holidays, just as you'll have.'

'But you think this is the beginning of your freedom.'

'Yes. Because it is.'

'And that's the difference between us. You want to be free of something but you don't know what it is. I know what I want to be free of, and it isn't home.'

'It's Mother,' Flick said frankly. 'You want to be free of her.'

'Free of her control,' Brinny said. 'Which is different.'

'But you will be,' Flick said, suddenly passionate. 'You will be, and you'll be in complete control of your life. She'll give you whatever you want. She'll let you be free because she expects you to be. But me? She won't want to let me go. Ever.'

'If you marry—'

'If I marry! That's just giving control to someone else! I want to be free and independent. And that means I might have to leave for ever. It could be the only way.' Flick gazed out of the window. They were about to go through the gates of Caundle Court. How many times had she passed between them? She knew that this wasn't the last time. But it might be one of the last. *Good.*

'Two hours or so to Oxford,' Brinny said. That was his way after a heated moment: to leave a pause. Move on. Say something uncontroversial. 'And it's a lovely day for the drive.'

Flick settled back to watch the world pass by as they headed for the main road towards Salisbury.

They arrived in Oxford in the early afternoon, having stopped for lunch at a pub outside Newbury, and went first to Magdalen. While the delivery of Brinsley's luggage was arranged by the porters, another showed them to Brinsley's rooms. The quads were thronging with undergraduates, the freshmen looking lost and the older years confident and sophisticated as they greeted each other after the long vacation.

'It's so beautiful,' Flick said, awed, looking about at the ancient cloisters, velvet green lawns and stately old buildings. 'Lucky you to be living here. Can't you just feel the dedication to learning?'

Brinsley gave her a sideways look. 'Dedication to something. Drinking probably.'

'You're just trying to make me feel better about not coming myself.'

'You could hardly come here.'

'One of the women's colleges. You know what I mean.'

A gang of blustering young men in their old school ties went by, loudly asking each other if they knew where the Turf was to be found.

'Horse racing?' Flick said, surprised.

'A pub, I think,' Brinny said as the porter led them to the gothic arched entrance of a stone staircase. At the bottom, a painted board listed the occupants of the rooms off the staircase. Gold lettering spelled out that B. D. M. Templeton Esq. was in rooms on the second floor.

The porter gave Brinsley his keys, lifted his hat, and left them. They climbed to a stout oak door studded with iron and Brinny's name next to it. It opened into a small sitting room with arched stone windows overlooking the deer park, and a smaller bedroom leading off it.

'Oh, it's lovely!' Flick said, overcome with envy. 'Lucky you, all this to yourself!'

36

'It's half the size of my room at home,' Brinny said wryly. 'And no sign of any bathroom or dressing room.'

Flick was already sitting on the sofa, gazing about at the bare walls and plain furniture. 'You know what I mean. I think it's brilliant. You can easily find some things to dress it up and make it interesting if you want.'

Brinny put his hat on the desk and gazed out of the window. 'The view is very fine.' He looked back at his sister, frowning. 'Caundle would benefit from a deer park. I should mention it to Mother.'

Flick laughed. 'Don't think about home! You're here now. You've got three years to study and meet new people and do new things, in this amazing and beautiful place! Lucky, lucky you.'

There was a knock on the door and a college servant put his head around the door. 'How do you do, sir. I'm Bates, your scout. I'm welcoming a lot of young gentlemen today, but wanted to introduce myself.' He came into the room, looking practical in canvas trousers and an apron, his shirt-sleeves slightly rolled. 'My cupboard is at the bottom of the staircase if you need me. Formal hall is at ten past seven, the buttery opens at six. I trust you have a gown, sir? If not, I can loan you one until you get to Ede and Ravenscroft tomorrow.'

'Thank you, Bates,' Brinny said.

The scout's gaze moved to Flick but he said nothing.

'This is my sister, Miss Templeton.'

'How do you do, miss,' Bates said, looking faintly relieved. 'Are you at one of the ladies' colleges, miss?'

'Sadly not,' Flick said cheerfully. 'Nothing so interesting for me. But I am in Oxford, you're bound to see me.'

'Lady visitors are most welcome in the afternoons,' Bates said with a bow.

Just then their cousin Edmund came bounding through the door, handsome as ever in a tweed suit with wide-cut lapels. 'Brinny, you've arrived!'

Flick jumped up to greet him. 'Edmund. I forgot you'd be here.'

'How on earth could you forget that? My rooms aren't far, Brin, if you want company.' Edmund kissed her cheek. 'And where are you going to be?'

'Some grim place in North Oxford.' Flick made a face and checked her watch. 'Oh dear. I'd better go. I said I'd be there by three. The cars will be waiting for me.'

'I'll chum you to the gate,' Edmund said. 'I'm going out to the High for some tobacco.'

Brinny said, 'I'll wait for my luggage.' He smiled at Flick. 'I'll see you soon, old girl. I hope the school is very nice.'

'It's not going to be as nice as this.' She gave her brother a peck on the cheek. 'Enjoy yourself. Edmund will watch out for you and I'll come for tea as soon as I can.'

'I think Brinny should be looking out for me,' Edmund said with a grin. 'Come on, let's get going.' As he walked Flick to the entrance of the college, he said, 'You must call on me soon. There are lots of excellent chaps to introduce you to.'

'You can save me from desperate boredom,' Flick said, feeling brighter.

'And you can bring a pretty friend or two.'

'So that's your game.' She smiled. 'I'll do my best. Don't drink too much. Don't smoke too much. Don't set Brin on the road to ruin.'

'As if I could.' Edmund laughed. 'Drop me a note soon, won't you? Give me the telephone number for your school. I want to see it.'

'Happy hunting ground.' Flick rolled her eyes. 'Now, I must go. I'll be so late.'

She was very late, but no one seemed to mind.

It's like a baby college, she thought, as the motorcar pulled into the driveway. The thought cheered her up. The school did not have the ancient grandeur of Magdalen College but it was still impressive: a very large Victorian house built in dark red brick, set back behind a wall and a high hedge. It was in the neo-Gothic style, with arched columned windows, ornate brickwork and bandings in dark brick, and many high chimney stacks. A flight of stone steps ran up to an arched front door under a portico and it had the air of a fine educational establishment.

Miss Wynne Finch, the headmistress, a busty lady in a businesslike navy dress and sensible shoes, welcomed her without rebuke. She had a curiously youthful face compared to the steel-grey hair brushed back into a tight bun, but she had to be at least fifty.

Now in the hall, Flick admired the colourful tiles on the floor and the ornate plasterwork while Miss Wynne Finch directed where the luggage should be taken. A nervous-looking woman in a shapeless dress, her grey-streaked dark hair in an untidy bun, emerged from a drawing room.

'There's tea in here, dear,' she said to Flick with a smile. She clasped pudgy hands together. 'I'm the younger Miss Wynne Finch. So we are both Wynne Finches. Confusing, I know. You're the first to arrive. The other girls are coming tomorrow. So it's just us this evening, I'm afraid.'

'Oh.' Her spirits swooped. This could be worse than being at home.

'Things will get much busier tomorrow. Now, tea?'

It's very Oxford, thought Flick, as she followed her into the drawing room. The walls were covered in William Morris paper in a dense pattern of dark blues and purples, and hung with many paintings and drawings, many of them of Oxford, as though it was not enough to have the place just outside the windows. An old Broadwood piano with delicate carved wood scrolling and candle sconces stood against one wall, and the room was crammed in the Victorian manner with sofas, chairs, bookcases, lamp stands, occasional tables, and many overflowing ferns in large cache-pots. Everything that could be patterned was, from the swirling Persian rug to the floral curtains.

On a low table, a tea set was waiting, with a large silver pot and delicate china cups and saucers. The younger Miss Wynne Finch settled down to pour.

'We're so happy to welcome you, Miss Templeton. You're our most important pupil this year by some way. We were so thrilled to get your application. Mary said you'd raise the profile of the school enormously.' Miss Wynne Finch widened her eyes and put her free hand over her mouth, shooting Flick an agonised look. 'I'm not supposed to say that. Please don't tell my sister, she'd be so annoyed. Naturally, all our pupils are equally as important to us.' She passed over a cup of tea to Flick. 'But it is rather lovely to have you here. How was your trip?'

Flick had taken her place on a velvet armchair opposite. 'It was fine, thank you. My brother went to Magdalen today.' She took the offered teacup. 'Thank you so much.'

'Magdalen! Oh, a fine college, very fine! One of the finest. The president is most impressive. I met him once. I'm sure your brother will enjoy himself there.'

'So am I.'

'I hope you'll be comfortable here. We're not as distinguished as Magdalen but we are fine in our way. Last year we had a princess *and* a duchess, and although I'm sorry to say they were both only European titles, they still count for something, don't you think?'

Flick tried not to laugh. 'Oh yes. Very much.'

'We like to think we offer the best kind of education to our ladies,' Miss Wynne Finch said. Her voice was high and childish but gentle and sing-song.

Just then, her sister came striding in. 'Ah, good, tea!'

She is obviously the sister in charge.

Miss Wynne Finch settled next to her sister and took up her own teacup. 'Now, Miss Templeton, a few small rules. No gentlemen friends in your rooms but you may have callers in the drawing room at agreed times. Male relatives may stay for supper and after six o'clock but only until nine. You have a curfew of nine, which is ten p.m. on Saturday. Although you may apply to us for special circumstances such as a lecture, play or other cultural pursuit. Naturally, Oxford is rich in such things.'

'Naturally. I'm looking forward to them.'

'I'm sure you're frightfully cultured already,' the younger sister said, smiling, somewhat breathless now her older sister was here. Her pale blue eyes darted everywhere as though looking for problems that might be raised later.

'Not so very,' Flick said. 'Not by Oxford standards.'

She was sure she had read a large amount of books. She had been taken to the National Gallery and to plays and pantomimes. But the great and meaningful world of art and culture, philosophy and politics, was yet to reveal itself to her. She felt a sudden rush of excitement. She had not wanted to come to this place; she had felt deprived of Brinsley's opportunities. But suddenly she realised that Oxford was, after all, Oxford. She was far from her mother's beady gaze, and close to a great seat of learning, and only a train ride to London. Brinsley was right. This was an opportunity and she would have to make the most of it in whatever way she could. Charming the Wynne Finch sisters would be her first task, and it helped to know she was already their prized pupil. 'Your school is simply beautiful,' she said warmly, 'and I already feel at home here. I'm so looking forward to learning all you have to teach me.'

The older Miss Wynne Finch raised her eyebrows over a small smile. 'I'm terribly pleased to hear that.'

The sound of a bell echoed through the hall beyond and

both sisters looked surprised, the younger clattering her cup into her saucer with a nervous start.

'Who can that be?' the younger sister said, as the older got up. 'Betsy will answer the door!'

'I will also go and see who it is,' announced the older Miss Wynne Finch. 'We're not expecting anyone until tomorrow.' She strode out through the drawing room door.

'I do hope it isn't bailiffs!' said the younger sister, gazing after her. Then her gaze whirled round to Flick and her hand went over her mouth again. From behind it, she whispered loudly, 'Oh, I shouldn't have said that!'

'Your secret's safe with me.'

There were voices in the hall and then the older Miss Wynne Finch reappeared, now followed by a very young woman in a smart hat, tweed coat and an ebullient fur at her neck. Flick could see at once that she was extremely pretty.

'Well, we have an unexpectedly early arrival,' said Miss Wynne Finch, as her sister clambered to her feet, her eyes wide.

'I'm so sorry,' said the arrival in a rich, almost sultry voice. 'I sent a telegram to say I'd be early. I can't think how it didn't arrive.'

'You're here now,' said Miss Wynne Finch in a gracious voice, though Flick sensed her annoyance. 'Sister, Miss Templeton – this is Miss Ravenbrook. One of your fellow pupils.'

The girl looked at Flick, a frank, likeable gaze from candid brown eyes. She went straight over as Flick stood up, holding out one gloved hand. 'How do you do? I'm Diana.'

'I'm Felicity. But you can call me Flick.'

'Flick?' The other girl laughed as she shook Flick's hand. 'Terrific name. I think I had a pony called Flick. Or was it Flicker? Splendid little jumper. Dog food, now, I should think.'

Flick laughed, liking her at once.

Diana was already taking off her gloves. 'Is that tea? What joy. I'm parched after the journey.' She tossed her gloves on a chair, then her fur, and then started unpinning her hat. 'I feel as though I've just traversed Russia. I mean, Kent is a long way, but . . .'

'I'll call the maid to take your things,' said Miss Wynne Finch, looking at the gloves in their crumpled heap.

'I'll take them.' The younger Miss Wynne Finch jumped up, scooped up the gloves and fur, and waited for Diana to take off her coat and took that, along with her hat, before hurrying out.

'Silly woman. I was going to tell her to inform Cook it's four of us for dinner,' Miss Wynne Finch said crossly. She got up and followed her sister out, saying, 'I'll do it myself.'

Diana threw herself into a chair opposite Flick and smiled at her. 'Well, here we are! Those two are a scream, aren't they? I can tell already. It's going to be a non-stop party in this joint.'

Flick laughed, a little taken aback. *What a pretty thing! Those brown eyes. She looks like a film star.*

Diana smiled back, curving her luscious lips into a smile. 'We're going to be friends, aren't we? I can just feel it. I hope you do too.'

Flick stared at her, then nodded. 'Yes. I can too.'

Chapter Three

FLICK

1951

Flick could not imagine what life would have been like at St Pandionia's – Pandy's, they called it – without Diana, but she suspected that it would have been painfully boring. She might have got on with Gwendolyn Percy or Margaret Henderson, who were the most sparky girls in the school otherwise, but there was no way that life would have been half so much fun.

As it was just the two of them that first night, it was entirely natural they should get to know one another before the others arrived.

They each settled into their rooms, which were handily both on the second floor and on the same hallway, and had the same plain iron bedsteads with candlewick covers, dark mahogany wardrobes and chests of drawers, with a mirror over a basin, and a horsehair-stuffed armchair. Then Diana changed into a plain skirt and jumper, although she still looked a knockout, and came to Flick's room.

'I can't think why they are still teaching us all this stuff about menus and flowers,' Flick said, lying back on her bed, having kicked off her shoes. 'It seems a waste, really.'

Diana was wandering about, inspecting Flick's things.

'This is like our housemaids' bedrooms at home,' Diana observed, before going over to the arched window that looked down to the road and opening it. She perched on the window seat beneath it and lit a cigarette, blowing the smoke away through the open window.

'Gosh, are we allowed?' Flick said. She had already tried cigarettes at home, filching them from ladies' purses or from the cases abandoned by gentlemen after the long and late raucous parties her parents had hosted. It had taken a while to get used to the rancid taste and the bitterness in her lungs but she had persevered.

'I shouldn't think so,' Diana said, exhaling another plume. 'But when in doubt, assume it's not allowed, and take the appropriate steps.'

'I wish I could be a proper student. We're going to be treated like children here.'

'Women are always treated like children, unless they have their own money,' Diana replied, looking over her shoulder at Flick. 'And of course this whole finishing school malarkey isn't about teaching us anything.'

'I suppose not.'

'We're being trained to find the kind of men who will look after us financially, so that we're marginally less helpless than the women who marry without money.'

'Those women can work.'

'Work?' Diana laughed, taking another drag. 'I say, do you want one of these?'

'No thanks.' The long journey that day had made her feel

vaguely out of sorts and the mutton stew for supper had not helped.

Diana slipped her feet out of her shoes and tucked them up underneath her. 'Who wants to work, darling? We're getting married so that we don't have to do anything beyond running a house and having children. And that is hardly nothing. It will keep us very busy indeed.'

'But not being able to work is just what makes women helpless,' Flick replied.

'Do you really think working women are so independent? They have to do all the other things as well – looking after a house and a husband and children – *and* manage a job or whatever it is they do. Unless they're single. And who wants that?' Diana crinkled up her pretty nose. 'Not me. I can't imagine life without a man in it. What's the point?' She smiled at Flick. 'Besides, you don't have to worry. You're going to have money, aren't you?'

Flick sat up on her elbows and frowned, tossing her head to send one long dark blonde strand back from her eyes. 'Who told you that?'

'No one. But I know you are, of course. You're Felicity Templeton. One of the famous Carrington family. Everyone knows you're swimming in cash, so you're bound to have something, aren't you?' Diana said it matter-of-factly, without envy or prurience. But she waited to hear the answer.

'I suppose so. My mother says I will have something from her. But who knows? She likes her little games. She might dangle it in front of me for years, to make me do what she wants.'

'But if she does give you money, you've got freedom. You can live life as you like, on your own terms. That sounds pretty good to me. Whereas I . . .' Diana laughed merrily. 'I'm a squire's daughter. The youngest of five children, all the older boys off to school and university and needing to be put into careers or the army or whatever . . . There's nothing much left over for me. If the worst comes to the worst, I suppose there'll always be a spare room in my mother's house, wherever she ends up when Daddy dies.'

Flick eyed her, smiling. 'I don't think there's much chance of that.'

'Well, neither do I. I'm young, I'm pretty and I'm clever.'

Again, so matter-of-fact, thought Flick, liking Diana all the more for it.

'So I don't think there's much fear that I'll end up an old maid,' Diana continued. She shot Flick a mischievous look. 'And that's why I let them put me here. They're already terrified what I might do if they don't contain me somehow. I had the most tremendous flirtation with one of the grooms and they were horrified. That's when this Oxford scheme was cooked up.' She took a last inhale of her cigarette, ground it out on the windowsill and tossed the end into the bushes below. 'They needn't have worried, I'm not going to do anything stupid with a groom.'

'You mean, do *it* with him?' Flick said, half amused and half aghast. 'Like a naughty book?'

'What books have you been reading, darling Flick?' Diana laughed again. 'Of course I would do it. Much better to get it out of the way if you can. But I didn't. I didn't even really fancy him, if I'm honest, though he was awfully sweet and touched my leg in the loveliest way when he was tightening Razzle's girth. But it was fun to make them think I might run away with him. I'd never be such a fool as to spoil my prospects like that.'

'Oh, good.' Flick considered her own romantic experience. There was none. Her parents had had a couple of nice-looking friends, but they were all ancient of course. The only other boys she really knew were family. The men she loved were the ones she read about. The Count of Monte Cristo had been one of her first crushes. She had longed to marry Edward Beverley, the eldest of the Children of the New Forest. She had felt his anger and pride when his family was reduced in the Civil War, admired his honour and chivalry, and walked with him on those very long deer stalking expeditions through the forest. If only he had really existed. She had, she realised, never really shaken her passion for him, although she had also secretly loved Mr Darcy, Mr Rochester, and several of the Knights of the Round Table as well.

What a fool I am. I might as well love the White Rabbit or Peter Pan.

Diana got down from the window seat and drifted to the armchair, showing off her wasp-waisted hourglass figure. 'Oxford is going to be where we find nice rich husbands.'

'Clever, interesting ones.'

'Well – all right, that's always a bonus. The key thing is to meet the right people. I've got the names of some of my friends' brothers and so on.'

'My twin Brinsley is at Magdalen and so is my cousin Edmund,' Flick volunteered.

Diana's eyes widened and she looked pleased. 'Edmund Carrington? Oh! I saw him at a few parties last season, but didn't manage to meet him. You must introduce me! He's awfully handsome.'

'I suppose he is. Oh dear, I don't know if I'm going to be very good at this. I've never really thought of embarking on a mission the way you have.'

'Because you're not in the same position as I am,' Diana said frankly. 'I'm pretty low down the pecking order. I've no money. My family are not important, though we are respectable. I've got my physical appeal, but you know, I'm nineteen now. Older than you are. And you know how quickly all that fades.'

Diana looked so solemn at this that Flick couldn't help bursting out laughing.

'You needn't laugh,' Diana said a little tartly. 'If I had money, I wouldn't have to be quite so cynical and strategic about all of this. I would wait for the men to come to me.'

'The fortune hunters?' Flick said dryly. 'The delightful men who only want you as a sack of cash? Money brings its own problems. It isn't a surefire way to happiness.'

'It's also not a guaranteed way to misery, but not having it is.' Diana shrugged. 'Well, you don't have to bother on your own account but you could help me.' She twinkled and smiled at Flick. 'It might be fun.'

Flick smiled back. 'You know, I think it might be.'

'And you'll most likely find love too.'

'Oh, it's love we're looking for, is it? I thought it was a rich husband!'

'Ideally, both. After all, who wants a life without love? And I think it should be just as easy – if not easier – to love a rich man as a poor one.'

Flick laughed again. 'I bet you fall for some handsome pauper and follow your heart.'

'And you fall for a rich marquis, when you really don't want or need one,' Diana said. 'It will be like a Trollope novel.' She set her face. 'But I know what I want. And I'm going to make sure I get it.'

'You know, I think you will,' Flick said. 'I can't wait to see you do it.'

Diana lost no time in pursuing her aims. She went through the motions in the classes, hardly concentrating at all even though it was clear she was one of the most talented girls in school. She seemed to be able to do so much, so effortlessly, Flick thought. She wasn't jealous but she did envy Diana's panache.

'You're so good at things,' she said over lunch one day when Diana had once again been awarded top marks for her flower arranging. The dining room was on the ground floor of a hexagonal tower at the side of the house, and their window table, just for two, nestled between two heavy William Morris curtains, was their favourite spot. None of the other girls dared sit there, but remained on the communal table in the middle of the room.

'Oh lawks, no, I'm not.' Diana shrugged. 'It's only flowers.'

'If it's that easy, why can't the rest of us do it? I follow all the rules – three large blooms, six contrasting or complementary smaller ones, one point of interest, a sprig of greenery per bloom – and what a mess I make of it. You don't even follow the rules, and your arrangements are beautiful.'

Flick meant it. Diana could pick up a pencil and sketch anything she saw. She dressed with a style all her own that the other girls were desperate to copy, but it never looked as good on anyone else. Her room was the same as everyone else's and yet her touches made it so elegant, from the silk scarf she draped over the lampshade, to the way she nailed up a collection of watercolours that had taken her fancy in a local junk shop. Flick would have put them in a row, but Diana arranged them on one wall in an interesting offset way that drew the eye.

'I can't read books the way you do,' Diana said frankly. 'And I'm not desperately interested in them, though I know they're clever and I ought to like them. You can write anything you like, and I can hardly spell my own name. So there. We all have talents. Now, show me that card again.'

Flick pulled the invitation card from her pocket and put it on the table. 'Here.'

The card was dark purple and printed in flowing black script.

The Trojans invite you to cocktails in the Cardinal Wolsey Room, Magdalen College, Wednesday of Second Week, 6 o'clock till 9 o'clock.
RSVP 'Hector', Magdalen College

'So exciting,' Diana breathed, looking down at the card with wide eyes. She looked up at Flick, whose name was scrawled on the top of the card. 'Are you sure I can come as well?'

'Of course. I told Brin all about you when I went round last week. He was delighted. I think they would like as many young ladies as possible.'

'Good. And who is Hector, do you think?'

'I have no idea.' Flick sighed lightly. 'But I did fall completely in love with him when I read *The Iliad*. Gorgeous Hector. Terrible Achilles.'

Diana gave her a sideways look. 'You are so strange. We're going to meet real-life men. Our first proper party. This is the way it's all going to begin, you'll see. We'll be invited to more and more, that's what it's all about.' She waved her hand around the dining room. 'That's what all this is for. To get us close to them. The men.'

'I don't find all that much exciting about seeing my brother.'

'His friends!' Diana said impatiently.

'I don't think he is going to have many, and they will probably be like him.'

'They can't all be! Anyway, let's see. The sooner we can escape sketching class, the better.'

They spent that afternoon in sketching class, doing their best to recreate a vase of lilies on a table beside a cup and saucer on large pieces of flimsy brown sketch paper with charcoal pieces that left the fingers pleasingly black and smudgy. Flick enjoyed smudging with her fingertips so much that her sketches were in danger of looking simply like vague shapes through smog. Diana, of course, managed to draw something in her own unique style of flowing dark lines, perfectly capturing the trumpets of the lily and the pollen-furred stamens emerging from them. She hadn't bothered with the cup and saucer.

'Only there to trap us into ruining our pictures,' she murmured to Flick, who agreed.

While they were sketching away under the tutelage of the very shy and quite elderly Mr Drummond, the older Miss Wynne Finch knocked at the door and came in. The art room had been created from an old conservatory, perfect for the light that poured in but stiflingly hot at times. Flick looked up to see Miss Wynne Finch almost wincing as the warm air hit her. She came in followed by a shy-looking girl with dark hair and very large, sad grey eyes.

'Young ladies.' Miss Wynne Finch clapped her hands together importantly. 'This is a late arrival to our happy school. Countess Marissa von Schulenberg. Please be kind to her as she knows no one.'

Everyone stared, then there was a general murmur of welcome but it was understated to say the least.

A German, thought Flick. Germans were still regarded with great mistrust and dislike, with the war so recent. The atmosphere in the room turned chilly.

Miss Wynne Finch said, 'I'm taking the countess to her room now and she will join you later.'

'Not if we see her first,' whispered Diana. 'But at least we know Winnie is busy.'

She had dubbed the sisters Winnie and Finchy – Finchy being the name that suited the younger, twittering and bird-like Miss Norah – and talked about them so openly by those names that everyone had picked them up without realising. Flick was constantly afraid she would inadvertently use these names when addressing one or both of the Misses Wynne Finch.

Diana put her charcoal on the easel and wiped her black fingers on her art smock. 'Come on, let's bunk off early. Let the others suck up to the countess if they want. We won't be missed in the excitement.'

Flick and Diana marched arm and arm down the Banbury Road, exulting in being free of the house for a few hours. In fairness, they had quite a lot of freedom, allowed to go into Oxford every day, and to walk around the University Parks for their exercise, but somehow it was never enough. There was always something to get back to, and this evening was really no different. They were due at the Sheldonian Theatre for a piano recital at seven o'clock. Diana had very naughtily treated Mr Drummond as though he had some kind of authority in the school, when really he had none, asking him brightly if she and Flick could please be excused and get some tea in town before the concert. He had hardly opened his mouth to protest that he couldn't possibly give them permission before they were discarding their art smocks and rushing to wash their hands.

'Thank goodness for you,' Flick said sincerely to her friend, as they walked together, kicking some of the freshly fallen leaves out of their path.

'Thank goodness for *you*,' Diana said. 'Friends for ever.'

They walked into the heart of Oxford, chattering together, Flick feeling quite overcome. She had never had a friend like this before, another girl, from a different background, whose company was endlessly entertaining, whose jokes she enjoyed and who appeared to enjoy hers, and with whom there was no shortage of things to discuss. It was a delightful thing and she was now wondering how she had gone so long without a friend like Diana. They were passing the Martyrs' Memorial on the way into Cornmarket when a large bus motoring by sent up a sweep of oily, leafy water from a puddle by the curb, and soaked Flick's coat from shoulder to hem.

'Oh, how horrid!' she said crossly. 'Look at me, what a mess.'

Diana clicked her tongue in sympathy. 'Bad luck. Let's go into Fuller's and order tea, and you can go to the ladies' room and wash off as much as you can.'

'Very bad luck,' Flick said gloomily.

'Fuller's is just there, past the church. Come on.'

They walked along, Flick conscious of the dark stain all over one half of her coat. As they walked past the church, she saw a man in a dark overcoat standing just inside the iron railings and smoking a cigarette. He had a thatch of thick dark hair and had buried his chin in the turned-up collar of his coat. Nevertheless, she could see him laughing.

What a rude man, she thought indignantly, embarrassed

nonetheless to be seen in such a state. *Most likely a tramp or a vagrant.*

'Do I look so bad?' she asked Diana.

'No, of course not. And it's getting dark now anyway, no one will notice. We'll get Betsy to sponge it all off later when we get back. Here are the tea rooms now.'

They went into the brightly lit, steamy interior of the tea room. A waitress showed them to a table but Flick disappeared off to the lavatories to soak the water off her coat as best she could with waxy lavatory paper. Coming back into the tea room, she saw that Diana had already ordered tea and was gazing about.

'Look at all the students,' she said as Flick sat down. 'That looks much better, darling. I'm sure it's going to come clean when Betsy has a go as well.'

The tables were crammed with students: dashing young men, studious ones or shy-looking ones, some with a gang, and plenty of young women, some with older people who might be parents, guardians or tutors. A clergyman was drinking tea with two young ladies who were probably his daughters.

'Oh,' Flick said, surprised. 'There's Brinny.'

She got up and went over to a table where her brother was sitting with Edmund and another young man, the latter two puffing away at cigarettes between gulps of thick brown tea.

'Hello, darling, fancy seeing you here,' she said, dropping a kiss on her brother's cheek.

Brinny and the others stood up. 'Flick! How nice. Join us, won't you?'

'You'll have to have Diana too,' she said, waving in her friend's direction.

'Of course.'

Flick beckoned her friend over. Diana wove through the busy tea room, looking flushed and bright-eyed.

'Goodness,' she said, 'I could tell right away you're Flick's brother.'

'Brinny, this is Diana Ravenbrook. Diana, my brother. Edmund, my cousin. And . . .' She looked at the third man.

He bowed. 'Alfred Beresford-Jones. Delighted.'

They all shook hands. Diana, Flick noticed, was emanating a kind of glow that she had never seen before, as though a little pink force field was shimmering around her. Brinsley did not seem to notice, but the other two men appeared to sense it, Edmund intrigued in the way a child might be on spotting a particularly delicious cake, and Alfred flustered, rosy in the cheek and unable to look long at Diana.

And there's that charm of hers.

They had barely sat down and asked the waitress to bring over the tea things from their table when Diana was regaling the table with stories of life at St Pandionia's, which Diana of course called St Pandimonium's, and making them all laugh. Flick felt proud of her clever and funny friend who was charming the table so effortlessly.

'What are you doing out?' Brinsley asked, when they had stopped laughing and Diana declared herself in need of her tea.

'We're going to the Sheldonian,' Flick said before checking her watch. 'I suppose we'll have to be there soon. It's Beethoven. Or Mozart. Or both.'

'I know it, I'm going too,' Alfred said, pulling a leaflet out of his pocket. 'Here we are. Gregory Cheadle is playing. He's very well known. He's just done the Wigmore Hall and they say he's going to be performing at the Albert Hall next summer.'

'I say, let's see that.' Edmund took the leaflet and scanned it. 'Very good stuff.' He looked up at Diana, his blue eyes sparkling. 'I wouldn't mind hearing this myself. You're going, are you, Miss Ravenbrook?'

'That's right.' Diana fixed him with a stare over the top of her teacup.

Flick noticed the connection. She had had no doubt that Edmund would be intrigued by Diana, it was no surprise at all. And how could he resist whatever force it was that she was projecting so powerfully?

Sex appeal. That's what it is.

She knew the phrase from reading about film stars. It was very important that they had it – that mysterious quality that was more than simply looks. The appeal of sex. As though whatever happened in the bedroom with someone who possessed it was going to be simply mind-blowing. Diana was alive with it. No wonder Edmund could not resist.

'Let's all go,' Edmund said. 'Come on, Brin, you too. You actually like all this classical piano stuff, I've seen it on your gramophone player.'

'Yes, I actually do.' Brinsley shot his cousin an ironic look. 'Perhaps you'll find you like it too, if you give it a chance.'

'I'm sure I will,' Edmund said heartily. 'Drink up, everyone, and we'll make our way there.'

It was a short walk from Fuller's to the Sheldonian, no more than two minutes or so. They strolled down Cornmarket and into the Broad. This was the heart of Oxford, with colleges everywhere. There was Balliol, Trinity, St John's and Wadham tucked just around the corner, for starters. It was a hop and a skip from the Turl colleges: Jesus, Exeter and Lincoln. And behind the turquoise cupola dome of the Sheldonian Theatre, with the stone emperors' heads sitting so massy and solid on the pillars that surrounded it, was the magnificent Bodleian Library, the repository of every single book published. No wonder its stacks reached far into the ground beneath them.

The five of them went through the gates and joined the queue of people going into the recital. Brinny and Edmund were going to try their luck for tickets on the door.

'Oh bother,' Diana said, dismayed. 'There's Winnie and Finchy and all the others.'

Sure enough, the two ladies were standing by a group of girls, looking like guards in their raincoats and bowler hats, each holding an umbrella. They were fussing over who had the tickets.

'We'll have to join them,' Flick said to the others. 'Thanks so much for tea.'

'You can join them if you like,' Diana said. 'I'm staying here.'

'Oh.' Flick saw how determined her friend was. 'All right. I suppose if they don't see us, we're all right.'

'Let us conceal you from the dragons,' Edmund said gallantly. 'Here, stand close to me, Miss Ravenbrook. You can hide.'

'You are kind.' Diana moved closer to him and bent down slightly to conceal her dark head. 'Come on, Flick, don't get us in hot water.'

Flick moved around to the other side of her brother and her gaze was caught at once by the light of a cigarette. By the railings she saw the man who had been in the churchyard they'd passed earlier. She was quite sure it was him even though she couldn't make out his features in the light of the street lamps; he had the same square shoulders and long dark coat and thatch of dark hair.

She felt vaguely chilled. Was that vagrant following them? To her relief, the queue moved forward and she made sure that she was in the middle of a group of ticket holders.

Before long, they were entering the theatre and finding their seats in the sides of the circular room. Flick glanced up at the magnificent painted ceiling, where goddesses and winged cherubs struck poses among the clouds. It was no doubt some obvious allegory although she couldn't recognise any of the figures. A grand piano drew the eye, ready for the concert. To her relief, Winnie and Finchy were sitting out of their eyeline, in the circle above, and they were unlikely to spot their rebel pupils sitting with young men below. Nevertheless, she felt guilty. Diana, talking quietly with Edmund, did not seem concerned at all.

The time for the concert came and the room began to quieten down. After a while, there was a certain restlessness and after fifteen minutes, a discontented murmur. After another five minutes, a balding man in a tweed suit and tiny round glasses came forward, looking distinctly embarrassed.

'My apologies, ladies and gentlemen,' he began, 'for the delay in commencing our musical programme. Our pianist, Mr Cheadle, has not arrived. He is coming from London and we assume he has met some difficulties on his journey. You are welcome to wait a little longer but we shall also understand if you feel you would prefer to leave. We will of course refund the cost of your ticket. My apologies again.'

The murmur of discontent grew louder. A couple of people began gathering their things and standing up, evidently meaning to leave.

A loud voice suddenly echoed out across the theatre, carried by its excellent acoustics. 'I'll play!'

The tweed gentleman at the front had been about to retire, but now he frowned into the audience, looking for the source of the voice.

A man in the main auditorium had stood up. 'I know all the pieces. I'll play them for you.' He gestured to the room. 'You've all come to hear some music, I can provide it. I'm not Cheadle but I'm not bad.' He shrugged. 'If he turns up, I'll withdraw.'

'Play this programme?' said the tweed gentleman, astonished, holding up his playbill as though he couldn't believe that the man had even looked at it.

'Yes.'

Flick stared at him, astonished. She could not be sure, but he looked very like the same man she had now seen twice already. The dark overcoat, the huge shoulders, the dark unruly hair. Was it him? The tramp she'd seen earlier? How could it be? Tramps didn't play Beethoven. Did they?

'Goodness,' Edmund said quietly. 'He's got a nerve.'

'Outrageous,' said Alfred Beresford-Jones, who had gone quite pink. 'Such arrogance.'

The young man – she could see he was young now, in his early twenties – made his way along the row and walked down the central aisle towards the piano. 'You can all go home,' he said, 'or you can hear some of what you wanted to hear. It's up to you.'

'Well, this is most irregular,' said the tweed gentleman uncertainly, but the young man had already gone up to the piano. He took off his overcoat to reveal baggy dark trousers, a deep red shirt and a brown jumper over the top. He looked louche compared to the smartly dressed audience and the tweed suit man.

'I rather admire the gumption,' murmured Diana, looking at Flick, who said nothing.

'I think I'll leave,' announced Alfred, standing up.

Tossing his coat on the piano, the man went to the stool, sat down, raised the piano lid and ran his fingers over the keys in a trill of notes. More of the audience got up to leave but others were intrigued and began to quieten down. Alfred was putting on his coat.

'The *Pathétique* first, I think?' enquired the young man.

'Yes, yes . . . that's right.'

'Ah. Lovely.' He went very still, then took a breath and began to play. The deceptively simple opening was elegant and beautiful. After a moment, Alfred sat slowly down in his seat.

The liquid piano music filled the air, acting like a calming drug on the audience.

'He's very good,' Edmund whispered.

'Did you think he'd get up if he weren't?' Diana replied.

'Shh,' Flick said. 'I'm listening.'

She was rapt. The pianist seemed to feel the music in every part of him, his fingers fluid and nimble and yet utterly connected to the instrument. The music was divine but she couldn't take her eyes off him: the dark flowing hair, the movement of his shoulders, his gaze intent at times while at others his eyes were closed altogether.

He played beautifully. When he finished the final movement, there was a communal intake of breath and then a roar of applause from the audience, Flick clapping until her hands stung. The pianist looked around almost in surprise, and then smiled, evidently pleased by the reaction. The tweed gentleman appeared again, now beaming. As the applause died down, he spoke.

'Well, a very pleasant surprise indeed. May I ask your name?'

'Knolle. Caius Knolle.'

What a very strange name, Flick thought, staring.

'If you'd like to continue, Mr Knolle, I'm sure we'd all be very pleased. Do you know our next piece?'

'Of course.'

'In that case—'

One of the doors slammed. A middle-aged man in black tie and a hat came hurrying down the aisle, puffing and sweating. 'I'm late, I'm late!' he called as he went.

'Mr Cheadle! Oh!' The tweed gentleman blinked from behind his glasses.

Caius Knolle immediately stood up, took up his coat, bowed first to Mr Cheadle, who was now almost at the piano himself, then to the tweed gentleman, and then to the audience. 'My job is done,' he said loudly, a smile on his lips. 'I bid you goodnight.'

A moment later he was striding back down the aisle towards the doors. As he passed, Flick drew in a breath. The intensity of his presence, even so fleeting, was overwhelming.

'What a shame!' Diana said lightly. 'Who wants to see fusty old Cheadle after that? But we're all stuck here now, aren't we?'

Flick knew that she didn't. But she also knew that she had to stay now, and possibly take the heat from Winnie and Finchy later for not sitting with the school. That didn't matter. She sat through the rest of the concert only wondering what it would have sounded like, and felt like, if it had been Caius Knolle playing the piano instead of the distinguished Cheadle.

Chapter Four

FLICK

1951

Flick and Diana were in trouble for sneaking off and going, apparently alone, to the recital. Winnie had even threatened that they would not be permitted to go to the cocktail party in Magdalen, but she relented. She even arranged a taxi to and from the school for the girls and, much to the envy of everyone else, they went off in their silk dresses and high heels, hair carefully set and faces carefully made up, feeling extremely mature and sophisticated.

Brinny was waiting at the lodge and escorted them to the party. Diana seemed in her element and was the focus of much attention in her clinging black dress with a halter-neck that set off her shoulders very nicely indeed. Flick felt a little dowdy next to her, in her flared pink silk, but Diana had said it suited her. The room was suitably atmospheric, with ancient beams, old portraits in gilt frames hung on the panelling, and thick velvet curtains pulled shut against the autumn night outside, and it thronged with men in dinner jackets and girls in frocks, many smoking and most clutching one of the violently coloured cocktails being handed around on silver trays by college butlers.

'Here,' Edmund said, coming up to them with two glasses of bright green drinks. 'These are called Achilles. The blue ones are called Hectors; don't drink those, they're filthy. The yellow ones are Paris. If you have one of those pink ones, it's raspberry lemonade, and it's called a Helen.'

'I'll have an Achilles,' Diana said with a smile. 'What's in it?'

'Curious mix of green chartreuse, some sort of peppermint liqueur and some soda.'

Diana sipped it and shuddered. 'Oh my goodness, that's horrible. What on earth must the Hectors taste like?'

Edmund summoned a butler, put her drink on the tray and said, 'Bring us two Helens with gin, won't you?'

'Why couldn't you have champagne like normal people?' Diana asked.

'One of the great questions of our time. It isn't done. The Trojans invent cocktails. It's one of our unique qualities.'

'Then I'll have to help you invent something decent.'

'I like that idea very much.' Edmund smiled at her. He looked rakishly handsome in his black tie, his blond hair neatly cut. 'Come and have a cigarette with me and we'll discuss recipes.'

As they went off together, Flick said to her brother, 'I think there's something going on between those two.'

'Oh, there most definitely is.' Brinny grinned. 'There have been letters written.'

'Diana didn't say!'

'I didn't say they'd been sent. He's very smitten. But he wants to play it carefully.'

'Obviously I'm going to tell her every word you say.'

'I should think it won't matter by the time you do.'

They both looked at where Edmund and Diana were standing in close and flirtatious conversation, their chemistry plain to see.

'I think you're right,' Flick remarked. 'But Diana is a champion girl.'

'She certainly is,' Brinny said.

'Oh, do you like her?' Flick was surprised. She didn't think of Brinny as noticing any girls, not so far.

'Of course I do. She's terribly entertaining.'

'I wouldn't have thought she's your type.'

'I'm not saying she is. Just that I like her.'

'Good. So do I.' Flick took a cigarette from her purse and lit it.

Brinny looked horrified. 'You're not smoking, are you, Flick?'

'Clearly, yes. It took a while but now I can do it quite well.'

'It's very bad for you.'

'Who says? Anyway, who cares . . . That's the point.'

Her brother looked at her gravely. 'That's the difference between us, isn't it, Flick? You want what's bad for you. Why? Revenge?'

'Revenge?' Flick laughed. 'On who?'

'On Father, for leaving you, getting himself killed like that. On Mother, for being the gorgon she is. But you'll only hurt yourself, you know that, don't you?' Brinsley looked serious.

He took his sister's hand. 'You see, I intend to make my life better if I can. That's the revenge I want. A better life. You know what we went through.'

Flick looked away, smoking furiously. 'Damn this awful smoke, it's making my eyes sting. The whole room is full of it.'

'I think you had it worse than I did,' Brinsley went on. 'In fact, I know it. And perhaps that's why you seem so furious with things.'

'I'm not furious,' Flick said, 'I'm just eager to get on. I want to grow up and get away.'

'All right. If that's the way you want it. But you won't find the answers you're seeking in cocktails and cigarettes.'

'They seem like a pretty good answer to me!' Flick picked a drink off a passing tray, a bright blue one. 'I always loved Hector!' She tossed it back. 'That's better.' She coughed at the strength of it. 'Oh . . . gosh.'

'Flick . . .' Brinsley let go of her hand. 'Do be careful.'

'You'll look after me, won't you, Brinny?'

'Of course I will. But I might not always be there. That's the rub.'

Flick knew she was drunk on the way home. The street lights moved in curious ways outside the taxi and she felt sick and numb. Her mouth wouldn't exactly obey her, slurring over her words and refusing to form the thoughts she wanted to express in coherent sentences. Diana had wound down the window to get lots of fresh air into the taxi.

'You can't be this drunk in front of Winnie and Finchy! They'll be ever so cross.'

Somehow Diana had managed to stay quite sober on her gin cocktails.

Despite Diana's efforts, it was obvious how inebriated Flick was. It was, she thought, very liberating even though she felt queasy. The cocktails were the problem, she thought, as she swayed up the steps. Mixing everything like that. The Hector had been nothing short of disgusting and was probably the problem. Purity was key. She'd learn that lesson next time.

But the Misses Wynne Finch were so cross at the state of Flick that she was told she could not leave St Pandionia's for at least a week. She would miss all the outings, all future parties and recitals, until she had repented.

But she didn't repent at all.

Diana was not in trouble, which Flick thought was rich, considering that she had drunk plenty and had kissed Edmund quite shamelessly in the quad before they said goodnight. While she, Flick, the eternal virgin, was in disgrace. To cheer her up in her isolation, Diana smuggled in a bottle of vodka, which they mixed with lemonade and drank in their tooth mugs, while smoking out of Flick's window. Diana tried to send smoke signals to Edmund in the direction of Magdalen but the smoke resolutely drifted the wrong way.

'This is the way to drink,' Flick said, holding up her mug. 'My problem was that awful mix of nasty things. But this is pure vodka, except for the lemonade. What's it made from?'

'Potatoes?' wondered Diana. 'The Russians invented it. I'm sure they drink buckets of it in Tolstoy.'

'Or Dostoevsky,' Flick said wisely.

'I haven't read either,' Diana said frankly.

'I've managed a bit. But not *War and Peace*.'

'You haven't been alive long enough to read it.'

They both laughed and drank more.

'Why is it so nice to be drunk?' Flick said, feeling the familiar numb feeling begin. All the things she cared about and that bothered her and made her unhappy began to float away. The things she enjoyed and wanted and cared about became more important. *Love is important. I want to be in love. Diana might be – lucky, lucky her.* 'Are you in love?' she asked abruptly.

'Of course,' Diana said dreamily. 'Of course I am. Lovely Edmund.'

'What was it like to kiss him?'

'Bliss. Utter bliss on earth.'

Flick sighed. 'You are lucky. No one will ever want me.'

'You silly girl, you're a mighty catch. So pretty, so clever, so interesting. You're going to be fighting them off.'

'No one wanted me at the party.'

'Well, you got rather tipsy rather fast, and Brinny was there looking after you. Plenty would have talked to you if they could. So next time, you had better just pace yourself a little, that's all. You'll see, they'll come flocking.'

'Will you go to bed with Edmund?'

'I might. If I get the chance. It's not so easy to arrange.

But . . . yes, I probably will if he wants to.' Diana sighed happily. 'It's so hard to resist, isn't it?'

'I couldn't possibly say.'

They laughed again.

Flick said, 'Now I'm stuck here for a week, while you get to go out and have fun.'

'Hard cheese, that's for sure. But a week will be over in no time.'

Except that it seemed to take for ever. It dragged, Flick found. As soon as lessons were over for the morning and the house emptied as the girls went off on their cultural pursuits, usually accompanied by Winnie, Flick found herself alone and moping. All she could do was read. She started *War & Peace*, wondering if she could finish it before the week was up.

She was curled up in the drawing room trying to make sense of all the Russian names and their diminutives when Miss Norah, the younger Miss Wynne Finch, came fluttering into the room.

'Oh, there you are, Felicity! You must come at once.'

Flick looked up from her book. 'What?'

'*What?* So rude! You must come at once for a piano lesson.'

'A piano lesson? I haven't had one of those since I was ten.' Flick laughed. 'Unless you want me to teach someone? I can't do that either, I'm afraid.'

'No, the young man has arrived. Didn't you hear the bell?'

'No.' Flick heard nothing when she was reading.

'The young man is here who's offered to become our piano teacher. You know, the one from the concert.'

Flick shut her book with a snap. 'Caius Knolle?'

'Yes, that's the one. He's in the hall. You're the only one here so you will have to have the lesson. He wrote to us. We promised him a trial, you see!'

Flick jumped up off the sofa and said, 'Of course, of course I'll have a lesson.'

She followed Miss Norah out into the hallway, and there he was. As intense as a pool of shadow on a sunny day. He was in that huge black coat but now with a blue scarf of extraordinary length encasing his neck and shoulders. His hands were deep in his pockets and he was staring over the top of the blue scarf with coal-black eyes under the hair that was even more windswept and disarrayed than before.

'Here is your pupil,' Miss Norah said breathlessly, indicating Flick. 'I'll show you both to the music room.'

Caius Knolle looked at her without any recognition and they followed Miss Norah along the tiled passage to the grandly named music room, which was not much more than a bare room with a piano and some instrument cases and music stands.

'Here we are,' Miss Norah said, ushering them in. 'You can give Miss Templeton a lesson now, if you please.' She departed rapidly, closing the door fast behind them as if eager to make her escape, and they were on their own.

'Hello,' Caius said. His voice had a rasping quality and he spoke in a cultivated way, much more than she had expected.

She realised that in her mind he was still half the vagrant she had thought him to be at first sight. 'This is all rather sudden.'

'It is rather.' *I sound so priggish*, she thought, so quickly added, 'The last thing I expected was a piano lesson.'

'What were you doing?'

'Reading *War and Peace*,' she said truthfully and was surprised when he started laughing. 'What's so funny?'

'Nothing. Now sit down at that miserable piano and we'll see what you can do.' He pointed at the piano stool and she went over and sat down. 'I didn't bring any music, so we'll see what's on the stand.'

Flick obeyed and went to sit down as Caius drew up a chair from the side of the room and sat next to her. She smelled the aroma of cigarettes on the wool of his jumper and caught a fragrance of sandalwood. Her skin prickled and she wanted to shiver, but she hid it. She felt so sensitive to his presence beside her, it was all she could do to stay still and to hide it as much as possible, but a heightened feeling of being alive possessed her as he leaned across her to examine the music propped up on the piano.

'Can you play this?' he asked, taking off a piece of sheet music. 'It's by Mendelssohn.'

She looked at the complex rows of notes and laughed. 'No, but I can play this.'

She strummed out a simple two-hand piece that she had learned aged ten and knew by heart. With a couple of errors, she managed it well enough, thumping out the notes, frowning as she recalled them. When she had finished, she put her hands in her lap, feeling rather pleased with herself.

There was a pause and then he said, 'Oh.'

'Wasn't it any good?'

'Frankly, no. Do you want to learn the piano?'

'Not particularly.'

'I see.'

She turned to look at him, and saw that his dark eyes were glistening with amusement. His features were strong, as intense as he was. He looked as though he'd been outlined in dark marker pen where most people were pencil sketches, his strong cheekbones and nose defiantly well structured. He was almost too much to look at.

He said, 'Well, there isn't that much point in a lesson then. But we may as well have a go. You can read music?'

'Only very simple stuff.'

'Fine.' He stood up and looked through some of the music books on top of the piano, selecting one from the pile. 'Easy classical pieces. We'll do the simplest of these.'

He made her find her way through the short fugue, first one hand and then the other, and then helped her put the first couple of bars together.

'You can be a little lighter with your hands,' he instructed. 'The musicality is just as important as the right notes. You need to find the light and shade, the emotion. The story the music is telling us. This is just a little piece about spring: it needs verve, lightness, a rippling quality. You're telling a story of sunshine and blossom and birdsong. Look, this little set of quavers is like the trill of a bird.' He played the bars for her, on the upper octaves.

'I suppose it is,' Flick said, surprised. She hadn't thought of music as telling anything, just as something pretty or evocative.

'Let's try again.'

Within half an hour, she was playing the little piece nicely, and enjoying her ability to coax something so musical from the piano, instead of thumping away as she might otherwise do.

'There, you see, you can do it.' Caius smiled at her again.

Flick smiled back, more relaxed now that her attention had been taken by the music. Then she saw that he was staring at her in that way of his, as though he could see her in a way that others couldn't, and those odd feelings returned, of being hyper alive and alert to something.

'Were you really reading *War and Peace*?' he asked abruptly.

'I really was. I've only just started, though.'

'What are you doing here, in this silly school?'

'I'm only here to get away from home.' She laced her fingers together in her lap to hide the slight tremor in her fingers. 'I saw you playing the other night in the Sheldonian.'

'Ah. Did you now?'

'You were marvellous.'

He laughed. 'I saw you there too.'

'You did? I didn't notice.'

'I'm good at hiding things. You crossed my path a few times that day, and I noticed you each time. You're very striking.'

'Striking? I'm like a dish of milk. You must be confusing me with Diana, she's the striking one.'

76

'The sexpot you were walking with? Oh yes, she's all right. Earthy. At her peak right now; she'll run to fat with motherhood. She'll age young and turn drab before she's forty.'

Flick laughed uncertainly. That didn't seem a very nice thing to say and yet it felt like a kind of reverse compliment to Flick herself.

Caius moved his chair so that he was even closer to her and stared at her more intently. 'You are something else, I saw that at once. Those eyes of yours. There's something in them. Has anyone ever told you that you have an ethereal quality?'

'No. No one has ever really said anything much about me, except that I need to brush my hair and sit up straight.' A thought struck her. 'Did you know I was at this school?'

'No. But it was a possibility. I'd seen your little sexpot friend around here before.'

'Don't call her that, she's Diana.'

'Diana, is she? And what's your name, Miss Templeton?'

'Felicity. But my friends call me Flick.'

'FFFF-lick,' he said, rolling the name around his mouth, and she got the overwhelming feeling of something almost obscene gripping her: something awful and wonderful and maddening and arousing. She shivered. 'Are you cold?'

'No . . . no, not at all.' She began to blush instead, feeling hot rather than cold.

He had smallish hands, for a piano player, with blunt-ended fingers, and he ran one through his hair, pushing the locks out of his eyes. For a moment she thought he was going to touch her but he only said, 'Shall we meet, away from here?'

'Oh, well, I don't know. I suppose we could.' She knew she wanted to, very much.

'I'll write. We'll go out.'

'I'm not allowed to stay out late.'

'Of course you're not. We'll work it out.'

Flick looked away, unable to bear his intense gaze. She felt she might melt or sigh, or cry, if she looked back into his eyes.

The door opened and Miss Norah came in. 'Is the lesson over?' she asked. 'I've heard no music for a while.'

'We are talking about theory, Miss Wynne Finch. That is almost as important as the music, you know.' Caius sounded quite stern and Miss Norah looked flustered.

'Oh, of course. I'll leave you alone.'

Caius stood up. 'As it happens, the lesson is over. If you would like me to return and tutor the girls on a regular basis, then you or your sister know where to write to me.'

'Yes, yes. I'll show you out.'

A moment later, he was following Miss Norah out to the hall, where his dark coat was hanging on the stand. Flick stayed where she was, her mind racing. Had he been looking for her? He seemed to have seen Diana, noticed her, worked out where she was at school. Perhaps it was coincidence that he had applied to the school, he seemed to imply that. But what if he had tried his luck here on purpose to meet her? Or even to meet Diana? Perhaps despite what he said, Diana had caught his eye.

Flick didn't know whether Caius scouting out the school was a good thing or a bad thing.

But what did all that matter? He had noticed her, and been struck by her, without knowing anything about her family or her money or any of it. He had seen something in her eyes in a way that no one had ever seen her before.

That was exciting. More than exciting. It gave her a sense of incredible possibilities. She would of course see him again if he asked. How could she dream of saying no to that?

Flick put her hands to the keyboard and picked out the little fugue again. It sounded impossibly pretty. He had taught her that.

'Oh my goodness,' she said aloud. 'Oh my.'

When the other girls got back, Flick went into the hall to greet them.

Diana came breezing in, rosy-cheeked and hard to miss in a very noticeable black-and-white checked coat and high heels, a black hat perched on the back of her dark curls. Behind her came the others, the sad-eyed German girl bringing up the rear. She had not yet settled into the school and had not made any friends, as far as Flick knew. In fact, she had received some unpleasant remarks about her nationality and still appeared to be getting some cold shoulders.

'Come upstairs,' Flick said urgently to Diana, desperate to share her news, but Diana was in no hurry. She was interested in the post and whether there were any letters for her. There were two. 'Tea, first, Flick, I'm parched.'

So they went into the dining room where tea had been laid

out, and sat in their favourite window seat while Diana opened her letters and Flick buttered crumpets for them both.

'Gorgeous Edmund,' she said with a happy sigh, having read his letter, and pressed it to her chest. 'Imagine, Flick, if he and I marry, then you and I will be family. Wouldn't that be lovely?'

'Of course. But I suppose marriage is a way off.'

'Yes, I suppose so.' Diana put her letter down and took a buttered crumpet off the plate. 'So, what excitement happened while we were out?'

Flick quickly told her about Caius's visit. Diana laughed heartily.

'It's too good! It's lucky for you we were out or I suspect he would have been teaching Margaret, who can actually play the piano!'

'Yes, wasn't it lucky? He was very friendly. He said he was going to write to me, and perhaps we can go out.' Flick smiled conspiratorially. She had decided not to tell her friend either that she was a sexpot, which Diana would like, or that she was bound to age badly, which she would not like at all.

'Go out?' echoed Diana, looking puzzled. 'You don't want to go out with him, do you?'

'Of course. He's very attractive, especially up close. Burning eyes. Dark looks like . . . like Heathcliff.' She had been wondering who he made her think of, and now she realised. The dark intensity of the brooding hero of *Wuthering Heights*.

'But he's a piano teacher, darling! You can't go out with

him, that's not the point of us being here at all! You should go out with that nice Alfred. He's the nephew of an earl.'

'You could be a bit romantic, Diana, just for a second,' Flick said, a little hurt.

Diana bit her crumpet and ate it carefully. 'I am romantic. And if anyone can afford to marry a piano teacher, I suppose it's you.'

'I'm not going to marry him!' Flick said crossly. 'I might go out for tea. That's all.'

'Mmm, if you say so.' Diana regarded her with a mischievous look. 'But we'll see. You're a hundred times more romantic than I am, and that's your fatal flaw.'

Chapter Five
FLICK
1951

It was agonising waiting for a letter from Caius. Every morning, Flick looked hopefully at the pile of letters by Winnie's plate, hoping to be called up for her post, but nothing came. When she was finally called for a letter, she was disappointed to find it was from her mother. Gloria was planning a trip to Oxford to see her children.

'That'll be nice,' Diana said.

Flick gave her a look. 'You don't know my mother. Nice is not the word.'

It had been three days since her piano lesson and still nothing. She was almost at the end of her period of seclusion and was desperate to get out of the house.

'When is she coming?' Diana asked.

'In a week or so.'

'I'm looking forward to meeting her.'

'Mmm. She's here to see Brinsley. I don't even know if she'll come to this place.'

*

The longed-for note didn't come by post. It was pushed through the letter box one afternoon and she found it on the hall table on her way past. Thick black letters on the envelope read *Miss F. Templeton* with a strong line underneath her name. She knew at once who it was from.

> *So Miss Flick,*
> *I enjoyed our lesson. Shall we meet for tea? I'll be*
> *waiting by the Martyrs' Memorial on Monday at 4 p.m.*
> *Caius*

There was no telephone number or address to reach him on, she noticed. She would either be there, or she would not.

'Of course you'll go. You're allowed out at last.' Diana made a face. 'Imagine what the birdies would think if they knew! They'd much rather you were getting tipsy at a college cocktail party than going out with a piano teacher.'

'It's just tea, I'm not going out with him,' Flick said, trying to sound cool about the whole thing, but she was really desperately excited. She slept Sunday night with her hair rolled up in rags to give her soft silky locks a proper curl, and she and Diana secured permission to go out to a lecture on the Monday afternoon.

'I'll go to tea with Edmund in Magdalen,' Diana said, watching Flick carefully brush out her curls and then apply red lipstick. 'And you can go wherever he takes you. Fuller's, I expect.'

Flick turned around, anxious. 'Do I look all right?'

She was wearing a neat blue suit, with a nipped-in waist, and Diana's black high heels.

'Very nice.' Diana consulted her watch. 'Well, come on. Let's be on our way or you'll be late.'

They took a bus down the Banbury Road to St Giles, where Flick got off. Diana waved as the bus pulled away, and Flick made her way towards the memorial. It was already dark, the lights of the Randolph Hotel glowing against the late autumn afternoon. A bitter wind whipped up leaves and dust and rubbish and sent them swirling through the air, making her eyes gritty.

Flick was nervous. She had a feeling that something was going to hinge on today and while she felt a longing for whatever it was, she was also afraid. There would, she felt, be no return.

There's another path that isn't this one. But I don't know which one is right.

Life was these little steps, day after day, small decisions that led to huge happenings. Gloria had picked St Pandionia's. There Flick had met Diana, and from there, Diana had met Edmund. And now lives might change, children be born, all because Gloria had picked that school rather than another. It was odd to think about.

And here I am, walking down St Giles. Another decision, another step.

Caius was standing by the memorial, as she had known he would be, exactly as she had imagined him: in his black overcoat, a cigarette between his lips, hair as wild as ever. Except that he was, she saw now, very beautiful. She knew those hands now, and had seen his face close to hers, lips moving, eyes blinking. He was already familiar. How had she once thought he was a vagrant when there was so much obvious poetry about him?

Oh dear, I think I may already be lost.

Caius saw her approach and the flare of his eyelids showed his pleasure. 'There you are, right on time,' he said, flicking away his cigarette. 'Come on then.'

He stuffed his hands in his coat pocket and they began to walk, Flick hurrying slightly to keep up with him. 'Aren't we going to Fuller's?' she asked, as he turned towards the Ashmolean Museum.

'With all your undergraduate chums? I don't think so.' He laughed. 'This way.'

Suddenly he reached for her arm and tucked it through his own, holding her hand down on the rough wool of his coat. He looked down, straight into her eyes, and smiled. 'I'm so happy you came. I've been longing to see you.'

'Have you?' She was thrilled that he had been thinking of her.

'Of course. I've been counting the minutes until we could be together again.'

'Where are we going?' She was a little breathless as Caius was striding and she had to walk quickly to keep up.

'You'll see. Somewhere we can be ourselves.'

That sounds wonderful. It was what she wanted most: just to be herself.

They went past Worcester College and, heading up towards Jericho, Caius made a sudden turn and then another and then, down a narrow terraced street near the river, he led her into a small, steamy cafe; men in donkey jackets and caps sat at most of the tables.

'Here we are,' he said. 'Good to be out of the cold.'

It was indeed much warmer, and a thick savoury smell filled the small room. They slid into chairs on either side of a Formica-covered table. Around them, the working men were eating plates of pies or stew and chips, drinking coffee out of mugs, smoking over toast smeared in dripping.

A waitress came up with her notepad. 'Yes?'

'Coffee.' Caius held up two fingers.

'Anything to eat?'

'No.'

The waitress walked off.

'I might have wanted something,' Flick said, although she wasn't in the least hungry.

'You don't want anything here,' he replied. He fixed her with his dark stare and his lips curled slightly into a small smile. Those eyes weren't as coal black as they had seemed; there were small inner wheels of hazel around the irises. 'The coffee's bad, like it is everywhere, but at least it's off the ration. I suppose this is rather different from what you're used to.'

'You needn't think that because of my background, I don't know a different life. I do.' She had a flashback to being in a cottage in the grounds of Caundle Court. She'd been called in by the kindly woman who lived there, and given a bowl of soup alongside her own scruffy children. Flick had been hungry, she remembered that, and very glad of the soup. How was that possible, when she was a Templeton, when she lived in the big house?

'I don't believe you've ever been in a place like this,' Caius remarked, shaking his head and smiling.

Flick looked around. 'All right, I haven't. Not quite like this. But I'm not as spoiled as you think.'

'So what is your background then?' He looked curious.

Flick opened her mouth, then closed it again. The last thing she wanted to do was talk about her family or start describing her background. She wanted her relationship with Caius to be untainted by all that. So she said, 'My life is comfortable, I suppose. I'd be silly to pretend otherwise.'

'And your parents hope you'll marry a nice undergraduate or a don or even a vicar, and settle down to married life?'

'That's about it.'

'And is that what you want?'

The waitress came over and put two large mugs of steaming coffee in front of them. Flick stared into the thick dark brown liquid, watching the overhead striplights reflect in its surface.

'Well?' Caius was staring at her intently. 'Do you want that, Flick?'

'No. I want more than that. I don't think that life is for me.'

He put his hand out and covered hers, so that it lay warm and heavy on the back of her hand. 'I don't think it is either.'

'And you? What's your background?'

He began to talk. They smoked cigarettes and drank their

coffee as he told her that he was a music student, the son of two professional musicians. They had left Germany before the war, sensing the direction of things, and from earning a good living as members of the Berlin Philharmonic, they had moved to a more humble life, living in one of the poorer areas of Oxford. His father taught the cello in local schools and his mother took in piano pupils. She had taught Caius from the earliest age to play. 'My destiny,' he said with a shrug. 'I really had no choice about it.'

'What do they want for you?'

'They want the concert stage, they want fame, they want me to conduct, they want greatness for me.'

'Do you think you'll be able to get it?'

He stared at her, almost uncomprehending. 'Of course.' Then he laughed. 'Like I said. Destiny. The only question is how it is all going to unfold. I'm not prepared to spend too much of my time on drudgery.'

'Like teaching silly girls in precious little schools,' Flick said, taking a drag on her cigarette. The exhalation swirled up to join the fug of steam, food aroma and tobacco smoke that sat below the ceiling, muting the electric light.

Caius shrugged. 'Money is money. Teaching young ladies in a comfortable house for good pay is nicer than a lot of my work.'

'Do you live at home?'

He shook his head. 'I have digs in a house not far from here. It's easier that way. The relationship at home is complicated. Mothers can love in all sorts of different ways. Mine means well but her love is not easy to experience.'

'Yes,' Flick said feelingly, thinking of Gloria. 'I know exactly what you mean.'

He had taken his hand away from hers some time ago while he talked, but now he put it back. 'So. You will have to tell me about your family.'

'Yes, I will. At some point.'

'Come and see my place,' he said suddenly.

Flick looked at her watch. It was half past five. 'I have to be back quite soon.'

'It's nearby. Come, just for a minute.'

Caius paid for the coffee, and they pulled on their coats before venturing out into the inky cold darkness outside. Street lamps gave out a faint yellow glow, barely penetrating the dark.

'I don't know where we are,' Flick said, looking around.

'Follow me.' They walked along the dark leaf-blown streets until they reached a tall Victorian house with six storeys that descended into the basement below the railings and climbed up to the attic windows at the top. 'This is my place.'

Caius unlocked the front door and led the way into a drab hallway with a few old pot plants and some cheap pictures for decoration, and up a staircase that was once grand but now looked old and chipped. They went up to the first floor and along a passage to a door at the rear, which Caius unlocked. 'I took this one because of the view of the garden,' he said. 'Even though you can't see anything of it right now, and it's a mess when you can in any case.'

He switched on a light just inside and revealed a bed-sitting-room. Along one wall ran a length of Formica countertop with cupboards beneath and a small primus stove on top. It was furnished with a table and chairs, an armchair, a basin and a bed. The lightbulb was bare above the table.

Flick looked about. It was sparse and plain but neat and clean, as far as she could see. 'It's very nice.'

'It's mine, that's the main thing.'

'What do you do about playing the piano?'

'Mrs Briggs, the landlady, has an instrument in her parlour downstairs. I'm allowed to play it more or less when I like. If anyone complains or wants to use the parlour, I have to shut up.'

Flick looked at the stove. 'And you can cook here?'

'We're not really supposed to. Breakfast and dinner are included in the lodging, served downstairs in the dining room. But we can make tea and toast in our rooms if we wish.'

Flick stood there, suddenly awkward. So now she had glimpsed his private life and it felt like too much. It was so intimate, to be in this space where he ate and slept and dressed and cleaned his teeth.

He turned and faced her. 'I wanted you to see this. So you know what you're getting into.'

'What?'

He stepped closer to her and took her hands. 'No nasty surprises.' Then he leaned forward and quite suddenly put his lips on hers. He pulled away after a second, smiling that half-smile of his. 'You know we're going to be lovers, don't you?'

She gasped. A burning sensation swept through her. Something in her rejected this. She was a nice girl, a lady. She didn't sleep with music teachers in bedsits in lodging houses. Something else in her was wild and elated, as though she'd been chosen for an adventure denied to most. 'Are we?'

'I don't mean to frighten you, but yes, of course. Kiss me now.' He pushed his mouth on hers again and this time his hand, strong, holding the secret of music in its fingertips, pulled her head into his and he kissed her properly.

When he let her go, she was breathless and trembling. 'Oh.'

He laughed and said teasingly, 'Oh! Oh my. Oh me, oh my.' He rubbed one fingertip down the side of her face and looked at her almost tenderly. 'It's a good start. Come on now, I'll walk you back.'

'So how was it?' Diana asked later.

'It was very nice,' Flick said honestly.

'Did anything happen?'

Flick didn't say about the room, only that he had kissed her after the cafe.

'Well . . . that's quite a nerve on your first ever date!'

'Rich, coming from you.'

Diana laughed. 'Perhaps you're right.'

She looked at Flick wisely. 'You've got a crush. Just be careful. He looks a bit like trouble to me. Are you going to see him again?'

'Oh,' Flick said carelessly, as though she'd hadn't really thought about it until now. 'I suppose I might.'

He hadn't asked but she knew it was only a matter of time.

*

Gloria arrived for her visit that weekend. Flick was mortified that her mother turned up in a Rolls Royce, the driver in full uniform and peaked cap. She got out, dressed in a long white wool coat trimmed with white fox fur, and wearing a Russian-style Cossack hat, also in white fur. Under one arm she carried her chihuahua, Mrs Kemp. Mrs Kemp's pink tongue hung permanently from one side of her open mouth, giving her the look of a simpleton. An attendant followed bearing a basket of gifts for the Misses Wynne Finch and for the girls: boxes of chocolates and candied fruit and nuts that had them all sighing with delight. Flick was embarrassed that rationing didn't seem to affect Gloria, but no one else appeared to mind. It was clear that they all thought she was marvellous. They didn't seem to notice that she had nothing for Flick, spoke very little to her after an initial extravagant embrace, and was soon on her magnificent way to Magdalen, although she took Flick with her. After a tour of the college and tea in Brinsley's rooms, Gloria took the twins to the Randolph for dinner, then had the car take them back to their respective school and college after she had retired to a grand suite for the night.

It was, agreed Flick and Brinsley, very typical of Gloria. Showy, ostentatious and full of performance but with very little heart.

'She hardly asked me one thing,' Flick said. 'Of course, I'm used to that.'

'I got lots of questions,' Brinsley said. 'But not much interest in the answers.'

'Well, there we are. Sound and fury, signifying nothing.'

Flick sighed as the Rolls Royce drew up in front of St Pandionia's. 'Do you think we'll ever reach her?'

'Do you want to, though?' Brinsley asked cryptically.

Flick gathered her things. 'I suppose not. Do you?'

'You know me, I prefer a quiet life and Mother is not that.'

'Very true. Goodbye, Brinny, see you soon.'

'See you soon, old girl.'

She watched as the silver car purred away, bearing her brother back to his college, then turned to go into the school.

Gloria left the next day without seeing the twins. Flick, keeping a careful eye on deliveries to the house, was surprised to find a card that morning waiting for her on the hall table, written in flowing blue script.

Let's take a drive to Whytefield. My parents are away. I'll collect you after lunch. Edmund.

Edmund arrived in the early afternoon in his smart coffee-coloured Fiat, an expensive car but nowhere near as showy as Gloria's Rolls, for which Flick was grateful. As Edmund was a cousin, she was allowed to go off with him for the afternoon and they were soon motoring out of Oxford and into the countryside beyond, heading north into the stark wintery beauty of the Cotswolds. Not long before Burford, Edmund turned off the main road and headed down into a valley, crossed a bridge and drove slowly through a village of stone and thatched cottages, with larger houses behind high walls and iron gates, and then finally through the grand pillars of his parents' estate.

'Where are they?' Flick asked. She had been to Edmund's home a few times on family visits, when it had been full of people.

'Spain, I think. Somewhere warmer and brighter than here in any case.'

He drove the car along the gently winding drive to the end, where the house sat large and square, a red-brick Queen Anne creation with rows of elegant windows that felt quite different to the brown thatch and honey stone of the Cotswold houses that surrounded it.

'So why have we come here?' Flick said, as they left the car and walked towards the house.

'Oh, I don't know.' Edmund turned to smile at her. 'I saw the way you looked yesterday when your mama came to the college – quite crushed!'

Edmund had joined them in Brinsley's room for tea the previous day.

'And you decreed emergency measures?'

'Emergency champagne.' Edmund rang at the door of the house and after a while a butler opened it, flustered to see him and protesting that he was not expected. 'It's perfectly fine, Wilson, we can look after ourselves. It's not a grand visitation. We're just popping in. I wanted to show my cousin some of my father's latest collection.'

'Has he been shopping?' Flick asked as they went in.

'Naturally,' Edmund said. 'But champagne first.'

They sat in the orangery – the warmest room in the house,

Edmund said – and the butler brought them the family champagne, bottled at the extensive vineyards they owned. As if the family had needed more money, their wine and champagne was famous, named after their French estate, Château Mournier.

'You must think I need cheering up,' Flick said, sitting on a rattan lounger, her feet crossed at the ankles and holding up a glass of the pale golden liquid. 'And there was me, thinking I had the perfect poker face!'

'Cheers, old thing,' Edmund said and they saluted each other. When he had taken a sip, he said, 'Whenever I think my parents are dreadful, I only have to meet your mother to appreciate them so much more. Cousin Gloria is the most monstrous woman I've ever met.'

Flick laughed. 'What put you off this time?'

'I couldn't bear the little rat dog under her arm with its tongue sticking out. Was it my imagination or did she have a sort of Russian accent half the time?'

'I noticed that.' Flick laughed. 'I think it was the hat. It seemed to set something off in her.'

'She screeches. She tells awful jokes. She doesn't seem to care about anyone. She embarrassed poor Brin. I can only think how she affects you.' Edmund shot her a sympathetic look.

Flick shrugged. 'I'm used to her.'

'She's your mother. It must be hard. She must be hard to love.'

'Love?' Flick echoed. 'I don't know. Yes. I'm not sure what

it feels like to love.' She looked at him over the rim of her glass as she took a sip. 'Do you?'

'Of course. My mother is a ninny but she means well and she thinks the world of me.'

'Boys do get thought the world of.'

'She loves Charlotte too.'

'Lucky her.'

'Come on.' Edmund got up. 'Let's take our champagne and go and see the latest acquisitions.'

They went to the china cupboard, a name that under-played the beautiful hexagonal windowless room that led off the dining room. It was painted the palest green and lined with shelves carefully lit to show off the stunning beauty of the china and silver that filled them. Edmund's father col-lected the finest Sèvres and Meissen, along with antique French silver, and had recently bought new tureens, fruit stands and wine coolers that took pride of place in the china cupboard.

'They're amazing,' Flick said, admiring the display.

'They are, but after a while, one gets blasé. One Sèvres dinner service looks much like another.'

Flick laughed. 'That's one of the most spoiled things I've ever heard you say.'

They examined the china and then Edmund took her to the gallery on the third floor where glass cases held the family collection of miniatures, snuff boxes and pocket watches. They spent a happy hour or so peeling back the silk damask covers that kept the paintings and boxes in the safety of dark-ness, to examine the treasures beneath.

'I suppose we ought to be getting back to Oxford,' Edmund said, when they had exhausted the gallery. 'It's going to be dark soon.'

'This has been very nice,' Flick said as they went back downstairs to the grand entrance hall. 'Your side of the family lives rather differently to mine. It's like a beautiful museum here. A palace. Not like poor old Caundle, falling down and leaking.'

'It's nice enough but it's hardly a home. It's empty most of the time. At least a museum has visitors. If this is mine one day, I'll probably get rid of most of the stuff to real museums so other people can enjoy it all.'

'What a lovely idea.'

They arrived in the hall and Edmund suggested they go back and finish the champagne before they drove back.

'I did have one thing I wanted to say,' he said with a trace of awkwardness as they sat down to their drinks.

'Yes?'

'Flick . . . you know, we could do a lot worse than get married.'

She laughed. 'Who to?'

'To each other.'

Flick stared at him, astonished. 'Are you serious?'

'Well, it's worth thinking about.'

'We're cousins.'

'Second cousins. And that's the point.'

She frowned, still puzzled. 'Is this about family money? Keeping it all in one pot or something?'

'No . . . it's about . . . I don't know.' He sighed. 'I know you and Brinsley seem to think your lot is under a dark cloud of some sort. Some kind of bad luck. With your father dying like that, and all the other horrid things. Well, I feel that my side is the same. We're under a cloud too. And I thought, well, maybe the two clouds would cancel each other out. Or at least, we can stop other people marrying us and suffering.'

Flick was amazed, then laughed again. 'I never heard anything so ridiculous. And you are involved with Diana. Why on earth are you proposing to me? You don't love me, not like that, and I don't love you like that.'

'You're sensible, that's why.'

'I'm just immune to your deadly charm, and you should be pleased. I'm a friend, a real friend. You can't possibly mean we should get married.'

Edmund stared down into his champagne. He seemed very sad, suddenly. 'I suppose I don't mean it. Perhaps I'll marry Diana instead. I don't know. We're very young for all that, aren't we?'

'Very. We're only starting out. And we wouldn't make each other happy, Edmund, even if you are a handsome devil. I'm not right for you at all.'

Edmund looked up at her. 'I'm afraid, that's all.'

'Afraid of what?'

'Of what I'll do and who I am and what will happen.'

'What can I do about all that?'

'Nothing, I suppose.' After a moment, he put his empty glass on the table. 'Come on. I'll take you back to Oxford.'

*

Diana was amused that Edmund had taken Flick out, if a little put out that she hadn't been invited.

'I'd love to see Whytefield. Is it very fine?'

'Very. You'll see it one day, don't you worry.'

Flick didn't tell her that Edmund had made his ridiculous suggestion that they marry. He hadn't meant it, that was clear, and it certainly wasn't based in anything like love. Nevertheless, it would be better for Diana not to know.

Whether or not Edmund would propose to Diana, Flick didn't know. He liked her but that didn't mean he would consider her the right person to be a Carrington wife, with all that implied.

It's all so stupid, she thought. *Why can't we just do what we want?*

That, she decided impulsively, was what she would do. No dynastic marriages, no worries about houses and money and social standing. Just love. That was all she wanted.

Chapter Six
FLICK
1951

Flick felt powerless in her relationship with Caius and yet she didn't mind. She was happy to be swept up in the intense feelings that were engulfing them both. From the moment he told her that they would be lovers, they had become increasingly obsessed with one another, only happy when they were together.

Caius took charge, encouraging Flick to make use of every spare moment, giving her the courage to break the rules so that they could be together as often as possible. Notes would arrive from him.

Sweet Flick. Tell the governesses that you're going into town, drop the sexpot and meet me at the Ashmolean. I'll be waiting for you at 3 p.m. Longing for you. C x

She would do just what he said, hungering for his presence, barely able to wait to see him again. Even without his direction, she would have broken any amount of rules to spend a few moments in his intoxicating presence. Each meeting made their passion for each other more intense. The touch of his hand on hers made her tremble, his fingers stroking her palm left trails of hot fire, the kisses they shared melted her inside and burned away her resistance. She was obsessed with his mouth, wanted to lose herself in his eyes, and longed for him to possess her completely, but, so far, they had only held hands and kissed, occasionally reaching below coats and jumpers to enticing warm bodies beneath. Even that was unbearably exciting.

This is love, at last!

It was everything she'd hoped: thrilling, intense and utterly enthralling.

Then a letter arrived:

Darling,

I can't wait any longer, you're driving me wild. Can you come to my rooms this afternoon? I'll be there from 4 p.m., waiting and dreaming and hoping.

C x

Flick gasped when she read it, her cheeks flaming. Thank goodness she had not been with Diana, or she would surely have been rumbled. As it was, she kept the assignation a secret. Caius had told her it was best to confide in no one, not even Diana, at least not for now. There would come a time when they could live freely, but not yet. She knew he was right. No one would consider him a suitable match for her; they would try to talk her out of it. So she kept it all to herself.

On that cold November afternoon, she escaped the school, telling the Wynne Finches and Diana that she had a dentist's appointment, and made her way to Caius's lodging house, almost overcome by nerves and excitement. She had no doubt what would happen now – the desire between them was like a tinder-dry forest catching flame. If she didn't want it, then she should not go, but she was no longer capable of saying no to something she craved so much.

When Flick arrived, Caius was waiting in the hall. Mrs Briggs, the landlady, did not permit female visitors in the gentlemen's rooms but she was in the basement kitchen, so Caius swept Flick up the stairs, then shut the door of his bedsit behind them, grinning wickedly, his eyes shining.

'The old bat would probably love imagining us here in any case,' he said, turning the key in the lock. 'I don't know where Mr Briggs is. Killed in the war, she said. Probably living it up in Brighton with some dancing girls.'

Flick laughed. She had thought she would be nervous but being with Caius felt like the most natural thing in the world. 'Hard lines on Mrs Briggs then.'

She took off her coat and hat as Caius put on the heater and shut the curtains, sending the room into green gloominess.

Caius came and stood opposite her, taking her hands and staring deeply into her eyes. He wasn't much taller than she was and yet he seemed entirely overpowering, as though he was able to surround her completely.

'Beautiful Flick,' he murmured. The heat from his hands was making her breath come faster and her heart pound.

Then, he bent his head to hers and began to kiss her, gently at first but then with more power and passion. She sensed the intention: these kisses were thorough but transitional, heading somewhere else entirely, and she determined to surrender to the journey, letting her own body and desires take over completely. His hands rested in her hair briefly but did not stay still. He was stroking her arms, her neck, playing them up and down her front as though she herself were an instrument, and soon she realised that he was unbuttoning her blouse, and then his warm hands were inside her blouse and roaming over her back and chest, strumming the lace trim of her brassiere, playing on the fastening at the back.

It was exciting, and bewildering, like setting out on a dance with no knowledge of the steps. She could only be led. He brought her somehow to the bed, and his shirt was off now, revealing a dark mass of hair across his chest. How had he done that? She had no time to think about that, not when the sensation of their skin touching was so overwhelming. The warmth, the coarseness of his dark hair against her, the smooth skin of his upper arms, the latent strength of his muscles, and the urgency of what he wanted from her: it was leaving her gasping and unanchored. He murmured words of passion and desire until she was trembling with longing. She closed her eyes and retreated into sensation alone as he gently pushed her back onto the bed, and climbed on top of her, his body covering hers entirely, his weight pressing breath from her in a soft moan.

She felt his hands and lips all over her. He pulled her skirt down and pressed his fingers in below the waistband of her knickers. Her eyes flew open. One hand reached instinctively for him and held his wrist, trying to hold him back. 'Wait – should we?'

He half sighed, half laughed. 'Of course we should, my darling. It's right. It's our destiny.'

She was reassured, comforted. This was passion, the point of being alive. She wanted it. She was falling in love with him. Being with him was like being in the grip of something elemental and close to madness and there was no more chance of stopping themselves than in taming a tornado.

'You're made for this,' he said breathlessly, as he stripped away all her defences, her outer layers of clothing. 'You're so incredibly beautiful. Will you, darling? Will you let me? I can't resist you. I love you.'

'Yes . . . and I love you,' she sighed, as she yielded to her instincts and took all the pleasure he could give her.

'Where did you learn that?' she asked afterwards.

Caius was smoking, lying on his back. He turned to her and smiled, and she was possessed with love and desire for him. 'I'm a musician. I was born knowing how to coax beauty and passion from whatever I touch.' He took her hand with his free one and looked at her anxiously. 'Did I hurt you?'

'No. No. I thought you might . . . but it was fine.' She thought for a moment. 'How many lovers have you had before me?'

'Two. Does that matter?'

'I don't know.'

'Don't let it. I didn't feel for them what I feel for you. I don't need anyone else now.' He rolled over so that she could see his eyes glittering. His lips curved into a smile. 'I warn you, if you ever have another lover, I'll kill you.'

'And will you have another lover?'

'I'll probably have plenty.'

Flick was hurt. 'Oh, that's terrible!'

He laughed. 'I'm joking, my darling. I love you. I'll always be true to you.'

'I'll always love you like this.' She traced a finger down his nose, as if in awe of its perfection, and then over his lips. 'I'll never change.'

'Then all will be well.'

Flick didn't tell Diana what had happened. Diana was perfectly frank about her experiences with Edmund, which were growing in adventurousness whenever they could find the time and the opportunity to be alone, but Flick somehow couldn't admit what she had done. She pretended that she and Caius merely drank tea and went on sedate tours of the Ashmolean, or visited churches of the city.

'He took me to see the tomb of St Frideswide in Christ Church Cathedral,' she said, which was true, but she didn't explain that he had pulled her by the hand to a door, unlatched it and seduced her rapidly, standing up, in a dark and empty corner of a back cloister.

'Don't you kiss him?' Diana asked, surprised, as she took rollers out of her hair in front of Flick's mirror. She was testing a new style, fluffing up the ends of her hair, smoothing the top quite straight.

'Oh yes, sometimes.'

'And do you like it?'

'Very much.'

'Hmm.' Diana gave her a sideways glance in the mirror. 'I'm sure he's intriguing. But honestly, how can it go on? Besides, you're missing some excellent parties.'

One way for Flick to spend more time with Caius was to pretend she was going to Magdalen with Diana to see her brother and cousin.

'You'll never meet anyone decent,' Diana went on, releasing a tight spiral of brown hair. Then she stopped still and stared at Flick in the mirror, before turning to face her. 'Wait – you're in love with that piano teacher, aren't you?'

Flick looked up and her cheeks began to burn scarlet. 'Well . . .'

'You are! I'm right.' Diana put down her hair roller. She looked anxious. 'I don't think your mother will approve. Are you sure you can't be happy just with a fling?'

'I don't know. Perhaps.' Flick could hardly hide her burning face. 'But I'm afraid it's a little too late for that.'

Diana gasped. 'You're not pregnant, are you?'

Flick laughed, but felt slightly sick. There was no point in pretending now. 'I'm not pregnant. But we are . . . in love, and you know . . . you know what that means.'

Diana rushed over, sat on the bed and took her hand. 'You know you mustn't have a baby, don't you? You're so young. Your life would be over. You'd have to marry him.'

'We won't. He . . . there's something . . . he knows how to stop it.'

'Good.' Diana's brown eyes stared into hers. 'So it's gone pretty far then. I hope he's making you happy.'

'Very, very happy,' Flick said sincerely. 'You can't think how much fun we have just talking.'

It was true – she was happy just listening to him, hearing him play the piano. She loved it when he put on the gramophone records he loved so much and explained where the piece was succeeding and where it was failing. They had private words, intimate jokes. He called her Pug, because, he said, her big blue eyes were as round as a pug's. She sometimes called him Keys, the way his name was pronounced in Cambridge, where there was a Caius College, and, of course, for the piano he loved to play.

He was the sun and moon now. Nothing mattered except being with him. He was intoxicating and maddening and loving and all she could ever imagine wanting. He drove her to exquisite delight while telling her how beautiful she was and how much he adored her. Love was exactly what she had hoped: exhilarating, delicious, overwhelming. It was also intensely addictive, and all else paled into insignificance beside it.

She hardly knew how to put that into words for herself, let alone for Diana. She mostly just felt it.

'What will happen?' Diana asked.

'It all depends on what Caius decides,' she said honestly. 'It's all up to him.'

'You can't let him dictate your life,' Diana protested.

'We'll decide together.'

Diana looked pained. 'Just be careful. You are just on the brink of everything. You have so many chances, so many opportunities. Don't throw it all away for him.'

'Of course not,' Flick said. Diana didn't realise that there was no life without Caius worth having. She had obviously never been in love, or she would know that.

The rituals of Christmas were upon them far too early, it seemed to Flick. She didn't want to go back to Caundle but the tree in the school drawing room, the Christmas cards, the wan threadbare tinsel that Miss Norah draped over things, all told her that Christmas was marching towards her.

They went to beautiful carol services across the city, did their charitable work of hosting a party in a church hall for the poor children of Oxford, wandered about enjoying the displays in the shops. There was still so much scarcity, and so much remained rationed, and yet there was an unaccustomed feeling of opulence and feasting, with the sweet ration increased in December. Besides, the butchers in the Covered Market had plenty of hares, pigeons and rabbits hanging up, which looked properly Christmassy. Cornmarket, the High and Queen Street were jammed with motorcars, vans and delivery boys on bicycles, and thronging with people.

'What will you do for Christmas, Diana?' Flick asked, as they walked arm in arm. They were muffled up now, in scarves and mittens and woolly hats, and wore sheepskin-lined boots instead of high heels.

'I'll be home with all the family,' she said. 'My two eldest brothers are married now, so there will be a houseful, I expect. It will be jolly. The hunt will be with us on Boxing Day. I'll miss you, though, and that wretched Edmund, who still hasn't invited me to meet his family or go to any of their places. I thought he might take me to one or two of their grand London parties but not a word. What about you?'

'Back to Caundle, I suppose,' Flick said drearily. She clutched her friend's arm. 'I can't wait to come back! How long till we're together again?'

Diana laughed. 'Come on, darling, don't pretend it's me you're going to miss! Your dark-haired musician is the lure for you.'

Flick laughed. 'Yes, you're right. I'm going to miss him like crazy.'

'Come on, I'm freezing. Let's go to the pictures. There's that Bette Davis thriller still playing at the Ritz and I'm keen to see it.'

'Yes, let's.'

Gloria sent the cars to collect Flick and Brinsley and home they went to Dorset, clattering down the A34 towards the South West. Gloria was still enjoying the social whirl of London, and had Prudence with her, so the house was quiet. The twins had their own round of local parties and gatherings to attend. In the morning, Flick walked for a couple of hours, or sometimes rode out, then returned home to bathe and read until lunch.

It was pleasant to be mistress of her own time again, but

Flick missed Caius desperately, waiting keenly for a letter from him.

Their last meeting had been agonisingly sweet and sorrowful, with neither of them able to bear any kiss to be the last one. She has asked him to write to her care of the Caundle Parva post office and he had promised he would write as soon as he could. She had arranged for any letter to be forwarded to her at the house, but there had been nothing at all.

By lunchtime, with the morning post delivered, she had given up, sloping sadly to the dining room to where the table was laid with linen, china and crystal and, now that she and Brinsley were considered grown-ups, there were decanters of wine as well.

The food was better than at school because it all came from the estate. There was no shortage of the milk and butter that had been carefully rationed at St Pandionia's, and there was meat instead of the endless fish at school. Most of all, Flick found she liked to pour herself large glasses of wine from the decanters. Before lunch she'd make vodka and tonics from the tray in the drawing room, and then, usually eating with Brinsley, she would drink a few glasses with lunch. By the end, when coffee was brought up from the kitchen, she would feel thick-headed and dozy with it. She'd go upstairs to fall asleep, waking groggy in the afternoon to prepare for their evening engagements, when she would drink more of whatever was on offer.

She found that the doziness and sometimes sick feelings were worth that delicious numbness that came over her at the end of the first vodka and stayed with her through the wine. Troubles, loneliness and despair at herself melted away. The

pain of not hearing from Caius disappeared and she felt longing instead, composing long, intense but illegible love letters
to him, which were never quite fit enough to post. She listened to piano sonatas on the gramophone, and dreamed
about him. She had never had much patience with the social
round, and now her longing for Caius poisoned the parties
she went to, making them unbearably boring. The tedium
was only relieved by the fuzz of champagne and punch. She
took a flask of vodka with her to parties so that she could
doctor the virgin punches served to the girls.

After all, I'm a woman now.

Sometimes she wondered if Brinsley had had his first experiences of lovemaking but she assumed he hadn't. He showed no
interest in girls. Only she had the secret knowledge of the world
of adults. She looked differently at everyone now. At those
awful parties, with the fire of vodka burning through her, she
would imagine all the stuffy old married couples doing what
she and Caius had done so passionately and recklessly and it
would make her giggle as she was steered awkwardly around
the dance floor by another pink-cheeked boy.

But nothing from Caius. No word.

At last, to her breathless relief, a letter came from him. He
was contrite; he'd been summoned to join a series of concerts
in Edinburgh and the whole thing had absorbed all his time:
travelling, lodging, rehearsals, performances . . .

*I'm so sorry, darling Flick. I miss you so terribly. Only
work has helped comfort me. It's the only thing that
could stop me longing for you.*

She was elated. He hadn't written because he'd been so busy. But the concerts were over now. He was going back to Oxford. Everything was all right.

Now she celebrated rather than wallowed, taking big glasses of her vodka and tonic back to her room, and writing passionate long love letters to Caius, legible ones he could actually read. They sat like fat little packages on the hall table to be taken down to the village in time for the last post.

Gloria and Prue returned from London for the Christmas period, the motorcar loaded with gifts. Hampers arrived in trucks, and two large trees were felled on the estate for the house. As soon as Gloria was back, quiet Caundle became busy, and noisy. Extra staff came, and the place was polished up, cleaned and decorated. Suddenly, Caundle looked beautiful, the large rooms swathed in greenery, sprigs of holly on top of picture frames, and huge logs burning in the vast fireplaces. The thick velvet curtains were drawn against the dark afternoons and lamps glowed, making even the largest rooms feel cosy. Flick realised that, quietly, Brinsley was taking charge a little more, directing the staff, making sure things were being done properly. The bedroom fires were lit and didn't smoke. The hearths were well supplied with logs and the coal buckets were full. Surfaces were dusted and leaks had been mended.

Gloria's arrival brought a certain chaos with her: her presence was dramatic and her voice boomed through the house. She brought home two more chihuahuas, Mrs Siddal and

Mrs Morris, and the three little dogs yapped around all day, skidding over the stone floors and leaving dainty messes on the Persian rugs if they were not taken out. The energy in the house changed, and Flick found she preferred staying in her room to the lunches in the dining room, though she had to come down for dinner, suitably dressed, as Gloria insisted on appearing in long evening dresses and in full jewellery. Visitors arrived: Gloria's usual coterie of admirers and hangers-on, as well as neighbours and friends. There were barely five minutes to spend alone with her mother and she was glad of it. Nevertheless, Gloria still seemed to have her beady eye on her daughter. Housemaids regularly arrived at Flick's bedroom door bearing missives on silver trays, addressed to Flick. On the cards, adorned with an embossed golden G, were notes in Gloria's flowing black script, usually admonishing Flick for perceived slights.

Darling, you didn't greet me with a kiss when you passed me in the hall this morning. How do you think that made me feel? Like a leper, darling! Kiss your mother when you see her! Your loving mother xxx

Sweetest F, I'm sorry to say you need to take more trouble with your hair. No one likes looking across the dinner table at a scarecrow. I hoped your school would have taught you such things, even if you won't listen to me! A hairbrush is arriving from Harrods tomorrow. Please indulge me and use it. Your loving mother xxx

Flick read them, and then enjoyed burning them with her cigarette lighter, letting the leaves of black ash float away up the chimney of her bedroom fireplace.

Prue came in to lounge about and ask her sister about her adventures. She brought with her some of her own rebukes.

'I don't even know how she's got the time,' Prue said, shaking her fair head over the cards. 'It must take all day to put that paint on her face.'

'There's always time to administer a telling-off.'

'Given with *love,* darling,' Prue said, in a perfect imitation of her mother's voice.

'How was London?' Flick asked, examining the hairbrush that had arrived that day. It had a tortoise-shelled back and her initial carved into it. She dragged the bristles through her hair, then put it down on her dressing table.

'Surprisingly fun. I had lots more freedom. She was so occupied with everything – her parties, her dinners. Of course I had to show my face, but she seemed more pleased with me than anything.'

'You're so sweet and pretty, Prue. Always her lovely baby. I'm just the extra child she got free with her heir.'

Prue looked over at her. 'You can't mean that. She's ever so proud of you and your brains. She thinks you'll make your mark.'

'Really?' Flick felt vaguely comforted by this. 'She's never said anything like that to me.'

'That's her problem, she can't do it. But she boasted about you quite a lot. Told people you were at Oxford and that you got all your brains from her.'

Flick laughed. 'What college did she say I was at?'

'She said she couldn't remember.'

Flick and Prue giggled again.

Prue said, 'She has plans for you. Lining up likely husbands. She's taken an unlikely shine to a boy from Cornwall, Henry something.'

'It's no go,' Flick said crisply.

'Why not?'

'I'm not going to marry anyone she tells me to, that's why.'

'Have you got your eye on someone?' Prue enquired, curious.

'Of course not.' Flick picked up the hairbrush again and concentrated on smoothing the top of her hair, like Diana did. Somehow it never looked as good as it did on Diana. 'Come on. Dinner calls.'

It was only after Christmas that the inevitable confrontation with Gloria took place. Flick felt she had done very well, keeping under her mother's radar and generally avoiding her quite effectively. She had taken to extending her country walks, all the way out to the ruined belvedere at the end of the Long Walk. The belvedere was like a miniature version of the house, with two towers linked by a central hall, but all of it was in disrepair and there was a chain over the door with a sign warning about going inside. It had been the scene of picnics and parties in the nineteenth century, the ladies and gentlemen strolling there from the house while their lavish feasts were transported on carts and laid out ready for their arrival. Flick walked around the outside, wondering what the view would be like from the towers. It must stretch for miles over the fields and woods. No doubt it was magnificent; that was what a belvedere was for, after all.

All of this helped keep her mind off the fact she had not heard from Caius since just before Christmas.

Flick had just come back in through the boot room, discarding her stiff walking boots and tweed coat, and was heading to her bedroom to change when a footman stopped her to say that she was summoned to her mother's room. Flick considered changing first, but then went straight there to get it over with, hoping her walking trousers and yellow jersey would slightly annoy her mother.

Gloria was sitting up in her four-poster bed in a puffy mountain of silken feather-filled eiderdowns, her face slathered in her usual white grease. Her hair was pulled back tight under a cap, and a small rim of grey sat at the roots between the dark red hair and her pink scalp.

As Flick came in, her mother turned her face away in disgust. 'Can't you ever wear a dress?' she demanded.

Flick opened her mouth to protest that she was, more often than not, in a skirt or dress, but then closed it. There was no point. Gloria enjoyed provoking her, enjoyed the conflict. There would be a squabble about it, with Flick enumerating all the recent times she had worn a dress, and Gloria dismissing them or otherwise arguing. It was familiar, and simply Gloria's way of warming up to the real issue.

'What is it, Mother?' she asked, sitting down on one of the spindly French armchairs by the window.

'I am disgusted,' Gloria hissed, turning her white shiny

116

face towards her daughter. 'Disgusted!' She picked up some opened envelopes and dropped them on the bed in front of her. 'Explain these, you . . . you trollop.'

Flick stared at the envelopes, a sick feeling forming in her stomach. She could see Caius's bold black handwriting and knew at once what had happened. 'You took my letters!'

'It's my duty as your mother to keep you safe.' Gloria's face seemed to melt like a candle and suddenly it was scrunched up and she was crying, reaching for a lace hand-kerchief on her bedside table. 'Felicity, how could you do this to me?'

'Do what?' Flick said, pushing down her fear and growing cold inside. She would show nothing, admit nothing.

'You are *sleeping* with someone.' Now Gloria was indig-nant again, bringing her fist down on the eiderdown in anger. 'You've ruined yourself! If you have a baby or catch some-thing frightful, don't come crying to me! Who is he? Is he decent?'

Flick stared back, her face stony.

'He can't be! Caius?' Gloria said it Kay-us instead of Kai-us. 'It sounds foreign. Very foreign. Please tell me, Felicity, that you are not sleeping with some . . . *foreigner*.' She picked up one of the letters between the tips of her fingers with a look of disgust. 'The things he writes are obscene. Utterly obscene.'

Somewhere deep in her core, Flick felt ashamed and humiliated. *I will not feel that way*, she told herself firmly.

'I don't know how you can look at yourself in the mirror.'

Gloria's voice dripped with scorn. 'It's bestial. No better than farmyard animals.'

Flick had a flash of herself in Caius's arms, the unbearable bliss of being close to his body and having him make that addictive love to her. It felt heavenly, like being lifted beyond herself and into a new being made of the two of them.

'I shall give those two old biddies a piece of my mind for allowing this,' Gloria declared. 'I don't even know if you should go back to that school. I should report them. Sue them!'

Flick was startled out of her frozen state. 'No . . . no, don't do that! It's not their fault, they didn't have a clue. I lied to them.' She whirled around her thoughts, trying to sort them out. Why was it always like this? How did her mother always find a way to her weak spots? She would have to capitulate. 'I'm very sorry. It was a terrible mistake. He seduced me, I gave in, I didn't mean to . . .' She scrabbled around for excuses, and then began to cry.

Gloria's face softened. 'My poor baby! Come to me!' She opened her arms and Flick went over to the bed to sit by her mother and be enveloped in a silken, scented embrace. Her mother's oily face pressed against hers as she kissed her cheek. 'You've been taken wicked advantage of, my poor little girl!' She rocked Flick as though she was a child again. 'You will end it then? You can't walk out with a common little immigrant, you know that?'

Flick nodded. She'd say anything to be allowed back.

'If you promise you'll never see him again, I'll let you return to Oxford.' Gloria's tone had turned wheedling.

Flick knew she would have to promise. It was the only way. She crossed her fingers behind her back. 'I promise,' she said miserably.

Gloria's tears had dried. She pulled away from Flick, and said briskly, 'Perhaps it's not such a bad thing. Losing your wretched virginity and enjoying it is probably an advantage. But you must pretend on your wedding night, you know that, don't you? Now off you go. Write a letter to that man and bring it to me to check, and you can send it off this afternoon.'

She waved Flick away towards the door, and turned to her own letters. 'Goodbye, darling!'

Flick turned to go, still unable to take in her mother's mercurial moods and all she had said, and what she herself had just promised to do.

The only way was to shut herself down again, and try to feel as little as possible.

Chapter Seven
FLICK
1952

'So are you going to obey orders and break up with Caius?' Diana asked.

She and Flick had been joyfully reunited at the beginning of the new term, and had spent long hours in each other's rooms, swapping their gossip and making plans for the coming weeks. 'I think it's rotten that your mother opened your post like that!'

'It's absolutely typical,' Flick said with a shrug. 'She doesn't respect things like letters or privacy. In her mind, anything under her roof is hers.'

'Horrid. My mother would never do that. Cigarette?' Diana passed over a new engraved silver cigarette case. 'Pretty, isn't it? Edmund's present to me.'

'Very nice.' Flick took one, lit it and breathed out. 'Oh, I needed that. It's only been cigarettes and vodka that have helped me survive the ghastly holidays.'

'Me too,' Diana said, although Flick suspected that her friend hadn't needed oblivion quite as much as she had. Diana's Christmas sounded happy and full of family and exuberant parties and flirting and dancing. Nothing like Flick's lonely walks and hours in her room, and the tedious, soulless parties. 'So . . . what about Caius?'

Flick puffed again and said, 'She made me write him a letter. I had to break up with him. So I went away and wrote something extremely convincing. You'd have been taken in, I guarantee it.' She adopted a dramatic air. '"I'm so sorry, but it can never be! The gulf between us is too great for us ever to be happy! I cannot be with a poor piano player. I must ask that you never contact me again."'

'And you sent it?'

'Yes. She watched me address, seal it and send it.'

'I hope she was happy.'

'Very pleased.'

'So of course you wrote another letter . . .'

'Of course. I had already written and sent it. I got one of the estate children to take it down to the post office so she couldn't see it on the hall table. I just said, "Ignore my next letter, my mother made me write it, she knows all. I will see you in Oxford on the eighth, I'll come to the house. Don't write again." I knew Mother would be keeping a close eye on my post after that, and all my movements. So I was very careful, pretended to be heartbroken for a couple of days, and then got a little better. The main thing was that she didn't stop me from coming back.'

'Cunning,' Diana said. 'Very cunning. And this way you safeguard your inheritance.'

'Thank you. Not so cunning, but yes, it does make sure I

keep my independence. Once I get that, I'll be free. I know I'm lucky – as long as I keep Mother sweet.'

'She swallowed it. You're back here. That's the main thing.'

'I'm going to go to Caius tomorrow afternoon.' Flick sighed, feeling happiness seeping back into her bones, waking her up again. 'I can't wait!'

It felt like an age since Flick had been at Caius's lodging house. She knew the quickest route there now, cutting through to Jericho from St Giles, slipping along Little Clarendon Street, past the shops and houses, most owned by various colleges. A few roads away was the lodging house, already swathed in late-afternoon darkness and lit by the glow of the old lantern hanging over the front door, a remnant of the house's grander days.

Flick went to ring the bell but saw that the door was ajar, so she pushed it open and stepped into the hall just as Mrs Briggs, in her house dress and headscarf and holding a duster, came bustling out of the lodgers' parlour. 'Oh, Miss Templeton,' she said, seeing Flick. 'Did I leave the door open?'

'Yes, I hope you don't mind my coming in.' She gave her most charming smile.

'Not at all.' Mrs Briggs had a soft spot for Flick, who had won over the otherwise formidable landlady, and had been turning a blind eye to her visits upstairs to 'study music theory in peace' as Caius had solemnly told her. 'Have you got a lesson, dear?'

'I think so, that's what we arranged. Is he in?'

'That's right, I heard him go up earlier. I thought you might be with him.'

'No, I couldn't get here before.'

'Ah, well, he's upstairs, dear.' Mrs Briggs lifted her duster towards the ceiling to indicate where she meant.

'Thank you.' Flick headed up the stairs, eager to see Caius again. It had been weeks and she was longing for him, desperate to feel him in her arms again and no doubt he was just as eager for her. She reached his door and rapped on it. She waited but there was no response from inside, so she knocked hard again and said, 'Caius, are you there? It's me!'

She heard a sound within. 'Are you asleep? I'm here! Answer the door!'

There were more sounds of movement and a mumble.

Flick turned the handle but the door was locked. 'Caius, open the door!'

Footsteps approached, there was the turn of the lock and the door opened just an inch or so. The room beyond was in darkness, but she couldn't see much of it as Caius's face and body filled the space between her and it. He was bare-chested, she noticed, and his hair messier than usual. 'What are you doing here, Flick?' he asked, squinting against the light in the hall, his voice thick.

'Didn't you get my letter? I said I'd come today!' She smiled happily. 'Do let me in, I can't wait to see you!'

'I did get your letter. You broke up with me in no uncertain terms, unless you've forgotten.'

She was confused; her smile fell away. 'Yes, but I sent

another letter just before, telling you to ignore that one. My mother made me send it – I told you that!'

'I didn't get your other letter.' His voice was curiously blank. 'I only got your rather cruel letter telling me to get lost.'

'Oh no,' she said emphatically, panic curling in her stomach. 'I didn't mean that, that was just for show.' She stared at him. His eyes were blank, his expression impossible to read. There was no recognition or joy in his face. It was as though nothing had happened between them. 'Let me in, I'll explain.'

'I can't do that.'

'Why not?'

'I'm . . . I'm busy right now.'

She laughed disbelievingly. 'You've obviously been asleep. How can you be busy?'

He opened the door, his pose now insouciant as he gestured back with one bare muscled arm, his expression sardonic. 'Well, see for yourself.'

She blinked at the gloom beyond and then her eyes adjusted and she saw the woman in his bed, a sheet pulled up around her chest, plump shoulders above: a tousled blonde with her lipstick kissed off.

Flick gasped. 'Who . . . wait, what are you doing? Who is she?'

'You broke off with me,' he said sharply. 'It's your fault.'

She turned to stare at him. Hurt and despair gripped her. 'How could you?'

'You said some terrible things to me. Unforgivable. If you

didn't mean them, you shouldn't have said them.' Then he said again, 'It's your fault.'

Flick closed her eyes, trying to take it in. 'I see,' she said in a shaky voice. 'Yes, I suppose it was. I'd better go.'

'I think so.'

'Come back to bed, Caius,' called the blonde. 'I'm getting cold.'

Flick turned and hurried to the stairs, running down and out through the front door before she had to hear that voice again.

There's pain, and then there's pain, Flick thought dully as she walked back through the dark streets. She didn't want to get back to the school, where life would be going on as if this terrible thing hadn't just happened, so she kept walking.

She remembered the pain of Gloria telling her that Father was dead and was never coming home. It was the confusion and sadness she had felt when her pony died, and when Bobby the spaniel had been lost on the railway line, but much worse. She understood that while ponies and dogs could be replaced, her father could not, and that something that had kept her safe had left her life. Now she was profoundly unsafe, with only her mother to see to her needs. That pain had not, as they'd told her, got better in time. It had got worse.

There was the pain of knowing her mother didn't love her as much as she loved Brinny, along with the fact that she somehow fell short all the time of whatever it was her mother wanted her to be. Gloria just wanted a different daughter – simpler, more subservient, more conventional.

Which was rich, considering Gloria herself. She dropped in and out of her daughter's life when she chose, threw it into chaos and then left again.

There was the pain of feeling so lacking in herself, never as good as she wanted to be. She had thought darkly that she would never be loved, and then Caius had come along. He was something special, she knew that, and if he liked her, that made her special too.

She had lost him. It was too much to bear.

And he was right – it was her fault.

Flick arrived back at the school just in time for supper, and managed to make a plausible excuse for her late return. She joined the others in the dining room for their evening meal of fish pie and carrots, but could hardly eat a thing.

'Are you all right?' whispered Diana, concerned. 'You look awful.'

'Caius is seeing someone else. He thought I'd broken up with him.' It still seemed so impossible to believe. 'He didn't get the other note.'

'Oh darling! I'm sorry.' Diana's eyes filled with sympathetic tears. 'You must feel rotten. What bad luck! Are you sure it's too late?'

'Quite sure,' Flick said simply. She couldn't get the picture of the blonde in Caius's bed from her mind. The thought of him doing to some other girl what he had done to her fractured something inside her. 'Do you mind if we talk about something else?'

*

Flick existed in a limbo of numbness waiting for the letter from Caius that she was sure would come. What had happened to the other note she had sent? That child from the estate must have made some kind of stupid mistake – lost it or something. She should have gone herself to the post office that day to be certain. But she hadn't.

Each day she hurried down to check the post before breakfast, but there was never anything. How could he stand it? Didn't he miss her? How had he given up so easily?

Diana helped her to forget. They smuggled their bottles of vodka to their rooms and spent hours smoking and sipping their contraband, while Flick talked incessantly about Caius and what had happened and how it might be repaired.

'You'll see,' Diana would say wisely. 'I don't think that the story is over yet.'

'Oh yes it is. You don't know him. He's very proud.'

'I think he'll be back, one way or another.' Diana twirled her glass so that the vodka within became a tiny whirlpool. 'Are you going to write to him?'

'I'm not sure yet.' She had composed reams, writing endless letters in her diary that she never sent. She begged his forgiveness, begged him to take her back, begged him to give up the other girl. Or she disdainfully told him she had wasted her time on someone like him, and that she was glad she had found out in time what he was really like. She wrote him poems, she wrote short stories about him. He took up all the room in her head.

At last, desperate with no word from him, she wrote a heartfelt letter, explaining everything and declaring her endless love for him. *If you ever want me,* she said, *I'll be yours. You only have to come and get me.*

But still there was nothing.

As the term moved on, life got a little better. It had to. She couldn't be so sad all the time, not when there was Diana to chivvy her along and encourage her. And now there was no Caius, Flick was free to spend her time with her brother and cousin, and their social circle. That meant more parties and amusements. Plenty of young men paid her a great deal of attention, but it meant nothing to Flick.

She even gained a new friend: Marissa, the little sad-eyed German countess who had never quite managed to settle into the school and yet seemed to have nowhere else to go. Flick had come across her sitting in the small room lined with bookcases that the Wynne Finches called the library, curled up on a chair with her nose deep in a book.

'Oh, hello,' Flick had said, startled to see her as she went past to the shelves. 'I didn't see you there.'

'Hello,' said Marissa. 'That's all right. I'm used to it.' She went back to her book.

'What are you reading?'

She held out the book. *The End of the Affair* by Graham Greene.

'Is it good?'

'Very.'

'You don't have a German accent at all,' Flick observed.

'No. We spoke English at home when I was small. My mother is English.'

'Oh, I see.' Flick was painfully aware that she had said very little to this girl, despite noticing more than once how lonely she looked. She had just assumed that one of the other girls would pick her up. After all, she was a countess, surely one of them would like the cachet of Marissa as a friend? But no one had. Her nationality still counted against her, no doubt.

She thought of Caius. His family were German too. They had brought him here when he was just a boy. Imagine if he had been friendless because of it. Perhaps he had been. Full of sudden sympathy, she sat down on the chair opposite and regarded the other girl. She was the opposite of Diana: slender and quite small, her soft brown hair cut short and parted at the side with a fringe that brushed over her sad eyes.

Why are her eyes so sad?

The countess wasn't beautiful but she had a soulful quality about those grey eyes, and her mouth was full-lipped and sensitive. She had a chin with a tiny dimple that was just slightly off kilter and might have ruined her face if it weren't for the charm of her tilted nose.

'Where do you live?' Flick asked.

'When I'm not here, I live in Northumberland with a very old friend of my mother's.'

'Not with your parents?'

Marissa shook her head. 'My mother is in a hospital in Scotland. She'll never come out. My father lives abroad. So I live with this old lady. I call her my aunt, though we're not related.'

'No brothers or sisters?'

Marissa shook her head.

'That's rather sad.' *It must explain the eyes.*

'I don't know anything else.'

Flick hesitated and then said quickly, 'Why don't you come with Diana and me to dinner tonight? My cousin Edmund is giving a grand dinner at a restaurant in town, the Adelaide. Have you heard of it?'

Marissa shook her head. 'No. I don't know if I'll come.'

'Please do. You never know, you might enjoy yourself.'

Once she had convinced the quiet, shy Marissa to come out to dinner with her and Diana that evening, Flick rang the porters' lodge in Magdalen to leave a note for her cousin to expect another guest.

'Why on earth did you do that?' Diana asked, half annoyed, as they got ready that evening. 'Why do we want that little mouse with us?'

Diana had poured herself into a sky-blue strapless lamé gown that gave her very noticeably pointed breasts. Her dark hair had been set into sleek curls that almost touched her shoulders and she was painting her lips a glamorous scarlet.

'You look wonderful,' Flick said sincerely, wishing she could look like a bombshell too. She felt wan in her black evening dress, her hair refusing to obey the curlers and falling in soft waves instead.

'I really have to get Edmund to take me seriously,' Diana sighed. 'It's getting embarrassing.'

'He's keen, isn't he?'

'Frightfully keen on all the physical stuff. But no word of a proposal yet and it's been months.'

'I'm sure he'll do it soon.'

'Has he said anything to you?'

Flick remembered her cousin's proposal to her. He hadn't really meant it, she was sure, but she could hardly tell Diana about it. 'No.'

'My patience is getting a little short.' Diana put another slick of scarlet on her lips. 'If only I didn't actually love him.'

'Come on, we'll be late.'

Marissa was waiting in the hall. Flick felt a jolt of surprise as she came down the stairs and saw her. Where Diana was a sexpot – as Caius had always called her – Marissa was something more ethereal. She looked unexpectedly stylish in a pale pink tulle gown with a white silk wrap. Her hair was glossy, curled just at the short ends, and she had darkened and thickened her brows so that her grey eyes were all the more noticeable.

'You look very nice,' Flick said to Marissa, putting a hand on her arm. 'There's no need to be nervous.'

'I'm not nervous,' Marissa said in her high, clear voice. 'I am perfectly all right.'

'Good,' Diana said briskly. 'Then let's get going.'

The Adelaide was famous for its celebrated diners. At one time it had been a club but now it was open to anyone who wanted to sit in the same grand wood-panelled room where Evelyn Waugh and Max Beerbohm and any number of aristocrats and prime ministers had sat and eaten their dinners, enjoying the view of Christ Church which stood imposingly across the road, its honey-coloured towers and spires piercing the Oxford sky while its meadow opposite stretched out towards the river. Edmund had booked the entire place for his dinner party.

'My cousin is prone to extravagance,' Flick explained as their taxi pulled up in St Aldate's just outside the door to the restaurant. The ground floor was a tobacconist's, closed now, and they climbed the stairs to the first floor, where a maitre d' in white tie ushered them to a fine wood-panelled room, a fire blazing under an ornate wooden surround and pillared overmantel.

'Ah, my adorable cousin!' said Edmund, coming forward to greet them from a knot of students. While the others were smart in dinner suits, Edmund was wearing striking leopard-print trousers with his dinner jacket, a mustard-coloured bow tie and red velvet evening slippers. The effect with his blond hair and intense pale blue eyes was striking. Edmund kissed Flick on the cheek, then greeted Diana the same way, complimenting her dress, which was drawing many admiring glances from the undergraduates. He looked at Marissa. 'This must be your new friend.'

'Edmund Carrington – Marissa von Schulenberg,' Flick said, making the formal introduction.

Edmund looked at Marissa, frowning. 'Oh. Wait. Have we met?'

'Yes. You know my cousin, Otto. I think we met in his rooms, and at the river, for the Michaelmas regatta.'

Edmund raised his eyebrows. 'Of course we did. Please excuse me not remembering. Otto tells me you have two popes and a saint in your family tree.'

'That's why no one ever dares to disagree with me.' Marissa smiled.

Edmund laughed. 'It's an honour to have you here, Countess. And if I'd known, I'd have invited Otto as well.'

'I don't mind,' Marissa said. 'I see him quite enough.'

Diana came forward, taking Edmund by the arm and telling him that he simply must get her some champagne, and they moved away.

'I'm glad you came,' Flick said, pleased to see that she had done the right thing inviting Marissa.

'I think I am too.' Marissa looked out of the window. 'Look at that magnificent view. I could never get tired of Oxford, could you?'

'No, it's wonderful. Come on, let's get some champagne. Edmund always has plenty of Château Mournier, lucky us.'

Even with no word from Caius, life seemed to improve a little. Flick enjoyed her new friendship with Marissa, who had fitted in very well at the dinner. Despite being so quiet, she had somehow charmed everyone and she had instantly been accepted into Edmund's social circle, which had put Diana's nose a little out of joint.

'Don't be silly, she's no threat to you,' Flick said when Diana talked frostily of the new member of their group. 'No one possibly could be.'

She meant it. Diana threw all the other girls in the shade with her blatant appeal and eye-drawing style.

'All the same,' Diana said tartly, 'I didn't much like it. She and Edmund chatted for ages about the blessed panelling at the Adelaide. She seems to be as much of a nut about pilasters and lintels and architraves as he is. Which is annoying.'

'You have quite a lot that she doesn't,' Flick remarked with a laugh.

Diana gave her a sideways look. 'Don't invite her too much, will you?'

'Quiet Mouse? I wouldn't worry.'

'Just don't, for my sake?' Diana gave her a kiss. 'Thanks, darling.'

Marissa, though, was part of what improved things for Flick. She asked the birdies for English literature classes to balance out their flower arranging, sketches and domestic management, and Winnie agreed, for extra fees, to employ a postgraduate research student to come to the school and teach literature to Marissa and anyone else who wanted to join in. The only other volunteer was Flick – Diana had no interest at all – and so the two of them enjoyed afternoons with an impressively brilliant young woman from Somerville who talked to them about Virginia Woolf and George Eliot and Thomas Hardy and James Joyce. Flick loved it. Talking about books and writing were the only things that could lighten her heart and help lift the sadness that sat with her daily, and the hunger for Caius that she couldn't seem to banish.

It was true, though, that she was finally beginning to enjoy herself. There were parties in the college gardens, in the boathouses and at various smart Oxford clubs and societies. The Misses Wynne Finch let the girls socialise as much as they wanted, as long as the company was respectable. There were plenty of cocktail parties, bottles of champagne and wine-fuelled dinners, and plenty of flirtations. Flick found the various levels of tipsiness helped numb her misery, and she and Diana enjoyed comparing hangovers in the morning, trying to hide their heads from the birdies, who didn't guess quite how hard the girls were partying.

By the time the vacation loomed, Flick was wistful about losing an entire term without seeing Caius – two whole months! How had she borne it? – but Gloria had decreed a trip to Italy, to the villa on Lake Como that she often rented at this time of year, before the heat became what she considered unpleasant. She would take her children with her. The trip, Flick felt, might at least keep her mind from veering back to her broken heart and her lost love.

But the truth was that nothing had worked so far. Despite everything, she thought about him every day and night.

Lake Como was one of the few places where Flick could bear her mother. The circle of society figures who rented villas on the lake were exactly Gloria's kind of people. She loved tempestuous, eccentric Europeans, and smart, sassy Americans. She adored the wits, dandies and entertainers, the famous writers and the rich and aristocratic from across the world.

For the first time, Flick enjoyed the stay. She felt able to hold her own and it was novel to be respected as a person in her own right, instead of merely a child. She was still ignored much of the time but that was fine with her. She liked spending days on the deckchairs by the lake, reading under striped umbrellas, or in the pergola draped in showy bracts of dark pink and purple bougainvillea. Sometimes she, Brin and Prue took a boat out on the lake, or went swimming, or strolled into the nearest town to have cold drinks at a taverna or a cafe.

The late afternoon was for sleeping and then it was time to dress up – not too formally, smart linen dresses and pearls were fine – for martinis by the lake with whoever Gloria had invited that night.

It was halfway through the holiday when the Leighton Harcourts, the rich American couple from the next-door villa, brought their latest friend, Chase Dupone, to amuse Gloria.

'You are going to love him,' purred Lauren Harcourt, a statuesque blonde with the most polished looks Flick had ever seen. How did Americans do it? 'He's all the rage at home, quite the wunderkind of literature. He's come out to write his latest novel and he has deigned to stay with lucky us! I have to supply his favourite brand of Scotch and his Lucky Strikes, or there is hell to pay. He says he can't write a word without them!'

Flick looked with interest at the friend, who was holding court in the lakeside pergola. He was a small, plump man with pale skin, ashy hair and little round glasses, and he seemed to have gathered all the other guests around him and was telling some sort of funny story that was making them all howl with laughter.

Lauren leaned into Gloria. 'I'll tell you something else, darling. He's the biggest bitch I've ever met.'

Gloria laughed. 'He sounds *tremendous*. I can't wait to know him.'

'And you shall. Come on, let me introduce you.'

Flick followed them to the pergola and lingered outside, not brave enough to go in, but keen to listen. Dupone was telling them about writing his book.

'I hate talking about it,' he said with a soft, Southern twang, holding his cigarette aloft. He shuddered theatrically. 'The tyranny of that blank page, you can't imagine. My editor is expecting a torrent of genius and I'm afraid I can only produce a trickle of banality.'

As the guests reassured him of his brilliance, Flick thought with surprise of her own blank notebooks and how much she loved the virgin pages waiting for her to pour out her thoughts and dreams upon them.

She listened to Dupone. His speech sounded almost too rehearsed and polished to be natural. He delivered a steady stream of wit and jokes that sounded half sour, half childish, as though he revelled in pointing out other people's gaffs and foibles. Whatever, he was amusing. At dinner, he went on in the same way, and the next night, when they gathered at the Harcourt villa for a change, it was the same. Flick never spoke to him beyond being introduced, and he didn't seem to notice her, until almost the end of the stay when he found her in the garden of their villa, smoking and gazing out into the blue, starlit night.

'Well, there you are.' The little voice sounded crackly as he came drifting down the steps to join her by the stone balustrades at the lakeside. 'I've been wondering when I'd get you to myself. We were introduced, weren't we? But I've not spoken to you at all.'

'I'm not very interesting,' Flick said with a smile, trying to look sophisticated as she smoked her cigarette.

'Au contraire. I think you're very interesting. I'm intrigued. Are you adopted?' He was standing beside her now, blinking behind his glasses in the twilight.

She laughed. 'Oh no. What makes you think that?'

'I don't see how you and Gloria can be related. She is a gaudy old parrot and you're a quiet little dove. I'm fascinated.' He took out his own packet of cigarettes and lit one. 'Tell me about yourself.'

'What do you want to know?'

'Begin at the beginning.' Dupone sat down on a stone bench and patted the space next to him. 'How old are you? Where did you grow up? What's it like being the child of Gloria Carrington?'

Flick sat down beside him, feeling the cool of the stone through her satin skirts. Gloria had decreed formal dress for that evening's dinner. It was a curious feeling to have someone interested in her and Dupone's interest felt real.

'Come along, dear,' he urged, puffing on his own cigarette. 'I want to hear it all. Tell your Uncle Chase everything.'

So she began.

Chapter Eight

FLICK

1952

Flick lay on a rug in the garden of St Pandionia's with Marissa and Diana, whiling away a sunny May afternoon. They were discussing the grand birthday party to be held at Caundle next month, and all the arrangements that were in train for it.

'I'll have to be primped and prettied to within an inch of my life,' she said.

'What's wrong with that?' Diana said. She was protecting her white skin with a wide-brimmed straw hat and a parasol, as well as cat-eye dark glasses. 'You'll be the centre of attention. My family would never do that for me. I'll be lucky to get a birthday tea.'

'That's just the problem. I don't particularly want to be looked at like that. Perhaps you can take my place?'

'I'd love to, darling, but I don't think it would work.'

'I wish I could come but I have to visit my aunt,' Marissa said wistfully. 'I'm sure you'll enjoy it in the end.'

Flick looked up, suddenly alerted by the sound of her

mother's voice coming loudly from inside the house. 'Oh no. What on earth is she doing here?'

Within a moment, she had been summoned inside and found herself shut in the drawing room with her mother, who was pacing up and down on the hearth rug, dressed in a huge satin fur-trimmed coat in violent pink.

'Hello, Mother,' she said awkwardly, going to kiss her. 'What an unexpected surprise.'

'All surprises are unexpected,' Gloria said abruptly. Then she stopped, and stared icily at Flick. 'Did you know?'

'Know?' echoed Flick. She was suddenly cold after the warmth of the garden sunshine and gave a little shiver. 'Know what?'

'Know about this!' Gloria pulled a magazine out from under her voluminous coat and threw it on the table. It was *Mademoiselle*, an American magazine that Flick vaguely recalled seeing on the shelves of the larger newsagents', with other imported titles.

'No,' she said, bewildered at the unexpected turn of the conversation. She gazed at the cover which showed a slim, smart lady in a modern boxy jacket, full skirt and neat small hat, with the strapline *New Romantic Fashion for the Fall*. 'It's a fashion magazine.'

'Fashion and society,' Gloria said crisply. 'And your new little friend is a contributor.'

Then she saw it. On the cover in large print was the name Chase Dupone and underneath: *His Penetrating Study of England's Poor Little Rich Girl.*

Her stomach somersaulted. 'Oh no.'

'Oh *yes*.' Gloria's eyes were blazing at her. 'It's hot off the press. Lauren got an advance copy from Chase, and she sent it urgent airmail to me. It arrived this morning.'

'I had no idea!' Flick said, stuttering slightly. 'He never said.'

'Who cares what he said? It's what *you* said.' Gloria scooped up the magazine again and turned quickly to the pages she had folded down. Holding it out in front of her, she began to read. '"Miss Felicity Templeton, heiress to a famous fortune, has to be one of the saddest girls I've ever met. Blessed with beauty and a sharp intelligence as well as her riches, she nevertheless has known suffering . . ."'

'Oh dear,' Flick said, appalled. She remembered sitting on the lakeside that balmy evening with Dupone, as he gently coaxed from her the story of her childhood, her hopes and dreams and circumstances. *Did I tell him about Caius?* she wondered in panic, and then, with relief, was sure that she had not. *Even so . . . how could he?*

'It goes on in the same vein for some time,' Gloria said sourly. 'How *awful* your life is. Forget what your mother has done for you, how many sacrifices she has made, all she has lavished on you . . . it's all just too *terrible*.'

Flick decided she could only front it out, bearing in mind she hadn't read it, though she longed to snatch the magazine from her mother's hands and find out what he had written about her. 'I thought it was all private!'

'He's a journalist, my sweet little idiot. Nothing you could say would be private.'

'I had no idea,' Flick said in a small voice. She was trying desperately to remember what she had said. Had he written the things she had said about Gloria? *Oh God, I hope not! How could he?*

Gloria fixed her with a beady look. 'I had no idea you'd *suffered* so much.'

'I told him how hard it was when Father died. You know how miserable I was.'

'Of course. That's only natural. But my dear – we all have our burdens! We all lost people in the war, you're not the only one! Do you know how self-pitying you sound? It's really quite awful.'

'I've been stupid,' Flick said, her head drooping. 'I can't tell you how sorry I am.'

The apology seemed to mollify her mother and Gloria sank onto an armchair with a long sniff, her chin tilted upwards. 'You have been a gullible little fool. And you've brought yourself a great deal of the attention you claim to hate so much.'

'I didn't mean to. It's the last thing I would want.' Flick gulped. A tear escaped and ran down her cheek.

After a moment, Gloria said in a lighter tone, 'Well, I suppose it could be worse. He's rather sweet about me, in fact.' She lifted the magazine again and read out: '"Her mother is the famous Mrs Gloria Templeton, the society hostess renowned for her flamboyance and outrageous sense of humour."' Gloria looked up. 'That's rather charming, isn't it? "With a huge circle of intimate acquaintance, including crowned heads and the British royal family, Mrs Templeton is unmissable wherever she goes, dominating every gathering with her wit and unusual panache." I rather liked that bit too.' Gloria smiled. 'Dupone is a little monster but I can't help loving him.' She put down the magazine. 'And I suppose it's one way to launch you into society. I was rather hoping *Country Life* would feature you for your eighteenth, but this has a little more about it, in many ways. It's more international, at any rate.'

'I shouldn't think many people will read it here,' Flick volunteered. 'I've never read a copy in my life.'

Gloria gave her a pitying look. 'Oh, it will be picked up, my child. Just you wait. Well, it's done now. I was half wondering whether to cancel the party but I suppose we will simply have to live it down. And a personal profile by Chase Dupone is rather a cut above what most girls get. As long as it doesn't put off the right types, that's all. Now. I've come all this way. Shall we go and see Brinny and go out for lunch if he's not busy?'

Everyone was too polite to mention the *Mademoiselle* article to Flick, although of course they all soon knew about it. Flick could not bring herself to read it completely, but skimmed over it before slapping the magazine shut in horror. How could she have revealed so much about herself? And how could Chase have behaved so badly and shared her confidences with the world? It was mortifying. Gloria was right, the piece was quickly noticed by the British press and soon there were articles about Flick and her family in the newspapers and publications, although the tone was respectful. There was no mistaking the interest in Flick, though. The mix of a famous name, money and the hint of sadness was clearly intriguing.

Flick did not like it at all. Brinny reproached her for being so silly as to share all her private circumstances with a journalist but he accepted that she had not meant what had happened. He was sure that the fuss would die down and they would return to relative anonymity quite soon.

'I hope so. I hate this more than you can guess,' Flick said.

'Come out with me,' he suggested. 'I've found a rather excellent little basement club in town. Late at night, there's music – jazz and blues, from America.'

'I didn't know you liked that sort of stuff, Brin,' Flick said in surprise. 'I thought you were strictly a classical man.'

Brinsley laughed. 'I've surprised myself. But I like it very much. There's a record shop in St Peter's Road that I've taken to visiting and the fellow there knows all about it. He recommends lots of good things. Django Reinhardt, Oscar Peterson, Charlie Parker. I'll lend you some records if you want to hear them.'

'I'd like that. And I'd like to come to this club as well.'

They went out together one Friday, with a special late curfew for Flick, permitted as she was with her brother. Besides, the Wynne Finches seemed rather impressed by the *Mademoiselle* article – Gloria had left the magazine in the drawing room when she departed – and the press attention that followed, and they had accorded Flick a little more freedom since then.

Brinny explained there was no point in going early, so they went out to dine first, in a little place just off St Giles, before making their way to the club situated underneath what was once a Methodist chapel. Descending the stone steps, they entered a smoky, dim basement, full of tables where patrons sat, sipping drinks, smoking and waiting for the music to begin. The audience was a mix of all types and ages, and colours too. It felt simultaneously strange but also familiar, as though Flick had discovered somewhere she might feel at home.

'I like this place,' she whispered to Brin as they sat down at a table.

'You've only just arrived.'

'I know. But there's something about it.'

'Perhaps it's because it's the last place anyone would think of looking for the society heiress Miss Templeton.'

Flick laughed. 'That must be it.' She lit a cigarette and exhaled. 'Order us some drinks, won't you, Brin? I'd like vodka and tonic.' She looked around. 'No one cares about us, no one knows us. There are no rules, no formality.' Her spirits were beginning to lift. 'This is the first time I've felt free since that wretched article came out. I can't tell you how much I've hated those stupid articles in the press. As if I want to be known as the most miserable heiress in Britain.'

Brin laughed too, and took out the pipe he had recently taken up. He began to stuff its bowl with tobacco. 'It's a rather ridiculous moniker. I'm sure you'll shake it off. And I'm glad you like it here.' He ordered the drinks from a waiter and told her what to expect. 'A saxophonist, he's very good. A jazz trio. And a rather fine guitarist at the end.'

'Wonderful. I hope they hurry up with our drinks.'

It was after ten before the first act came on the stage, and once the music began, there was no more chatting. Flick sat back and let the melancholy song of the sax float over her. It was accompanied by a guitar and drums, and that seemed all that was needed to conjure extraordinary sounds of wistful melancholy that floated over the room and swirled around it like the smoke of the many cigarettes glowing at the tables.

'Beautiful,' breathed Flick as the trio's final piece finished. 'Who's next?'

'Another jazz trio. Pianist, double bass, drums.' Brinsley picked up the programme that lay on the table. 'Here we are. The pianist is Caius Knolle. I say, was that the chap who played at the Sheldonian that time?'

But the pianist was already walking out onto the stage. Of course it was him. Somehow it was no surprise. She'd always known she'd see him again, just not how. He was in a white shirt and dark trousers, his black hair longer than she remembered, the locks at the front falling over one dark brow. The bassist followed carrying his instrument, and the drummer slipped behind the kit at the back.

Flick felt as though her body had just been switched on after a long period of darkness. Her very skin seemed to prickle with current: the hairs on her arms stood up, her skin bumped and she shivered and sighed.

Oh Caius.

He was at the piano now, lolling against it before he sat down and squinting out into the darkened room. The room fell quiet. Then he spoke. 'I'm going to play a piece I've written.'

His voice seemed to move through her, and everything she had felt for him came rushing up to seize her again.

'This is for someone I know,' he said, moving towards the keyboard. 'I've called it "Little Girl Lost".'

He sat down and nodded at the other musicians so that they all began at the same time: the slip and punch of the drums, the thrum of the bass and then the liquid melancholy of the piano.

Flick was entranced. Little Girl Lost? Who was that? *Could it be me?*

It was probably that buxom blonde from Caius's bed, she thought miserably. And yet the music spoke to her. It talked to her about the hours she had spent in Caius's bed, the feeling of being in his arms, their whispered confidences and jokes, the way he would call her 'Pug' and tease her.

She listened, soaking in the music. She'd had no idea he liked jazz, or composed. But of course he did. It was very Caius. He was modern and subversive and creative. That was why she loved him.

When the mournful, beautiful piece ended, the room erupted in applause. Only Flick didn't clap; she couldn't. It was taking all her control to stay still, rather than run onto the stage to embrace him.

The trio played another piece, but Flick fled to the lavatory and sat in a stall, her heart pounding, her breath coming in small gasps. Should she talk to him or not? What would she say?

By the time she returned to the table, Caius had left the stage and the last performers of the night had taken his place.

Brinsley had paid the bill and was knocking out his pipe. It was after eleven now.

'You missed most of it,' Brinsley observed mildly.

'I know, I was feeling a bit dicky. But I heard the best bit.' She tried to sound normal. 'I ought to be getting back to Pandy's. I know they worship you there, but they'll be cross if I'm late.'

'Of course. I've heard what I wanted. Let's go.' Brinsley stood up to help her with her coat. 'I'll walk you back if you like.'

'I'll get a taxi,' she said.

'Really? Will you find one at this time of night?'

'There's bound to be one on St Giles, there's a rank there.'

'All right, if you're sure. But I'll walk you there.'

They walked amiably through the cool night air and Brinsley left her at the taxi rank, heading on his way to Magdalen. Flick climbed into a cab and asked for Caius's address.

Five minutes later, she was sitting on the steps of the lodging house, smoking and wondering what on earth she would do when he pitched up, or if he arrived with another girl.

I'm making a terrible mistake, I'll go home. She stood up.

The sound of footsteps came echoing down the pavement in the cool darkness, and she froze under the great lantern that hung over the front door.

'Well, well,' Caius said as he emerged out of the darkness. 'Little Girl Lost has been found.'

'I was never lost,' she said. 'You knew where I was.'

'You were lost to me.' He came up the steps towards her.

'I tried to explain.' His nearness was overwhelming her

148

and she began to tremble with longing. 'You wouldn't listen to me. I never wanted us to part.'

'And yet you sent that letter.'

'My mother made me do it!'

'You didn't have to do what she said. It destroyed me to receive it.'

'If I hadn't, she would have stopped me coming back to Oxford. I couldn't have borne that. I needed to come back to you. I did what I thought I had to do.'

He was standing close to her now, his eyes dark holes in his face in the semi-darkness. She couldn't read his expression but she caught the scent of tobacco and sandalwood, and cramped inside with need. She longed to kiss him more than she'd ever wanted anything.

'Ah,' he said softly. 'And this is how paths diverge – misunderstandings, accidents, mistakes.'

'Can't you forgive me? Now you know I didn't mean it? Our paths could come back to one another.'

'I'm not sure about that.' He reached out and put a finger on her lips, stroking his finger across her mouth. It was agonising, like the promise of water in a desert.

'I love you, Caius. I had to tell you, in case I never see you again. I don't know if I'm coming back next year. I'll be gone soon. I just want you to know that I meant what I said when I wrote – if you ever ask me, I'll come to you. No matter what.'

'That's quite a promise, Little Girl Lost.' He smiled. 'Perhaps one day I'll take you up on it. Now, come on, I'm going to find you a taxi to take you back to that school of yours.'

She felt the crushing blow of disappointment. For a moment she'd thought he would take her upstairs and make love to her, something she violently wanted. But no. He was going to take her home.

She hoped he would kiss her when he put her into the taxi, but instead he lifted her hand to his lips and then smiled at her.

'It was lovely to find you again,' he said. 'If only for a moment.'

'But why? Why won't you take me back?' she asked desperately.

'Things happen on my terms, Pug, not yours. You need to understand that. If you don't accept that, nothing can happen between us.'

'I do accept that, I do.'

'Then be a good girl, and wait.'

He turned and sauntered off and, as her taxi pulled away, Flick watched until he disappeared into darkness.

I'll probably never see him again. How can I possibly bear it?

PART TWO

Chapter Nine
ETTA
1975

'One for fun, two for you, three for me, four at the door . . .'

Etta, concentrating and muttering as she climbed the stairs, was startled when she heard a loud laugh coming from the top landing.

She looked up to see her sister Mary there with a gang of friends, all clutching books and bags. Mary was at the centre, always achingly cool with her long blonde hair and stylish clothes. Today she was wearing a pair of flared, flowered overalls over a sky-blue cropped-sleeved T-shirt, and looked great. No wonder other girls flocked around her to soak up her glamour.

'Who are you talking to, Etta?' she called down over the landing balustrade.

'One of her imaginary friends, I expect,' said one of the other girls. 'The only kind she's got.'

Mary gave her a sharp nudge with an elbow. 'Shut up, leave her alone. If anyone's going to insult Etta, it'll be me.'

Etta grinned up at her big sister. She knew Mary would

never let anyone hurt her, even if she could be distinctly prickly with Etta herself.

Lucky me. Mary is just the coolest sister in the world. She's like a movie star.

As the older girls came down the stairs, Etta flattened herself against the wall, trying to make herself as invisible as possible, though she smiled shyly as Mary went past. Mary took no further notice of her, flicking one long lock over her shoulder as she went by, and taking a casual drag on her cigarette.

The headmaster was standing at the bottom of the stairs as the girls approached. He stood back and waited for them to come down, smiling at them. 'Afternoon, everyone!'

'Hey, Frank,' Mary said, as she reached the ground floor. The others greeted him the same way. 'How are you?'

'Fine thanks, Mary.'

'Cool potatoes.'

'How are things with you? Are you going to lessons this afternoon?'

'I'm not sure.'

'I think I'll go to history,' said one of the other girls with a shrug. 'But I haven't decided.'

Mary said, 'I'm going to sit in the orchard for a bit. The weather is kind of great today, you know?'

Frank Creed smiled again. 'Good idea.' As the girls went by, he said, 'Oh, have you seen? A senate this afternoon. We're sitting in session at four p.m., if you want to come.'

'Maybe,' Mary replied with a shrug. 'All depends.'

'Barry Johnson has called it. Someone stole some money from his locker, so we're going to decide the consequences.'

'Yeah, okay, thanks. Gotta go.' Mary drifted past, taking another drag on her cigarette as she went.

When the girls had passed, Frank looked up the stairs to where Etta was still standing with her back against the wall. He was a nice enough man, dressing younger than his age in cord flares and a floral shirt with pointed collars, but his balding head and grey comb-over gave the game away.

'What are you up to, Etta?'

Etta looked down the stairs. 'I thought I might go to maths with Rosie.'

'Good idea,' Frank said. 'She's working with Domino Group. You'd fit in well there.'

Etta knew what he was saying. At Armitage Hall, there were no set year groups or forms. The pupils chose where they wanted to go on the basis of their interests and abilities rather than being categorised according to their age. There were minimal rules, and freedom, democracy and tolerance were the founding principles. Things like uniforms, lesson bells, or any organised activity except the school meetings – called senates – were unknown.

Opinion was divided on how effective the regime was. Somehow enough pupils scraped through their exams to keep the school open and passing inspections and its adherents were passionate about it.

On the one hand, Etta enjoyed the freedom but on the other, she sometimes wished for someone to tell her what to do, instead of having to fret all the time about making her own decisions. Wouldn't a timetable take some of the stress out of the day? Sometimes she seemed to spend most of the day dithering about what to do. There weren't many team sports she could play, as enough people for two sides could never be mustered at any one time – except in boys' football, which seemed to be an endless rolling game taking place all over the grounds and school – and there was no one to provide the equipment or teach them how to play in any case. Etta stuck more or less to tennis as it was easier to find one person who wanted to play with her, and Dan, one of the teachers, would sometimes coach her if she asked and he had nothing else to do.

When Etta complained, her mother rolled her eyes.

'Why would you want to run around with a load of jolly-hockey-sticks braying girls anyway?'

'But I've never played netball, hockey or lacrosse, like other girls.'

'Lucky you. It's so lovely to be able to do what you like. Games are horrible, everyone knows that. Just go to the library and get some books out. That way you can teach yourself anything you need to know. Or ask a teacher.'

Etta found it odd that she was supposed to have ultimate choice, but in the end, the school had been chosen for her and now she had no choice but to be a part of its liberal philosophy, which meant she was extremely hazy about what formal education involved, and she didn't get the choice to play games, or wear a uniform or go to standard lessons. As for chapel and hymns and prayers – they were considered anathema, a pursuit for the brainwashed and terminally simple.

Mum sat back in her chair and gazed anxiously at Etta. 'Don't you like school, darling?'

'Of course I do.' She knew her parents wanted her to go there, and it was important to please them. She wasn't like Mary, who raged and shouted and stamped and made demands. She quietly got on with it and seethed in private about being pushed around and ignored. It felt like in Mum's world, writing was most important. Then came Dad, then Mary, then Etta last of all.

Mum stared at her, frowning, as if trying to read Etta's thoughts. 'If you want to go somewhere else, then tell me! But you'll have to decide soon, or I'm sure you won't get in anywhere else with your education. Now, go away, sweetie, I have to write.' Her mother put her glasses back on, and turned back to her typewriter, surrounded by her towers of books, a cigarette glowing in the ashtray beside her.

But how did Etta know where she could go? And anyway, at least she was here at Armitage Hall with Mary, even if her sister acted as though she did not exist.

Now she said to Frank, 'Yeah, Dominos maths class is good.'

Dominos was for children younger than Etta, though no one ever said that. All lessons were for anyone and everyone. But in reality, Dominos was for children of around the age of twelve.

'Excellent,' Frank said heartily. 'Enjoy yourself, Etta!'

'Thanks. See you later, Frank.' Etta left the main school building and started heading for the Dominos maths class. Classrooms outside the main building were made from old railway carriages placed about the grounds, and she walked past the orchard on her way to Rosie's lesson. She plainly heard a peal of Mary's laughter and smelled the rich incense-odour of marijuana as she went past. The sounds of boys' and girls' voices came over the hedge – there was a bit of a party going on in the orchard.

And that's another thing, thought Etta, as she went past. *If you want to just take drugs and party, then you can.*

No consequences. No punishment. Did the parents know? Did they know how the upper years of the school were awash with drugs? The girls and boys slept in different boarding houses but there were plenty of opportunities for all sorts of mischief and the staff simply didn't seem to care. The rumour was that the school sanatorium handed out the contraceptive pill like smarties to whoever wanted it.

As she trudged towards the railway carriage, Etta felt the familiar prickle of anxiety about Mary. Her sister had been a studious, quiet type until about a year or so ago, when she had suddenly blossomed into a very pretty girl, and had started to become much more interested in clothes, and looks, and being stylish, than she ever had before. The older years were always more sophisticated and glamorous, and suddenly who you were and who your family were seemed to matter and change things.

As Etta approached the carriage, she could see that Rosie was already inside, writing some equations on the black-board. Hopefully today quadratic equations would mysteriously become clear to her. She was tempted to give up entirely but something kept making her come back to attempt to master them.

'Hello there, Etta,' Rosie said cheerfully, as Etta came in. 'How are you?'

'Fine, thanks.'

'Back for equations?'

Etta nodded.

'We'll get you there, don't worry.' Rosie put her chalk down and examined her handiwork. Then she sighed. 'God, I'm dying for a fag.' She pulled a packet out of her jeans pockets and lit up. Sitting on the desk, she exhaled and said, 'Some of the others should turn up soon.'

The younger years tended to be more obedient and turn up for lessons but around thirteen, they'd discover the unlimited freedom and start using it.

Etta sat down at a desk and reached in her bag for a notebook and pen. 'We could always start?'

'Sure, if you like.' Rosie squinted at the board through the haze of cigarette smoke. 'Right, let's go back to the beginning.'

Just as Rosie started to work her way through the formula for quadratic equations, and Etta was finding it unexpectedly comprehensible, the railway carriage door opened and one of the younger children stood there.

'Etta, you're wanted in Frank's office. Blue card,' he said breathlessly, then slammed the door and disappeared.

Blue card meant you had to go.

So much for choice, Etta thought grimly, closing her book.

'That's a shame,' Rosie said cheerfully, 'but we can start again any time you like.'

'Thanks.'

Etta hurried off, back to the main school. She couldn't imagine ever having Mary's insouciance and turning up when it suited her, making it plain to the headmaster that she didn't consider him particularly important. But when she got to his office, she was surprised to see that Mary was already there, along with her grandmother. Granny was sitting in one of the chairs in front of Frank's desk looking quite a sight in a huge purple kaftan. It would have been quite attention-grabbing on its own, but her lavender hair set in rolling waves and her huge diamanté-encrusted glasses and thick make-up made the whole effect overwhelming.

Etta blinked, caught between the surprise of seeing her grandmother and delight. Granny was always fun, generous, exciting company and she was Etta's heroine.

'Etta, darling!' Granny said with a broad smile. 'Kiss your granny!' She scrunched shut her eyes and pursed her lips into a big pout, staying perfectly still while Etta went over to kiss her grandmother's powdery cheek.

'Hello, Granny,' she said, smiling broadly. 'I didn't know you were coming today!' Then, suddenly anxious, 'Is everything all right?'

Mary was looking sour, no doubt annoyed to have been summoned away from the fun and joints in the orchard. She heaved a huge sigh and stared crossly at the ceiling.

'Feeling tired, Mary?' Granny said innocently. 'Perhaps an early night is called for.'

Etta stifled a giggle. The way Granny could puncture Mary's attitude so easily was also something she loved about her.

'Sit down, Etta,' Frank said from behind his desk. 'Your grandmother has asked if she can take you and Mary out for tea. Would you like to go?'

'Yes, of course.' It was just a tea. There was nothing serious about the visit after all. She was relieved.

'Mary, you'll go too?'

'I suppose so,' Mary said sulkily.

Granny beamed, not apparently noticing her older grand-daughter's reluctance. 'Good! Thank you, Mr Creed, I'll whisk them away and have them back for supper.'

'No hurry,' Frank said amiably. 'Whenever they want to come back is fine with us.'

As they walked to the front door, Mary said, 'I don't think he'd care if we never came back, as long as Mum keeps paying for us.'

'Darling, *I* pay for you! And I can't think why I do, this place is a terrible dump. I said Benenden. I said Roedean. Your mother wouldn't listen. She banged on enough about wanting to go to proper school herself when she was a girl. That's all forgotten. And you know what she's like. Everything has to be done her way. Come, chop chop, we've no time to waste. Stop loitering, Mary.'

Etta had to be fair to Mum – this was a bit outrageous coming from Granny, considering the control she seemed to exert over everyone and the fact that she did whatever she wanted – but she also wished Mum had listened and sent her off to a normal school.

Granny's Rolls was also in her new favourite colour: purple. And she'd had it upholstered in swirling purple and brown leather. 'Like something one of those lovely Beatles would choose,' she'd said happily when she first showed them. 'I'm so fond of them. I believe I'm one of the few people who can give them musical advice.'

'They broke up years ago,' Mary had pointed out, giggling.

'That's exactly what I told them to do,' Granny had replied.

Now they settled back on the zany leather seats and Granny's driver steered out of the school grounds and towards the local town. There was only one decent hotel, The Grosvenor.

'It really ought to be done for some kind of trades description violation,' Granny said as they parked at the back near the bins. 'It is nothing like the *real* Grosvenor.'

As usual, Granny's appearance and manner of supreme self-confidence seemed to inspire terrified awe in the hotel staff, and soon they found themselves in a private lounge, with a special afternoon tea being made for them to accommodate Granny's request for cucumber sandwiches. Granny asked a few questions about school while they waited for the tea to arrive, and once it had been served out, she gave a long sigh.

'Well, girls, it's always a pleasure to see you. I talked to your mother last night.'

Mary snorted. 'That's good because I'm not going to.'

Granny gave her sideways look. 'Why not? Has she annoyed you?'

'Yes, she has! Her stupid newspaper column came out again on Sunday and she's written about me in it, and I fucking hate it.'

'Language, Mary,' Granny said serenely. 'What did she say this time?'

'She wrote all about my shopping habits and my favourite places in London, and how different it was to when she was young. Like, yeah, Mum, of course it is! It's like twenty years later, of course. But she makes me sound like a child and an idiot and I hate it. I've asked her not to do it. Etta, you hate it too, don't you?'

Etta nodded. She didn't think of it much, but perhaps that was because her friends didn't seem to be aware that their family life was being dissected in print all the time. But also, Mum mainly wrote about Mary, probably because Mary was more interesting and the older one. Mary was much more like Mum, as well, and not just in looks. She had Mum's fair hair and big blue eyes, while Etta was dark and more sultry looking. Mary also had Mum's sharp intelligence and impatience, mixed with a certain self-absorption.

'You should tell her not to,' Granny said, seeming more pleased than anything else by Mary's fury.

'I have! A lot!'

'And what did she say to that?'

Mary snorted again and crossed her arms, flinging herself against the back of the sofa. 'She said it's her job and she isn't writing, like, *shit*. She's writing proper serious journalism, and meditations on growing up and motherhood, like, *litera-ture*, and that she's given me a false name so no one will know it's me, but everyone bloody well does know it's me.'

Etta thought that this was fair enough. What was the point in giving Mary a false name, when most people knew exactly who her mother was, even if Mum wrote under a different surname? But still, Mary must know that she was just going to do it, and that was that. There was no point in getting cross about it. The crosser you were, the more likely you were to get written about, which was another reason why Etta kept so quiet.

She seemed to spend her life both longing for her mother's attention and fearing it. When those large, pale blue eyes turned on you, with their piercing quality and the sense that they could see into your head, it could feel very unpleasant. But there was nothing nicer than seeing them bright with praise and approval, or scrunching up in laughter.

'I shall have a word with your mother, Mary, and tell her you're not happy.' Granny looked keen at the prospect. 'She'll listen to me.'

Etta and Mary swapped glances. They knew that Mum did listen to Granny and then, when Granny had left, went on furious tirades against her monstrous selfishness, hypocrisy and interference.

'I have no idea how she can lecture me about being a good mother!' she'd cry, and go over all of Granny's worst actions one after the other, as though the girls had never heard them before. Then, after a while, and a few drinks, Mum would get tearful and beg them for reassurance that she herself was a good mother and nothing like Granny, and they would reassure her, and this could go on for ages. It would be a relief for the girls to escape back to their own flat at the bottom of the house. They'd knock on Dad's front door on the way down and tell him he was needed upstairs, and he'd go up to comfort Mum and drink more with her, and help her recover from the trauma of Granny's visit.

Granny did not visit much any more. She had declared the house a scandal that should be condemned and Mum's flat a disgrace. So they tended to be summoned to Granny's house, which Etta loved. It was like a fairy tale of sparkling opulence, utterly different from their mother's flat, which was always drowning in books, papers and ashtrays.

As they ate the cucumber sandwiches and fruit cake and drank their tea, Granny regaled them with stories of her London life, which sounded very glamorous and included many occasions where Granny had wowed entire roomfuls of people with her style and witty conversation.

They were just finishing up and thinking of their return to school when Granny suddenly became very solemn.

'Now, girls,' she said, 'I'm afraid I have something serious to tell you.' She looked very grave but the effect was undermined by a crumb stuck in her lipstick and Etta couldn't help watching it as she talked. 'It's something your mother told me last night.'

'Yeah?' Mary's attention was wandering and she was clearly thinking of getting back to Armitage Hall before too much longer.

'I'm afraid your poor dear father is back in hospital. Your mother asked me to tell you.'

'Dad's in hospital again?' Mary was alert now, her blue eyes round and anxious. 'Is he okay?'

Etta felt the same anxiety coursing through her. This was the fourth time Dad had gone back into hospital. 'How bad is it, Granny?' she asked in a small voice.

'I'm told it's quite bad this time,' Granny said carefully. She dabbed at her mouth with a napkin and the crumb vanished.

Etta's anxiety increased. If Granny was being careful about what she said, it must be awful. 'What did he do?'

'He's still digging for treasure, I'm afraid. And he got rather overwhelmed with that.'

Etta's eyes filled with tears. Lately Dad had become convinced that there was treasure buried somewhere in the walls of his flat and had been digging for it. No one could persuade him for long that there was nothing there. Mum wasn't even bothering to get the holes filled because it would only give him fresh places to search. She'd even considered putting chicken wire over all the walls so he couldn't dig into them. Sometimes he would be more like his old self and appear quite bemused by the damage and laugh at himself for believing something so absurd. And then, one day, it would all be different. He would be agitated, obsessed, unable to rest or sleep because of the desire to find the gold he knew for certain was in the walls.

'Is he okay?' Mary asked, losing some of her sophisticated adult veneer.

Granny looked sympathetic. 'Poor girls. It's hard on you. All I know is that he's responding to treatment. But he'll be staying a while.'

'How's Mum?' Etta asked. It seemed to her that Mum needed looking after and when he was well, Dad was the one to do that. How was she managing? And wasn't she lonely all on her own in that tall house, with the other flats beneath her empty? She might be perfectly happy. Etta was never sure how her mother would react to anything.

'She's just fine, don't worry about her. She's visiting your father and keeping the show on the road. You can write to him if you like, it's the usual address. No telephone calls at the moment.'

The girls nodded sadly. They knew the routine now.

If only Dad would get better, Etta thought sorrowfully. His illness was something that blighted their lives horribly. Surely there was some kind of treatment or medicine that would fix him?

'I'm afraid the curse has struck again,' Granny said with a sigh.

Mary rolled her eyes. She did not believe in the family curse that Granny often talked about.

'None of us can escape it,' Granny said, standing up and smoothing out her kaftan. 'Perhaps you will, Etta. But I doubt it.'

'Why Etta?' asked Mary. 'Why not me?'

'Well, perhaps one of you will. But none of us seem to escape unscathed. I know I've suffered badly.' Granny sighed again, shaking her head. 'What can one do? How does one lift a curse? Now, girls, let's go to the car and get you both back to school.'

In the car, Etta reached out for her sister's hand, and for once Mary held it without demur and squeezed it too. They both seemed to find comfort in the contact.

Then her big sister leaned over and said quietly in her ear, 'Don't worry about that stupid curse. It doesn't exist. I promise.'

Chapter Ten

FLICK

1955

Flick let herself in through the front door of the tall building in Meard Street, Soho, and checked for their post. More bills addressed to her: Mrs F. Knolle. She was still not used to her new name. It didn't seem like her at all.

She went down the backstairs to their basement flat. It had not mysteriously tidied itself in her absence, and so chaos greeted her. She was almost grateful for the gloom that concealed so much of the mess but it was painfully evident when she switched on the light. There were books and musical manuscripts everywhere, and clothes flung around, cushions astray from chairs, ashtrays overflowing on the coffee table that was covered in old newspapers and magazines. Shoes and slippers were scattered about singly, and there were coffee cups and sticky wine glasses everywhere.

'How do women do it?' she said out loud, putting down the shopping. She seemed to slave every minute of the day and yet still it was never done, and as fast as she cleared up, more mess was created.

By the door was a bag of laundry she had been supposed

to take to the launderette in Noel Street but she had not yet had time. There was still supper to cook, and supper was a mystifying thing to have to produce. She didn't know a single thing about how to cook, so she had gone to a bookshop on the Charing Cross Road to find a book to tell her what to do. She had managed to find one that promised her simple and delicious recipes, but even these involved a huge amount of effort and equipment. The flat was equipped in a basic manner and she didn't seem to have half of what was required. The supper she had produced was nowhere near as simple and delicious as had been promised.

'We're going to need some help,' she had said to Caius one afternoon. 'I don't think I can manage it on my own.'

Caius had been sitting on the sofa with his feet up, legs outstretched, reading a newspaper while smoking and drinking the coffee she had made him. He looked over the top of his paper, fixing her with a sardonic look. Then he gazed around their very small flat. 'This is too much for you, darling?'

'Well . . . I suppose I'm not trained for it, that's all.'

'How hard can it be to learn? I think it will be an excellent thing for you to acquire domestic skills.' He went back to his paper, then bent down one corner to look over it and say, 'We can't afford help, you know that. Not with your mother behaving this way.'

Gloria, incensed by Flick's elopement, had put a halt to the passing over of Flick's inheritance. All Flick had was the small allowance she had enjoyed as a schoolgirl.

'Perhaps you could help me a little?' she suggested to Caius. 'You're used to living in a bedsit after all.'

Caius laughed. 'That was before we got married. Anyway, Mrs Briggs cleaned the place. She provided meals. That's what women do. You really are going to have to learn, Flick, or we'll both starve and that's no good.'

'I suppose I will have to. I'd hate our emaciated skeletons to be found, all because of me.'

Now in the empty flat, she felt overwhelmed by it. Married life had started in such a blaze of excitement. They had run away to London and applied for their marriage licence at the register office in Chelsea. It had felt amazingly, powerfully naughty and thrilling. No one knew where she was, no one could tell her what to do. She and Caius were together again and all was right with the world. She was lost in the bliss of their reunion and the extraordinary power of the love between them. They stayed in a shabby hotel in Hammersmith, where no one cared if they were married or not, and Flick paid by writing out cheques. Thank goodness she had remembered to bring her chequebook with her when she left home. She'd also gone to the bank with her passport and cashed a cheque for a hundred pounds, which seemed to give her limitless funds as far as she was concerned. The hotel was cheap at only twenty shillings a night for the two of them. They ate their evening meals at cafes and bistros, also cheaply. It was all enormous fun, and the London she knew – of tall houses in elegant squares – felt a world away from this one: busy, dirty, crowded, with street markets, grimy shops, betting joints, and pubs every few yards, full of men drinking during opening hours. London's terraced houses seemed packed with people. Shabby children were everywhere, scampering over bomb damage and rubbish piles. There were still boarded-up ruins of buildings long condemned, waiting for the time and money to be made available to demolish them.

During the day, they explored London together, arm in arm, floating on their cloud of love, until the day they could be married. They bought rings in a jewellery shop in the East End, where, according to Caius, they could get gold cheaply. Flick wrote to Brinsley and Prue and told them when the wedding was to be. She wrote to Diana too, care of her family home in Kent, hoping that the letter would reach her somehow. But she did not write to her mother. She tried not to think of the towering rage that had surely followed her dramatic departure from the birthday party.

Her August wedding day dawned hot. In the morning, in the hotel room that was plagued with flies in the hot weather, she had put on the green satin ballgown she had worn at her party when she ran away. Then she put on the pearl necklace and earrings that her mother had given her that day.

She stood and stared at her reflection in the mirror screwed into the door of the wardrobe.

I look ridiculous.

How incongruous it was to wear such a dress in a room like this. She felt starkly the change in her circumstances. She was no longer the jewelled heiress, but the soon-to-be wife of a struggling piano player. But she had been miserable and she was happy now, so she might as well embrace it sooner rather than later. She took off the ballgown and put on a flowery, full-skirted dress she had bought a few days before in a shop in the outskirts of Kensington. Over it she put a light blue cardigan that matched her eyes, and some high-heeled sandals. She took off the pearls and put them back in their case.

Caius came back from the barber's freshly shaved and neat, and put on his usual clothes, except adding a tie, and they headed off on the bus to the register office. Caius bought her a posy from a flower stall on the street and that was her wedding bouquet. As they waited their turn at the register office, Flick looked hopefully at the doors, wondering if Brinsley or Prue would arrive. They would have to ask people in one of the waiting wedding parties to be their witnesses if no one else arrived. Gazing down at the posy of late roses in her lap, she felt suddenly afraid at what she was doing. It was a serious undertaking. She had been destined for a grand society wedding in St Margaret's, Westminster, surrounded by her family and the dozens of friends and relations who would expect to be invited. This was so very, very different. Could it really be right?

Caius seemed happy but unconcerned at this muted little wedding. He didn't appear to mind that his parents were not there, and that they had never even met Flick, or that he had no best man and no friends with him. He just seemed to want to get it over with, tapping his foot and smoking with impatience at their wait.

The happy couple before them emerged from the registrar's office, beaming with pleasure, surrounded by delighted family. On the steps of the building, they were pelted with rice and rose petals, the bride squealing with delight and shielding herself with her bouquet, and her father took photographs with a big box camera, trying to get everyone to stand still.

Now it's our turn!

She was so nervous, twittering inside with fear and excitement.

Their names were called. Caius took her hand. For the first time, he looked anxious himself. He squeezed her so tightly it almost hurt. 'Are you ready?' he asked.

She nodded.

'Let's ask those two to be our witnesses,' he said, nodding at some early arrivals for a later wedding. He began to walk towards them.

'Flick, Flick!' Diana burst in through the doors, chic in a tight, dark blue suit and neat veiled hat. Edmund followed behind, in a loud black-and-white checked suit. 'Are we in time?'

'Diana! Edmund!' Flick dashed forward to embrace them. 'I'm so happy you came, you can't imagine! You're just in time. Come on. I'm going to get married!'

The wedding went by in a strange flash. They walked in and it seemed that moments later, they emerged man and wife. Diana was sobbing as Flick and Caius made their promises, taking the handkerchief that Edmund offered to dab away her tears.

'So beautiful,' she sighed as Flick and Caius put the rings on one another's fingers.

Caius had planned that they would go to a pub for their wedding breakfast but Edmund wouldn't hear of it. They took a taxi to the Ritz, and had their wedding breakfast there – their wedding present from him, he explained. Caius accepted without protest, seeming just at home in the red and gold surroundings of the Ritz restaurant as he would have been in the pub, and completely unsurprised by the turn that events had taken. Diana was as ebullient and charming as ever, Edmund polished, polite and soigné, while Caius sat back and allowed them to amuse him.

'Is there a honeymoon?' Diana asked playfully.

'Only if you offer one,' Caius replied. He looked at Edmund. 'I'm sure you've got some houses, Eddie? Spare one for a honeymoon?'

Edmund laughed easily, though Flick could see the faintest hint of his embarrassment. 'It would be more than my life's worth to annoy my cousin Gloria.'

'Is she very angry?' Flick asked anxiously.

Edmund stared at the tablecloth for a moment and then said, 'Officially, she hasn't acknowledged what's happened. But I'm told that she is not at all happy. I don't suppose you're surprised by that.'

'And Brin, and Prue?'

'Shocked. Very sad.' Edmund looked at Caius, who didn't appear to be listening although Flick was sure he must be. 'Nothing personal against you, old man. But you have to admit, it's not what everyone hoped for Flick – not you, but the manner of it all.'

Caius shrugged and said nothing.

Somehow, afterwards, when they were back at the hotel on their first night as man and wife, it was this remark that dominated Caius's memory of the whole day. He started to go over and over it, getting crosser and crosser each time. When she protested that Edmund was simply telling the truth, not attacking Caius at all, and that he had after all bought them a wonderful wedding breakfast, Caius would not listen. He began to think that he had been personally insulted by Edmund. Then he moved on to Gloria, who had not softened, had not sent a present, was not going to be as easy to win over as Flick had promised. They started to argue, then Flick burst into tears at the way her wedding night was unfolding, and Caius, furious, stormed out and did not come back until much later, when she had cried herself to sleep in bed. He woke her to slur an apology and make drunken love to her, and she was happy again.

Marriage changed everything in a way Flick had not expected. It was as though the day before they were equals and the day after, she had been demoted in some ways – Caius made it clear that he would make decisions from now on – and promoted in others. She was now in charge of the domestic realm entirely and completely. It was not something she was in any way prepared or trained for. St Pandionia's had taught her how to manage staff. How to plan menus that someone else would cook for her. It had not prepared her for using a washing tub and mangle, or heating an iron over the fire, which was why she had turned to serviced washes at the launderette, paying extra for the ironing to be done, and for it all to be delivered in a little van that trundled up on a Wednesday morning to drop off the freshly laundered things.

They had left the hotel not long after their wedding, as soon as Caius had found them the tiny flat, thanks to a friend who was also helping him find work playing the piano in clubs, pubs and hotels while he attended conducting classes during the day, and practised his music. They had no piano so he had to go out to play, until they had the money to get one in their flat.

'Soho is the place to be,' Caius had decreed, 'because it's where the music is. It's where the interesting people are.'

So they had moved into their Meard Street basement, in an eighteenth-century townhouse, now divided into flats. Flick was grateful they had an indoor lavatory, at least. Many of the flats they had looked at shared an outdoor one with all the other occupants of the building and she didn't think she could have stood that. They had two rooms, a sitting room and a bedroom, with a galley kitchen and tiny bathroom tacked on the back in what was the old courtyard garden. There was electricity, supplied by the meter that had to be fed with shillings to keep the lights on. More than once, trying to conjure up a meal on the electric cooker, she had been suddenly plunged into darkness, the stove shutting off, and had stumbled in the blackness to find her purse, a coin and then the meter to feed it into. She had learned after a few times to put a small mountain of coins on top of the meter, and to keep a torch in the kitchen in case of another black-out. In the evenings, she would wait for the man to wheel up on his bicycle and light the gas street lamps, which let scraps of mellow illumination fall through the railings and down into their gloomy place.

She bought coal from a man who came by every few days with a cart; it was better than going to the coal yard herself to buy a bucketful. She kept the fire going for as long as she could, eking out the coal lump by lump. The flat was stone cold some-times, even on a hot day. It was hard to warm it as the fireplace was very large, a remnant of the time the basement contained the kitchen. Her trusty chequebook had almost run out and she was making each one last as long as possible. Her small allow-ance could not possibly support them, but it was all she had – as long as Mother was still paying it.

'This is real life, Flick,' Caius told her. 'Your gilded little world was never like this, was it?'

He seemed to be enjoying watching her struggle with her new life and that made her more determined to succeed.

She became accustomed to the chill and gloom below ground level, often looking up through their sitting room window to the sight of feet cut off at the ankles pounding past on the pavement above their heads, feeling like some-thing small and insignificant in a burrow somewhere.

The music might have been in Soho but it was a place like nothing Flick had ever experienced. There was a thriving sex industry, with many upper rooms glowing with red lights and theatres offering showgirls and naked revues, and blank-windowed shops that she knew had magazines, books and equipment that would never be seen on any decent high street shelf. A cinema a street away showed films that attracted many men, who slunk in wearing raincoats and hats pulled low. At night, women lingered on the pavements, heavily made up and smoking, their boyfriends in the shadows nearby. There was a sharp vinegary atmosphere of something cruel and selfish, mixed with the soothing oil of entertainment, escape and self-indulgence. It was about pleasure – drinks and wit and laughter and cigarettes and talking – mixed with a kind of numbness and misery and loneliness. When night came, there was a feeling of menace and violence she heartily disliked. Their sleep was often broken by someone getting over their railings, staggering down the iron stairs and pounding at the window, demanding a girl. It was the oddest place that Flick had ever known.

It was also lonely a lot of the time, for Caius worked in the evenings. She was glad when he got a regular gig in a louche drinking club above a restaurant in Lexington Street. Here, she could join him, and while away her evenings sitting at a small table at the back, or at the bar, getting to know the owner, Miss Chardonnay – or Barbie to her close friends – who was startling in a big blonde wig and enormous glittering evening dresses. Barbie ruled the club like an ancient queen-goddess, and when things got rough, she simply took off her wig, revealing a bald, stubbly head, dropped her voice to a snarling bass, and used her mighty strength to eject the miscreants.

When they were in the club, it felt to Flick that normal life had been resumed. She was no longer a failing hausfrau fretting over coal and eggs, but the pretty, young, glamorous Flick from before. Here, she sipped on glass after glass of chilled Polish vodka, smoked endless cigarettes, and gossiped with the regulars – a mix of artists and eccentrics – when she wasn't cosying up to Caius between his sets. When he did play, she listened, enjoying the smoky jazz, the dark notes he conjured out of the piano. Every now and again, he would play 'Little Girl Lost' and Flick would feel a rush of pride and love that he had composed it for her. Caius had a little band of dedicated fans, queer young men mostly, who sighed over his dark good looks and were in raptures at his playing. In the early hours, as the club began to close, they would be swaying in couples, dancing to the last moody bars of Caius's music.

It was a strange life, but Flick was happy and still madly in love with her husband. He was intoxicating and maddening and loving and all she could ever imagine wanting. He drove her to exquisite delight and could hurt her just as easily. He seemed obsessed with her one moment, and then barely knew she existed the next. He would lavish her with compliments, telling her how beautiful she was. Then, quite suddenly, he would say something horrible, hurtful, critical. If she defended herself, or handed out the same, he got worse. If she wept, he kissed her tears away and grew loving again. But, she was sure, that was what love felt like: a roller coaster, unpredictable, exhilarating; passionate conflicts, delicious reconciliations. Caius was a god and she was a supplicant. She was raised to the divine from time to time, up to golden heights of the empyrean, and then woke up on the floor of the temple, compelled to start worshipping all over again.

When things were sunny, they were marvellous: she and Caius made love all the time, and laughed constantly too. But the darkness was always close by, and it felt very dark and frightening. And, when she wasn't stressed by her inability to run their home, Flick was bothered by the way she was supposed to be elastic and flexible while he was unchanging.

Nevertheless, their strange half-lit life was exciting and satisfying, and she didn't regret it for a moment, or miss the gilded existence she had left behind.

'Caius, what will we do? How much money do you make from playing at the club?'

That morning, when she had gone to cash one of her cheques, the bank manager had come to tell her that her account was empty and there was no more money to be had. She had rushed home, anxious and confused.

Caius shrugged. He was infuriatingly unconcerned by their lack of money, as though she hadn't been paying for all their food, electricity, fuel and laundry, and everything they actually needed. 'I don't make much once we've settled our tab. You get through a fair amount of Barbie's vodka, you know.'

'We pay for it? Full price?' she said, dismayed. 'I thought it was gratis or at least cheaper.'

'Barbie doesn't run a charity, darling.'

'What about your other playing?'

'That pays for the conducting classes.'

'Well then, what will we do?'

'You'll just have to go and beg your mama, I suppose. You can't really expect me to support you with the family you come from.' Caius laughed. 'What is the point in marrying an heiress if she doesn't have any money?'

'You didn't marry me for that,' Flick said, hurt. 'You married me knowing what I might give up.'

'You promised me the old woman would come round. It's absurd to think we could manage without her,' Caius replied coolly.

Flick looked about their gloomy, messy flat. The small pile of coins on top of the meter was shrinking rapidly. He was right. They couldn't manage. And she had promised, even though she felt that Caius had implied it didn't matter if Gloria never came round.

'All right,' she said finally. 'But there'll be a price to pay.'

'I can sing for my supper,' Caius said, going back to his book. 'As long as it's a good one.'

Flick knocked on the door of her mother's house in Chester Square. After the months of living in Soho, she saw the reality of her family's circumstances through fresh eyes. It seemed absurd that these two worlds could exist barely a mile apart. In Soho, she saw grime and poverty and want all the time. She could hardly walk a few yards without passing what seemed like dozens of ragged, dirty children, some of them pushing even younger children in filthy prams, some begging, some clearly working. There was desperation everywhere, it was almost palpable. Even so, she would see women out every day, scrubbing the front steps of their buildings, and on Sundays, in their Sunday best and a hat, their husbands in suits, their children washed, as they made their way to church and chapel.

Here, in Belgravia, the pavements were clean, the garden squares lush, though many railings were yet to be replaced after being melted down for the war effort. The houses were lavish and spacious. Money made everything different. She had known that intellectually, but now she truly understood it.

And now I'm the one that needs it.

She had never thought this moment would come. Somehow, she'd always assumed that Gloria would hand over the inheritance she had promised when Flick turned eighteen, but there was no sign of it and letters to the trustees received evasive replies that seemed designed simply to play for time. Her allowance was not enough to cover their bills; it was gone almost before she had received it. Things that she had always taken for granted – stockings, haircuts, scent, lipstick – now seemed like crazy luxuries, when there was food and fuel to pay for.

She had finally sent Gloria a card asking to see her and now arrived at the time she had suggested to her mother, despite getting no reply.

A housemaid answered the door and led Flick to the grand downstairs drawing room with its set of five French windows over a white stone terrace and a stretch of garden beyond.

The trees were just on the turn, she noticed, before the thought popped into her head that they would be able to fit their flat at least twice into this room alone.

Flick wandered about, hearing only the solid tick of the silver mantel clock, before sitting down on one of the slippery damask sofas. She had never spent that much time in the London house with her mother, and she was struck by the air of monied luxury that had never settled on Caundle. Here, her mother lived like the royalty she loved to entertain, in the kind of comfort that took a great deal of money indeed.

Suddenly the door flew open and Gloria came sailing in, a sight in a bright yellow polka-dotted day dress, her hair a violent red and curled about her face. Flick stood up.

'Hello, Mother.'

'Felicity.' Gloria stood and waited for her daughter to come and kiss her cheek. Then she went and sat on the sofa opposite, crossing her feet at the ankles and putting her hands in her lap. 'Well. To what do I owe this honour?'

'I thought perhaps it's time to make up after our falling-out,' Flick began, sitting down herself.

'Our falling-out?' Gloria said icily. 'Is that what you call your act of terrorism?'

'Terrorism?'

'Of course. You ruined the birthday party I put so much time and money into, to make *you* happy. You ran off and disgraced yourself. I assume you got married – yes, I can see by your ring that you did. And how is married life with your common little piano teacher?'

'He's a musician. He's going to be a great man, I promise.'

'How touchingly loyal.'

'Married life is lovely.'

'Good. I'm happy for you. Obviously you enjoyed rather a lot of married life before the actual ceremony, but there we are. At least you knew what you were getting into.'

'Yes, well . . .' Flick decided to come straight to the point. 'We need money. I need a much bigger allowance. Or, ideally, you would make over my inheritance. I know you've done it for Brinny. It's only fair to do the same for me.'

Gloria's eyes glinted. 'But surely your wonderful husband, that great man, can support you?'

'Not yet.'

Her mother's voice grew cold. 'Can't you see he married you for money, you little fool?'

'He loves me. He knew nothing about my money when he met me.'

'How can you be so stupid? Of course he did.'

'He didn't, he knew nothing about me.' She was quite sure of it. 'I never told him about the family, not the detail.'

'Your picture was all over the papers!' Gloria exclaimed. 'Thanks to Dupone's article about you. Don't you remember? He wasn't so keen on marriage before then, was he?'

'You made me break up with him,' Flick reminded her.

'And he didn't care! Or so Prue tells me. She said you didn't hear from him again until he turned up to take you away.'

'That's not true,' Flick said hotly. 'I did see him after that! And I knew then he would come for me one day. And if you think Caius reads gossip in newspapers and magazines, then it's clear how very little you know him. He doesn't give a fig

185

for all that, and knows less than nothing about society and all its fripperies.'

'Fripperies! And yet, it's so hard to live without the money that buys them. Well, you've made your bed, Felicity, and now you must lie in it. A cold, miserable, poor little bed.'

Flick stood up, angry and upset. Her mother's words had made her uneasy and she did not like that feeling at all. 'So you won't help me?'

Gloria held up a hand. 'Wait. Sit down.'

Flick tried to control her emotions. She sat slowly back down as directed.

Her mother said, 'I'm prepared to forgive you and give you some money, simply because I hate looking like a fool. Everyone knows you ran away in that awful dramatic way. You've made us the subject of gossip and speculation. If I'm going to help you – which you in no way deserve – you must bring him here and you can both apologise in person. I want no further disgrace and I want my apology. Do you understand?'

Flick stared at her obstinate mother, thinking suddenly how alike she and Caius were in many ways. Stubborn, over-sensitive, sulky, just for starters. And she knew that Caius would not react well to being told to offer a grovelling apology to Gloria. 'Very well,' she said slowly. 'I'll do my best.'

Gloria smiled with satisfaction. 'Good. After that, we will see about the matter of your inheritance.'

To Flick's surprise, Caius was extremely agreeable towards going to visit her mother. Almost eager, in fact. She had been sure that he would be too proud to apologise, and too scornful of Gloria to want to be a part of her world, which was so very different from the Soho life he seemed to love.

Instead, Caius said brightly, 'If that's what it takes to make the old girl happy, then that's fine with me. When does she want us to visit?'

He dressed carefully for the encounter, putting on his suit and tie and getting a shave at the barber's beforehand. He even polished his shoes.

'We need to make the old girl like me,' he explained to Flick as they set out from Meard Street to walk to Belgravia. 'It's in our interests. Winter's coming. We'll freeze at home if we don't have enough money for fuel.'

It felt so odd to be talking in such a way as they walked towards her mother's huge house, ablaze with light and warmth.

'You'll behave, won't you, darling?' she asked. 'Don't spoil it by getting cross with her.'

'Don't worry about that,' he said serenely. 'I'll be an angel, you'll see.'

She was comforted, and faintly surprised. Caius didn't seem able to control his temper very well when he was with her – he was often tempestuous, moody, frequently flying off the handle for no reason at all – yet he seemed certain of his ability to rein it in now.

As soon as they went through the door to find Gloria in the hall, dressed to the nines, Caius was charm itself, praising and flattering her mother until she was as soft as warm wax in his hands. Flick was immensely proud of her handsome, charming husband, and delighted that he was clearly working his magic on Gloria. She might have known he would be irresistible when he wanted to be. In fact, she felt almost redundant to the whole thing, as Caius and her mother seemed to concentrate exclusively on one another. Gloria showed him around her treasures and he talked with informed intelligence and sensitivity about her pictures, china and objets d'art. Over dinner, he made her chortle and laughed uproariously at her jokes, begging her for more of her indiscreet stories about society figures behaving badly. Gloria blossomed under his attention.

Now she can see why I love him. And he has clearly charmed her.

Flick was delighted and relieved.

This is wonderful. It couldn't have gone any better!

And then Caius played the piano.

Gloria listened, entranced. Even though Flick had seen him play many times, she had to admit that he performed with rapturous brilliance. A cigarette between his teeth, he coaxed beautiful ripples of Chopin out of the keyboard of Gloria's grand piano, his eyes burning with intensity, dark locks of hair falling into his eyes, which he shook back as he played.

Flick glanced at her mother, who was staring intently at Caius.

She almost looks like she's in love with him herself.

It was a success, she was sure.

'Oh yes, the old girl will come right round, you'll see,' Caius said confidently as they went home, this time chauffeured in Gloria's car. 'It all went stunningly well.'

She squeezed his hand in the car. 'Thank you. You were amazing.'

He gave her an amused look. 'When am I ever not?'

'Never not.'

'Exactly. Never not.'

The following week Flick had a letter from the trustees with a date for her inheritance to be transferred. She would be receiving a large sum to be invested on her behalf and, from now on, an annual dividend, to be paid in monthly amounts to her. Caius was delighted, sleek with satisfaction at the success of his seduction of her mother.

'We need to move,' she told Caius, when the initial excitement had worn off.

'Why? Do we need more room?'

'Yes. There's going to be an addition to our household.'

He looked amazed and then misty-eyed as he reached for her hand. 'You mean . . . you're expecting?'

She looked at him, astonished, and then laughed. 'Oh darling, I hope you're not disappointed. No. We're getting a housekeeper-cook. Just as soon as we possibly can.'

Chapter Eleven

FLICK

1955

Everything should be wonderful, Flick thought. *It should be perfect. Or am I asking too much?*

Life was much easier in many ways. It was simply that her relationship with Caius had changed so much. She had imagined that when their money troubles disappeared, thanks to her, they would go back to being as blissful as they had been at first. Caius's temper and irascibility would calm down, and she would be restored to favour. But this hadn't happened, and she couldn't understand why.

They had moved to a larger flat in a slightly more salubrious area, closer to Piccadilly, and now there was Mavis, who had the back bedroom by the kitchen, and managed to bring some kind of order to their lives.

'I'm not really sure how you cause so much upset, ma'am,' she would say to Flick. She had a strong Cockney accent after growing up in Bow with her mother and four sisters. Her father had died young of emphysema and both brothers were killed in the war. Mavis had gone off to be a land girl, and had decided never to go to the country again.

'Seaside's enough for me,' she'd say tartly. 'Nice trip to Margate and chips on the prom. Then back to civilisation. I never want to see another hedge, that's for sure. I definitely never want to dig another potato.'

She seemed very happy to live in with the Knolles, cooking for them and managing the house.

'But I don't know how you do it!' she would say to Flick nearly every day. 'No sooner do I clean up than you've made a dreadful mess again.'

'Do I?' Flick said. She was so much happier now that she didn't feel oppressed by learning to keep house. But she felt the lack of something real to do. By marrying Caius, she seemed to have stepped out of the life she knew and into nothing at all. The only thing she could think of to do was to have a baby, but she wasn't quite ready for that either, feeling she needed to live for herself before she lived for someone else.

Flick sat down on a bench in Dolphin Square and took her library book out of her pocket. She was soon lost in her novel and hardly noticed who had sat down at the other end. Then a soft voice said, 'Felicity Templeton, is that you?'

Flick looked up and found herself staring into a familiar face but she couldn't place it. 'Yes?'

'I'm Rachel Donnelly. I taught you literature at St Pandionia's. Do you remember? It wasn't so long ago!' Miss Donnelly smiled at her.

Flick gasped with recognition. 'Oh yes, Miss Donnelly! How lovely to see you.'

'How are you, dear? So nice to see you with a book.'

'I can't imagine life without reading,' Flick said firmly. She held up her novel. 'George Eliot. You made me love her.'

'You were very insightful about *Middlemarch*, I seem to remember.' Miss Donnelly raised her eyebrows behind her little round glasses. 'And what are you doing now? Did you pursue your studies, as I advised? I hoped you might apply to a university to study literature.'

Flick flushed. 'Well, no . . . I got married, actually.'

'Married?' Miss Donnelly looked horrified. 'But you're so young!'

'It . . . seemed right.'

Miss Donnelly stretched out a hand and took Flick's. 'My dear, you must do something with that brain of yours. You mustn't be lost to tending house and having children, noble though those things can be. Don't you think you've been just a little reckless?'

Flick felt her face grow redder. Miss Donnelly was voicing her own darkest fears. Talk of disgrace and inheritance and society all meant nothing to her. But she had a creeping fear that she had thrown away the things she had longed for all her life: freedom, independence and the chance to do something that mattered. It was becoming clearer and clearer that Caius saw her as his support and provider, and that he would be happy for her to devote herself to him indefinitely. What was there for her, though?

'I don't know . . . I'm not sure. Perhaps I have been reckless.' A twist of fear turned in her stomach. What if she had made a mistake?

Miss Donnelly stared at her for a moment, and then stood

up briskly, a round figure in a green wool coat and brown hat, looking, Flick thought, a little like an acorn. 'I have just been to see my literary agent about my latest book on Woolf. His office is just there, across the square. Come along, let's go there now.'

Flick stood up too, and took Miss Donnelly's proffered arm, a sense of hope kindling inside her.

'I didn't think you could make this place worse,' Mavis said, bustling about in her apron. 'But you have. Look at all this blessed paper! Covered in ash as well. You smoke too much, ma'am.'

'Do I?' Flick looked at the overflowing ashtray. She always seemed to be lighting a cigarette, forgetting about it, and finding it burned out in the ashtray. She felt she was actually smoking very little indeed. 'Will you be an angel and bring me some tea, please, Mavis? I have to read three manuscripts and write reports by Friday.'

Miss Donnelly had taken her into her literary agency and introduced her to Mr Adams, the agency owner. Flick had been quite humbled by the way Miss Donnelly had described her brightness and discernment.

'Felicity should really be at Oxford, reading for a degree. Can you find her anything?' Miss Donnelly had asked. 'I'm certain you'd find her a useful addition.'

Mr Adams had scrutinised her, thought and then said, 'It's a happy chance that brought you back here, Rachel. We do need another freelance reader of manuscripts.' He looked back at Flick. 'If you are interested in the position, I can give you a manuscript to read and assess, as a trial run. After that, we would pay you per script.'

'I would love that!' Flick exclaimed. And then, remembering herself, she said more calmly, 'Thank you so much for the opportunity. I'll be sure to do my very best.'

Outside she had hugged Miss Donnelly. 'I'm so enormously grateful. What a marvellous chance to meet you.'

Miss Donnelly had grasped her hand. 'Make the most of it, dear. I hope it is the start of something. Visit me if you're ever in Oxford.'

'Of course I will. And thank you again!'

Flick had raced back to the flat, the pile of paper under one arm, desperate to start. She had read the entire script the same afternoon and by lunchtime the next day, she had carefully handwritten a report of it: strengths, weaknesses and what she would recommend to improve it. She dropped it into the agency, along with her telephone number, for they now could afford the luxury of a telephone, and waited. Two days later, a secretary called to ask her to come round.

'We liked your assessment very much,' Mr Adams said, gazing at her over the top of his glasses, her report in his hand. 'Although perhaps you didn't have to go into quite so much detail. The first requirement is to tell us if you think the script has a future. If you don't, a few points will do that we can pass back to the author with a rejection. But your analysis was intriguing.'

'I'm so very pleased,' Flick said happily. 'Would you like me to read more?'

'Yes. But we'll need you to type your reports. I assume you can type?'

'Of course,' she said immediately, although she could not.

'Good. Then we'll write to you with terms, and you can sign and return our letter.'

As soon as she'd left the offices, she went to buy a typewriter in a shop just off St Martin's Lane. She carried it carefully home in its case, hoping she could remember how to change the ribbon the way she'd been shown, stopping only to buy a book called *Teach Yourself Typing* on the way back.

From then on the flat was dominated by the click of typewriter keys as Flick practised her exercises, when she wasn't lost in reading her way through mounds of paper, cursing herself when she mixed up manuscripts or got the pages hopelessly out of order.

She loved the feeling of doing something useful that required thought and analysis. This was, she supposed, work, but it didn't feel like it. Work was what Mavis did: dusting and cleaning, and shopping and cooking. Reading, thinking and writing was not work, not in the same way, and it was such fun, she felt guilty being paid for it.

Caius seemed amused that she had a job. 'When we were poor as church mice, you did nothing. And now we have money, you want to work.'

'I did *everything*!' Flick exclaimed. 'I barely had a minute to myself. Don't you remember?'

Caius looked blank. 'No. Did you do everything?'

She sighed and went back to her scripts.

*

195

Flick and Caius were spending more time apart now. He slept until after lunch, when he went out to his conducting classes and then on to his evening gigs. He was still out at the club until late most nights, and in pubs or playing at parties and wedding receptions. He had recently got a regular Friday night slot at a jazz club where he played in a trio like the one she had heard in Oxford. While Flick still occasionally stayed out late, she now found she'd rather get to bed at a decent hour and be up to start her work in good time. They saw each other less as a result.

One regular fixture was going to see Gloria once a week, and she found she looked forward to it, as Prue was allowed to see her again and she enjoyed chatting to her sister, now eighteen herself and about to be launched on society. For some reason, Caius didn't think Prue should visit them at home and so she only saw her at Gloria's. Brinsley, in his last year at Oxford, was rarely there but the two of them wrote to each other often. And Caius did not like her visiting her family alone. He always accompanied her to her mother's house, and no matter how tired and grumpy he was, as soon as they stepped through the door, he became charming and attentive to Gloria, who had very much changed her tune about him. She was almost giddy around him, Flick noticed, and Caius in turn was quite flirtatious with his mother-in-law.

'Should you really put it on quite so thick, though?' Flick would ask. It made her uncomfortable. 'I mean, it's almost as though you're mocking her, telling her how beautiful she is.'

'She is beautiful. Quite stunning,' Caius said with a laugh.

'Do you mean that?'

196

He fixed her with a dark look. 'Don't worry, she's not my type.'

'I didn't mean that,' she said hastily, feeling a little sick. 'Just that I can't tell if you're teasing. You mustn't tease her so much.'

'And you shouldn't be so sensitive,' he replied.

Flick was quiet. She couldn't help noticing that Caius always hit back when she talked about his behaviour. If he was cross, then she had made him cross by not letting him sleep in peace, with her incessant typing. If he was rude, then she was far ruder, according to him. If he was unkind, then she was imagining it or overreacting. And in any case, it was something she had done that had made him unkind.

Yet, when she was kind and loving and patient, wrapping her arms around him and making love to him when he came in smelling of sour tobacco and tasting of whisky, more than half drunk at three in the morning, that was her duty and his right and not worthy of praise or gratitude. She was, he seemed to think, a very lucky girl indeed.

'You know that little piece of mine, "Little Girl Lost"?' he said one day. 'I think I should have called it "The Luckiest Girl in the World".'

She had no idea why that made her so uneasy.

On a cold spring morning, there was a sharp knock at the door.

'I'll get it, Mavis,' Flick called, hurrying to answer it. There, on the doormat, stood Diana, ravishing in a grey tweed full-skirted suit.

'Darling!' she said, opening her arms to Flick.

'Diana!'

They fell into a warm embrace. Diana took off her hat and fox fur, and they walked together into the sitting room, arms around each other's waists.

'How are you, dear Diana? It's been so long!'

'Well, sweetheart, I couldn't tolerate another year at Pandy's without you, as you know. They sent me away to learn drawing in Florence. I don't think they had a clue what to do with me.'

They sat down on the sofa in the cosy sitting room, Diana glancing about at the piles of books and manuscripts. On the piano were sheaves of music, and by the gramophone, heaps of records out of their sleeves. 'Golly, you are certainly settled in.'

'Don't,' Flick said with a laugh. 'Mavis despairs of us, she can't keep up with us and our mess. She'll bring in some tea soon.' She fixed her friend with a look. 'But how are you?'

Diana took off her fox fur and smiled. 'That's what I've come to tell you. I'm engaged at last.'

'Congratulations!' Flick said, jumping up to embrace her again. 'Finally! I'm so happy for you and Edmund.'

Diana held up a hand. 'Not so fast, darling. You're right. Edmund's engaged. But not to me. He's going to marry our mousy friend the countess. It's not announced yet, but a little bird told me all about it. Obviously you don't know yet.'

'What? Engaged to Marissa? I didn't know a thing!' Flick was dismayed. 'Diana, I'm so sorry. How did all this happen?'

'Oh, it was no surprise,' Diana said, tilting her chin up and looking proud, but Flick suspected she was just being brave. 'We broke it off – or at least I did. I had to give him his freedom once I went to Italy. I'm not the kind of woman to tether a man to her against his will. He's got to adore me, or what's the point? Anyway, I got a letter from a friend saying that he was romancing Marissa, and so I came back and confronted him, wanting to know what was going on. He'd said he'd wait for me, you see. He was still writing lovely letters, saying how much he missed me and all the rest.' She went pink at the memory and her eyes glistened. 'He had to admit it. He proposed to her only the previous night and she'd said yes. That was early this week. So I came to see you. I knew you'd understand. I'm sure it's going to be in *The Times* in a week or so, once he's managed to locate Marissa's father and formally asked his permission. I don't suppose he'll notify anyone until then.'

'We don't know anything about it,' Flick said helplessly. She felt awful for Diana, knowing she had truly loved Edmund and desperately wanted to marry him.

'I blame Florence,' Diana said feelingly. 'If I hadn't had to go, it all would have been all right. As it was, I left the citadel undefended and the Barbarians rushed in to conquer it.'

'But you said *you* were engaged.'

'Oh yes. I am.' She held out her hand and Flick saw that she was wearing a glittering diamond ring on her left hand.

Flick gaped, astonished. 'What? Who to?'

'Perhaps it was stupid but I went straight to Alfred Beresford-Jones and accepted his proposal.'

'Alfred had proposed to you? Even though you were with Edmund?'

'Not exactly. But he proposed pretty fast when I explained

what I wanted. Marriage, I told him. Almost at once. Alfred's joined the Foreign Office and he's being posted abroad to the embassy in Cairo. I'm going to go with him. I hear it's a jolly laugh out there with the British community. They're building a new embassy apparently, it will be quite the place to be seen. So I'll be off.'

'How can you marry Alfred without loving him?'

Diana shrugged. 'I know him, he's a fine man and a decent sort. He'll adore me and look after me. I banked on Edmund, you know, and everyone knew it. If I'm not careful, I'll be considered damaged goods and no one will want me. Better to become respectable as soon as possible.' She smiled at her friend. 'I don't have the money and name to be able to survive a scandal or live down a tarnished reputation. Not like you. But if I'm Mrs Beresford-Jones, niece-in-law to the Earl of Whatsit, I'll be all right.'

'Darling. I simply don't know what to say.' Flick looked up as Mavis came in with the tea things. 'Mavis, I think we need something stronger.'

'Vodka, for old times,' Diana put in.

'Yes, vodka and tonic. I'm sorry, I suppose. It must be awful, I can't believe Marissa did such a thing.'

'Oh, I can. It was clear as day to me. Anyway, don't be sorry. Come to my wedding instead. Mummy is frantically planning it, she's so excited. Church wedding here in London. It's in six weeks, and then we go away.' Diana sighed. 'Enough about me. You'll have to be happy for me instead. Is married life with Caius utter bliss?'

'Oh yes,' Flick declared. 'I'm terribly lucky. It is wonderful. And I've such high hopes for him, he's so talented.'

'No baby?'

'Not yet,' Flick said. 'I don't feel quite ready yet. Maybe soon.'

Diana nodded wisely. 'Don't get chained to him too hard.'

Mavis came in with the drinks before Flick could ask her what she meant, and then the moment passed.

Gloria was throwing a party for Prue, and had arranged for the garden of her Chester Square mansion to be covered in a marquee so that she had a large enough venue for the guests to eat, drink and then dance.

'Imagine how much it is all costing,' Caius said, as they got ready for the party. 'We could have done with that money.'

Flick said nothing as she carefully applied her make-up. It seemed to her that they were well off without more of her mother's money and how Gloria wanted to spend it was her business. She was glad Prue was getting a lovely party, when she and Brin had been so spoiled themselves. Her mother seemed to have a much less spiky relationship with Prue than she did with Flick, and Flick was glad about that.

Caius had become more oddly reckless lately. He seemed to be living on the edge of something and Flick had no idea what he was thinking. He was composing, he said, and was gone all hours. He said Barbie would let him use the piano into the early hours in the empty club – he could hardly keep Flick awake using their instrument.

He was always testy now, exhausted from his lack of sleep

and the pressure of composing, performing and his conducting studies. Flick was sure it would all get better in time but it was not easy to live with.

'Come on, let's go. Aren't you ready yet?' Caius looked irritated. He didn't seem to appreciate that her own preparations took much more time than his, when he only had to put on his evening clothes, drag a comb through his dark curls and he was more or less ready.

'Go and have a drink. I'll be done soon.'

Caius wandered off to the sitting room. She heard the clink of ice in a glass and knew he was priming himself for the evening. When she had put on the last coat of mascara and slick of lipstick, she pulled her wrap around her shoulders and went through to find him.

'I'm ready now,' she said.

'Good,' he said. He glanced at her briefly and said, 'You look nice.'

Something in her chilled. He had said those words in the same tone, the exact same tone, every time she had got ready in the last few weeks. It wasn't like the early days when he had seemed delighted by her appearance, when he was loving and flattering. He seemed bored. He put down his glass and sighed. 'Well. Let's get this over with.'

This ought to be so much fun, she thought, later. But it was awful. Caius was flirting outrageously with every young woman he saw. He was drinking fast and heavily, tossing back the wine with every course, then calling for more.

Luckily no one else seemed to have noticed, even though

she and Caius were on the top table with Gloria, Prue and Brinny, in full sight of everyone. Friends and family filled the marquee along with many distinguished guests. A band were preparing to play on the stage erected at the back of the tent. From her mother's barely suppressed excitement, Flick had a feeling that something was afoot. Sure enough, when the band struck up as coffee was being served, Gloria appeared on the stage, shimmering in her golden dress, her bright hair flecked with glitter, beaming at her guests and waving at friends.

Oh my goodness, Flick thought, and then she laughed inside. This was par for the course for Gloria.

The band played the introduction to a Cole Porter number. Flick knew it well. It was one of Gloria's favourite party pieces. Besides her love of costume and practical jokes, Gloria adored to perform and there was nothing like throwing a lavish party to bring out her need to show off. There had been one memorable night when Gloria had joined a line of dancing girls, wearing a spangled leotard and ostrich feathers, throwing up her legs in a routine she had clearly long rehearsed. Flick had been mortified for her mother, who had not been able to match the grace of the real dancers, but Gloria had loved it.

Now, as the band played an extended introduction, the bandleader went to the microphone and said, 'We welcome a very special lady to the stage. The woman of the hour, our marvellous hostess, a very great lady indeed. Mrs Gloria Templeton!'

'How fitting, on Prue's special night,' said Caius in a low voice, lighting up a cigarette.

'Shh,' Flick said anxiously, but the applause covered what he had said.

The bandleader turned to Gloria. 'We beg you to honour us with a song.'

'I couldn't possibly,' Gloria said serenely. 'Well, if you insist.'

The bandleader turned back to conduct the band and brought the long introduction to a conclusion, nodding Gloria in at the right moment. She began to sing.

With the first few notes, Flick curdled inside. She swapped an agonised look with her brother. Prue sat quite still, a smile stiff on her lips as she stared at her mother on the stage. Whatever singing voice Gloria had once had she no longer possessed. She was wailing and quavering, occasionally hitting a pure, true note, but mostly almost coming close.

'This is bloody torture,' Caius said. He was rocking next to her, clearly uncomfortable.

'It will soon be over,' Flick said quietly.

'Not soon enough. What does the old trout think she's doing? I've never known such vanity.' He gathered his breath and suddenly, loudly, began to boo.

Flick froze, then put her hand on his arm. 'Stop that at once!'

He only booed louder. Gloria was still unaware, but others were not. The guests began to look at him, embarrassed, disgusted even, as he continued to boo loudly.

'Off! Off!' he shouted, and started to clap.

'Caius!' Flick hissed. 'Stop it! How can you? Let her sing! What's the harm?'

He wasn't listening. There was a discontented murmur among the guests and one shouted, 'Let us listen, can't you?'

Another said loudly, 'Outrageous! How rude!'

Gloria at last seemed to realise that something was going on as she quavered through the next verse. She looked about for the source of the disruption.

To Flick's horror, Caius leapt to his feet, booing as loudly as he could.

'Flick, stop him!' said Prue, horrified. Brinsley went to stand up, white-faced and furious, his fists clenched, but Flick put out a hand to stop him. Fisticuffs on the top table would be even worse than what was happening.

Gloria stopped singing. The band's playing faded to silence.

'Thank Christ for that!' yelled Caius. 'You sounded like a goose being strangled. Get off the stage, Gloria, give us all a chance to mend our ears.'

Gloria stared at him, uncomprehending. There was a horrified silence from the guests, some staring crossly at Caius, others unable to look at the stage. Embarrassment covered the entire room.

Flick had never felt so mortified. Why had Caius done it? Why not just let Gloria sing?

Then, quite suddenly, Gloria burst out laughing. Into her microphone, she said, 'Dear Caius, what a wag you are! And what a very odd way to ask for an encore! Most people wait until the lady has finished! But of course I'll go back and start again.'

A wave of relieved laughter covered the room, followed by an outburst of applause, then cheers, and the room was possessed by a riotous enthusiasm for Gloria and her singing. The tension seeped away from Prue and Brinsley as they realised that she had saved the situation, and now the room was cheering and calling for an encore. Gloria was basking in the approval, glowing with delight at her adoring public. The band struck up their introduction again.

'I can't stand this,' Caius said, now obviously enraged. 'I can't take another minute.' He stood up, and stormed out, oblivious to the looks of disgust that followed him.

'What should I do?' Flick said to her brother. 'Go after him?'

'Your choice, Flick,' Brinsley said. 'Stay here, or go. But his behaviour was outrageous and completely baffling. Is he always this cruel?'

She stared at the tablecloth, ashamed to her core of Caius's behaviour. Was he always this cruel? Perhaps not outwardly. But she had sensed a change in him, a recklessness, as though he had ceased to care and could no longer be bothered to keep up a pretence or play a game that didn't interest him. 'I don't know,' she said at last. 'Perhaps he is.'

Brinsley leaned forward and looked at her seriously through his little owl glasses. 'Then you must be free of him. What kind of a life will it be with him? He can't come back into this house after that.'

'Mother will forgive him. Look how she turned it round.'

Flick gestured to their mother, warbling happily on the stage to her appreciative guests.

'She might. But I can't. It was inexcusable. You know it was. Whatever Mother is, she didn't deserve that after her kindness to him. What gives him the right to be so arrogant?'

Flick sat, miserable, her thoughts whirling. He was right. Caius was arrogant. He was utterly self-centred. She could see that almost everything he had done was for himself.

But he loves me. Or at least he did. We are happy together. This is a terrible phase, because he's unhappy and unfulfilled professionally. We'll get through it. Perhaps a baby will help.

She had often dreamed of the black-haired, black-eyed child they would surely have together but they had decided that a family would wait for a year or two. Perhaps now was the time to bond Caius to her in the way that only a baby could.

'Stay or go, Flick?'

'Stay,' she said.

Brinsley smiled in relief. 'Good.'

But she only stayed until her mother's performance was over, and the loyal toasts had been made, and the dancing begun. Then, quietly, she slipped away to go home and find Caius.

But he was not at the flat and did not return the next day either, or the one after that.

Chapter Twelve

ETTA

1976

Etta knew it was kind of weird to live downstairs from her mother, but that was just normal in their world. She wondered sometimes if it would be different if she and Mary lived with Mum.

Perhaps Mum would see that, alongside the incense and candles and ornaments, Mary's bedside table was covered in rolling papers and tobacco pouches, and little decorative tins where she kept lumps of resin and bags of weed. Mum could not fail to notice the row of decorative bongs on the cabinet in the sitting room. Mary spent a sizeable part of every day sucking smoke through the glass pipe of her water-filled bongs. Friends came round and did the same, passing the bongs around the table as they all got progressively more glassy-eyed and spacey. The whole place reeked of it. Etta sometimes thought that surely someone on the street would smell it and they would have the police round some time. The aroma of grass and weed and resin must surely waft up the stairs to the upper flats? But so far, no one appeared to notice.

'Come on, Etta, have a go!' Mary would urge, or one of

her friends would pass her a bong, or a pipe, or a joint, because she was there.

Etta didn't want to. She would always pass it on. Once she had tried it and had hated it. As soon as the fuzzy feeling had come over her, she had wanted violently for it to go away. And once that fuzziness dissipated, she had felt something else equally as horrible, if not worse: fear. A dark panic nipped at her heels, threatening to grab her ankles and pull her downwards into a swamp of fear. She had never wanted to do that again. She preferred the ice-cold sweetness of cider that she drank with friends at school, or the beer mixed with lime cordial and lemonade that she had at home or the whisky and ginger ale that she drank in the pub round the corner, where they didn't seem to mind serving her even though she was underage. If she had enough jewellery and eyeliner on, they seemed to think she was a grown-up. She didn't yet like the wine or vodka that her mother swilled all the time, but perhaps she'd grow to like their astringent qualities one day. At least these things made her happy, not afraid. They made her vibrant, not sleepy and spaced out, like Mary was after smoking her pipes.

Anyway, Mum was not in the flat and didn't appear to have noticed. She almost never came down, summoning the girls up to her instead. When the phone rang, the bell shrilling out at all hours, they knew it was her and in a minute they'd be climbing up the stairs to the top floor. Sometimes it was Granny, but usually it was Mum, in the grip of some crisis, needing their help to sort it out, from unblocking a plughole to helping her remember the name of a book or a poet.

Except that right now, Mum was home less. She was spending more time driving to the hospital out near Richmond where Dad was still recovering from his latest episode.

It meant that when the holidays had come, the girls had been collected from school by a driver and brought home to London, with no one there at all. Luckily their housekeeper Rosalie, who lived in the basement flat and looked after all of them, had stocked the flat with food for them, or they would have had nothing. It was a good thing she had put in plenty of snacks: Mary would eat nothing in the day, and then, after smoking her bongs, would go on huge late-night binges, cooking up vast omelettes or vats of spaghetti which she covered in cheese and sucked down by the plateful. Etta would wake up to the kitchen covered in dirty pans and plates, depending on how many people had been there the night before. She felt so guilty about Rosalie cleaning it up that she did it herself as best she could, running endless sinkfuls of water to wash the dishes with.

Everyone else seemed to have so many problems and she felt that somehow, she must do her best to sort it all out, even though she also quailed before such a task. And she felt vaguely envious of the other members of her family who could shout and cry and demand help, and then get it. Even Dad, although of course he couldn't help anyone now.

There seemed to be no room left over for her own troubles, and they had to be squashed away and ignored.

Etta worried about Mum all the time. And she worried about Mary. She couldn't help it. There must be a reason why drugs were illegal and why taking them was frowned upon.

But Mary insisted that drugs were, in fact, of great benefit to humankind and it was only their own stuffy, repressed culture that didn't see their advantages. Anyone who didn't smoke didn't know what they were talking about, and were hypocrites to criticise those who did.

'It helps me,' Mary would say cryptically.

'Helps you how?'

'It just helps me, you little twit. Now go away and read a book.'

That was how it was with Mary. She was nice to Etta but only up to a point, then she would snap and turn caustic, nasty, insulting, belittling. Etta never knew when that point would come. When Mary was being wonderful, there was no one more amazing in the world. When friends came around and Mary was happy, she was dazzling. Hilarious, clever, beautiful, and effortlessly the centre of attention, a sun that everyone orbited around. Etta loved her so much then, and felt so proud of her glamorous sister. Sometimes Mary talked about being an actress or a model when she left school, and Etta could totally see how she would do that, with her star quality.

But that star quality was doused by the drugs. Mary, glassy-eyed and remote, no longer had that magical spark. Her beauty got dull and draggy, her wit vanished. What made Mary want to go to that state? Wasn't it nicer to stay her wonderful self?

Mary didn't seem to think so. If anything, she wanted to find new ways to get into that altered state. One of her friends brought a little bag of pills into the flat and the minute Etta saw them, she knew that they were a new type of trouble in their life. But she had no idea what to do about it. How could she tell Mum?

Mary would hate her for it.

Mum would be desperate, unable to cope, sent into another frenzy when she already had so much to cope with. Dad was supposed to look after her, and be her rock. He was not supposed to crumble away like this.

I suppose I will just have to do all the looking after, Etta thought. *I think I'm the only one who can.*

Chapter Thirteen
FLICK
1957

Flick couldn't think how it had suddenly appeared, right there, at her feet.

Caius had been gone for three weeks now, without a single word. It was as though he had simply been erased from her life. But the flat was still full of all his things.

She was looking for a particular book she wanted, and had gone to Caius's study. She set about moving books and piles of old sheet music off shelves when she suddenly noticed a copy of *Mademoiselle* magazine lying on the floor.

She stared at it for a moment, remembering the day that Gloria had arrived in Oxford, so furious with her for talking to that journalist, Chase Dupone. That holiday in Lake Como felt like a lifetime ago.

I never read that article properly. I wonder what it actually said about me.

Picking up the magazine, she went to a chair and sat down. The pages fell open quite naturally at the article about her, illustrated with a black-and-white studio photograph of her looking demure and neat.

Flick blinked, not quite able to take in what she was seeing. The article was annotated: underlinings, circled words, notes scribbled in the margin. All in Caius's hand. It was clear it had been well read. Where Dupone speculated about the size of her inheritance, there were red underlines and question marks in the margin. The description of Caundle Court had been circled and the words *Dorset . . . drive?* scrawled nearby. The last few sentences were heavily underlined:

Miss Templeton doesn't seem so much a poor little rich girl as a little girl lost. She is lost in wealth and inherited fame, and doesn't know what to do. Only love can save a little girl lost, and let us hope she finds it.

Flick felt faint as she read.
Little Girl Lost.
'He knew,' she said out loud. 'Mother was right. He knew.' She had never before asked herself how Caius knew where to come on the night of her party. She had talked a little about her family and her home over the course of their love affair, but never given him the kind of detail that would enable him to go to the house without more instruction. She had even given her address as the local post office rather than the house itself.

She could see it now. He had read the article and finally learned exactly what she came from. Perhaps he felt something for her, perhaps he did not. But he hadn't wanted to marry her until he knew the extent of her riches. And then . . . 'Little Girl Lost'. The piece he wrote for her. He knew exactly how to touch her heart: he would offer her love, pretend to rescue her, pretend he was her saviour.

But he never truly loved me, she thought, despairingly. *It was all pretend, all of it. It was all about the money.*

Caius was the ultimate deceiver. She had seen him woo and seduce and win her own mother, in order to get money – of course he had done that with her too. Perhaps he'd even known from the very start that she was someone he could work on, from the time he glimpsed her in Oxford and then, mysteriously, arrived at the school to offer his services. As long as she had been in his thrall, willing to sacrifice herself to him and provide all he needed, he had given her love. No wonder that letter Gloria dictated had made him punish her for months with coldness and absence! And if he hadn't seen the article, perhaps he would never have come back at all.

As long as she tended to his needs and believed in him, he was happy. When she had sided against him in the humiliation at Prue's party, and then did not run after him to play her usual placatory role when he stormed out, he had suddenly and violently decided she was of no further use to him.

That was not how love behaved. That was something else entirely.

Her heart ached violently. She felt too numb with grief and pain to cry.

I'll never hear from him again. I'm quite, quite sure of it.

The divorce from Caius attracted little attention, for which Flick was very grateful. Gloria put it in the hands of her lawyers and it was dealt with away from Flick entirely. She simply signed where she was told to. Flick felt certain that favours had been called in to keep the news that England's most miserable heiress must surely be even more miserable now, with a failed marriage behind her so young.

She never heard a word from Caius. The only acknowledgement that their marriage was over was the arrival of an envelope addressed to her. When she opened it, a wedding ring slipped out from a folded sheet of paper. It fell into her palm and she held it, hot tears scalding her eyes.

So it's over. And that's all I will ever get.

It was brutal. Unkind. After everything, she deserved more, didn't she?

Surely this pain will pass. I must be strong.

If there was one thing she must do, it was not to let Caius win by destroying her.

She straightened her shoulders and took a long, trembling breath.

I will survive this. I will.

There was a strange sense of unreality about her marriage and its abrupt, almost invisible end. Sometimes it was hard to believe it had happened at all.

'We won't speak of it,' Gloria said with a wave of her hand when Flick tried to raise it with her during a visit to Chester Square. 'He was a grubby fortune hunter after all, just as we always suspected. I liked him, I can't deny it, but I always had a soft spot for gigolos.'

Flick wondered if her mother had ever had another relationship since her husband had died. Gloria had a coterie of admirers whom she kept close and yet not close enough for any single one to be her regular companion. She seemed to rotate them in her favour in order to keep them all devoted, like a queen at a court of competing favourites. Perhaps she had a fear of the gigolos she also liked, worried that she might lose her mind and marry one, and then risk everything, just as Flick so nearly had.

'It really was all your own fault. You were warned, I tried to make you break it off but you wouldn't listen and you paid the price. Perhaps you'll pay attention to your poor old mother next time.' Gloria shook her head sorrowfully before adding firmly, 'Anyway, my darling, he's gone now and that's that. You chose us, to stay with us, and it was the right decision.'

It has to be, Flick thought, as she walked home from Chester Square. She didn't mind Gloria believing the myth that somehow Flick had chosen her family over her rascally husband. In truth, she had had no choice: she had been deserted. She couldn't bring herself to tell her mother about the *Mademoiselle* article that confirmed all of Gloria's suspicions about Caius's motives.

Wanting to be free of places haunted by the memory of Caius, she left the Piccadilly flat for a new start, and found a small mews house in Kensington, with a bed-sitting room for Mavis at the top. Mavis had proved fiercely loyal to Flick in the divorce, hardly able even to speak Caius's name. She said '*him*' in tones of disgust that comforted Flick. At least someone remembered his presence in her life, considered her ill used and didn't mind saying so.

Mavis packed up all of Caius's things and they were collected one day when Flick wasn't there. Gloria's lawyers sorted that out and Flick asked in particular not to be told where he was living. She feared that she might be drawn towards wherever he was, unable to resist torturing herself by watching his happy new life. No doubt he had another lover by now. And no doubt he was much nicer to this new woman; no doubt he truly loved her and was kind and sweet. It was agony to think of it and so she tried not to.

Here I am, she thought, *barely twenty-five and already divorced. No children. What can I do?*

She felt it keenly first at Diana's wedding. That had taken place just after Caius had first left her, and she was still in the numbness of early grief, walking through life in a state of shock and misery.

The wedding at St Margaret's, the old church behind Westminster Abbey, was a solid and traditional affair, with everything as expected: a beautiful bride in white and a long veil, carrying orange blossom; a nervous and neatly dressed groom; six bridesmaids and two page boys, and a bevy of guests turned out in their wedding finery. Journalists and photographers and crowds of onlookers gathered as they always did for a society wedding, hoping to catch a glimpse of lords, ladies, MPs, magnates and young beauties.

Flick went with her mother and Brinsley, but remembered very little of the day itself, except that she felt that Diana was doing exactly the right thing. Marrying without love to avoid this horrible, all-consuming pain when it went wrong. Marrying someone who couldn't hurt you. That was definitely the best plan.

She got through the ceremony, strangely thanks in part to Gloria's rock-like presence, getting comfort from the nearness of her mother and her solid dependability. Her vibrant outfit drew attention away from Flick, who had to wipe away tears a few times during the day. And then there was Brinsley, her reliable brother, who made sure she had an arm to lean upon.

The wedding breakfast was at a nearby hotel, and after a short reception and a champagne toast, the happy couple were driven away to begin their married life and board a boat bound for Africa and their new life in Egypt.

Flick was sad to see Diana go, but wished her joy. She had lived for Caius when they were together. It was right that Diana should devote herself to her new husband now. She hoped they would be very happy.

Edmund's wedding followed hard on the heels of Diana's – which he had not attended – and it was much the same but grander. There were more titles and more distinguished and much richer guests, including his own parents, Lord and Lady Carrington, bearing the title bestowed a generation before in return for huge political donations to the government of the day. It wasn't only the elite of England who turned out for Edmund's marriage to Marissa. Distinguished German guests arrived too, an assembly of counts and countesses, dukes and duchesses and princes and princesses from across Europe, representing Marissa's roots.

Flick could see why this rich ancestry had appealed to Edmund and his romantic nature. Diana had been something so familiar to him, no doubt: the bouncing, almost brash English girl with her charm and wit, and her earthy sex appeal. Marissa had another quality altogether: that sad, aristocratic gracefulness married to her style, so ethereal where Diana had been solid; poetic and melancholy where Diana was grounded in the English upper class world of ponies and country life.

There was no doubt the bride and groom were in love. Their bliss was apparent in their faces on the wedding day. Flick wasn't sure whether that made it easier or harder to bear. But at least, in this gathering of grandees, she got little attention. Even her mother, resplendent in green velvet and a Robin Hood style cockade hat with green pheasant fathers, and dripping in pearls, was less photographed than the elegant German princesses, Austrian countesses and the duchesses of eastern European countries now lost behind the Iron Curtain.

While Diana and Alfred had gone abroad, Edmund and Marissa were heading north, to a beautiful house in Northumberland that they intended to renovate and restore. This would be the work to which they would devote themselves: rescuing buildings that time and taxation were leaving on the brink of ruin, and that were not significant enough for the National Trust to care for.

Work is the thing, thought Flick. *It's the only thing that can save people like us.*

Leisure was deadly, and the mixture of leisure and money

more deadly still. What was Gloria but the result of a monstrous boredom that had robbed everything of meaning? Without anything to do but acquire, she had become the shallow self-obsessed woman she was, only able to live in the moment of satisfying her every need.

That's what I have to do, just work. Work and work and work.

There was plenty of work coming in from the literary agency, but while Flick enjoyed reading and reporting on scripts, she wanted to do more. The sad truth was that the vast majority of the things she read were no good. They were often too derivative, obviously inspired by someone famous like Daphne du Maurier or Agatha Christie or Kingsley Amis. Ever since *Lord of the Flies*, she'd been reading about savage children until she couldn't bear to meet another set of ruffians. If they weren't derivative, they were often too eccentric or unusual, and something Flick couldn't imagine anyone wanting to buy. And even books she liked and enjoyed would often not find representation with the agency, precisely because no one could see a market for them.

'People don't seem to be reading books about rockets,' Mr Adams observed when she had been very enthusiastic about a futuristic story she'd been given. 'But spies and elves are doing well.'

Flick felt she wanted to write herself, but not a novel. She wasn't sure she would ever be able to do that. Instead, she hoped to channel her book reporting into something else, perhaps book reviewing or articles for the magazines. She went to a newsagent's and bought copies of all the literary and artistic magazines she could find, and visited the offices of each one in turn, asking to see the editor. She had typed up dozens of copies of a book review she had written of the latest du Maurier novel.

She was often turned away, but each time she left a letter and her review. Occasionally she was able to see an editor, or assistant editor, but they were often hurried and not particularly interested in talking to her.

Flick found only one who gave her even a sliver of a chance. The magazine was a newish one called *Viewpoint*, published from offices down on the Strand, on the edge of Fleet Street, and the editor was a young man, plump and ginger-haired with a slightly slack mouth and very white hands, called Matthew Reynolds.

He read her review while she was sitting in front of his desk. 'Very good,' he said when he'd finished, handing it back to her. 'I like your way with words. You must remember, though, that real criticism isn't about cattiness. No point in just being nasty to raise a laugh. It needs to be well thought out and well founded. If something is too terrible for words, we'd rather not review it at all but direct our readers to something more worthwhile.'

'Oh. Yes, I see that.'

'The only problem is that I don't have a vacancy for a book reviewer. I've got plenty of those. I do need a film reviewer, though. My last one has gone off in a huff after I told him I wasn't going to put his review of *Revenge of the*

Monster Titans of Mars in my magazine, no matter how hard he pleaded.'

Flick laughed. 'I can do films.'

'You can?'

'Of course I can. I'll go and see a film tonight and give you a review of it by tomorrow lunchtime.'

'All right. You're on. Happy viewing. If you're any good, you're hired.'

Flick discovered she loved reviewing films. There was nothing nicer than the ritual of buying her ticket to the first showing of something and then settling back in the dark with her notepad, pen and a tiny torch so that she had enough light to scribble notes by without inconveniencing her fellow filmgoers. For a short while, she'd be lost in another world, far from her own rather lonely existence. The art of filmmaking intrigued her almost at once, as she started to understand the language of lighting, viewpoint, camera angles, wide shots and close up, and the role of music in creating atmosphere. She began to appreciate fine editing. She had a feel for a script of quality or a dud, and for a work of creativity as opposed to workmanlike storytelling. She was no snob, she found, loving comedies and musicals as much as artier, more high-brow work, and she could easily see the way that film acting required a different skill and talent to acting on the stage. Film actors could convey so much through a blink of the eye or the twitch of a lip. Sometimes they simultaneously did nothing and yet said everything. She loved Hollywood, with its gaudy technicolour and the lavishness that was so different to the grey deprivation of London. But she adored British films too: the historical romps of the Gainsborough Studios, the Ealing comedies, the thrillers of Pinewood.

Matthew Reynolds loved her reviews, though he was a stern critic himself, sometimes sending back her work if he thought she was simply point scoring or being amusing at the expense of an honest appraisal of the film. Soon she was a regular in *Viewpoint* and the reader response was very good.

Her new career was not something that impressed Gloria, however, who thought that this was something else that was beneath her. Films were, for Gloria, inherently low class although, paradoxically, she adored film stars themselves and was always keen to have them at her lavish parties. She was always thrilled to spot them on her travels, boasting about dining with Laurence Olivier and Vivien Leigh on the *Queen Mary* as they all travelled to New York, or bumping into her favourite film star Michael Wilding, although annoyingly he had been with his wife at the time and seemed immune to Gloria's charms.

Flick didn't care. She had found a purpose, and the work that she craved.

It was always likely that love would find her again at some point. She had thought it might – after all, she was still young. But her heart had felt impervious after being so beaten and abused by Caius. For months, he had been the last thing she thought about at night, and the first thing in the morning. Her dreams were dominated by him. She simply couldn't imagine feeling that seismic passion for anyone else, ever again. And what was love if not that?

It wasn't that she didn't meet other people. There were plenty of parties connected to the magazine, usually in the upstairs rooms of the pubs around Fleet Street, or in a restaurant in Covent Garden. They celebrated book launches, or milestones or achievements, and usually involved writers and journalists on London's literary scene drinking a great deal of warm wine and eating lumps of cheese on cocktail sticks while they smoked and talked earnestly about politics and culture, or gossiped about the lives and loves of its own members. Gradually Flick made some friends, both at the magazine and beyond it. Her reputation was small but growing and it was surprising how many journalists told her that they enjoyed her film reviews. She was told she might be lured away by one of the big papers, but she doubted that very much.

What she loved was that no one seemed to know who she was. They were unaware that they were talking to England's saddest little rich girl, scion of the Carrington family. She wrote as Flick Templeton, and that was how she was known to them.

Usually, at the end of these parties and tipsy on the wine, she would leave alone, take a taxi to her little house and then open the bottle of vodka that was always chilling in the freezer and start to write her diary, the record of how she felt in the wake of her short and disastrous marriage, the thing she was sure would define her entire life. When she wasn't pouring out the words on her typewriter, she would scrawl letters to Diana, who wrote back from the heat and sun of Cairo, always begging her for the visit that somehow never happened.

'Busy tonight?' Matthew asked, his pipe clenched between his teeth. Flick had gone into the office for a meeting with him which was now over and she was preparing to leave.

'No.'

He picked up a card from his desk and held it out to her. 'A launch party, for an important book. If you're not busy, you can go for me. Give my apologies. But someone from *Viewpoint* should be there.'

'You can't go?' Flick asked, looking down at the invitation. The venue was a room above a pub near Leicester Square. She didn't know the pub but it was bound to be a little seedy, these places always were. The wine would be bad. If there was one thing her background had not prepared her for, it was drinking bad wine. The cellars at Caundle and at Gloria's had always been fine, and the Carrington family wine in plentiful supply.

'No. I'm spending the evening with my mistress,' Matthew said.

'Your mistress! I didn't know you were married.'

'I'm not. That's what makes the arrangement so very safe. Whenever she threatens to tell my wife about our liaison, I feel perfectly all right about it. Now, enjoy yourself.'

'All right.' Flick wanted to keep her editor happy. She would show her face and go home. Mavis had an evening off but would leave her supper in the fridge and she was rather looking forward to writing up her review of the movie she had seen that day, a brilliant comedy by a director she loved. It was going to be dismissed by most reviewers as a silly piece of fluff starring the latest Hollywood blonde, but she thought it was very clever and was going to say so. The blonde was a fine comedienne, she thought, and she already had a line in her mind: *No one can act dumb that convincingly without a good deal of intelligence.*

Flick arrived early and went upstairs to find the room still empty apart from one man standing near a table piled with books. He was tall, with thinning brown hair and hazel-brown eyes, and was holding a glass of wine, looking a little lost.

'Hello,' she said cheerfully, going over to him to offer her hand. 'You're one of the first too, I see. Well, the sooner we get here, the sooner we can leave, I suppose.' She glanced down at the books on the table and picked one up. 'God, this looks dry, doesn't it! *Modern Capitalism in Britain Today*. Thank God I don't have to read it. I'm only here to stand in for my editor. He's got a nicer option for his evening.' She looked up at the man. 'Have you read it?'

'Yes, I have,' he said. 'It's not so bad.'

Flick looked at the author's name. 'Where do you think this Jonathan Blair is? He ought to be here by now. They usually turn up with the full parade of agent and publicity girl, don't they?'

'Oh, he is here.'

'Is he?' Flick looked around. 'Where?'

'Right here. He's me.'

Flick flushed, looking at the author photograph on the back. 'I'm so sorry, I didn't realise.'

'I had a little more hair when that was taken.'

'How rude of me.'

'Don't give it another thought.'

'Your book looks very interesting!' she exclaimed, trying to sound enthusiastic.

'That might be overstating it a little. So what magazine are you from?'

'*Viewpoint*. Oh God, I shouldn't have said that, you'll know that Matthew cried off. I'm making such a mess of things.' She could tell her face was bright red now.

'You're making a very charming mess of it. What's your name?'

'Flick Templeton.'

'Hello, Flick Templeton. Let me get you a drink. I'll give you exclusive comments about modern capitalism if you like.'

She laughed. They went to the bar where trays of glasses of wine were laid out and Jonathan gave one to her. His features had seemed insipid at first but close up, she saw that he had a fine nose and surprisingly attractive lips as well, and the brown eyes were sensitive and kind. When they began to talk, she was aware at once of his sharp intelligence and sense of humour. Everything he said seemed to have a laugh hidden somewhere inside it.

'You're not what I expected from a financial writer,' she said, staring at him over the top of her wine glass.

'And you're not what I expected to turn up at my launch party,' Jonathan replied, gazing back at her. 'Not at all.

Beautiful, talented young women like you don't tend to walk into my life like this.'

She stared on, feeling a sudden and intense connection to him. 'Do you think I've walked into your life?'

'Of course you have,' he said simply.

The party rapidly filled up and soon Jonathan Blair was being feted as the man of the moment. His editor, portly and red-faced, made an overlong and dull speech about the book, and invited them all to toast its success and buy as many copies as they could. From the speech, Flick learned that Jonathan was also a financial journalist on a Sunday newspaper and this was his second learned publication, the first having won the Malthus Prize for political and economic writing.

Flick stayed, mingling and chatting, smoking cigarettes and sipping the nasty wine, always aware of where Jonathan Blair was. And he was aware of her, she knew that. His eyes kept meeting hers, those warm, hazel-brown eyes alive with sensitivity and intelligence. When he sat down to sign copies for his guests, Flick went and bought two hardbacks from the young lady selling them, and took them over, waiting her turn.

Jonathan Blair smiled at her. 'Two copies. Goodness.'

'One to keep and one as a gift for . . . my mother.' Flick tried to imagine Gloria's reaction to being given a book on modern capitalism and couldn't.

'So kind.' Jonathan scrawled in one, and then, as he opened the other, asked her mother's name and dedicated that to her. As he handed them back, he said, 'You're not leaving, I hope?'

'Well, I was going to,' she said.

'Please don't. Please stay. Everyone else will be leaving soon.'

'Don't you have a dinner to go to?'

'Oh no. Nothing like that for a dry old book like mine. But you and I could have dinner if you like.'

'I would like that,' she said, feeling a warmth flowering inside her. She had been looking for this, she realised. That sense of warmth and security that came from being in the presence of someone solid and reliable. Caius had been a tempest and she wanted refuge from that kind of storm. She craved someone safe, sane, modest and kind.

She had the most curious feeling that she had, quite unexpectedly, found that person.

Jonathan Blair seemed to feel the same. After the party, which emptied out as rapidly as it had filled, they were alone. He walked with her to a nearby Italian restaurant and they ate olives and then veal chops and potatoes fried in olive oil, rosemary and garlic, with a flagon of Valpolicella to accompany it.

They talked unceasingly, in a gentle flow of conversation that moved back and forwards between them as naturally as a game of tennis. There was no grandstanding, or boasting, or domination. She didn't feel she was in the presence of someone who wanted to overwhelm, impress and mesmerise her. It was give and take.

Nevertheless, she was careful what she said. There was no

point in revealing her background too soon, no matter how wonderful this man seemed. It could poison things, she knew that, and she wasn't going to make the same mistake again.

'Where do you live?' he asked, as they finished their coffee and walked out onto the street.

'Not far. In Kensington.'

'Do you live alone?'

'Just my maid, Mavis, and me.'

They stood in the glow of the street lamps together, oblivious to the traffic going past and the late-night commuters heading for the stations. 'I don't want to let you go,' he said, taking her hand. 'I feel that fate has brought us together.'

'I feel the same,' she said simply.

'Then how about I don't let you go? I don't want you to walk out of my life as easily as you walked into it, Miss Flick Templeton.'

'You don't have to worry, I won't do that.'

He gazed down at her. 'I believe you. I can trust you, can't I?'

'Yes. Of course. I don't tell lies.'

'Then can I see you tomorrow?'

'Yes.'

'And the day after?'

'Any day, every day.'

'That's exactly what I want.' He stooped and kissed her lightly on the lips before pulling away.

'And so do I.'

Chapter Fourteen

FLICK

1957

Normal life, Flick thought, felt good. It was what she had hoped. Jonathan was safe and normal, something reassuringly familiar even if she had never known anyone like him.

It felt so safe and right that he quickly moved into the house with her, charming Mavis with his jokes and good humour and kindly chat. A short time after that, he proposed to her.

'I don't like living in sin,' he said gravely. 'I like to be respectable.'

'So do I,' Flick said, meaning it this time. Ordinariness was all she wanted now. She had been Bohemian and it had only led to misery.

It was only after they were engaged, a modest diamond sparkling on her finger – her first engagement ring as Caius had never provided one – that she finally revealed to him her past. She had to do it, as he had to meet her family and there was no way it could be concealed.

He was astonished to discover the truth about her background.

'I did wonder how you could afford this place in Kensington at your age, and all on your own,' he said. 'But I assumed that your ex-husband gave you the money.'

'My ex-husband gave me nothing,' she said crisply. 'I'm afraid this is all bought from family money, of which there is a lot.'

'I suppose my left-wing socialism ought to make me highly disapprove,' Jonathan said, laughing. 'But there's not much I can do about it. You are who you are. And I suppose there are advantages.'

'I'm afraid my mother will want you to sign some documents renouncing a claim on the family money.'

'I understand,' Jonathan said with a shrug, 'and I'm very happy with that. I'm not after your money, my sweet, you know that.'

'I do,' she said, kissing him. 'I know it very well.'

Flick assumed that her mother would be all in favour of Jonathan after the madness of Caius. And his respectable profession as a writer would surely appeal to her more than Caius's life as a musician. But Gloria seemed curiously unmoved by Jonathan.

'He's nice enough. I can see why you like him. He's steady. Rather dull, let's be honest, darling. Not like that first husband of yours. A thorough rogue . . . but you must admit, Caius was exciting and interesting.'

Flick felt half exasperated. 'You loathed him at first!'

'Yes, of course. And he was really quite awful. But he had

charm. And lots of sex appeal, like the best bounders. I'm afraid the sex-appeal fairy passed over Jonathan's cradle.'

'Mother! Please!'

'Sorry, darling,' Gloria said, unrepentant.

'Who do you want me to marry?' Flick demanded. 'What would satisfy you?'

'Darling, a lovely duke would be absolutely wonderful. It's these people from the ordinary side of life who seem to lure you in. Why can't you marry an important house, a *name*, like most girls of your background?'

'Because I don't want to marry a house or a name, and I don't need to. I have my own security. I want to marry a husband, a real husband.'

'Well then, let's hope you've found one this time.'

Jonathan did not seem overwhelmed by Gloria and her house, magnificent though it was. 'It doesn't seem real,' he confided to Flick as they left. 'It's like visiting the Queen or something. It's hard to believe she goes on existing after we've left.'

But he loved Caundle, when they went down to visit Brinny, who had moved there after Oxford and was working on improving the house and starting up the farm around it as a going concern. Flick was delighted that her fiancé and her brother got on so well, both serious, thoughtful types, with similar steady outlooks. Jonathan took a real interest in the house and what Brinsley was doing with the estate.

'Were you really brought up there?' Jonathan asked as they drove away after a very pleasant visit.

'Dragged up,' Flick said. 'It wasn't as lovely as you might think. My mother was not particularly good at raising young children. And it was in far more of a state then than it is now, I can promise you.'

He looked at her quietly as he drove, and then turned his gaze back to the road. 'I can hear that there's quite a story there.'

'I don't really like to talk about it. It wasn't easy. I don't know why it was so manically tough, or why my mother couldn't look after us . . . but she couldn't. We all pay the price for it today. Brinsley is painfully shy, I'm a tortured soul, and Prue just wants to bury herself in marriage and children as soon as she can, no doubt hoping to please our mother along the way. She's bound to marry someone just to win Mother's approval.'

'I'm sorry to hear it was all so awful. It makes my childhood sound positively boring in contrast. I was rather happy.'

'I'm looking forward to meeting your family.'

'I don't think that's terribly possible – my father is long dead, as you know, and now that my mother has retired to Australia to live with my sister, you're not likely to see them any time soon, unless you're prepared to go to Sydney.'

'What a shame. I'd love to meet them.'

'They would adore you, don't worry. We'll see them one of these days.' Jonathan smiled at her. 'But I want to think only of you right now. I'm going to fix you, Flick Templeton. All those wounds you've got, all that sadness in your heart. I'm going to make it all go away. I promise.'

Flick smiled at him, happiness rising in her. This was what

she wanted and needed to hear. Stability and security was all she wanted, and she knew that Jonathan was the man to give it to her.

'Your weddings are destined to disappoint me,' Gloria said loftily on the day that Flick married Jonathan. It was another register office wedding, this time in Marylebone as Flick had not wanted to marry in the same place twice.

'I'm so sorry, Mother,' Flick said dryly. They were on their way to the ceremony. Flick wore a dark blue satin dress with a full skirt and a tight waist, her hair curled and pinned back with diamond clips, a white fur wrap on her shoulders.

'Look at me, after all!' Gloria indicated her own white satin gown, thickly encrusted with crystals. She was even wearing a baby tiara in her red curls. 'Anyone would think I was the bride! It should be me getting married!'

'I think Jonathan might object. And don't worry, Prue will give you the wedding you long for.'

'Yes, she will,' Gloria said with satisfaction. 'She's done so well.'

Prue had recently got engaged to the young heir to a minor earldom, a solid young man entirely devoted to the pursuits of fishing, shooting and hunting when he wasn't working in a bank in the City. There would be a traditional society wedding the following year of the kind that Gloria enjoyed so much. Flick was happy for her sister, who seemed delighted with her fiancé and keen for her new life to begin.

'Ah, here we are!' her mother announced as the Rolls

pulled up outside the register office. 'At least we've arrived in some kind of style, even if you're determined to marry with none.'

Passion was dangerous, and life with Jonathan was easy and safe. He was placid and easy-going, always keen to devote himself to Flick and to her needs. He encouraged her to continue her writing, and when, after a year of marriage, she was pregnant, he told her that even when the baby arrived, he would understand if she wanted to continue working.

'I don't think you're the kind of woman who will be fulfilled just by motherhood,' he said. 'I think you need to keep busy.'

Flick was grateful to him. She was never afraid to tell him how she felt and what she wanted, as she had been with Caius. She knew that he would put her first and make her his focus at all times. He was an ideal husband, she was sure of that, and when the baby came, he would be the ideal father as well.

Her daughter arrived at the Chelsea and Westminster Hospital, delivered by Mr Pringle, the consultant who had hurried back from his round of golf when he heard that Mrs Blair was in labour at last. It was a hot summer day and Flick found the heat unbearable. She panted and sweated and screamed, while Jonathan paced up and down outside in a state of high anxiety. It was a long labour that ended after twenty-four hours, by which time Flick was exhausted and longing for it all to be over somehow. She had just begun to wonder at what point she would rather be dead than have to go on suffering like this, when there was a general uprush in activity, she was told the baby was crowning and it was time to put all her efforts into pushing.

As if I have any effort left to give!

But from somewhere, she found a reserve of strength, and pushed down with all her might. Something deep within her seemed to move and, with a start of surprise, she realised that she was actually about to have a baby. That aspect of the whole process had been forgotten in her struggle with the exhaustion and heat and pain, and the endlessness of it all.

With a rush and a kind of slither, the baby came out into Mr Pringle's arms, and a moment later, the cord had been clamped, cut and tied and the baby wiped down and checked for her vital signs. Then, to Flick's astonishment, the tiny bundle was put into her arms and she was looking down on the red scrunched face of an actual baby. Her baby.

'You have a healthy little girl,' Mr Pringle said proudly, as though he had made her himself and simply handed her over. He was taking off his gloves. 'And all is well. No tearing. No need to cut you. We are pleased.'

'Thank you,' Flick said, her fatigue mysteriously vanished and replaced by deep delight. 'Is my husband here?'

They called him in. Jonathan wept as he saw her, horrified by what she must have suffered while he couldn't comfort her, and then moved by the sight of their little girl, nestled in her mother's arms.

'Oh Flick, she's so beautiful. You clever, clever thing. What a gift you've given me!'

'It took both of us.'

'What nonsense, you did all the work. Oh my. She's

gorgeous.' He put one hand on her, as gentle as any father could be.

'I'm going to feed her myself.'

'Of course you are, you clever girl.'

The nurse came and helped her latch the minute mouth onto a nipple. The tiny creature knew what to do, and pulled hard on it, fitting her little nose over the curve of Flick's breast and nestling in to her. 'What should we call her?' Flick asked, full of bliss now that the agony was over.

'If you don't mind, we could call her Mary after my mother.'

'Mary. Yes, I like that. Mary she is. I don't think we can use my mother's name. Mary Gloria sounds like a religious anthem. Mary what?'

'Mary Felicity Blair.'

'Oh yes. Perfect. There. We've named her. Just like that.'

Now they were a family, happy in their little mews house, although with the addition of a rather fierce maternity nurse, who seemed to want to whisk the baby away from Flick as often as possible. Her attitude was that a mother's greatest wish was to see the baby as little as she could, and that the baby's interests were best served by a nanny. She highly disapproved of the breastfeeding that Flick insisted on, and was constantly trying to introduce bottles to the baby. It seemed that every half hour, the nurse was heading out of the door with the huge pram, Mary a little swaddled bundle in the middle of it.

Eventually, Jonathan sacked that maternity nurse and

replaced her with another, and then, when Mary was well established and thriving, they decided on a day nanny, as Mavis did not like having the nannies living with them.

'It's too small here, ma'am, I find it too cramped with an extra person,' Mavis said. 'There just isn't the room for us all to live comfortably.'

'Oh dear, I suppose we shall have to move again,' Flick said, wondering how she could cope with such an upheaval when Mary was so tiny. She was still doing her reviewing as it was not so hard to get to a cinema and then write her pieces. Jonathan took the reviews around to the *Viewpoint* offices on his way to his own work.

One day he said to Flick, 'Listen, darling, the editor has said something that indicates he's thinking of an over-haul. I've been thinking . . . why don't I give up the office altogether? I can write at home, after all, and I've been want-ing to do another book for a while. We don't need the money, do we?'

'No, of course we don't.'

'Then, doesn't it make sense for me to be here? I can find us a place, sort that all for us. I can help look after Mary while we don't have a full-time nanny, I rather enjoy it – strange, I know. And you'll be free to concentrate on what you love doing.'

Flick looked at him in amazement. 'You're one in a mil-lion, Jonathan Blair, you really are! I think it sounds like a marvellous idea. Of course you must give up that dreary office and write the book you've always wanted to.'

It seemed like no time at all before Jonathan had found

them another house, not far from their little mews place, and now there was room for a full-time nanny. He gave up the newspaper, and the three of them, Mavis and the nanny, lived a placid and pleasant life of regular routines. Jonathan seemed to have plenty to keep him busy, spending days in the British Library researching his book while the nanny took care of the baby. Flick, tapping away at her work between the time she spent with Mary, was the happiest she had ever been. The madness of her life with Caius had been shut up in a box and stored away somewhere deep within herself.

Gloria had become a doting grandmother, adoring little Mary and turning up every other day with gifts for the baby. She seemed, at last, pleased with Flick for giving her such a precious gift as a perfect, fair, blue-eyed little granddaughter. And with Prue married in a blaze of glory the proper way, she seemed satisfied at last with her children. Only Brinny now wanted a wife but there was no hurry for that. Gloria liked things just as they were for now.

At last, Flick thought, *I'm happy.*

Her failed marriage to Caius seemed like a bad dream. Jonathan was comfortable and reliable: he doted on her, cared for her, built his life around her. The safety, warmth and protection of her second marriage was exactly what she needed, and if she sometimes yearned for a little more adventure, and sometimes still sat up late at night with her vodka and cigarettes, pouring her hopes and dreams into her typewriter . . . well, that was just her being greedy.

*

'Oh!' Flick stared at the printed sheet she had been sent through the post that morning.

Jonathan looked up from his breakfast of toast and marmalade and thick, dark tea. 'What?' he asked at once. He was always interested in what was going on in her life.

'I've been invited to the preview screening of that film everyone's been talking about, *The Girl Who Stole the Ritz*.'

Jonathan looked mystified. He was not much of a filmgoer. 'Should I have heard of it?' He picked up his toast and took a big bite, munching thoughtfully. 'Well, anyway. Nope. I don't know it.'

Flick regarded him sceptically. 'You haven't heard of Chase Dupone?'

'I've heard of him, of course.'

'Well, this is the film based on his novel. The one that won those prizes . . .'

Jonathan nodded, pleased. 'There you are, you see. I'm not so hopeless. I might be a specialist in economics but even I have heard of Chase Dupone.' He gave her a sideways look. 'Is this film of special interest to you?'

Flick laughed, flushing slightly. 'Well, it is a little. I met him once, years ago.'

'Of course you did.' Jonathan rolled his eyes, laughing. 'I might have known you'd have a connection with him. You usually do. So come on then . . . how do you know him?'

Flick scanned the pre-screening information, taking in the hyperbolic language praising Chase's wit and skill to the skies, ramping up the excitement for this film as much as it could. She had followed his career ever since he had changed the course of her life with his article: Caius had come to Caundle to claim her once he had realised the extent of her family's wealth, and that was down to Chase.

I ought to be furious.

And yet, she had never forgotten the charm and wit of the American, and now felt rather honoured that someone so famous had written about her. In the few years since she had met him at the Lake Como villa, he had exploded into fame and prominence with two books, first a prize-winning meditation on life in the deep south of America, and then this delightful and astringent comedy of love and sex, *The Girl Who Stole the Ritz*.

She gave Jonathan a potted history of how she and Chase had crossed paths, though she didn't talk about the role that the article played between her and Caius. As a rule, she mentioned him as little as possible.

'How funny!' Jonathan sat back in his chair, shaking his head. 'I've been a fan of his for a while. Perhaps I read that piece in *Mademoiselle*, never realising we were fated to be together!'

'I highly doubt it.' Flick put down her screening information and turned back to her coffee. 'I know you well enough to know that you would never read a copy of *Mademoiselle*!'

'You know me better than anyone,' Jonathan agreed. 'Well, I hope you'll give him an honest review!'

'As if I'd give anything else.'

It was true. Flick certainly felt that she knew Jonathan. He was an open book, a man incapable of dissembling. When, occasionally, she heard muffled and urgent telephone calls going on behind the door of his study, she thought nothing of it. The very many official-looking letters he received meant nothing either. He was the kindest and most sensitive man she could imagine, and she trusted him entirely. When she ever asked about these things, he hastened to tell her not to worry. Everything was fine. He had some family matters to deal with, but nothing awful. He wouldn't worry her with them. She was far too busy for that, and it was all nothing anyway.

The following week, Flick went to the private cinema in one of the mazy streets near Leicester Square, the home of the big picture houses. It was plush and warm, and one of the many reasons why Flick loved reviewing films. She adored the cocoon feeling of a cinema and the anonymity of the darkness. No one knew who you were when you were watching a film and the film didn't care either. It was the same for everyone, and it was always predictable and always the same. No worries about the actors having an off night or forgetting their lines. It was always exactly as it should be.

The film opened with a burst of music and a series of comic credits, and then the music faded over the bright opening scene, a street in Manhattan where a pretty girl was meeting a handsome man for a date at the Ritz hotel, a melange of the London and Paris Ritzes with a New York feel all of its own. Flick settled back to enjoy it.

It was just as good as she had hoped and she wrote very few notes except the odd aide memoire. She was too busy enjoying it, and the shining central performance that would make a superstar of the young actress who played the heroine.

At the end, all the critics broke into applause, a rare thing in the hardened world of film reviewers, and Flick was delighted to find that they were all of her mind. Then came the moment she had waited for: the lights came up to reveal the screenwriter, a balding man in heavy square glasses, and Chase Dupone. She stared. He looked hardly any different to how he had in Italy that spring, except with a little more of the polish that wealth had brought him, his suit clearly expensive, a silk Hermès scarf at his neck.

The question and answer session began and Chase easily dominated with his witty remarks and funny stories about how he had conceived and written the short novel the film was based on. Occasionally the screenwriter would hold forth but it was really Chase's show and he charmed the audience with ease. Flick had prepared a question but she was too nervous in the end to ask it, afraid of what Dupone might say if he realised who was asking. Instead, when the session was over and everyone was filing out to go and write up their review, she lingered in the foyer of the cinema until Chase came out, still chatting with the screenwriter.

She stepped forward as he passed her, half afraid but knowing she would regret it if she didn't. 'Mr Dupone – do you remember me?'

Dupone stopped with a world-weary air, as if this happened to him all the time and there was no chance he would remember her, and peered at her through his little round glasses. Then his expression cleared and he said, 'Well, if it isn't my favourite poor little rich girl! Felicity Templeton, is that you?'

'Yes.' Flick smiled, relieved that he had spared her the embarrassment of not recognising her. 'It's me. Although I'm Flick Blair now.'

'Flick Blair? Ugh. Go back to your old name, my dear!' He turned to the screenwriter. 'Excuse us, my dear. I must talk to this radiant creature!' The writer moved on while Chase stepped forward, took her hands and pressed his cool lips to her cheeks one after the other. 'What a delight. I was wondering how to pass an evening in gloomy old London, and now there's you! I was half considering giving your mother a call, but I have no idea how she feels about me these days.'

'Since your article.'

'Since my little article. Lauren Harcourt told me she was incensed! I don't want to beard that particular dragon if I can possibly help it.' He grinned at her mischievously. 'So how about it? Will you come for a drink with me?'

'Just one,' Flick said. 'I have a daughter now, I mustn't stay out too late.'

'Oh, don't be so silly. What good will you do her not having a martini or two with your old friend? I'm just shocked you didn't ask me to stand godfather – shocked, do you hear? Now come along, we're a hop and a skip from the Ritz and that's definitely the place to go this evening, don't you think?'

It was like being with one of her oldest friends, even though she hadn't seen Chase in years. They ended up in the bar at the Ritz at a table in a dark corner – 'I must avoid my fans if I can,' Chase said, 'they do bother me so when they find out who I am, and it's only going to get worse with this film' – drinking very dry Martinis and eating little salty crackers with them.

'Tell me everything and don't leave out the juicy bits!' Chase demanded, and so she told him about her elopement with Caius and the crazy time she had spent in Soho.

'Sounds right up my street, dear,' Chase said. 'I like the sound of this guy. Just how I prefer them myself – dark and dangerous.'

'A little too dark and dangerous. He left me. He walked out one day without a word and I never saw or heard from him since.'

'Inevitable. That's what they do. And how are you now? Has the heart mended?'

'Oh, I'm so much happier now!' She told him about wonderful, placid Jonathan and adorable Mary, and her life as a reviewer.

'Mmm,' Chase said. 'I'm sorry to hear that.'

Flick laughed. 'What? I have a happy ending!'

'Oh, it's not an ending. It's a slightly stalled beginning, that's all.' He nibbled on a cracker and then said, 'I think you need a little more excitement in your life. Have you thought about coming to New York?'

'No . . . not lately. I went with my mother years ago, after the war, but I don't remember that much about it, except very big hotel suites and even bigger ice creams. That was the best bit in fact.'

'I think you'll be interested in more than ice cream these days. New York is where it's at. Vibrant, alive, creative. Why don't you come visit?'

'I have a husband . . . a baby . . .' Flick said doubtfully. New York sounded marvellous but her life was here in London, with her family.

'Bring them with you! Or would it kill you to take a few weeks away? You have a nanny for the kid, don't you? I'm sure she's sweet but they don't get really interesting for another few years, that's what my girlfriends tell me. Although to be honest, none of their children have got to that stage yet and it's been years and years.' Chase smiled his tight little smile. 'Come over. I can arrange things for you. Why not interview me in my own milieu? I tell you, I'm going to be all the rage quite soon, even more than I am now! You can have an exclusive sneaky peek and a cosy chat that only you and I and millions of readers will share.'

'I'll think about it.' It was tempting, she had to admit that. Her life was placid and calm and maybe just a touch predictable. Being shown New York by a celebrity of Chase's stature sounded more than a little exciting.

'You'd better. I'll give you all my details. Now I want to hear more about your monstrous mother. What is she up to these days?'

Chase was as good as his word, and on his return to New York, he bombarded her with postcards and even telegrams, demanding, begging and wheedling her to come over.

Flick told Jonathan all about it.

'You simply must go,' he said, dandling Mary on his knee, making her chortle. 'Chase Dupone? Even I've heard of him. It could change the course of your career. *Viewpoint* is all very well, but it's so tiny. You could get a reviewing gig on a major magazine or at a prestigious paper.'

Flick sat back in the chair at her desk, where she had been typing up her latest review. 'But leave you and Mary? You know how she's changing every day.'

'We'll be fine. It won't be for long. I've got Mavis and Nanny Elspeth to look after us, I'm very spoiled. I even have your mother dropping in all the time to see the baby. You'd be crazy to pass this up. I think you'd regret it.'

Flick smiled at him. He always put her first. That was one of the things she loved about him. He was utterly, utterly devoted to her, and that was a wonderful feeling.

Chapter Fifteen
FLICK
1958

Flick's transatlantic flight was exciting, if slightly scary.

The PanAm flight from London took over fourteen hours with stop-offs for refuelling, but that seemed like no time at all to traverse the ocean and land on another continent. Despite all the excitement of her trip, Flick began to miss home and Mary and Jonathan almost as soon as she set off. Halfway through her flight, she felt such yearning for them that she had to lock herself into the tiny lavatory and let herself cry it all out. Feeling better, she came out, wiping her eyes, and resolved to put that homesickness out of her mind for as long as she could and enjoy the adventure ahead.

A car – the longest and sleekest she had ever seen – was waiting to collect her at the airport, and before long she could see the Manhattan skyline ahead of her, its high-rise office and apartment buildings glittering against the crisp blue of the day. As they crossed the bridge into the city, she felt as if she were entering some magical land, unlike anything she'd known. Chase had been right: the vibrancy was something else. Everyone seemed to be in a rush. An endless stream of traffic waited impatiently at every junction to be on its way. There was a sense of things to be done right now, this minute.

Flick gazed out of the window of her car, drinking it all in. Would she ever really find her way in this great place? She felt so insignificant here.

But, she reminded herself, her entree was Chase Dupone, who had set up all manner of opportunities for her. And he was not her only ally.

The car headed down the long straight blocks of the city until they reached the area around Central Park, where elegant old buildings with awnings over their grand front doors lined the avenues. Flick's car stopped in front of one of these and the uniformed doorman came forward to guide her out onto the wide pavement and deal with her luggage.

Flick got a glimpse of the greenery of the nearby park before she was led into the marbled interior of the apartment building, and then into a lift, in which she and the doorman and all her suitcases rose smoothly upwards.

The lift opened onto an elegant and carpeted hallway dominated by a polished and panelled door. As Flick stepped out, the door opened and a woman came rushing out, hurrying over to embrace her while the doorman took Flick's luggage inside the apartment.

'Flick! You're here. I can hardly believe it!'

Flick put her arms around her old friend. 'Hello, Diana. I can hardly believe it either.'

Diana pulled back and looked mistily at her. 'It's been so long. Too long. Come inside, you must be exhausted after your flight. It will take you a day or two to get yourself back to normal but I have some wonderful pills that will knock you out and give you the twelve hours' sleep you need to recover. Come on, come in!'

Flick followed Diana into a palatial apartment, formally decorated with large chandeliers, antique furniture and gilt-framed paintings. The windows were swagged in tasselled, fringed damask drapes and gave a magnificent view over the park below, a field of green in the great city. 'Goodness, what a place!'

'It's nice, isn't it?' Diana said casually. 'There's almost too much space, but it's excellent for parties and I have a lot of those.'

Flick stood back to look at her friend. 'You've lost weight.'

'I am a little less chubby,' Diana admitted. 'I couldn't eat much in Cairo, the heat was something else. I never got a taste for the food out there either, even the English stuff they made us. It was never right. After the baby came, I just got thinner somehow.'

'You look wonderful,' Flick said sincerely.

'Thank you. So do you. Motherhood must suit us. I want you to meet Madeline just as soon as her nurse brings her back from the park. She really is the sweetest little thing, I'm so in love with her! Sit down. You must want a drink or something. Let me ring for the maid.' Diana pressed a button by the fireplace and, when the maid appeared, ordered tea.

'And Alfred?' Flick said.

Diana looked blank for a moment. 'Oh, Alfred. Well. He wasn't quite what he seemed. A bigger and more pompous

bore you never knew. It began on the night of the honeymoon. He read me great chunks of something quite
tedious – history of some sort – as a way to seduce me. Can
you imagine? It was quite awful. I knew from the start that I
wouldn't be able to stand it for long. We were utterly different and had nothing in common at all.'

'I could have told you that,' Flick said. 'I think I might have
tried.'

'Edmund had spoiled me,' Diana said mournfully. 'I will
never forgive him for dropping me the way he did. I thought
marriage would be easy if I just tried hard enough, but
it wasn't at all. Alfred and I rubbed one another up the
wrong way in every conceivable manner and life was soon
intolerable.'

'Respectable, though?'

Diana tossed her head. 'Respectable enough. And that's
when I decided. I am just not made for self-sacrifice. I can't
be a married matron and miserable. I would simply have to
live for happiness instead. But a woman can't live on happiness alone, she needs money.'

Flick looked around at the apartment. 'She certainly does!'

'I was pregnant with Madeline by then, and if there is one
good thing to come out of my marriage to Alfred, it's my
darling little daughter.' Diana's expression softened. Then she
looked sharply at Flick. 'Oh my dear – look at you, you're
practically falling asleep right there! I'm being selfish. Take
the tea, and I'll show you to your room.'

Flick had found her eyelids becoming heavier as Diana
was talking. 'I might have to have a nap.'

'Of course you have to. We can catch up on all the gossip later and you can meet Madeline. And don't worry – New York will wake you up soon enough.'

As Flick recovered from her journey in the luxurious surroundings of the Park Avenue apartment, Diana told her the story of how she had finally left Alfred not long after the birth of Madeline. When marriage had become unsupportable, she fled with the baby to Paris and there she had found someone to look after her.

'Hartley rescued me. I met him at a dinner not long after I arrived, and I've been with him ever since.' Diana gestured about the lavish drawing room, where she and Flick were chatting after she had woken from her nap. 'This is his place. I lived in Paris a while, and he came to visit me often. Then we realised it made sense for me to live here.' There was the sound of the hall door opening and a loud voice bellowed her name. She jumped up, smiling. 'He's here now!'

She rushed out and, a moment later, reappeared with a stocky man in a smart suit with big lapels, shiny shoes and a vivid blue tie. He had strong, sensual features: heavy brows with bright eyes below and a wide mouth over a broad chin. Not handsome but striking and attractive.

Diana said, 'Hartley, this is my friend, Flick. You remember I said she was coming to stay?'

'I sure do,' Hartley said expansively, holding out a hand to Flick, who had stood up. 'How are you? Any friend of Diana's is a friend of mine. You're very welcome.'

'Hartley is joining us for dinner,' Diana said.

'How lovely,' Flick said politely, although she'd hoped to have Diana to herself.

Dinner, though, was all about Hartley. Diana focused her attention entirely on him, touching his arm frequently as they talked, and bringing Flick into the conversation only to tell her more about Hartley. Flick didn't mind; she soon found that she was fascinated by his career. He was a theatrical producer, with several hit shows playing on Broadway. Before that, he had been a talent agent in Hollywood, starting the careers of a raft of great stars and building his own fortune in the process.

'Hartley's amazing,' Diana cooed. 'He has the magic touch. Have you heard of *Starshine Parade*?'

'Of course,' Flick said. Everyone knew the songs of the hit musical. It was playing in the West End and Broadway simultaneously, to packed houses.

'I found that,' Hartley said frankly. 'Got it polished up from nothing. Commissioned those talented boys, the songwriters who do all the big shows. They wrote some crackers for me. Huge hit!' He opened his hands expansively. 'Huge.'

Flick was impressed and wondered if she could write an article about his work. She was fascinated by his time in Hollywood, keen to pick his brains about its talent and personalities and the power brokers behind the glossy facade, and urged him to keep talking, which he was happy to do until eventually Diana put a stop to the business talk.

'Hartley needs to relax,' she purred. 'Don't you, darling?'

'Work is my relaxation, honey,' Hartley replied. 'It makes

me happy. I work in the business of dreams, not many people are lucky enough for that.'

'I love that,' Flick said. 'The business of dreams.' She filed that away for later.

After a wonderful dinner, far more lavish than Flick had eaten at some restaurants, they went through to the drawing room for brandy, cigarettes and coffee, and Diana put some big band music on the record player. Soon, she and Hartley were dancing and smooching in the centre of the room.

Realising Hartley wasn't going to leave anytime soon, Flick quietly said her goodnights and slipped away.

She didn't get up until late the next morning, but even so, she was up earlier than Diana, who finally appeared just before lunch, exquisitely dressed and made up.

They took Madeline out for her walk together, Diana holding the white leather reins that stopped the child from stomping off on her chubby legs. The park was beautiful and Flick at last felt rested after her journey, with her internal clock adjusted to the new hours.

'So Hartley is the reason you are in that amazing apartment,' Flick said, as they walked.

'Yes, he is.'

'But you're not married . . .'

'Not yet! But we will be. As soon as he divorces his wife.'

'Oh . . . I see.'

'She's the second Mrs Hartley Silverman. I'm going to be the third.' Diana sighed happily. 'I can't wait, Flick. Life here is a dream. You can see what it's like – there's everything here.

We just live on a different scale. I meet such fascinating people, and Hartley's so immensely successful and talented and the most incredible lover I've ever had. It's bliss.'

'That's wonderful,' Flick said. 'And where is the current Mrs Silverman? Doesn't she mind her husband as good as living with you?'

'Things aren't so strait-laced here, although of course there are still some niceties to be observed. Hartley's wife and children live on the estate in Connecticut. I guess they'll stay there until the divorce. I don't know what will happen after that or where she'll go, but I'm rather looking forward to taking over the place and making it my own.'

Flick raised her eyebrows at her friend. 'Isn't that rather cold? Don't you care what happens to her? It must be miserable for her that you've come along.'

'Survival of the fittest,' Diana said. 'I had the love of my life stolen.' She shrugged. 'I suppose now it's her turn. She might find another husband she prefers, you never know.'

Flick was silent, watching little Madeline in her coat, bonnet and white leather shoes as she toddled along the path, stopping to examine pebbles and leaves that interested her. Diana had clearly hardened. Life with Alfred must have been very difficult if she had been able to stick it out such a short time. She seemed to feel justified in whatever she did now. And who could blame her? She was clearly infatuated with Hartley.

Diana said in a low voice, 'I'm sure you don't approve, darling, but I'm not asking you to. We don't get so long to enjoy ourselves and I intend to make the most of every minute.'

'I don't judge you,' Flick said, although she wondered secretly if she did, a little. 'I just want you to be happy.'

'And I want the same for you.'

'I am happy,' she said truthfully. She thought of her solid, dependable husband. He might not be as glamorous and successful as Hartley but he was warm, loving and true.

'Good.' Diana clutched her hand and squeezed it. 'And we both deserve it.'

After spending a few days with Diana, sightseeing and indulging in some serious shopping – or at least, watching Diana shop – Flick moved out of the Park Avenue apartment and into a hotel. Hartley could manage a short time with a guest in the place, but he wanted Diana back to himself so that he could enjoy evenings with her in peace, and not feel uncomfortable about staying over.

'You don't mind, do you? You must come back to some of my parties,' Diana said brightly. 'You can be my star guest! I have some wonderful people for you to meet.'

Flick was happy to move a few blocks over to a very comfortable hotel on Madison Avenue. She wanted to explore not just the great department stores and the most famous sights, such as the Empire State Building and the Rainbow Rooms, but also to wander, soak up the city and explore a little off the beaten track. Wherever she went, she was struck by the energy of the place. Everywhere she looked new buildings were going up, thrusting upwards into the sky, as if to win some vital race to the future.

Despite all the distractions, Flick also missed home horribly. An attempt at telephoning had been protracted, expensive and unsatisfactory. She hadn't been able to hear Jonathan clearly, let alone Mary's gurgles when he held the receiver to her. She decided to stick to letters after that.

It was hard to be away from them but New York was an excellent distraction. She was half in love with the city already.

Flick's promised interview with Chase Dupone seemed to be taking an age to arrange. She called his apartment not long after she arrived, and at first he seemed to have forgotten that she was coming at all. Then he said that they would have lunch in his favourite bistro, La Chanson du Printemps, and she could interview him there. He changed his mind and decided on the interview in his apartment. Then finally he said that it should take place in the offices of his literary agent, Robert Gerstein, and from there they would go out to lunch at the bistro, which was not far away.

'It was darling Robert who introduced me to the place,' Chase said down the line to Flick, after she had called for the third time to pin him down. 'You'll love it.'

'Are you sure your agent's office is the right place for our interview?' Flick asked. 'It sounds a little businesslike, not very relaxed.'

'Of course it is, dear. Then I don't have to worry about you judging my own little place.'

'As if I would!'

'You wouldn't be able to help it, no one can. Here's the address. Are you ready to write it down?'

On the appointed day, Flick found herself outside a huge white office building in Lower Manhattan. It stretched over almost a whole corner plot, soaring upwards for at least twenty floors, and was subtly grand with ornate stone-work and carved bronze decoration that had turned verdigris with time.

A modern temple, dedicated to the business of making money.

Flick went inside through vast glass doors. The interior was as large as a railway station, and at the huge desk, a smart young woman directed her to a long bank of lifts. When one opened, a uniformed boy in a cap and white gloves inside selected her floor from one of the many illuminated buttons and they rode smoothly to the fifteenth floor.

Outside the lifts the corridors bustled with activity. At another reception desk, Flick was directed along a carpeted hallway, past door after door of agencies and businesses, to one emblazoned in gold with *Gerstein & Gerstein Literary Agency*.

She opened the door to see a secretary typing behind a desk, surrounded by filing cabinets and neat piles of papers.

Seeing her, the secretary stopped typing and stared over the top of her cat-eye glasses. 'Can I help you?'

'I'm here to see Mr Robert Gerstein and Mr Dupone. I have an appointment.'

'Of course. Mr Dupone isn't here yet, but Mr Gerstein is in his office. Please follow me.'

Flick followed the secretary and a moment later was being led into an office. She felt instantly at home. The antique desk was covered in piles of scripts and more paper surrounded it, in wonky towers. The bookshelves were crammed with volumes of all kinds and the walls were covered in pictures. A comfortable sofa with a reading lamp over it took up one wall, and a Persian rug added colour and cosiness to the room.

Behind the desk, a good-looking man, broad and well built with warm brown eyes, was standing up, smiling and coming around to greet her as the secretary gave her name.

'Hello there,' he said in a pleasant New York accent. 'How do you do, Miss Templeton. I'm Rob Gerstein, and I have the dubious honour of being Chase Dupone's agent. It's a pleasure to meet you.'

Flick felt a jolt of recognition. She smiled as she took his hand. 'Have we met before?'

'I don't believe so. Amy, could you bring us some coffee, please?'

The secretary turned to go while Flick stood in confusion. She had the strangest feeling that she had met this person before, but she couldn't think how. Surely she would remember a New York literary agent, particularly one who looked like this? He was talking to her, offering her a seat and apologising for Chase's late arrival. Then he sat back down behind his desk and smiled at her. 'Tell me how you like New York. Is it what you expected?'

'It's simply wonderful even if somewhat overwhelming.'
She began to tell him impressions of the city, even making
him laugh a little, while she was half bemused at the feeling
of connection that was still snapping and flickering through
her. It was an illusion. Obviously they had never met. And yet
everything about him, from his dark brown eyes to his broad
smile, to the scattering of dark hair she could see at his wrists,
even the shape of his fingers and the way he moved his hands
when he talked . . . it was all so oddly familiar.

*He's handsome, but not in a stop-the-traffic way. He's the
kind that the more you look at him, the more you see about
him that's nice.*

The secretary brought in the coffee and went away, the
conversation continued pleasantly, and all the time Flick kept
being distracted by that odd feeling that they had met before.

Chase arrived half an hour late, a whirlwind of charm and
apologies. Rob showed them into the next-door office and
left them to it so that Flick could conduct her interview. She
had bought a tape recorder specially, a bulky machine with a
built-in microphone and tapes that ran reel to reel. She had
been shown how to operate it in the shop and could only
hope it was working correctly. She planned to leave it behind
in the US and take the tape home with her.

'At last, we get to have our little chat,' Chase said, lighting
a cigarette and sipping on the coffee that Amy brought him.
'And then lunch. Rob will come with us. You will like him.'

'I already do.'

'He's a mensch, you know what I mean? One of the gang.

One of the ones who knows what it's all about. I have a theory about it.' Chase leaned forward. 'Turn your tape on and listen to this. You know what I think? I think childhood suffering is a gift. I think monstrous mothers and fathers can be the people who open your soul to the universe. I sometimes wonder if there's a divine plan that puts open hearts like ours in the hands of the cretins and the demons and the wicked, in order to create artists. Humans. The ones with the key to all of it.'

Flick stared at him, trying to understand. 'You mean, suffering makes artists?'

Chase sat back, waving his hand. 'We're all flawed, of course. Don't think an artist is any more perfect than anyone else! Au contraire! We can be selfish and mean; sometimes we positively have to be, in order to be artists. But . . . we see the beauty and pain of life. We are exposed to it, as though our painful upbringings ripped off several layers of skin and left us raw to it. And we communicate to others. We see others. We know they exist.'

'Is that it? The answer? I mean, the answer to why some people seem to understand life more than others?'

'It's *an* answer,' Chase said carefully. 'But there's almost more than one explanation for everything. And it doesn't change anything much. You won't be able to help messing your own kids up, don't worry about that. You're not granted special exemption from anything.'

Flick thought of beautiful Mary, and her eyes filled with tears. She adored her daughter's innocence and potential and had convinced herself that she would not make the mistakes that Gloria had, or make Mary suffer as she had. Mary would have the chances she hadn't had. She, Flick, would be a wonderful mother. And here was Chase telling her she was destined to fail and to make Mary unhappy. It was awful.

'Hey now, don't get upset, dear,' Chase said, repentant, seeing her tears. 'You're human. That's what I'm saying. You're not a monster, you won't torment her in that way. But you'll upset her and make her need to leave you. It's the way. It's the right way. Now come on. Let's talk about my stunning career and huge talent, and all about my very, very glamorous life.'

The interview lasted over an hour and when it was done, and Flick had her tape and her notes, she knew it was something special. Chase declared himself starving and Rob reappeared to accompany them to the bistro for lunch.

The feeling of familiarity had died down a little, perhaps because of Chase's presence, but Flick still felt at ease in his company, as though he was someone with whom she had everything in common.

Over lunch, when Flick asked, Rob told them briefly about growing up in Brooklyn, how he got himself as much education as he could before becoming a mailroom boy at a big agency and working his way up rapidly, until finally he and his brother felt able to launch their own business, finding great new talent and placing their work with publishers and the press.

'You found me, you lucky boy,' Chase said as they ate lobster in butter and caviar sauce, and drank Sancerre.

'You found me,' Rob countered with a laugh. 'Don't you remember?'

'Across a crowded room . . . our eyes met. It was love.' Chase laughed. 'For me! I had to hunt you down and make you sign me.'

'We have an amazing working relationship,' Rob countered diplomatically. 'And, Flick, you're going to sell this interview?'

Flick nodded. 'I think it's going to be wonderful. Usually papers commission interviews but I'm going to write this up, take it to the editors and see what happens.'

'We'll need approval.'

'Of course.'

'I'll approve it,' Chase declared, with a wave of his hand. 'I approve of anything Flick does.' He checked his watch. 'Well, darn it, I have to go. I'm going to a fashion show this afternoon and it starts in twenty minutes.' He turned winsomely to his agent. 'How about you take a little time off and show Flick some of the cultural sights of the city?'

Flick was embarrassed. 'There's no need, really, I wouldn't want to take up your time. I've been to the Met and some wonderful galleries.'

Rob eyed her as he finished his coffee. 'Have you been to the Frick?'

She shook her head.

'Then we'll put that enormous bag of yours back in my office building, and I'll take you there this afternoon.'

'Good,' Chase said, satisfied. 'I think that's a wonderful idea. And it makes me feel a great deal less guilty too. We'll catch up soon for cocktails instead.'

The Frick Collection was, Flick thought, the most perfect museum. It was housed in a grand beaux-arts mansion built by a wealthy industrialist who had amassed a collection of beautiful art and wanted to display it. Paintings were hung in splendid rooms and galleries, with the house and collection now bequeathed to the public and open to all.

'How magnificent,' Flick said, as she and Rob wandered through the galleries.

'You see why you've got to love New York. This is how a Brooklyn boy gets educated,' Rob said. 'Look at what's on offer. I didn't come from a fancy background, there weren't a lot of books and pictures in my house. But all this was on my doorstep.'

Flick thought of his office, crowded with just those things. 'You've made up for it.'

'When I discovered how much beautiful stuff there was in the world, and how much there is to learn about it, I couldn't resist wanting to know all I could about it, and enjoy it too.' He smiled at her, his dark eyes crinkling at the edges. 'I think you're from a different sort of background, aren't you? I read the piece that Chase wrote about you years back.'

'And what did you think of it?' They were walking slowly through a large, dark green gallery hung with masterpieces.

'I thought Chase wrote it brilliantly, as you'd expect. But I felt sorry for you. What eighteen-year-old girl needs something like that written about her? You were only just beginning and your life was spread out on the page for anyone to read and judge you for it. It was so sad. And you know Chase, he is always present in everything he writes. It was half as much about him as you.'

'That's true.' She was touched by his sympathy. No one else had thought of it that way.

'But he captured something that meant I had faith that you'd overcome all of that.'

'What did he capture?'

'Soul, I think. I think that's what it's called. Now come over and let's look at that Velázquez together. It's quite the painting. Imagine having to do a portrait of your boss and he's as ugly as sin and also has the power to sling you in prison if he doesn't like it . . . what would you do, huh? Let's go see.'

Flick went back to her hotel feeling elated. Her day had been a great success. Not only was the interview with Chase better than she'd hoped, but she had made a friend. She had spent a happy afternoon with someone who made her feel entirely comfortable. Being with Rob had felt as natural as breathing. They talked away without any awkward pauses, laughing at the same things, either feeling the same way about the things they saw or interested in the differences between them. Flick found it easy, pleasant and fun.

When he left her at the end of the day, he seemed to feel the same way. 'It's been fun,' he said. 'I mean it.'

'I enjoyed it too.' She smiled at him.

'There's nothing like seeing your own city with a visitor to help you appreciate it.' They were standing at the entrance to the subway, where they would part. 'Listen, I'm owed a few days' vacation. And I'm the boss. So how about I take a day or two and we go and look at some other things? I like the idea of being a tourist.'

'Are you married?' she asked suddenly.

'No, I'm not. But you are, aren't you?'

She nodded. 'Miss is my writing name. I'm Mrs Blair in real life.'

'Well, there you are, it's very respectable. I wouldn't think of offering to take you about if you weren't,' he said, smiling back.

Flick laughed. 'When you put it like that . . . all right. I'd love to see the city with you.'

'Good.' Rob touched his hat to her. 'I'll pick you up tomorrow at ten and off we'll go.'

The next few days passed in a whirl of activity. They did not visit fancy French bistros or go shopping in Bergdorf's, but they did eat pretzels from a stand in the park, go to a baseball game and attend an off-Broadway performance of a work by a new and unheard-of playwright, someone Rob told her would be famous one day. They ate sandwiches with something called pastrami and pickles, washed down with Coke, while sitting in booths in a cheap restaurant. Rob took her out to Ellis Island, to the funfair, and, in the evening, to a club in Harlem to hear a black artist sing the blues while the band wailed behind her. He took her to a huge cinema, as fancy as any London theatre, and they saw a marvellous movie about gangsters that left Flick in tears. Afterwards they ate burgers in a late-night diner.

'This was what I hoped New York would be,' Flick said happily. They had ended up at a bar down an alley, with the entrance hidden under a fire escape, where lone men sat at the bar sipping beers and spirits, and couples hunched together over tables lit by red-bulbed lamps.

'New York is so many things,' Rob said, 'but one thing is for sure, there's a place for anyone here. It's impossible not to fit in. No one is a misfit in this city, we're all misfits who belong together. You never understand till you've been here.'

'I do understand,' Flick said sincerely. 'I want to thank you so much, Rob. You know I'm going home in a few days, don't you?'

'Uh-huh.' He sipped on his whisky and rattled the ice cubes in his glass.

'And you go back to work tomorrow. So we won't be going out together any more.'

He pursed his lips and nodded, frowning. 'Yup.'

'It's just been amazing and I'm more sorry than I can say that it's over. You've made my trip incredible. Thank you.'

'I should thank you. You've made me see my town afresh and given me the best vacation ever.'

They clinked glasses and drank, and then sat in an awkward silence, the first between them.

'I guess you're going home to your husband, huh?' Rob said quietly.

'Yes.'

'Will you tell him from me that he's a lucky guy?'

She laughed. 'I think he'd be quite surprised if I told him that. He might not understand what friends we are, even though we've known each other for such a short time.'

'I guess he would find that hard to understand. In a way, so do I.' Rob squinted at the table, frowning again. He put down his glass suddenly. 'Come on, I'm gonna walk you back to your hotel. The party's over, I guess.'

'Oh, are you sure?' Flick said, disappointed. She didn't want the evening to come to an end.

'It's late. I'm going to get you home. Come on.'

She knocked back the remnants of her whisky and reached for her wrap.

Back on the street, she slipped her arm through his and they strolled back through the city towards her hotel, chatting as they always did in perfect companionship.

'I can't believe it's the last time I'll see you,' she said as they drew up outside the hotel. 'Will you come and see me in London perhaps?'

'Maybe I will.' Rob smiled at her and then they were staring at one another, their smiles fading. He put his hand over hers where it sat on his arm. 'Flick, if you weren't a married woman, you know I'd be kissing you right now, don't you?'

She dropped her gaze and nodded, biting her lip. She had a sudden wild desire to tell him to please kiss her anyway, but she knew that would be very wrong. She couldn't betray Jonathan. He had been nothing but good and kind to her. He didn't deserve it. She knew how painful it was to be betrayed, she could not inflict it on someone else. 'We can't do that.'

'I know. But we will be friends, won't we?' he asked in a low voice.

'When I met you, I felt like I knew you already.'

'Huh. That's strange. I know what you mean, though. I felt that too.'

'So how could we not be friends?'

'You're right. It's meant to be. Goodbye, Flick, and don't forget me.'

'I won't,' she said. 'Don't forget me either.'

'As if.'

Rob dropped one warm kiss on her cheek, lingering just a little longer than he should, and then smiled, turned and walked away. Flick watched until he was just a dark shape in the distance and sighed.

I have a new friend. A good friend. I don't know why that makes me feel sad.

Chapter Sixteen

FLICK

1958

Flick had only two more nights in New York before flying back to London. She was desperate to see Mary again, and of course Jonathan, but her longing for home itself had diminished. Her stay in New York had been so fabulous. She had felt truly alive for the first time in her life.

Diana threw a dinner party in Flick's honour in the Park Avenue apartment. Hartley was there, playing the host alongside Diana as though they were already married and his actual wife had been neatly disposed of. The star of Hartley's Broadway hit was there, glamorous in black lamé with an extremely penetrating voice, along with some other society couples, a senator from Washington and a frozen food magnate and his wife from California, both incredibly tanned. It was all very civilised and cultured and lavish, with plenty of witty and brittle conversation. But as they drank cocktails before dinner, Flick wished like anything she was back at the baseball or eating burgers with Rob.

They were about to go in for dinner when the maid showed in a late arrival.

'Oh Henry, you're here, thank goodness,' Diana said. She looked ethereal in a white evening gown. 'You're just in time, you naughty boy! I was about to get cross. You're taking Flick in.'

She brought the new guest to Flick. He was tall and handsome, elegant in black tie, and he bowed to Flick. 'Henry Morfield at your service,' he said in a cut-glass English accent.

Flick smiled and frowned at once. 'Henry Morfield?'

'Ah, do you remember me, Miss Felicity Templeton?'

'You have a moustache now, but yes . . . of course I do.'

'Your birthday party. The unforgettable occasion when you turned me down flat and then ran away with one of the guests and married him instead,' he said with perfect dryness and humour, with a charming smile.

Flick laughed. 'You put that beautifully. I hope you've forgiven me.'

He bowed politely. 'It is all forgotten, of course. Only the memory of your delightful charm remains.' He offered her his arm. 'Please.'

'Thank you,' she said, taking it.

As they went into the dining room, she slid her gaze over to look at him properly. She remembered him now, sitting on the fountain edge at her eighteenth birthday party. Age suited him and he was now more handsome, with short dark hair cut in the classic English way, a small moustache and fine-boned features. He looked like an archetypal English gentleman, which was exactly how he spoke as well.

Henry was charming company over dinner, witty and

acerbic with a cosmopolitan air. He seemed to know every-one in London and regaled her with lots of funny stories.

'You surprise me,' Flick said, shaking her head at him. 'I thought you were just going to be a country gentleman, like so many of the rest.'

'I'm sure you didn't like people making judgements about you based on your background,' he said, sliding a look at her.

'You're quite right, I didn't. I'm sorry. So you weren't inter-ested in being a farmer then?'

'I couldn't bear horses – horribly allergic, actually. I hate the countryside, loathe hunting, abhor fishing. So to be quite honest, it wasn't exactly my cup of tea. I wanted to go on the stage.'

'Oh! How unexpected!'

'That's exactly what my father said, although not in quite those words. In fact, he nearly had a stroke at the very idea. He was certain that a desire to act made me not quite a func-tioning man, if you know what I mean. He was wrong about that but I just loved acting. Only one problem.'

'Yes?'

'Not very good.' Henry shrugged. 'I'm not bad-looking, I can make a decent fist of a drawing-room comedy or a detect-ive drama. But no one was ever going to rave over my Hamlet or swoon at my Romeo. I thought I'd try my hand at movies, so headed out to America. Turns out I'm better at writing words than speaking them.'

'You write movies?' Flick was impressed.

'I've done some rewrites. I fix things.' Henry nodded at their host. 'Hartley used me a bit in Hollywood and that helped me get on the circuit. Scripts arrive with me when they need a fresh eye, sharpness, sophistication and jokes. My forte.'

'Fascinating!' Flick said. 'Does it pay?'

'Very decently. I cannot complain. And I like the life here very much. Lovely food and drink. Generous people. Lots of excitement. I prefer New York to LA but I don't mind travelling here and there as necessary. Writing can be done anywhere, of course.'

'Do you ever miss home?' Their last plates were being cleared, the coffee laid out. Henry poured her a cup.

'Sometimes. I love meeting people like you from the old place. Someone I can talk to properly. I can't think how Diana can bear being surrounded by Yanks day in and day out. But she manages. Then again, Diana isn't much of a woman of the mind, is she? I love her, but she isn't.'

Flick smiled and shrugged. 'She is a wonderful hostess.'

'She has the very mostest!' Henry gave her a wicked look. 'And offers such a comfortable berth to anyone who needs it.'

Flick drank her coffee and after a while, Henry murmured, 'Listen, I know exactly what's going to happen next. We'll retire to the drawing room, and then that Broadway baby is going to start singing show tunes with her acolyte over there on the grand piano. We'll all applaud and ask for more, and more we will get. More and more and more until we can't stand it. So . . . here's a plan. Why don't we make our excuses and I'll take you to a splendid little club I know? There's

275

late-night jazz. Wonderful stuff. And you and I can have a much quieter, nicer late-night drink.'

Flick looked over at him, and then at Diana holding court opposite Hartley. She knew she would not get another word with her friend tonight, Diana was in full hostess mode. She also knew that Henry was right, and that things would unfold exactly as he predicted. The sound of a smoky jazz club sounded more appealing. In fact, it sounded like the kind of place that Rob would take her. He had taken her to that Harlem club with the incredible singer. Perhaps he might even be at this place himself.

The minute she thought this, she was keen to see if he might be. *Wouldn't that be funny? If we crossed paths again by chance?*

The idea tickled her.

'All right,' she said, 'as long as I tell Diana first.'

'Of course. I'll make my excuses first and wait downstairs. You get your wrap and meet me there.'

It was a little awkward to get away, and Flick could see that Diana was not pleased, but Flick was keen to escape. Diana's parties were fun but exhausting and she had heard Hartley holding court many times now. Henry was very good company and she was looking forward to her nightcap. Then she would head back to the hotel to sleep.

They took a yellow cab downtown to Greenwich Village to a nondescript bar, half full of patrons, with a stage set up for music but without any musicians on it yet. They settled down at a table, both lighting cigarettes. The waiter brought them some drinks, bourbon on the rocks. Flick looked around but of course there was no sign of Rob. It had been ridiculous to think that there might be. Suddenly she rather regretted leaving Diana's dinner party, but she'd done it now.

I hope she isn't cross. She has a right to be. And I hope I didn't offend Hartley. I should just have seen it out. I didn't need to come here. A quick hour, and then I can go home to bed.

'The music is going to be something special, you must stay and hear a little,' Henry said, as if sensing her desire to go back to her hotel. 'I've heard great things.'

'Of course,' she said politely.

He smiled at her, and she noticed that when he did his fine straight teeth were edge to edge, making his smile much larger than a normal one.

'And how is your husband?' he asked easily.

She gave him a look. 'I take it you know that my elopement escapade did not work out?'

'Yes, I did know that. And I also know that you married again – to Jonathan Blair. A fine man.'

Flick was surprised. 'Do you know him?'

'Oh yes, we crossed paths a while back. He and I were at Cambridge together, same college, both reading history. We rowed in the same boat. Both tall.'

Flick was taken aback. 'He never mentioned you, at least not that I remember.'

'We weren't that close. Besides, I was good friends with Anne, you see.'

'Anne?'

'Yes. You must know who Anne is.'

'No,' Flick said slowly. 'I don't know who Anne is. Who is she?'

'She's Jonathan's first wife, of course. I can't believe you don't know that.'

Flick sat there, stunned, then picked up her drink and took a hearty slug of the ice-cold whisky.

Henry regarded her sympathetically. 'Oh dear. You didn't know, did you?'

Flick shook her head. She felt frozen inside. Of all the people to lie to her . . . Jonathan? So steadfast and open? Unless Henry was lying. 'Is this true?'

'Of course it is. They were married in our college chapel while still undergraduates. I was there, I watched the whole thing. Anne was at Girton, I can't remember what she was reading. They had a boy together – Samuel, I think his name was. He must be around six by now, I suppose.'

'He has a son?' Flick whispered through numb lips.

'My dear girl, you can't seriously be telling me that you don't know your own husband has a first wife and a son?'

'He never said. He never said a thing about them.'

'He must have been waiting for the right time.'

'We're married. We have a daughter. The right time was some time before those things happened.'

'I'm sorry to be the bearer of bad tidings. Here, you'd better have another drink, you look like you need one. And the music is going to start in a bit. Cheer up, it's not like he's a bigamist, they at least did get divorced before he met you!'

At least I think he did. Sorry, only joking, I'm awful.' Henry signalled for another drink to the waiter.

The first act came out, a trumpeter and a pianist, and they played while Flick tossed back her drink, and started on her next. She felt shocked and horrified, unable to take in that Jonathan – safe and trustworthy Jonathan – had lied to her. She had put her faith in him. He had betrayed that.

Flick didn't say much as the music filled the bar: edgy, scratchy jazz that matched her mood. She drank more of the cold bourbon, layering it on top of Diana's cocktails and fine wines and not caring that it made her woozy, fuzzy-headed and miserable.

How could he?

It felt as though the world had twisted on its axis. Caius . . . at least she had known that he was capable of cruelty. Maybe not from the start, he had hidden it for quite a while, but she had sensed it. He had the aura of danger and light of unpredictability in those dark eyes of his. Jonathan, though . . . mild, sweet, sometimes stuttering, always wide-eyed and candid. How could he tell such a lie?

She was washed with despair. She signalled for another drink.

'Steady on, old girl,' Henry said. 'You might have had a bit too much, you know . . .'

She ignored him. What did he know about any of this?

Do I deserve it? Is that it? Do I draw the kind of men who are dishonest and don't care what they do to me?

It wasn't so much that Jonathan had been married – that he was a father! – but that he had concealed it. Why? Did he think she'd be angry? And surely he must have known she would eventually find out? How could he hide a son from her for his entire life? It was impossible. All those letters and phone calls made sense now, if he had a son to manage. He must have known he'd be found out one day. But he still lied to her.

The next bourbon came. And the next.

She drank them all, not caring.

Flick woke in the morning feeling absolutely terrible as well as confused about where she was. Looking about, she saw she was alone although the bed where she was sleeping was rumpled on both sides.

Looking down, she also saw with horror that she was naked.

Did I do that? she wondered.

She must have. Her clothes were in a heap on the floor beside her.

She climbed out of the bed and went to the basin in the corner, rinsing her face, drinking some water from the tap and cleaning her teeth with her fingertip and a spot of toothpaste from the tube in the tooth mug.

Putting her head around the door of the bedroom, she saw a warehouse-style sitting room, sparsely furnished and empty. But she could hear the sound of a shower running in another room.

She thought of the night before, remembering being in the club with Henry, the news about Jonathan and the black despair that settled on her. Then nothing more.

I must have gone home with Henry. Now he's in the shower. I must go before he gets out. I can't face him.

Feeling mortified, she went back into the bedroom and started pulling on her underwear and then her evening dress. She would simply have to go and hail a taxi and get back to the hotel, while living down the obvious fact that she had stayed out all night. When she had put on her dress and found her shoes and wrap, she found a raincoat on the back of the bedroom door and decided she must borrow it and then would post it back, so she slipped it on. At least she looked marginally more respectable.

Flick tiptoed back through the sitting room. She let herself out of the apartment and took the stairs down to the front door, and was out in the street below. She managed to find her way to where she could hail a taxi, and from there was able to get back to her hotel, desperately in need of coffee.

It was her last day in New York and Flick felt terrible. The hangover had set in back at the hotel, although she had tried to cure it with coffee and dry toast. It had taken a long sleep to feel like herself again and when she woke in the afternoon, she felt better in her body but worse in her mind. Depression had settled there like a heavy blanket.

She knew in her heart that what Henry had told her the previous evening must be true. It would be an extraordinary lie to tell her, and one easily disproved. Jonathan had concealed an ex-wife and a son for all this time. It was unthinkable.

No wonder she had got so drunk last night. No wonder she felt so low.

Then there was the question of exactly what she had done with Henry in his apartment.

She couldn't bear to think about that. It only added to her sense of being wounded and hurt and miserable.

I need something. I need a friend. Not Diana. She'll be cross about last night, not surprisingly. I let her down too.

Flick took a shower, dressed in a sensible skirt and jacket, and put the raincoat she had borrowed into a bag. She would go back downtown and return it to Henry's building. Surely she could find the way?

Out in the late-afternoon sunshine, she made her way to the subway and took a ride down to the station nearest where the club had been. She remembered where it was well enough now she had a map in her handbag to consult. But when she reached the stop for the jazz club, she stayed on another two stops and got out at Lower Manhattan, near the white building in which Rob's office was located.

What are you doing? Are you insane? she asked herself as she crossed the road and went in through the big glass doors. At the reception desk, she asked if they might phone Robert Gerstein and tell him Flick Templeton was waiting downstairs. Then she sat down by a pot plant in the lobby and waited.

It took five minutes, and then she saw him exit the lift and come hurrying across the marble floor towards her, his expression anxious.

'Flick, are you okay?'

She stood up and, at the sight of him, her control faltered, and even though she nodded that she was okay, she began to weep. Rob's arms went around her and hugged her tight.

'Hey,' he said in a low voice. 'Don't cry, honey. Has someone hurt you?'

'Yes . . . no. I don't know.' She pressed her forehead against the scratchy lapels of his jacket.

'Has something happened?'

She nodded.

'Want to talk about it?'

'Yes . . . please.'

'Come on then.' Rob tucked her arm through his and led her out of the building. They walked through the busy Manhattan streets, uptown, not saying anything until he took her into a hotel bar and they sat down in a quiet corner.

'So . . .' He took her hand, gazing earnestly into her eyes. 'What's happened?'

She told him about the dinner at Diana's, and then her escape with Henry and the whisky at the club and how drunk she'd become. She told him what Henry had told her about Jonathan and his previous marriage. Rob's expression changed to a kind of grave astonishment and he let out a low whistle.

'Sheesh. That's bad. What are you going to do?'

'Confront him, I suppose. When I get home.' She felt wretched just thinking about it. 'I don't want it to be true. I want to go back to how things were. You know how you and I have got on so well over the time we spent together . . . I felt so guilty. I felt guilty at how easy it was to be with you, when Jonathan was sitting at home so innocently, looking after our daughter.'

'And now he's not so innocent after all.' Rob shook his head. 'But he's faithful to you, don't you think?'

'Yes, I think so. He's physically faithful, I'm sure. But you see . . . lies. I hate them. They rock a world, shake its foundations, like nothing else. If we don't have honesty and trust, what do we have? I was going to tell him all about you, and be honest that I had made a good friend, and that while we obviously like each other, nothing would happen because I'm married and I know where to draw the line. I wanted him to know he could trust me. And now I think – well, what's the point? What's the point in being honest if you can't be sure of getting it back? I didn't ask to meet you but I knew where to draw the line between us when we did meet. I would never have crossed it.'

'And now?' Rob asked. 'Has all that changed?'

She gazed at him, looking into the deep brown of his eyes. She could read hope there. 'I don't know.'

'I don't want to push you one way or the other, Flick, but you must know I'm crazy about you. You do know that, don't you?'

She nodded slowly.

'And you like me too, don't you?'

She nodded again.

'It's up to you to decide what to do next.'

'I can't make any decisions until I see Jonathan and ask him to explain. Rob, he has a son! A six-year-old son! I have no idea when he sees him, if ever. How did he think he could keep a secret like that from me?'

'I think people often don't set out to deceive. But then an omission becomes too hard to correct. A lie is too difficult to untangle. They justify what they've done to themselves. Maybe convince themselves that you are too difficult or sensitive to explain things to. Who knows? I guess you're right, and it all depends on what he tells you.' Rob reached and rubbed his thumb over the top of her hand. 'But it's going to be too late for us in any case.'

'Do you think so?'

'You'll be there and I'll be here. No matter what happens.'

'If it doesn't work out . . . I could come back?' she said hopefully.

'You'll change your mind on the plane. You'll want your marriage to work and that's the right thing to do. You've got a daughter and a home and a life. You've got a good heart too.'

'But the lies,' she whispered.

'You'll forgive them. You'll see.'

There was a long pause. They sat in silence, sipping their drinks, lost in their thoughts until at last Flick said, 'So I suppose this really is goodbye.'

'Can't we have a few more hours?' Rob asked. 'Just a few more hours? Have dinner with me?'

'I don't know what will happen if we do that,' Flick said, unable to meet his eyes. 'It's harder now that we both know, now that it's been spoken out loud.'

'The temptation is there, I guess.' Rob considered the tabletop carefully, then looked up at her. 'But I still want you to have dinner with me. Will you?'

She took his hand, warm and smooth, and held it tightly with hers. 'Of course I will.'

The following day, Flick took a car out to the airport and boarded her flight for the long trip home.

The time she had spent with Rob had helped to ease her sore heart. He was kind and understanding like no one else she knew.

What a blessing that I met him.

She felt at peace even though she was apprehensive about what lay ahead and the talk she must have with Jonathan.

She was still hurt and sad, but she wasn't angry any more. She would accept what he said. She would ask him to introduce her to his son, Mary's half-brother. She would tell him he was forgiven and that they would move forward into their lives together.

The trust was shattered but she didn't expect to have that in her life any more. They could both have their secrets, if that was the way it was. The balance of the scales had been righted.

She had spent the night with another man, in his apartment. There was little doubt what had happened. She had to acknowledge that.

It was said that two wrongs did not make a right, but she felt that, in this case, that was not quite true.

I've reset everything. I've done what I had to do. Revenge? Or justice? Whatever, I won't feel guilty. I can't.

She settled back into her seat, and opened her copy of the newest Chase Dupone novel, dedicated to her in a bold black hand:

> *To the saddest little rich girl in the world,*
> *I hope you find your happiness soon.*
> *All my love,*
> *Chase*

PART THREE

Chapter Seventeen
ETTA
1979

For as long as Etta could remember, life had had a kind of stable instability. That was how she thought of it. For a huge stretch of her childhood, from her earliest memories, the family had lived in a country house on the outskirts of London. Dad had been a sort of househusband, looking after them all, cooking and tending to the house and garden, while Mum had worked at her writing and her journalism, spending most of her day holed up in her office, typing away or on the telephone. She'd emerge towards the end of the day, smelling of the many cigarettes she'd smoked while writing, and looking for her glass of vodka tonic and ice. One of the first things Etta learned to make was a good vodka tonic with a slice of lemon nestling in the ice cubes.

There had always been Mary, of course, three years older than her, and her heroine, nearly as glamorous and important as Granny. They had shared a nursery that was always full of games and books and toys. They spent hours building dens in the grounds, cycling about on their little red bikes, playing tennis or going on long adventures dictated by Mary and usually based on whatever book she had been reading. They couldn't be the Famous Five so they were the Terrific Two – the dogs were too stupid to solve mysteries and couldn't be relied on to stick around, so they weren't included – and, when Samuel came to visit, they were the Terrific Three. Even though he was much older than they were, he still played with them like a proper brother and joined in with the right spirit. He invented some terrific games, such as Mad Cows and Grass is Greener, chase games that had them screaming with laughter and excitement. Sam came to see them every other weekend and for great chunks of the holidays and they were always happy when he arrived for a visit.

Etta didn't remember when exactly she found out that Sam had the same father as her but a different mother. It seemed to be something she had always known. Sometime in the distant, murky past, when ancient kings and queens were on the throne, before motorcars and aeroplanes, when her parents were young, her father had been married to someone else, Samuel's mother. This lady had been seen only once or twice then, when Sam was young, and Etta didn't remember her although Mary said she did and the lady was perfectly normal. That lady had been a mistake. Then he and Mum had got married and everything was the way it should be, and so she and Mary were born.

She had always had faith in the rightness of things.

Having a brother who appeared and disappeared seemed like a wonderful thing. When she and Mary went to the village primary school, lots of girls seemed to hate their brothers.

'You live in that big house,' some of them would say to her. 'You must be rich.'

Perhaps they were, but she didn't feel particularly rich, she felt normal. And their house, inside, was not luxurious. The furniture was shabby, the wood scratched, the rugs had holes, there was dust everywhere even though they had a cleaner, and nothing matched. She went round to one little girl's house for tea and it was much grander than their house in some ways: the sitting room had all been in white with matching furniture, a pale pink rug, and white cushions and a marble coffee table. Everything was perfectly arranged and neat and their mother had a special flowery tea set that she brought out when Etta came over, and served two types of cake from a platter: Battenberg and Jamaica Ginger Cake.

Whereas at home, they didn't have a tea set, just piles of mismatched plates and cups and teapots, and Dad made things like courgette cake and carrot cake, and let them whip up fairy cakes with violently coloured icing whenever they wanted. They would sit on the wooden floor of the kitchen, scraping out the empty bowls of mixture and icing with their spatulas, and sucking on the rubber tongues to get all the sweetness off them, trying to keep all the dogs from licking the bowls until they'd finished.

'No chocolate!' Dad would shout. 'It's not good for dogs!'

Dad was always doing something while he was in the middle of doing something else, and his half-finished projects were all over the house. Mum would swear when she tripped over rubber hoses that were for his brewing project or stubbed her toe on a demijohn. The kitchen table was always a chaos of papers and letters, and tools and pairs of spectacles, and stray batteries, ornaments, broken toys and cigarette lighters. When mealtimes came, Dad would sweep the lot into a laundry basket and say, 'There, all tidy!'

Several cleaners left in fits of despair until they got Saskia, who stayed and eventually moved in for a while. She didn't seem to mind the chaos. She also didn't do all that much, except clean the bathrooms and do the laundry, but they were all grateful for that. Plus, Saskia was funny and kind and didn't swear at them or shout. She'd go off in the evenings to her sitting room and they could hear all the television they weren't allowed to watch: game shows and comedies that Mum said rotted the brain.

Etta had always thought of Dad as looking after Mum, who had seemed to be increasingly unhappy over the years. She didn't laugh as much as she had once. When the girls were little, Mum had looked after them and played with them, sung to them, hugged and kissed them all the time. As she grew sadder, she did that less. Sometimes, she would weep and hug them and tell them she loved them and that she was sorry, although they didn't know what for. Perhaps it was the outbursts of temper and frustration she had sometimes. She could go for weeks perfectly fine, and then swoop down into a pit of misery. At times like that, her vodka tonics didn't seem to cheer her up at all, even though she said they were all that kept her going.

Dad preferred red wine, the first bottle opened as he started the evening meal, the second as he served up. On one frightening occasion he had knocked back a whole bottle of his own homemade elderflower wine. He got incredibly drunk very fast, and then was violently ill, running out of the kitchen to throw up on the grass outside. Mary said later she had seen the dogs eat it up and then get drunk themselves, but Etta didn't believe her. It had been horrible to watch him transform like that, from normal lovely Dad to someone incapable of talking or walking straight.

Dad stuck to normal wine from the shops after that.

Perhaps the most curious part of their stable instability had been their visits to and from Granny. Etta kept Granny a secret from her primary school friends. While she thought her grandmother was simply amazing and probably the best person in the world, she knew that Granny had a kind of power over others like being a queen or a prime minister and other people didn't always exactly like that.

For reasons Etta did not understand, Mum found Granny very tricky and tried not to see her that often. Granny had a nose for knowing exactly when Mum was least able to cope with her, and turned up then to spend a weekend with them.

Etta didn't know why Mum couldn't stop herself from going into meltdowns over Granny when, really, Granny was a very funny and interesting person.

Although Etta hadn't told her friends about her grandmother, she didn't remain a secret. On one incredible occasion Granny turned up to sports day, a simple occasion of a few races run on a field near the school. She arrived in a Rolls Royce with a chauffeur, who drove the car actually onto the field, and then laid out a grand picnic on a trestle table under a gazebo, with bottles of champagne chilling in a silver bucket. Granny herself had worn a vast hat festooned with flowers and a floating chiffon dress that was cut very low at the front.

Etta had been delighted with the sensation that Granny caused, but Mum and Mary had both been cross about it.

'Not that kind of sports day!' Mum had said crossly to Granny. 'This isn't Eton or Harrow. It's a village primary school!'

Granny had saved the day by sending her chauffeur to the local shop where he bought up all the ice creams and lollies and brought them back for the children. But Etta had known that all the parents and some of the children had looked at her differently after that.

She couldn't imagine what they would think if they ever saw Granny's house in London, which was exactly like a palace. In fact, in her mind, Granny was a kind of wonderful queen: powerful and magnificent.

When primary school came to an end for Etta, Mary had already been at Armitage Hall for two years and Etta had known she would go there too. In some ways, it felt very much like an extension of home, with its freedom and lack of rules. Anyone could do anything they liked. Lessons, if they wanted, or whatever.

Etta had gone to lots of lessons; she liked learning. But sometimes she just felt like spending long hours in the art department, painting pictures and thinking.

Etta had been less conspicuous at Armitage Hall, where there were children from rich homes, whose parents had big cars and all the rest of it. But while she was there, things changed, and the golden life she had enjoyed until then came to an end.

Mum suddenly sold the house in the country. She said she wanted a change.

'I've been mouldering here for too long. It's making me depressed. I need to get back to London where the literary scene is happening,' she said. The girls were home for half-term, but only Mum was there, valiantly trying to cook them decent meals out of whatever she could find.

'Where's Dad?' Mary enquired, looking around as if he might be hiding in a cupboard.

'He's on some kind of retreat,' Mum said vaguely, banging some pans around as she looked for what she needed, eventually pulling a frying pan out of the cupboard.

'What's that?' Etta asked. She thought of armies retreating, people withdrawing and going away. It made her a little nervous to think of Dad retreating.

Mum took some eggs out of the wire basket on the counter and looked at them thoughtfully as if wondering what to do with them. 'He's made some new friends,' she said after a moment. 'And he likes to hang out with them. In tents. In fields. They stay up late and look at the stars and think about things. Spiritual things.'

'How fucking boring,' Mary remarked.

Etta was watching Mum. She had the distinct feeling that Mum did not like Dad doing these harmless-sounding things.

When Dad came back a few days later, he was in a wonderful mood, chattering away about everything he had learned on the retreat, but it didn't make much sense to Etta.

She let his words flow over her: a long ramble about spirits, medicine, a federation of light and existence on the fifth dimension.

But she noticed that Mum didn't laugh or joke about it, as she would have expected. Instead, Mum looked, listened and asked questions. But Etta could see that her eyes were sadder than ever.

It wasn't long afterwards that Mum and Dad sold the house in the country, rehomed most of the dogs, and they moved to London, to a house in Kensington, on the edge of a garden square, with black railings around it and old-fashioned lamp posts topped with lanterns like the one in Narnia. The houses were like something from a Dickens novel, tall and slightly tipsy brick buildings with many windows and chimneys. Their house was divided up into four flats, and it started off with her and Mary living with Mum in the upstairs flat, Dad below on the first floor, and then the ground floor flat was left for guests and Samuel if he wanted it, while the house-keeper was in the basement.

'Why does Dad live downstairs?' Etta asked once. Mary had been out visiting a friend, or shopping, which were her favourite things when they weren't at school.

'We came to a decision,' Mum said. 'We were driving each other up the wall. This is a much more sensible solution as we can each have our own space and not bother each other, but we're there for the nice bits and when we need help.'

That made sense. Besides, Etta had long known that her parents lived by their own rules. Mary still insisted it was bloody weird for a married couple to have different homes but couldn't she see that Dad was becoming more taken up with the ideas and thoughts that had started in the country? And that Mum couldn't bear to hear about it all? She, Etta, didn't mind. It all sounded quite amusing and she didn't believe that Dad really took it seriously – aliens zooming about, or manifesting as sasquatch to hide in the forests of North America; why on earth would they? But she did mind when he started smoking a lot of weed, and when he also offered some to Mary, who took the joint enthusiastically. It felt as though a lot of trouble had started then.

It was only at Caundle that she felt truly happy and relaxed. Now that they lived in London, they spent their holidays at their Uncle Brinsley's house, Caundle Court, where Mum had grown up, although she said it was very different now with Brinsley there. According to her, they had lived in terrible conditions of great hardship, but Etta had found that difficult to believe. It was a beautiful house that seemed to sit somewhere between the shabby, ramshackle qualities of their own house and the luxurious perfection of Granny's, combining beauty with warmth and a sense of homely comfort. The atmosphere was serene and, somehow, permanent. She loved Caundle, and her funny, eccentric and interesting uncle, who lived there with only dogs and herds of cattle for company, as well as the cast of characters who helped him with the house, garden and farm. Caundle, huge, honey-coloured and draped in wisteria, became her touch-stone of stability in the unstable world.

Dad stopped coming. He went on his own strange retreats

when they were there, and so Caundle remained untouched by his eccentric world view. This was Mum's place, full of what occupied her: beauty, peace and books.

Perhaps, Etta thought, it was part of why she loved it so much.

Mary started getting properly into drugs around the time that Mum suggested that she and Etta move out of the upstairs flat altogether and go to the ground-floor flat. Mum's flat, occupying the top two floors, was the largest but this one had access to the garden down a flight of stone steps. Samuel still lived there but he was now a postgraduate at the London School of Economics, hoping to be a professor one day. He spent most of his time at the LSE and would move out to his own place before too long.

Etta had moved downstairs happily enough, still feeling as though she was essentially at home, but Mary had been upset about it.

'Can't you see how fucked up this family is?' she'd asked Etta. 'What kind of mother makes her children move out and live downstairs? She's insane. She hates us.'

Etta didn't think that was the case. Mum just marched to the beat of her own drum and she always had. She loved them, but it was hard for her to have all of them around her when she had to work.

'I suppose she grew up used to plenty of space,' Etta suggested.

'Then why did we leave our big house in the country? Typical,' Mary countered, even though she loved living in

London. She never seemed happy with Mum. And, Etta thought, most teenagers would kill for this independence but it seemed to make Mary miserable.

'I'll just spend more time with Dad,' Mary said.

Etta knew that they sat at his kitchen table, smoking joints, Mary getting high while Dad rambled on. It made her worried but she had no idea what to do about it. Mary started to acquire her own supply, Etta had no idea how, and to smoke in the downstairs flat. She came back from Camden Market with more of her pipes and bongs to smoke her cannabis and weed, stayed up late with a steady stream of friends who liked to smoke with her, and just seemed to get into the whole scene more and more.

Now Etta herself had left Armitage Hall and was living full time at home in London, having managed to just scrape herself two A levels. Mary was a student at fashion college and Etta was working at whatever she could find while she decided what to do. Sometimes she waitressed at the dinner parties of her mother's friends, sometimes she did a shift in the pub down the road, and sometimes she did some nannying work. But really, she was waiting until she was struck by inspiration about what she wanted to do with her life. Some evenings, to avoid the thick marijuana smoke in the flat and Mary and her spaced-out friends, she would go upstairs and sit with Mum, and eat whatever concoction Mum had created on the stove that night.

'You should go to college, darling,' Mum would say, stirring a pot, a cigarette in her free hand. She always seemed to look the same: flared jeans, a black jumper with a jumble of gold jewellery at her neck, and her shoulder-length fair hair tied back out of her face while she worked. Mum looked so young to her, like Mary's older sister, with the startling big blue eyes that dominated her face, and the girlish mouth. She never looked matronly like some of her friends' mothers. 'Study something. The world is your oyster. There're so many opportunities out there.'

But Etta didn't know what she wanted to study and, in truth, her generous allowance meant that she didn't need to earn that much money. She really wanted to keep her eye on Mary and on Mum, who seemed lonely now that Dad lived more or less all the time in hospital. While once he would spend more time home than away, and he was always expected to return, there was no talk of coming home any more.

Etta didn't know what to make of it or even how she felt about it, except confused and sad. This condition of his, whatever it was, had started slowly when they were still living in the country. At first, he had just seemed a bit eccentric, with his retreats and theories about aliens and alternative dimensions. It wasn't until they were in London that it had turned into something serious and permanent. Dad had always been odd and prone to doing whatever he felt like, but once he started excavating the walls for hidden treasure, Mum had begun to panic. At first, they tried to talk him out of it, but nothing they said to him made any difference. Then Dad announced that he had an alien snake living inside him who was giving him directions and that he had been selected for a special mission to aid mankind before the return of the star people.

They'd laughed at first and thought he was joking.

One day, Dad took Etta to one side and said very seriously, 'Of course I know that people who hear voices are usually mentally ill. But what you have to understand, Etta, is that the voices I hear are actually real, and that's the difference between me and them.'

Etta had nodded. Weirdly, she believed him. He was, after all, still Dad. She even half believed in the snake in his innards and the idea that star people were on their way to collect everyone and take them to another, better planet.

'They're already here,' Dad said solemnly. 'But the elite don't want you to know that.'

'Why don't they just come out and talk to us then?' Mary said, rolling one of her little cigarettes. 'Why are they disguising themselves as sasquatch and running around the forests trying not to get spotted?'

They were sitting at Dad's kitchen table, having lunch with him in a period after he had come back from a hospital stay. When Dad started talking like this, Etta's heart would sink. She would know then that the hospital had made no difference. She hoped Mary wouldn't get too punchy with him. What was the point?

Dad had poured another glass of red wine. 'Because,' he said loftily, ignoring the sasquatch comment, 'our human brains would explode if they did. They are preparing us to accept the incredible. That's where people like me come in. I've been selected as a steward to act as a bridge of communication between them and mankind, and prepare the way. When the time comes, I will be called upon to usher the terrified masses aboard the starships that will take us to another planet.'

Etta wasn't sure if she wanted to believe this. or not. It might help at the end of times to have a father who was a chosen steward. But deep down, she knew it was nonsense.

Later Mary said, 'I bet the aliens are regretting choosing Dad. Cos he's not very effective, what with being carted off to hospital every time he tries to spread the message.'

When Dad told Samuel that he and Jesus were really close friends and had a good working relationship, Samuel went up to talk to Mum, looking sad and serious. Things took a turn. Etta heard words like 'paranoia', 'psychosis' and then 'schizoid delusion'. A carer, strong steady Sid, had moved in to keep a permanent eye on Dad, and Mum saw him less and less, unable to cope with it. Etta was scared, as well as miserable in a way she could not explain. It was easier to keep her distance and think about it as little as possible.

'It's living death,' Mum said to Etta one night when it was just the two of them. 'It's seeing someone you love disappear while their body remains the same. There's nothing we can do about it. I'm sorry, darling, it must be so hard for you.'

'I just wish he was better.'

'So do I, sweetheart. So do I. The strange thing is, I think he's happy. His mission seems to give a meaning to his life. But I wish he were better too.'

One night Etta had come home from a shift at the pub

to see a small crowd gathered on the pavement in front of their house and her heart had sunk. This could not be good news.

Sure enough they were staring up at the balcony outside Dad's window and he was standing there, a tall, rangy figure against the lights blazing out of his sitting room window.

'The time is coming!' he was calling to the crowd beneath. 'Soon, the world you think you know is going to vanish. You are being controlled by vicious forces who want your destruction, and who intend to enslave you in pursuit of the wealth and power they crave so much! You are so many living batteries, designed only to provide energy through your labour, kept in a state of docility through the opium of money and a popular culture designed to numb you into submission!'

Oh no, Etta had thought, her heart sinking and her stomach rolling with apprehension. *What now?*

As Dad carried on his great speech, the people below were sniggering or murmuring, some of them thinking they were witnessing a bit of impromptu outdoor theatre. Etta stood below wondering what to do, too embarrassed to go in through the front door and show them all that she belonged there. But her heart went out to her father. Then Sid appeared on the balcony and managed to persuade Dad to go back inside, even though Dad protested that he had not yet finished the message, and that he had to relay it to the people before it was too late.

During the night she heard shouting and scuffling in the

flat upstairs. She pulled her pillow over her head and tried to shut it out. The next day, Dad went off by private ambulance to the hospital near Richmond and had not come back.

It was Mary who said what Etta had been thinking: 'Maybe this curse of ours is real, that's all. I used to think it wasn't but now I wonder. It's just so unfair that this should happen to Dad. Which of us is next?'

Samuel, too, was sad and bewildered. He would sit up late with his sisters, looking enough like Dad for it to be both comforting and heartbreaking. 'I don't know about a curse,' he would say, 'but let's hope Dad's illness is not genetic. Otherwise, any of us could have it.'

That frightened Etta more than anything. Going into that world of delusion and false belief looked terrifying. Like being detached from reality and going off to live in a lonely world that didn't exist, a place of craziness where no one else could go with you. How awful was that?

One evening, Mary got back from college with some records she had bought at a shop on the Tottenham Court Road that day.

'Listen to this,' she said to Etta, putting one on the record player. Out came the sound of a melancholy jazz piano trio. 'This guy is really cool.'

'Which one?' Etta asked, picking up the album sleeve and seeing a photograph of a pianist, a bassist and a drummer on the front.

'The pianist. I mean, he's old but like, wow. He writes all the music.'

Etta stared at the photograph, which showed a craggy-faced man in his forties, but who had undeniable good looks, with his strong features and thick dark hair, greying a little at the temples. More than his looks, he had an intensity in his black eyes that meant you couldn't help looking at him.

The girls listened to the music while Mary rolled a cigarette. 'This is the kind of music to get stoned to,' she said.

When Samuel came in, he heard the music and said, 'Oh, that's Knolle.'

'You know these guys?' Mary asked from where she was curled up on the sofa.

'Of course.' Samuel put down his bag. 'I'm much older than you guys. Knolle hit the big time in the sixties. Now they're really well known but still kind of cult. But you know, it's like Blondie. There are five people in it, but everyone thinks it's just Debbie Harry, right? It's the same with Knolle. The main guy is Caius Knolle, he's the one everyone thinks about when they hear the band.'

'Are you a fan?' Mary asked, stubbing out a little roll-up in the nearest ashtray.

'Yeah, sure. I think they're great. Actually, they're doing a gig in London soon, if you fancy going. They travel all over the world so you'd be lucky to catch them.'

Mary looked interested. 'Yeah,' she said. 'I'd be on for that. I think they're really cool.'

Etta looked at her sister, surprised. Somehow she had expected Mary to be more into punk or hard rock. Something edgy from the States with dark overtones. Instead, she had a taste for folk music and now, it seemed, moody jazz

307

with a bitterly nostalgic air. Perhaps it was worth a listen. Etta loved Abba, the Bees Gees and 'Bright Eyes' made her cry, especially when she thought about rabbits.

'I'll get you tickets for your birthday treat,' Samuel said. 'Want to come, Etta?'

'Yeah . . . yeah, sure. I'd like that.'

The Knolle gig took place on a Thursday evening in a small theatre near Covent Garden, rows of seats packed cosily around a small central stage. Samuel, Mary and Etta had cheaper seats near the back, and they settled in with drinks in good time. The audience was an eclectic mix of young and old, from geeky-looking students to cool old blokes in leather jackets. There were lots of women too, no doubt brought in by Caius Knolle's dark good looks and stage presence, as well as the magical sounds he conjured out of the piano.

The lights dimmed and Knolle strode out of the shadows, taking centre stage and acknowledging the rapturous applause of the audience. When the other two musicians took their place, they were different from the ones on the album cover, and there was no pretence that they were of any interest to the audience. Knolle was all about the pianist, pure and simple, and the audience listened intently to every note. As he played his opening piece, the music floated around the room like scented smoke, relaxing and touching everyone there.

Amazing, Etta thought. *Fancy being able to do that. He doesn't have any sheet music, it's all just coming out of his fingers as though he's channelling it.*

She had never played an instrument. There had been no

piano in any of their houses, and Mum had never arranged a lesson for her. At Armitage Hall, she had not bothered with music apart from singing occasionally, which she had enjoyed. Someone told her once she had a lovely voice, but she didn't think it was anything special.

She watched the man at the piano, and the way he swayed and moved as he played, sometimes bending low over the keyboard and sometimes stretching back, his eyes closed, as the music flowed through him and out through his fingertips. He was magnetic, that was for sure. Next to her, Mary was stock still, staring at the pianist through wide blue eyes, evidently enraptured, while Samuel listened, nodding his head slightly in time, or tapping his fingers lightly on his leg. The music went from sultry and smooth to vigorous and passionate, and back again.

As the show approached the conclusion, Etta felt the audience growing twitchy for something. And then, suddenly, Caius Knolle turned to them, and said in a gravelly voice, 'I'm going to play you one of my most famous pieces.' There was a murmur of excitement and approval from the audience. 'I wrote it years ago, and called it "Little Girl Lost", because it really is about a lost girl. And here it is.'

He took a breath, nodded to his musicians and then it started: a deliciously melancholy melody of beautiful, painful sweetness. Etta knew it, of course. It was famous. She'd heard it in shops, on car radios, at parties and on television advertisements. Everyone knew it.

So this is the man who wrote that.

Mary was still transfixed beside her and, when the piece

was over, she was the first on her feet, whooping and cheering, clapping her hands fiercely. But the whole room soon
joined her, applauding and calling for an encore.

Knolle played two encores before he signalled that there
would be no more, made a short bow and left the stage.

'Oh my God, that was amazing,' Mary said as they left the
theatre. 'Thanks for taking us, Sam.'

'You're welcome, I'm glad you enjoyed it. Did you like
it, Etta?'

'I did,' Etta said, as they came out onto the pavement. 'But
not as much as Mary!'

'I bloody loved it,' Mary said. She glanced up at the poster
outside the theatre. There were two more nights, both
labelled sold out. 'And I'm going to come back tomorrow and
the next night. There's bound to be a ticket if I wait for long
enough.'

'Wow, you really liked it,' Sam said.

Mary nodded. 'Come on, let's go for a drink. It's still early
really. Sam can pay!'

It was one of life's odd coincidences, Etta thought, that once
you hear of someone, you suddenly hear more about them.

The Sunday paper had been put through their letter box
that morning, as usual, and Etta had gone out in her pyjamas
to take it in. It was the paper that Mum wrote for, and it was
really destined for her mother's flat upstairs, but she was
never up until lunchtime at the earliest, so no one wanted the
paper until then.

Ever since Mum had landed a column a few years ago, one

that gave an insight into her own life and family, Etta found it was a good idea to read it as soon as she could on the day it was published, just in case Mum had dropped some kind of almighty clanger. Mum seemed to be able to write about her children and her thoughts on world events and the literary scene and some of her friends, but she never addressed the one thing that affected all their lives, and that was Dad's illness. It drove Mary wild.

As Etta picked the newspaper up off the mat, she saw that just under the masthead was a headline advertising the contents inside: *Caius Knolle: the truth about the coolest man in jazz.*

Weird, she thought. *Just after we saw him.*

He was probably on some kind of publicity drive to promote his tour and new album.

Mary had been as good as her word and gone back to the show both of the following nights. Obviously she had managed to get a ticket again last night as she had not come home until after Etta was asleep.

Etta took the papers back into the flat, made herself a cup of instant coffee and a piece of toast and jam. Then she sat down to read the piece. She would read about Knolle before she read Mum's latest, and she flicked to the review section, which was adorned with a big black-and-white photograph of the famous pianist at his keyboard, his expression intense as he played.

She ran her eye over the opening paragraph.

Knolle is famous for composing classic jazz and for an overpowering talent – as well as for his womanising and many marriages. Here is the inside story of his tangled love life and the effect it has had on his work. Has the Little Girl Lost been found at last?

Etta thought this sounded promising, took a bite of her toast and began to read.

Chapter Eighteen

FLICK

1979

Flick woke up and lay awake, staring at the ceiling and wondering how Jonathan was, and what they could do to solve all the problems.

Then, seeing the time, she dragged herself out of bed. Last night had ended like so many Saturday nights, with her sitting up until after midnight, drinking and smoking and watching a late movie on the television. She'd woken up at two to find herself slumped fully dressed on the sofa and had padded through to her bedroom, groggy, to strip off and fall into bed and back to sleep.

Making coffee in the pot on the stove, she also picked up the telephone to call Etta and remind her to bring the Sunday paper up now she was ready for it. There had been no answer, which surprised her. Sam was probably at his girlfriend's. Maybe the girls had stayed out. That was normal for Mary, her wild child, who was in the process of discovering nightclubs, but not so much for her little staid baby, Etta. They were so different in so many ways: Mary was fair and fiery, glamorous and ambitious, with a hedonistic edge, while

Etta was dark and more soulful, with a little more of the vulnerability that Flick remembered about her own younger self. What had Father said all those years ago? Oh yes, that her eyes showed how easily she could be hurt. Or something like that.

She loved both girls equally but sometimes Mary was testing, while Etta was always obedient and biddable.

I must be careful of turning Etta too much into my handmaid, she thought. *She never says no to me.*

Mary was always furious about something. Flick thought of her latest column, which she was sure would not upset Mary as it was about the virtue of window boxes and the pleasure they could bring to a city flat, and from there she'd done a general meditation on the value of flowers and what roles they played, from the elaborate displays to simple posies or even a daisy in the grass.

Sometimes Flick laughed wryly to think how impressed her younger self would have been to see her as an established Fleet Street journalist, still reviewing films and now writing her weekly column for a broadsheet newspaper. It had been quite a climb and taken a lot of work, but she had to admit that she had Chase Dupone to thank for a good deal of it. That interview had brought her to the attention of editors, and it had been the kind of piece every journalist prayed for: an article that spawned dozens of articles about the article. From then on, she had a platform. At first, the angle was that the tables had turned. From being the subject of Chase Dupone's penetrating pen, he was now the subject of hers. The sad heiress had rejected her wealth and learned to use her own talents for success and fulfilment. It was neat and satisfying. Soon, the old *Mademoiselle* piece was more or less forgotten, and Flick's connection to her family money made even more obscure when Gloria reverted back to her maiden name of Carrington, creating a little distance between them that Flick was grateful for. She wrote as Flick Templeton and so they weren't endlessly linked together.

Flick decided to go downstairs and get the paper herself. It was quite the climb but it kept her fit and sometimes was her only exercise, if she had a deadline and had to keep writing. Mary said she could tell the proximity of the deadline by the state of her mother. The wilder her hair, the older her clothes, and the more dishevelled she looked, the closer it was.

She let herself out and went down the stairs, feeling a pang of sadness as she went past Jonathan's empty flat. She had more or less decided to offer it to Samuel, who would no doubt welcome moving out of the flat he shared with his two sisters, much as he loved them. A bit of independence was what he needed. Lovely Sam. He had been a blessing.

At the bottom of the stairs, Flick was surprised to see that the paper was not on the mat as she had expected. She looked about, and then heard voices behind the girls' door. They were raised and almost frantic. Concerned, Flick went over and knocked on the door.

'Girls?'

She pushed it open, as it was not locked, to see Mary and Etta standing in the sitting room in their pyjamas, Mary redfaced and wild-eyed, Etta looking shocked.

When they saw her, Etta froze. She was holding a section of the newspaper and she dropped it down at once. But Mary's eyes blazed at her.

'Why the fuck didn't you tell us?' she shouted.

Flick was confused. 'Tell you what? About the window boxes? What's wrong with that? You can't be upset about that, Mary, you really can't.'

She walked into the flat, wanting to soothe her upset daughter, but Mary backed away from her. She looked almost tearful.

'Window boxes? What the hell are you talking about?'

'Are you cross about my column?'

'No!' Mary gave a bitter laugh. 'Show her, Etta.'

Etta slowly handed over the newspaper section, looking frightened. It was the review section, where her column was usually on the back page. But she could see that the splash article was about something quite different. The huge black-and-white photograph of Caius made her stomach turn over with fear.

Despite the initial discomfort, she had grown used to seeing him in the press ever since he rose to prominence over ten years ago. She had managed to cope with the growing fame of 'Little Girl Lost', and had forced herself to forget its power to hurt her. She had done it through dissociation, simply forgetting about it as much as she could. She refused to talk about it, even when Jonathan occasionally tried to raise the subject with her, in the days when he was well.

'Mum,' Etta said in a small voice. 'Are you the Little Girl Lost?'

She gaped at her younger daughter, still not able to take it all in. So it was in the paper? Everyone knew? How?

Mary broke in. 'You never told us that you were *married* to Caius Knolle! What the hell?'

Flick put up her hands, still shocked. 'But . . . I don't understand. What does it matter? Why should you care?'

'I think it does matter,' Etta said, facing her with a firm expression. 'We know about Dad's previous marriage. Why shouldn't we know about yours?'

Flick looked at them both, Mary so angry and Etta puzzled. 'It was over years and years ago. I was very young, and the marriage was barely started before it was over. I have nothing to do with him and he has nothing to do with me. It never occurred to me that you needed to know.'

'That's not good enough!' Mary shouted, her eyes fuzzy with tears and her cheeks bright with fury. 'Why didn't you tell us?'

Flick closed her eyes, unable to stand it. 'I didn't want to.'

'This family is full of secrets, awful secrets! How do you think we feel to find out shit like this? And you don't know what it does to us, what it means!'

'I don't understand,' Flick said helplessly, desperate to placate her. 'What difference does it make to you if I was married to Caius Knolle for five minutes before you were born!'

'Because,' spat Mary, 'you lied to us!'

Flick stared at her daughter. She had a sudden flashback to how she'd felt in New York all those years before when she'd found out about Jonathan's first wife and his hidden son. It had been the lies that destroyed her the most. Was she guilty of exactly the same kind of betrayal and deception? How could it be the same?

As she thought this, a pain gripped Flick's stomach, and she bent over groaning, clutching at her belly.

'Mum, are you okay?' Etta was beside her, trying to help her, but it was no good, the pain was intense and crippling.

'It's just a play for sympathy,' said Mary with a sneer. 'To take the heat off her!'

Perhaps she's right, Flick thought dully. The pain was surely connected to the fact that she had apparently done the very thing that had been done to her and that had caused such hurt. *Perhaps it is just self-pity.*

Etta turned to her sister. 'Don't be mean. She's not feeling well.'

'When did you start protecting her?' Mary demanded. 'You know she wasn't there for us when we were growing up! She was always shut away in that study, writing, ignoring us. It was Dad who cared! Not her! You thought the same as me.'

The pain in Flick's stomach gripped harder. *Is that what they thought? That I didn't care?* She had always tried to give them freedom to do what they want, to live as they wanted as independent people, who were still deeply loved. Couldn't they see that? It wasn't possible that they felt neglected, surely? She had tried to show them that work was the purpose of life, that women didn't need to be just decorative objects, just wives and mothers. And she had done all she could to protect them from what was happening to Jonathan.

I must have done it all wrong, she thought blackly.

Etta said in a small voice, 'Mum does her best.'

'You fucking turncoat!' shouted Mary. 'None of this is my fault. It's hers! If she told the truth and tried to be a proper mum instead of not even *living* with us, none of this would have happened!'

Mary marched into her room, moving about, clearly packing a bag while Flick moaned with the pain of her cramps. A couple of minutes later, Mary came out, dressed and with a bag slung over her shoulder.

'I'm leaving,' she said defiantly. 'And by the way, just in case you're interested, if you had been honest with us, then maybe I wouldn't have gone with Sam and Etta to Caius Knolle's gig last week.'

'You went to his gig?' Flick had known he was performing but had tried not to think about it. It had never occurred to her that the children might be interested in a jazz concert. 'You didn't say. But I don't mind that you went to his gig.'

'But I wouldn't have gone back. I wouldn't have hung around the stage door. I wouldn't have gone out for a drink with him.'

There was a terrible silence as Mary's words sank in. Etta gasped, her eyes round. Flick stared, trying to comprehend what she had just heard. An awful nausea swilled in her stomach, churning and roiling up.

Flick gasped, the words like a punch. She felt faint. 'You went for a drink with Caius?'

319

Mary was staring at her defiantly, her hands on her hips. 'Two dates, actually. And if you're wondering, you could have prevented all this by being honest. But it's too late now.'

She strode out, the slam of the front door announcing her departure.

Flick groaned again.

How on earth can this be happening? Aren't things bad enough? Mary, on a date . . . with Caius?

Oh my God. I can't bear it.

Etta, looking shocked and frightened, helped Flick back upstairs to her flat and gave her painkillers. It took an hour or so before the dreadful pain in her belly subsided.

Afterwards, when she was on her own, Flick opened a bottle of white wine and, after a glass or two, she checked on the time and then picked up the telephone. The long number took a while to connect but when it did, it only rang a couple of times before the familiar voice came down the line to her.

'Rob Gerstein, hello?'

'Rob, it's me. Flick.'

'Hi, honey. How are you? You do know it's nine a.m. on a Sunday, don't you?'

'Yes, I do and I expect you're already up.'

'Well now, yes, I am up. I've done my run. I'm having breakfast here with Mindy.'

'Oh, say hello to Mindy for me.'

'Flick says hi,' Rob informed someone with him, and Flick

heard a bright female voice in the background. 'She says hi back. We're really looking forward to coming over in a couple of weeks. It'll be so great to see you and the kids.' He dropped his voice slightly. 'So, everything okay?'

Flick stared down at her kitchen table, one hand on the phone and the other clutched around her wine glass. She could just see Rob now, in his sunny modern kitchen with his pretty girlfriend, the picture of health and contentment as they ate muesli and drank orange juice after their exercise. A perfect life. Here she was, alone, half drunk again, a cigarette burning in the ashtray, with a desperately sick husband she could not help and had ceased to love years ago, and a daughter who had stormed out furiously after saying one of the worst things Flick could imagine. It was so painful and so humiliating.

'Flick, you okay? Is it Jonathan?'

'No, no, it's Mary.'

'Oh no, is she all right?'

'Yes, but . . . the girls have found out about my marriage to Caius Knolle. It's in the paper here. They read it. I'd never told them.'

He let out a breath. 'And they were angry. I'm sorry, Flick. I guess it never occurred to you to tell them?'

'No,' she said wretchedly. 'And now Mary's gone. I can't think why she's so cross.'

'Honey, I'm sorry. It's complicated, isn't it?'

'It sure is.'

'You need to talk?'

'Yes please . . . if you've got time.'

321

'I've always got time for you. Tell me.'

She poured it all out, knowing he would have the wisdom she needed to put her life back together.

Flick sometimes wondered how she would have coped over the years without Rob Gerstein to support her. When he had told her all those years ago in New York that she would get home and forgive Jonathan, he had been right. The further she went away from America, the more it receded into memory and the more home, which had become dreamlike in her absence, became reality again.

Jonathan had been waiting at the airport, his face bright and cheerful, with Mary in his arms. She was waving a little windmill to welcome her mother home, the rainbow-coloured sails spinning round. Seeing her daughter again had been bliss, but when Jonathan had taken her into his arms to welcome her home, she had felt the first chill of disconnection.

Sometimes, afterwards, she wondered what would have been the outcome if she had either never learned about Anne Blair and the little boy, Samuel, and never met Rob Gerstein; or if only one of those things had happened and not the other. How could she ever know? She could not be sorry about either, for Samuel's arrival benefitted them all and Rob had proved to be the strongest friend in her life.

Flick believed that whatever happened, she had been destined to fall out of love with Jonathan because she never had been truly in love. She had loved what she thought he was: a man who was upright, true, utterly dependable and completely trustworthy. Life with him was like living with a good friend, and everything about their relationship was comfortable and predictable. They never fought, he wouldn't let it happen. If she was cross, he devoted himself to placating her. He agreed with all she said – not, she felt, because he thought the same way at all times, but because he was mainly concerned with keeping her happy.

Now she saw that this was not as good as she had believed it must be. While Caius had made her feel inferior, Jonathan made her feel like a queen endowed with a power she didn't entirely want. She was the centre of his world in a way that wasn't healthy. It was slightly obsessive.

And all along he had been lying to her, so it was just an illusion anyway.

At the airport that day, as he bustled about collecting her luggage and then taking her to the car for the trip home, she had felt as though she was in the company of a stranger.

Back at the London house, she had slept for a whole day and a night, not wanting to wake back into her everyday world again, and face what had to be done.

On the evening of the second day home, they had dinner in the kitchen. Mavis had gone out for the evening and the nanny was upstairs in her rooms watching telly. It was just the two of them.

'I think we need to have a talk,' Flick had said.

Jonathan had not looked in the least anxious, his hazel-brown eyes clear. 'Of course. I want to hear all about New York.'

'I'm going to tell you everything,' Flick had said. 'But first, is there anything you want to tell me?'

Jonathan stared at her over his plate of dinner, uncomprehending. 'No. Nothing. Everything was fine here. We missed you, of course, but it was all fine.'

'I mean, is there anything you think I should know? About you? Your life? Us?'

Jonathan gave a half-laugh and shrugged. 'No, of course not.'

'Nothing about your life you want to share with me.'

'You know everything.'

'Do I?'

'Of course.' He took a mouthful from his plate, and ate it slowly, regarding her with amusement. Then he said, 'Why, what do you think? Do I have anything to tell you?'

'You tell me, Jonathan.' She suddenly realised how familiar all this was. So often conversations felt like a game of hide-and-seek, in which the main aim was to avoid giving anything away. So often when she tried to pin Jonathan down, he slipped away, deflecting and diverting, or simply reflecting back to her what she had already said. She felt that one of the reasons they had felt so in tune with one another at the start was simply because he did this, echoing her, mirroring her, making himself into her twin so that she had faith in their compatibility. But it was a mirage. She had told him the truth, concealed nothing, been frank and honest, and he had only said what he thought she wanted to hear, and what would get him what he wanted: her love and protection. Her trust. All the things she had given him, from a daughter to a safe and secure home.

He looked thoughtful and then said, 'No, I don't think there's anything.'

'Would you swear to me?'

'Of course.'

'Would you swear to me on your life?'

He laughed. 'Yes, I swear on my life.'

Flick stared at him, wondering suddenly if she knew him at all. Where was her firm, stable, upright husband, that beacon of integrity? And why did he think she was asking these questions? Why wasn't he asking about that? He didn't seem in the least surprised at the line of questioning, or curious, or even suspicious. He was just utterly innocent and if she didn't know better, she would completely believe him.

'Okay,' Flick said slowly. 'And would you swear on Mary's life?'

There was a pause. Suddenly, and with all her heart, she wanted him to break. She longed to see a flicker of uncertainty, maybe reluctance, maybe a sense that perhaps he was going too far and that she, Flick, must have an inkling of his secret, and that it would be better for him to admit it than keep the lie going to the bitter end.

Jonathan made a face of surprised, almost amused capitulation, as though he was astonished at the request but if that was what she wanted, then fine. He said easily, 'Of course. I swear on Mary's life. There. Happy now? Can we just have dinner and you tell me about your travels?'

Flick tasted bitterness in her mouth, whether real or imagined she didn't know. *So he'll go that far.*

Afterwards she thought that perhaps her love for him had died in that moment. She had never thought him capable of it. And when she knew he was, then everything she believed about him withered and died.

She put her knife and fork down, and said slowly, 'So when were you going to tell me about Anne?'

Jonathan froze and went white. 'Anne?'

'Don't pretend any longer, Jonathan. I met Henry Morfield in New York, and he told me about your first wife. How on earth did you think I wouldn't find out eventually?'

Jonathan's complexion went from white to red and sweat broke out along his upper lip. He panicked and began to babble. 'Yes, I have a wife, he told her, an ex-wife. From when I was young. We married too young, it didn't last. She had an affair and left me. I put it all behind me. I haven't seen her again, I never think about her, I love you. You made the same mistake, didn't you? You had a bad first marriage, just like me. It's the same, isn't it? You can't really criticise me. You should feel sorry for me, if anything, because I suffered too.'

Flick listened to the stream of excuses, self-justification, the attempt to turn the tables and say that she was just as bad, the plea for pity. 'And is there anything else?'

'No,' he said frantically, and then fervently. 'No. I promise. Nothing else.'

She had slammed her palm on the table and screamed at him. 'What do you not understand about telling the truth? I know about him! I know about Samuel! My God, what's wrong with you? How on earth did you plan to hide this indefinitely? And why would you?'

He slumped. 'I don't know. I just don't know. I'm sorry, Flick.'

They had existed in a state of coldness and uncertainty for the next few days. Jonathan had apologised constantly, bringing her flowers and gifts, doing all he could to repair the damage. He had wept and begged and promised to change, until beaten down and somehow sorry for him and his suffering, she had taken him back into her bed.

It wasn't long after that that she found she was pregnant with Etta. When they discovered she was expecting another baby, they decided it was time to leave London and start anew. Jonathan would devote himself to Flick and to the family and their life in the country. Flick would take her Dupone interview and see what she could make of it. They would be a happy family again, Jonathan promised her. He introduced her to little Sam, and the secrecy that had surrounded him was swept away as if it had never happened. Flick couldn't help loving the little boy and they had him with them as often as they could, although she had had to pay for expensive lawyers to persuade Jonathan's ex-wife to allow him to resume his access to his son and to agree to Sam's visits. A large alimony and support payment from Flick helped to ease this. However, Flick never met Anne in person, staying out of the way at her request when she came to drop off or collect Sam.

But over the years, Flick always stayed in touch with Rob, first by letter and then by transatlantic telephone call, her one real extravagance. She had told Jonathan about her friendship with Rob, but not about the extent of their close-ness or about how often they were in touch.

There was no escaping that Rob was utterly unlike Jona-than. He understood Flick to her bones without needing to lie or pretend. He had no fear of her and no fear of who he was either. He accepted her as she was. He thought she was beautiful, brilliant and fascinating and hugely talented. He read everything she wrote and gave her the kind of insightful, kind and constructive criticism she longed for, even when he told her she needed to start all over. Flick knew he loved her wit, her turn of phrase, her kindness and her love for her children. He was all too aware that she was scatty, disorgan-ised, prone to panic, easily distracted, sometimes wilfully selfish, and that she could be irritable and snappy. If she turned her wit on someone, she could be hideously and hil-ariously mean. And of course he knew that she drank and smoked far too much. He still loved her.

They were living in the big house in the country when Jonathan moved into a separate bedroom.

He had begun to get involved in a world of spiritualism that bothered Flick. She didn't mind all manner of beliefs and practices but there was something about the intensity around Jonathan's beliefs that bothered her. He talked to her about astral planing, and soon claimed that he believed he had been reincarnated several times, each time becoming closer to his original being as a star person.

It all happened so slowly that she hardly noticed how it moved from being something normal to something close to absurd. Jonathan was adamant that he was being abducted by aliens several times a year before she truly began to suspect that he was not well.

But it was more than that. She had never been able to rebuild her trust in him. And once a liar, always a liar. She had learned that Jonathan couldn't really tell the truth about anything. It was no wonder that he was so prone to delusion, she thought. His grip on the difference between truth and fiction had always been shaky.

Her letters with Rob were her lifeline; they were the only thing that kept her having a shred of faith in the power of relationships to be solid and real, and to mean anything or achieve anything. It was ironic, she thought, that he was the most disembodied person in her life – a voice at the end of a telephone line, a pen on a page – and yet also the most real.

'Keep the faith, Flick,' he would say down the line. 'Keep the faith and you'll get there.'

And when she called late at night, half drunk, lying on her bed alone, it didn't seem to matter that it was his working afternoon in New York. He'd press the telephone close to his mouth and murmur, 'Tell me.'

And she would sigh out her griefs and miseries. Everything except her longing for him.

They had met again, when business brought Rob to London and Flick had taken trips to New York herself, sometimes to see Diana, who was enjoying a spectacular life at the peak of New York society, and sometimes for work. It was always a profound joy to be in his company.

But it was inevitable that Rob would find a companion. She'd prepared herself for that. He wasn't a monk, and besides, they were just friends. He might love her dearly but she wasn't his girlfriend. Over the years there had been a series of women, but their existence didn't seem to change their intimate connection and she never envied their emotional life with him. She believed that Rob's relationship with her was somehow richer and always would be.

Jonathan didn't seem to mind about her close friendship with Rob, whom he met on a few occasions over the years. Rob came out to stay at the house when he was in London for a publishing exhibition one year, and spent the weekend with them. He talked to Jonathan quite a lot over the stay.

At the end, he said quietly to Flick, 'Get the best help you can afford for your husband.'

She hadn't understood what he'd meant and had put it out of her mind. It was only later, when the symptoms worsened and began to manifest in unmissable ways, that she realised he had seen Jonathan's issues before anyone else.

Now there was Mindy, Rob's latest girlfriend, twenty years younger and a proponent of a healthy lifestyle. Rob's boozy literary lunches were anathema to her, and she was working on getting him trim and fit. Rob would laugh about it indulgently, as though he didn't mind humouring her. Flick could never work out what exactly he felt for Mindy, but it seemed almost entirely sexual as far as she could tell.

The connection between him and Flick was as deep as ever.

But even he would not be able to help if this nightmarish scenario were true.

If Mary is going to start seeing Caius . . . what on earth will I do?

I will not be able to bear it.

Chapter Nineteen

ETTA

1979

Etta felt traitorous making her way to Granny's house in Belgravia. But she was torn. She had a foot in both camps.

I can see it from Mum's side, and from Mary's.

She took the long route via Hyde Park, skirting the bottom of the Serpentine before crossing over to head past any number of grand stucco-fronted embassies on her way to Chester Square.

Mum should have told her and Mary all about what had happened with her first marriage. They might not even have gone to the gig if they had known. Caius Knolle's dark glamour and heartthrob appeal had definitely disappeared as far as Etta was concerned, now that she knew he had been married to Mum.

But she hadn't told them anything.

And Mary shouldn't have said what she had. It was obvious that Mum had been deeply wounded, first by Mary accusing her of not caring about them, and then by the absolutely dreadful revelation that Mary had gone on two dates with Mum's ex.

*It makes me feel sick. God knows how awful Mum
must feel.*

It was so weird to think that Mum had been married
before like that. The article in the Sunday paper had confirmed it, there was no mistake.

> . . . Knolle's little known, brief marriage to society
> heiress Felicity Templeton is a chapter they both seemed
> eager to close completely. Neither has ever commented
> publicly on their union, or been seen in one another's
> company. Templeton has since become a distinguished
> film reviewer and columnist for this paper, although she
> was not asked to comment on this piece. Knolle has
> gone on to become one of the great jazz pianists and
> composers of his generation, famous over the world,
> and not only for his music. His subsequent marriages
> and voracious womanising are well known . . .

Etta remembered the charismatic figure on the stage, playing the piano as though the music was being channelled
through him from heaven. It was impossible to imagine him
and Mum as a young couple, despite the photograph of
Knolle as a soulful youth with a mop of dark hair and intense
black eyes.

*It's ancient history, I suppose. I just can't believe the bad
luck of Mary meeting him like that! And now we all have to
deal with the results.*

This had included a barrage of telephone calls from
reporters wanting to talk to Flick about her marriage, and

even a couple of photographers chasing them about outside for a bit, but it had calmed down in the face of Flick's repeated insistence that there was no comment. Nothing.

Surely it will all just be forgotten?

Etta hoped so – and that Mum and Mary could reconcile before their separation grew permanent.

Etta dawdled on the walk but eventually reached the shiny black front door to Granny's house, and rang the bell almost reluctantly. It would be easier just to ignore all this. But she couldn't.

The maid showed her up to Mary's room. When she'd stormed out of the house, Mary had gone straight to Granny who, of course, had welcomed her with open arms. Etta suspected that Granny relished the opportunity both to offer Mary solace and somehow to rub Flick's nose in it.

Mary was standing at the door of her room as Etta came along the landing, casual compared to her surroundings in bare feet, denim shorts and a T-shirt, blonde hair pulled back into a long ponytail. She looked pleased to see her sister. 'Hi! Come in, come in!'

Etta went in, gazing around at her sister's new lodgings, which were exceptionally luxurious: a huge bedroom with floor-to-ceiling windows overlooking the garden square, a four-poster bed swagged with floral chintz, and an ensuite bathroom in pink and gold. 'It's nice here.'

'It's amazing. Like being a princess. You have to wonder why Mum is happy to live in such a shabby way when she could live like this.'

'Not so shabby,' Etta said cautiously, 'but this is so cool.'

'Everything's done for me,' Mary said, 'and such lavish meals, you would not believe. It's like living in *Dallas* or something. I can even roll up in my room if I want – but I blow the smoke up the chimney obviously. Don't want Granny finding out. She did come in once to ask about the smell and I told her it was incense.'

Etta sat down on the fluffy rug in front of the marble fireplace. 'Does Granny know what happened?'

She had wondered if their grandmother was aware of the nub of the problem. Despite her anything-goes attitude, she was old-fashioned in a lot of ways and would be horrified at Mary seeing Caius Knolle.

'She hasn't really asked about the row,' Mary said, sitting on her bed. 'And of course I'm not going to tell her.'

Etta squeezed her knees up under her chin, wrapping her arms around her calves. 'Did you really go on a date with Caius Knolle?' she asked in a small voice.

Mary sighed, and looked away. 'Do you really think I'd lie about something like that? Of course I did.'

'And did . . . did anything happen?'

Mary looked defiant. 'That's for me to know, and you to find out. It's private, okay?'

Etta felt miserable. This was not the reassuring answer she had hoped for. 'Does he know who you are?'

'Of course not, why would I tell him that? Besides, I gave my false name, the one I use in clubs and stuff. So he can't know.'

'Okay.'

Mary sighed again. 'It's so fucked up. I really like him.'

'Do you think you'll see him again?'

'You know what, Etta? I haven't decided. I mean, it's not my fault what happened in the past. Why should I have to give up something I want, because of what happened to Mum?'

Etta said nothing. It seemed to her obvious why it would be a terrible idea to pursue Caius Knolle. But one thing she knew about Mary was that she would do the very thing that everyone thought was wrong.

So it's best if I say nothing. And just hope that she hasn't already gone too far.

She changed the subject. 'Mum's having a party.'

'What?' Mary got off her bed, rolling her eyes, and went to get her cigarettes. 'Oh my God. Why?'

'I think she arranged it ages ago.' She didn't like to say that Mum was in no state to plan a party now, not since Mary's revelation. She was miserable and stressed, and Etta had moved upstairs to look after her, trying to keep her from staying up too late and drinking too much vodka.

'She's insane. Let's just hope everyone gets out alive.'

Mum's parties were always epic events, and were famous throughout London for their loucheness. She managed to gather sparkling mixes of literary types, actors, celebrities and eccentrics, as well as staid old aristocrats and bright young things. As soon as they had climbed the stairs to Flick's apartment, guests lost all their inhibitions and often seemed to lose their heads well beyond what they normally would, indulging in all kinds of reckless behaviour, from outrageous flirting to huge arguments. Emotions ran high, and there was always some kind of memorable incident, from a peer of the realm falling down the stairs, to a Nobel prize winner loudly throwing up in the bathroom.

'I don't know how it happens,' Mum would say helplessly. 'I don't think I do anything to encourage it.'

It was no doubt the free-flowing alcohol that encouraged the unrestrained atmosphere, along with the fact that the flat was never pristine or ordered. Its mixture of seductive style and disorganisation seemed to encourage everyone to become messy in their own behaviour. Etta and Mary, often serving as informal waitresses at the parties, watched it happen every time, no matter the changes in the guest list. One time, a guest got so drunk and angry about something, he had to be physically ejected from the flat, Flick and the girls and Samuel managing to push him out into the hall and get the door shut behind him.

Now Mum had another of these events on the way.

Etta looked over at her sister, who had opened a window so that she could exhale her smoke out over the leafy square below. 'Do you think you can ever forgive Mum?'

Mary looked away, out of the window, then took another drag. 'Depends. She needs to be sorry for how she's treated me over the years.'

'Do you really think she's been so bad?'

'She's been bloody awful. She complains about Granny. But she's no better.'

Etta wondered if Mary herself would be any better as a mother. But she said nothing. It would only be incendiary. 'If you're going to see her ex-husband, then she won't like it, will she? You should have seen how miserable and sick she was about it.'

Mary frowned, kicking one barefoot against the window seat. 'That's her lookout. I haven't decided. But unless she apologises, I'm never going home.'

Etta went home without seeing Granny, who had been off on some glamorous day out. She felt bewildered by Mary even hinting that she might go on seeing Caius.

Back at the house, she went in to check on her mother, who was sitting at her desk, sweating over a review deadline and the arrangements for her party.

'This party really is the last thing I need, darling,' Mum said forlornly, surrounded by notebooks and scraps of paper, her typewriter half lost in them.

'You could cancel?'

'Oh no. I won't cancel. I can't do that.'

Etta wondered what it would take. Mum was on the brink, anyone could see that. 'Perhaps we can have a quieter one than normal?'

Mum gave her a reproachful look. 'Darling, I always plan a quiet one! Every single time! It's a mystery to me why everyone goes so berserk.' Then, suddenly, she looked more cheerful. 'Do you remember my friend Rob Gerstein? The American?'

'Yes. I think so . . .' Etta remembered the friendly man who had come to their house a few times over the years when she was younger. He was kind, she remembered that, with an approachability rare in adults. He had always talked to her as though she was a fully rounded human being and not just a child with limited understanding. Instinctively she had felt safe around him. Mary often talked about aura and she knew that whatever it was, Rob had a good one.

'He and his girlfriend are coming over for a trip, and they'll arrive in time for the party.' Mum smiled, the first happy expression on her face for ages. 'I'm so looking forward to seeing him. I hope he has some advice about Mary.' She glanced anxiously at Etta. 'Have you seen her?'

Etta said cautiously, 'I've spoken to her. She's okay.'

Mum bit her lip, staring at the floor. 'I don't know what to do. I don't want us to be at odds. But it's so hard. Do you know if she's still seeing Caius?'

It was obvious Mum found it hard even to say that name. Etta said honestly, 'No, I don't know.'

'I will have to reach her somehow. I just don't know how.' Mum sighed. 'When the party is over. That's when I'll try.'

'Good idea,' Etta said. 'Let's get the party over first.'

Samuel refused to come to the party. He did not want to subject his new girlfriend to the experience, he said. She was too innocent for all that.

'Great, so I'm on my own.' Etta rolled her eyes.

'Sorry, sis. Just try watering down the vodka or something.' Sam had come upstairs to Flick's flat for breakfast and was shovelling down a bowl of Coco Pops on his way out to the LSE. Flick, a notorious late riser, was still asleep. 'But honestly, everyone survives in the end. It's always fine.'

'If you say so,' Etta said sarcastically.

'Any rapprochement between the warring factions?'

Etta shook her head. 'Mary won't go home till Mum apologises. I think Mum's going to try next week. She's so hurt by the whole thing but she knows why Mary is so angry. I think she's hoping it will calm down a bit. And she also needs to get herself together.'

'I feel a bit sorry for Flick,' Samuel remarked. 'But she should have come clean years ago. It's always the best way.'

'Yeah. Well.' Etta sighed. 'Too late now.'

Sam ate another mouthful, pondering. 'Do you think Mary was telling the truth – about going on dates with Caius?'

'I think so. That's what she told me.'

'She's smoking a lot of weed. A *lot*. Do you think she might have hallucinated it?'

'No, I'm sure she saw him.'

'And did something happen?'

They exchanged glances at the unpleasant picture this provoked.

Etta said, 'She didn't say. And she wouldn't tell me that it was over either.'

Samuel looked aghast. 'She wouldn't! Surely not now? Not now she knows? And won't he guess she's Flick's daughter?'

'She used a fake name,' Etta said unhappily. 'She told him she was called Miffy.'

Sam shook his head. 'Jeez. What a mess.'

'I would wish that it was a hallucination, but that would also be terrible. Too like Dad.' Etta sighed.

Sam gave her a sympathetic look. 'I'm going to go out and see him on Sunday, actually. Do you want to come?'

'Are we allowed?' Visits had been highly discouraged in the past.

'I rang up and they said that yeah, he can come out and sit in the garden for a short while. He's pretty sedated right now but he can get about.'

Etta felt a rush of yearning for her father. She had grown used to the sadness of being without him and tried not to think about it. 'Yes, I would like that,' she said.

'Great, we'll go together. Good luck tonight, don't drink too much!'

'Rosalie, you're an angel, I couldn't do this without you.'

Etta and Rosalie, the housekeeper, were climbing the stairs from the basement flat right to the top, where Mum was dashing about, full of anxiety and with a list of things to do but achieving very little.

'You're welcome,' Rosalie said calmly. She had whizzed up trays of canapés for the party and now they were carrying them carefully up to the flat. 'Let's hope it's not as wild as usual.'

'I bet it will be.'

Mum was delighted to see them as they came through the door, loaded down with stuffed tomatoes and cheese straws. 'Those are fabulous, Rosalie! Thank you. You're so clever, I don't know how you do it. I've been getting the drinks ready.' Mum pointed to rows of cans of stout on the sideboard.

'Will people drink that?' Etta said uncertainly. Not every-one liked the thick, dark, bittersweet taste of stout, after all. Etta certainly didn't.

'They should like it!' Mum declared. 'It's practically a health food. The alkaline properties counteract the acid of the wine. Result – no hangovers! Now, the champagne is in the fridge; I've had to move all the food downstairs to Dad's place to make room.' She sat down with a sigh at the kitchen table. 'We might be nearly ready.'

'No one will get here till six – that's two hours away.'

'But I've got to bath and beautify,' Mum replied. 'Etta, you need to show me your eyeliner trick. And help me pick a dress to wear.'

'Okay,' Etta said, mystified. Mum didn't usually care much what she looked like. 'I'll do your make-up for you, if you like.'

'Yes please!' Mum looked grateful. 'Do your best to make me look halfway decent, darling! If anyone can, you can.'

A rush of pleasure went through her.

That's strange. It's almost like Mum is seeing me for the first time. Really seeing me.

Mum's parties always started with a deceptive calm. The real rioters wouldn't show until at least 9 p.m. – when it was only an hour or so before the party was supposed to be ending – and so the earlier hours were quite pleasant, with quiet conversation and restrained behaviour from civilised guests.

Etta circulated with a tray of stuffed quails' eggs, enjoying the relative calm. Mum was drinking her trademark mix of stout and champagne, which was apparently called a Black Velvet, a drink that Mum considered barely alcoholic.

The intercom buzzed and Etta rushed to press the button. She was on general arrival duty including coat collection, so she put down her tray and stood by the flat door. To her surprise, the person coming up the stairs was approaching at speed. Usually guests were groaning by the time they reached the fifth flight of stairs.

A man appeared on the last flight, puffing only slightly as he bounded up towards her. He was broad-shouldered and slightly stocky, with warm brown eyes in an appealing face, his brown hair cut very short and sprinkled with touches of grey.

I know him. But how? Oh yes, of course, he's Mum's American friend.

'Oh wow,' he said as he neared her, obviously recognising her in turn. 'Etta, is that you?'

'Yes!' She smiled broadly at him. 'Are you Rob?'

'You got it! C'mere.'

The next moment she was embraced in a huge bear hug.

'Boy, have you grown! You're a young woman now. You were just a kid when I last saw you.' He looked her up and down, shaking his head. 'And what a young lady you are. Now . . . is Flick here?'

'Yes, come in!'

Inside the flat, knots of people stood about chatting and drinking. Mum was in a group by the fireplace and Etta called to her. She turned around and saw Rob. Immediately her expression transformed. She jumped slightly, and her whole face came alive with a look of pleasure, her eyes shining and a smile bursting on her lips.

'Rob,' she said. 'You're here!'

'You better believe it, Flick.'

Etta saw her mother disappear into the same bear hug that she had just experienced herself. Then Rob stood back and regarded her mother, smiling broadly. 'Flick, you look just the same.'

Mum laughed. 'You appalling flatterer. I do not. You do, though. How was your flight? And is Mindy with you?'

'She sends her apologies. She's zonked after the journey and asleep at the hotel. She's looking forward to seeing you another time, though.'

'Of course, that would be lovely. And no wonder she's exhausted. You must bring her over tomorrow for coffee instead.'

Etta watched them chat, completely at ease in one another's company, and almost oblivious to the rest of the room.

It was a relief to see Mum happy. At last there was something to make her forget all the stresses and strains of the last few weeks.

She looks better than she has for ages.

As usual, the madcap and the manic arrived late, to reinvigorate the party with fresh energy. Etta was suddenly busy again, finding food from the abandoned trays, opening bottles of champagne and trying to locate the tonic supply. Rosalie had gone back to her own place so Etta was coping on her own.

'Let me help with that.'

The warm American tones made her look up. 'Oh, thanks!'

Rob gave her a lopsided smile. 'Are these parties always so crazy?'

'Yep. And Mum can never work out why.' Etta gave an ironic shrug, pointing at all the bottles of wine and spirits on the sideboard.

Rob laughed. 'I guess we only live once. C'mon, let's get them all fed and watered.'

They reconvened in the kitchen half an hour later, having done their duty topping up glasses and trying to make people finish up the canapés.

'We deserve a drink ourselves,' Rob said, filling two glasses with champagne. The roar of partygoers talking ever more loudly came from the other room and Rob kicked the door shut and handed Etta a glass. 'Come and sit down. Let's have a chat away from the madness.' When they were settled, he said, 'So, tell me, how's it going?'

Before she knew it, Etta was spilling out the story of everything that had happened since the piece about Caius Knolle had been published, and Rob listened attentively, sipping his drink and interjecting only to ask questions. When she'd finished, he said thoughtfully, 'This is tough on all of you. And I guess it's thrown up a whole load of stories about your mom and dad and all the rest of it.'

'Yes, it has,' Etta said feelingly. 'Maybe Mary was a bit harsh, but she wasn't wrong. Dad was there for us. Mum was always working. I feel as though now Dad is ill, she just needs us to fill in for him.'

'Honey, I am not going to tell you about your own emotions and experience,' Rob said slowly. 'But you might see things a bit differently in time. Your mom has been looking after your dad for many, many years. I saw him a long time ago, and I knew he was ill. I had an uncle with a similar condition and I saw the signs right away. She's coped with a lot, and looked after you kids all the way through too.'

'I suppose so . . . But it felt like she was a bit removed, that's all.'

'She's no saint. But she's done her best. It's not been easy. She already had a failed marriage when she met your dad, don't forget.' Rob looked thoughtfully into his glass of champagne. 'I hope Mary isn't really getting involved with that guy Knolle, is she?'

'I just don't know. I hope not.'

'Me too. Not for Flick's sake but for hers. He's no good. He really isn't.'

'I know.' Etta shook her head. 'He's obviously trouble even without the connection.'

Rob fixed her with a penetrating look. 'And you, Etta? Any guys on your horizon?'

'Oh no. None. And I don't want any either,' Etta said firmly. 'I prefer to be alone.'

'Really? Why is that?'

'I don't know. It just feels safer, I suppose.' She had been wary of any boys interested in her at school. She'd kissed a couple she'd liked but held the ones who wanted to know her better at bay. 'It's just hard to know who to trust.'

'You're right to be wary and protect yourself. But I hope

one day you find someone you can trust. And in the mean-time, you'll need friends. I'm your mom's friend, but I want you to know that I'm here for you too. Any time you need me.'

She looked into his warm brown eyes and smiled. There was something interesting about him. A kind of quality of sunshine. Perhaps all Americans had it. He felt safe to her. 'Okay. Thank you.'

'So call me if you're ever in trouble or need a listening ear. I'm here for you. Deal?'

'Deal.'

'Good. Now let's get back to the party.'

The party took the usual turn, with the hours slipping by and people getting drunker and louder, but the atmosphere was a merry one. No fisticuffs tonight, Etta thought with relief. To her surprise, her mother clapped her hands at just before midnight and told everyone the party was over, and they had to go home.

'Ah, just another drink!' shouted one guest, as the others murmured with surprise at the early end to proceedings.

'No, no,' Mum said firmly. 'The bar is closed. Time to go home. Time, ladies and gentlemen, please!'

And she firmly began to usher people out of the door.

At last the sitting room and dining room were empty, with only Rob Gerstein remaining, standing by the fireplace, hold-ing a drink and looking surprisingly bright-eyed.

'Thank you for all your help, Etta.' Mum came over and

hugged her warmly. 'I need to talk to Rob, I haven't seen him in so long. So you head off and I'll clear up later.'

'Are you sure?' Etta said, realising her mother meant she should go back to the flat downstairs.

'Of course, I'm sure.' Mum put a hand to her back, almost gently pushing her to leave. 'And I'll see you in the morning.'

Etta went back downstairs to the ground-floor flat, where most of her things still were. She brushed her teeth, got changed and went to bed, waking only briefly when the front door closed, noticing that it was three in the morning, before falling immediately back to sleep.

Chapter Twenty
ETTA
1979

When Etta went upstairs to check on Mum the day after the party, she found the flat was already back in good shape.

Mum was sitting in the kitchen over coffee with Rob the American, and a slim, glossy woman with the blondest hair Etta had ever seen. She looked like she'd stepped out of a television show or a magazine. She was saying that she was so excited about visiting Scotland because she was Scottish.

'Goodness, are you?' Mum said, pouring out more coffee.

The woman nodded. 'Uh-huh. My great-grandmother was a Macdonald.'

'Oh,' Mum said, looking mystified. 'Ah, here's Etta! Come in, darling. This is Mindy, Rob's girlfriend. They're about to go exploring the British Isles. Isn't that nice?'

'Hi, Etta, great to meet you!' Mindy said brightly, showing dazzling white teeth.

Rob grinned at her. 'Any tips for what to see?'

'Oh . . . well . . .' Etta thought a moment and said the first thing that came into her head. 'Offa's Dyke?'

'Offa's what?' exclaimed Mindy.

Mum and Rob laughed, and Mum said, 'Out of everything to see in Britain, Etta . . . Offa's Dyke!' and laughed some more.

'But what is it?' asked Mindy.

'A sort of bank of earth that goes on for some time – near Wales,' Etta said, before starting to laugh too. 'Perhaps you might enjoy Windsor Castle a bit more, now I think of it.'

'I think I might,' Mindy said with a smile. 'But thanks for suggesting the . . . dyke, was it? Maybe next time!'

After they had gone, with promises to call in before they headed back to the States, Etta settled down with Mum to dissect the party and everyone who'd been there. 'Your friend Rob is really fab,' she remarked.

'Yes, he is.' Mum smiled. 'I'm glad you like him.'

'Were you ever, like . . . boyfriend and girlfriend?'

'No, no. Just really good friends. He's someone I can rely on.'

'Mindy's nice.' Etta looked curiously at her mother, just in case there was some expression that gave away something.

'Isn't she?' Mum shook her head. 'But so American! Where do they get their energy? Mindy seems to have added batteries or something. She gets up at dawn every day to go jogging! She does something called aerobics too. Isn't that strange?'

'So weird,' Etta agreed. 'I thought if you were slim, you didn't have to bother with exercise!' She helped herself to coffee from the pot. 'By the way, I wanted to tell you that Sam and I are going to visit Dad today.'

'Oh – that's nice.' Mum smiled at her. 'I should go myself. It's been too long. I don't find it easy, though.' After a moment she said, 'Is Mary going too?'

Etta shook her head. 'Just me and Sam.'

'Okay. I'm going to see Mary this week. I want to apologise to her and I hope she'll think about coming home. We all miss her.'

'It would be nice to have her back home,' Etta agreed, although she had not missed the constant smoking and fug of weed in the flat.

'And give Dad my love and a kiss from me. Tell him I'll visit him very soon.'

'I will.'

The gardens of the hospital were so calming that they had to have been specially planned to induce that effect.

Etta and Samuel went out from the main reception building, making their way through the rose bushes and knots of shrubs to where Dad was sitting on a bench, a dressing gown wrapped around him, and an orderly on the bench beside him, a tall man in a loose blue uniform.

'Hey, Dad,' Samuel said, as they approached. 'It's good to see you.'

Jonathan looked like a shell of his old self, his cheeks hollow and eyes sunken and yellow. His hair was longer than it used to be, and fluffed out in grey tufts over his ears. He seemed thinner. But the main thing, Etta thought, was the absence.

Over the years, she'd got used to Dad drifting slowly away,

but now she felt he was altogether gone, his spirit somewhere else, his thoughts looking only inward towards the chaos and chatter in the middle of his mind.

'Dad?' She went forward and gave his unyielding body a hug. 'It's me, Etta.'

There was no response. His misty eyes didn't seem even to register her presence. Even so, she kissed his cheek and sat down beside him, holding his hand, and the orderly got up to let Sam sit on his other side. They each took a hand and talked gently to him, but still without any response. After a while, they stopped asking questions and simply took turns telling him things about their lives, and eventually just had a conversation between the two of them, keeping everything calm and quiet while they chatted, hoping their father was comforted by their voices.

At last, Etta ran out of things to say and sat back. She looked over at Sam. 'Do you think he even knows we're here?'

Sam shrugged, looking sad and serious. 'I don't know. But we've come and we've done our best. I think we should probably go home and let Dad go back inside.' He squeezed his father's arm. 'We're leaving now, Dad. It's been so lovely to see you. We all love you.'

Jonathan dropped his head, frowning, then quite suddenly lifted it and looked around. 'Where's my daughter?' he barked, looking about.

'Here I am, Dad,' Etta said, thrilled that he had asked for her.

'Where is she?' He looked all around as if Etta were not there at all. 'Where's Mary?'

Etta's spirits swooped. 'Oh . . . oh, she's not here. She couldn't come, she's busy.'

Mary had not wanted a trip to the hospital she considered gruesome. She'd said that it was depressing to see a man who didn't know who she was. Now he was asking for her. It was awful.

'Where's my daughter?' Dad barked again.

'I'm here,' she said again, trying to get into his eyeline. 'I'm right here, Dad! It's Etta.'

His disconnected gaze at last fell on her. 'You,' he said. 'Don't you call me Dad. I want Mary.'

She was confused. 'What do you mean, Dad?'

Now he looked at her, with a kind of scorn. 'I want Mary,' he said roughly, and seemed to get more agitated.

'I think we'd better go,' Sam said quickly, standing up so that the orderly could take his place and put a firm restraining hand on Jonathan. 'Come on, Etta. We're going home.'

On the way back into central London, Etta was tearful. She felt deeply hurt by Dad's rejection.

'Why did he say that? Why didn't he want to see me?'

'He's mad, Etta, you know that,' Sam said sympathetically as he drove back along the busy roads. 'He never even said a word to me.'

'I know, but he said . . . he said, "Don't you call me Dad." What did he mean?'

'It meant nothing, Ets. He's not well. You can't take

anything he says seriously. He thinks he's a member of the star people and that he's on a divine mission for humankind. Don't let it bother you. Honestly. Don't.'

Etta couldn't help it, it did bother her. It left a bitter, unpleasant feeling that she couldn't shake off all day.

Etta went over that evening to see Mary at Granny's house. Granny was having what she called a beauty day, so she was a quite horrific sight in a green face mask and a huge flowery cap covering her hair as it soaked up the lavender dye she liked so much these days. Granny seemed to be becoming more and more of a caricature of herself, and was as flamboyant as ever, drawing attention to herself with her very loud clothes and huge purple hairdos.

'I won't kiss you, Etta,' she announced. 'I need to sit quietly while my skin absorbs. You two entertain yourselves, won't you?'

The girls were happy to be left alone. Mary had nicked a bottle of white wine from one of the party fridges in the basement kitchen, and now they were sitting on the terrace, drinking it.

'Did you see Dad?' Mary asked, inhaling the fragrant smoke of a joint and letting it out slowly with a long breath.

'Yeah.'

'How was he?'

'Fine.' Etta had decided not to say anything about Dad asking after Mary, in case she felt guilty for not going. And she wasn't going to mention his cruel words to her. They were the sort of thing that Mary would love, and would remember and make jokes about. Etta could hear it now: *You're the one Dad forgets!* 'I mean, he looked okay. He wasn't there. He didn't speak to us.'

'Oh God. How long are we going to have to look after him? He's like a vegetable!'

'Mary!'

She blew out more smoke, talking as she did so her voice came out thickly. 'Well, he is. What kind of a life is it, in a psych ward with no awareness?'

'We don't know. And it can't get better unless he's alive, can it?'

'Don't fool yourself,' Mary said crisply. 'He won't get better. He'll die. Sooner the better.'

Etta's eyes filled with tears. 'I can't believe you would say that.'

Mary stared at the table. 'I don't really mean it. I hate that Dad's like this. I feel like he's abandoned us. Like, why wasn't life with us enough? Why does he prefer to think about aliens and spaceships and all the rest? We all used to be happy.'

Etta thought about Dad and how unkind he'd been that day. Mary was hurt too. They both felt rejected by him. 'It's not him, Sam says. It's the illness.'

Mary didn't seem to hear her. Instead she said, 'Caius Knolle wrote to me.'

'What?' Etta was startled out of her sadness. 'How?'

'He wrote to my college. I told him I was a fashion student there. He used my false name, though.' She laughed. 'They still knew that Miffy Celesta was me, don't know how.'

Etta sat up straight, and reached for her wine. 'And?'

'He wants to see me again.'

Etta drew in a sharp breath. 'Oh my God, Mary. What are you going to do? You don't want to . . . go out with him, do you?' She had no idea how far the situation with Knolle had already gone. But this sounded serious. 'You've got to tell him.'

Mary said sharply, 'I don't have to do anything.' She took another long drag of her joint and stared mistily out over Granny's huge garden. 'It would fuck Mum up, wouldn't it?'

'You know it would. That's why you shouldn't do it.'

'Or maybe that's exactly why I should.' Mary let this sink in and then said mysteriously, 'And maybe it's too late anyway.'

'So is it?'

Mary remained silent, taking a final drag from her joint.

'Mum's going to try to make peace with you. She's really sorry. She misses you.'

'So now you're her little go-between, are you?' Mary jeered. 'You've been just as badly treated as I have. I bet you couldn't wait until I was gone to start worming your way in, turning us all against each other.'

'It's not like that,' Etta said in a small voice. 'I wouldn't do that.'

'Families are fucking fucked up,' Mary said, stubbing out the remains of her joint. 'But ours is worse than just about anyone else's I know. It's that curse, Etta. I'm a full believer now. We're all under a bad sign, and that's that.'

*

Etta was glad that her bad sign or whatever it was wasn't visible to the rest of society. She had gone for an interview for a part-time job in the florist's shop across the road, and the owner had not apparently noticed any kind of curse or emanation of evil. Instead, she offered Etta the job, which Etta enjoyed very much. She loved stocking the flower buckets, and making up very simple bouquets. The owner was in charge of the more expensive and complicated arrangements, from wedding flowers to funeral wreaths. When she was out the back making up orders, Etta sat behind the till and watched the world going by. From here, she could also see the end of their street, and often saw neighbours coming and going, on the way out of the square and heading to the busy shops of Kensington.

The roses made her think of the garden at the hospital, and the painful words that Dad had said to her. It was a mystery. Why would Dad say something so nasty?

Sam had been there, he had heard it. He had also dismissed it. And he was probably right. But even so, it bothered her.

She recalled quite suddenly something from last year. They had been having supper with Mum in her flat, and she was pretty drunk, as she often was in the evenings. She was never furious or cross-eyed and incoherent, or sick. Many people would not have known just how drunk she was. She just got slowly more blurry, sometimes repetitive, sometimes expansive. Occasionally a bit teary. That night Mary had been talking about Dad's illness and wondering if there was a chance that they could all inherit it.

'I hope not,' Etta had said. 'I can't bear the thought of going mad.'

And Mum had looked at her, almost kindly, and said, 'Well, darling, you're probably the only one who might not have to worry about that.'

'What do you mean?' Etta had said, taken back. 'Why not me?'

Just for a second, she had seen the four of them round the table. Three fair, blue-eyed blondes, and her, Etta: dark brown soulful eyes, heavy brows, a sensual full-lipped mouth, and the long burnt-umber hair.

'Why not me?' she'd said again.

'Because, darling, you're the most sensible soul I know, and the very last person who's going to go mad.' Flick had lit another cigarette, completely normal and at ease. Etta had felt reassured.

She had forgotten all about it until now. But Jonathan's words – *Don't you call me Dad* – were still ringing in her ears.

A horrible thought was beginning to form in her mind. But it couldn't possibly be true. How could it be?

Out of her pocket, she pulled the scrap of newspaper she had been saving, and unfolded it. It was torn from the article in the review: the old black-and-white photograph of Caius Knolle as a young man. Dark, intense eyes stared back. His thick black wavy hair fell over his brow. His full lips were slightly parted as he stared into the lens.

She went over to one of the decorative mirrors and held the picture up so that it was beside her own face. But it was

impossible to see if the small scrap of newspaper was anything like her own real, natural face.

Going back to the till, she put the paper into her pocket.
It was her imagination. By the time she was conceived,
Mum and Caius had long been divorced. According to the
paper, they'd never met again after that. And Mum was married to Dad, in any case, and had had Mary. When Etta
had been small, and Mum had combed out her hair after the
bath, she had said that Etta had hair just like her grand-
father, and that must mean Granny's dead husband from
years ago. It was perfectly possible for colouring to skip a
generation.

Etta felt guilty for even thinking it. And yet, that nasty
feeling was not going away.

From her vantage point at the till, she noticed movement
at the end of her street, and strained to see if it was anyone
she knew.

Then she realised that it was Mum, half running, half
walking towards the main road, and then standing at the
side, waiting for the lights to change, clearly agitated. Etta got
up. She couldn't leave the shop but she walked over to the
front window.

Mum was definitely in a state and coming towards
the shop.

Etta moved to the door and opened it, the bell above jan-
gling. 'Mum?'

Mum came bursting through and grabbed Etta by the
arms. Her eyes were round, her mouth dropping slackly
open. Then she said, 'Oh darling, I'm so sorry!'

'What? Why?'

'Dad . . . Dad is dead. They just phoned to tell me. I can't believe it. I'm really so sorry, so terribly sorry . . .'

Etta felt cold and numb all over. 'Oh no.' Then, as if in a stupor, she said, 'Mary. We have to tell Mary.'

Chapter Twenty-One

FLICK

1979

Flick didn't know why she should be surprised that Jonathan wanted to be buried at Caundle. After all, he had loved it despite a connection that was nowhere near as deep as hers.

I suppose I never truly understood what it meant to him.

The parish church, a tiny building in accordance with the size of the village, was hard by the house, surrounded by a picturesque graveyard. Brinsley had arranged for a plot by the south side, near a beautiful magnolia tree, which Flick was sure Jonathan would have liked.

The news of Jonathan's fatal coronary had been a horrible shock. It was a mild comfort that he had been in the hospital garden at the time, bearing in mind how much he'd loved being outdoors. Even though he had been absent from her life for so long, in so many ways, it was still an unexpected blow that he was gone from her for ever, without a chance to say goodbye. She had gone for a long walk and wept for him, remembering their years together and the life they had built, and the loss of what it could have been. Whatever, it was all vanished now.

The real pain, though, had been for her children, who had lost their father. Etta had dissolved into rivers of tears, standing in the florist's shop, and the owner had come out, full of sympathy, and sent her home. For once, it had been Flick supporting her daughter and it made her realise how much she had relied on Etta over the years, perhaps too much.

They had gone home and after weeping together at the kitchen table, Flick had left a message at the LSE for Samuel to come home. She wondered if she should phone Anne, Jonathan's first wife, but then decided she would let Samuel tell her. It would be strange, under the circumstances, for their first and probably last conversation to be about their husband's death.

Samuel came home after getting the message and they told him. He took the news calmly but was clearly stunned. He went off almost at once to see his mother, and reassured Flick that he would help as much as he could with all the arrangements.

The hardest thing was telling Mary.

Flick and Etta had decided not to telephone Gloria in advance, knowing that she would not be able to resist telling Mary herself in some melodramatic way that would undoubtedly feature lots of her own tears and grand gestures. So they had made their way to Chester Square, Etta crying quietly in the taxi, Flick holding her hand tightly.

Gloria had sailed into the drawing room when they arrived and were waiting, in a simple housecoat and a turban covering her purple hair.

'Goodness, to what do I owe this honour? You're lucky I was in!' Then she saw their faces. 'What's happened?'

Flick felt a surge of love for her silly, spoiled mother. She could still feel things. She still loved her. 'It's Jonathan.' Her eyes filled again with hot tears just having to say the words. 'He's died. He's dead.'

Gloria stared, her mouth a round, painted O in her white face. Then she said, 'How terrible. I'm sorry, darling.' She held out her arms and Flick went into them, weeping. 'You too, sweetie,' she said to Etta, and then the three of them were in a messy embrace, crying together.

When Gloria pulled away, she said, 'You want to see Mary. She's not here. But she said she'd be back to get changed before going out.'

While they waited for Mary, they sat together on the sofa, talking in low voices about what had happened and what might happen next. It was an hour before they heard the front door slam. The maid intercepted Mary on her way upstairs and a moment later, she appeared in the doorway, taking in the sight of her grandmother, mother and sister sitting together, tear-stained.

'What?' she demanded. Then her eyes were frightened. 'What is it?'

Flick stood up. 'Darling Mary, you have to be very strong.' And she told her.

It was not surprising that Mary's grief was powerful. The only good thing to come out of this was that it was only Flick she wanted, needing hugs of comfort and a listening ear as she sobbed out her loss and her guilt for not going to see him that last time.

Flick took her home, and Mary stayed upstairs with her, where Flick could look after her and Etta as they struggled with their shock and sadness. They felt again like a family, even if they'd been brought together by something so awful, and the situation with Caius was never mentioned. Flick wanted to make her apology properly, when Mary was in a stronger state. The right time never came, and she found it easier to assume that the whole thing had been a terrible mistake that luckily had not got serious. The article, horrible though it had been, had prevented something truly awful, and she was glad for that.

Now, here they were at Caundle and it was Jonathan's funeral.

Brinsley had stepped up. The place was at Flick's disposal, her friends welcome, and he sat up with her till late in the night with glasses of brandy while she wept and told him the whole story of her marriage. The real story, not the merry jolly front of family he had seen when they visited.

'You seemed to be happy,' Brinsley said, frowning. They were sitting in the library, one lone lamp casting a bit of illumination, as they did most evenings. 'I thought you'd found your safe port. And Jonathan's illness . . . I had no idea of its extent or how early it all started.'

'I couldn't talk about it. I couldn't say. I felt I'd made my choice and I had to live with it. I couldn't bear to fail again, not after Caius.'

'I'm so sorry. And the girls?'

'They're bearing up. They could live with him being ill because there was always the hope that he might get better. But now . . . it's so final. They've lost him. And Mary didn't go to see him for the last time, when Etta and Sam did. So she's finding it hard to cope with that.'

Brinsley nodded. 'Yes. Mary is not in a good way. We must take care of her.'

'She and I fell out badly recently, and she went to live with Mother.'

'I know. Mother was delighted and took every opportunity to let me know what a great replacement she was being. What was the falling-out over?'

'I . . . I can't say. It's Mary's private business. But it was incredibly painful for us both. We haven't had the chance to talk about it since Jonathan died.'

'I hope you can heal the breach.' Brinsley took a sip of his brandy. 'You know, you don't have to worry so much. You're a better mother than you realise. And you were a good wife to Jonathan. You did your best.'

'I tried.' Flick managed a small smile. 'I've always tried. I've often failed. But I've wanted to be good.'

'That's what makes the difference. The wanting.'

Flick looked at her brother with gratitude. 'Thank you for everything. It is such a blessing to have you. We haven't spent as much time together as we should.'

'We are separate souls, despite twinship. All of us are isolated, aren't we? Hardly ever brought back together like a normal family.'

'We should make an effort to reunite. We really must. And thank you for sharing this place.'

'It's your place too,' Brinsley said simply. 'Always.'

The funeral was held on a beautiful, late summer day. The coffin arrived at the church, covered in the bright blooms of roses and all the flowers of summer. Flick arrived last of all, with Samuel, Mary and Etta, and she was only vaguely aware of the congregation during the short service. She held the hands of her daughters, only letting them go when it was their turn to read poems. Samuel delivered a beautiful eulogy, managing to turn Jonathan's mental illness into something almost poetic in the recounting of his life. He said that his father left earthly life earlier than most, to live on another plane where a new reality had just as much meaning as theirs. The vicar gave a short sermon and said some prayers, and after the last hymn, they filed out to the little cemetery, following the pallbearers and the festooned coffin. Brinsley and Prue were there, Prue with her young family. But Gloria did not come.

'Death is so morbid,' she'd sighed. 'I think I would find it all a bit depressing. And all that weeping and wailing is not going to bring him back, is it?'

Flick felt that under the circumstances, it was a relief not to have her mother there, grabbing all the attention she could.

She gazed at the coffin as it sat by the graveside, waiting to be lowered into the huge empty hole. Flick could hardly believe that Jonathan was inside that box. She wished he had requested cremation; it seemed so strange to want to rot into the earth when you could fly away as a cloud of ash.

Standing opposite her, on the other side of the grave, were Rob and Mindy, both of them with heads bowed. They were still travelling in Britain when Jonathan died and the funeral coincided with the end of their trip. Rob had insisted that they would come, to pay their respects to Jonathan.

It was strange to see him, so apparently close and yet also so far away. He was holding Mindy's hand, and had not been able to do more than mutter a few words of sympathy to Flick when they'd arrived. The whole time he'd been in Britain, he hadn't been able to call her. Usually, they spoke frequently, their separation, and the disequilibrium of time, meaning that she lay in bed when he was still at his working day. But Mindy was with him. Talking had not been possible. Flick had missed him. Now he was here, and still she couldn't really be with him. She longed to go to him, fall into his arms and sob her heart out with the grief she had for Jonathan, and for the lost potential and the suffering in both their lives. Instead, she held Etta and Mary's hands, and thought of them and of her husband.

They stood together, shoulder to shoulder, with Samuel next to them, watching as Jonathan's coffin was consigned to the earth, the flowers they had thrown on top of it.

'I'm so sorry for your loss.'

Flick was standing in the drawing room in the middle of Jonathan's wake, on her own for a moment. The girls had slipped out to the garden. She had talked to the few members of Jonathan's family who had come. His sister and mother had stayed in Australia despite Flick offering to pay for their travel. After all the talking, she was relishing a few moments of peace. Now she was back on duty.

She looked up into a pair of dark eyes in a slim, handsome face. The man in front of her was a little older than she was, but with iron-grey hair cut short at the sides. He was tall and extremely elegant in a black suit and navy silk tie. She did not recognise him, but the drawing room at Caundle was full of people she did not know, the friends and colleagues of Jonathan who had not been part of her own life.

'Thank you,' she said with a smile. 'And thank you for coming. How did you know Jonathan?'

He gave her a half-amused look. 'You don't remember me, do you, Flick?'

She was startled to hear him say her name, and looked more closely into his dark brown eyes. He did strike a chord with her now he'd said that. 'Can you remind me?'

He raised his eyebrows and said, 'I had no idea I'm so forgettable. But then, it's been years and we've both aged since we met in New York. Do you remember? I stole you away from Diana's dinner party and we went to a club together.'

As he spoke, she remembered. 'Henry Morfield.'

'That's right.'

Flick stared at him. She had a flashback to that night, of sitting with him in that bar after he told her about Jonathan and Anne and Sam. The black misery. 'Of course I remember you.' Her voice came out blankly. 'How nice to see you again.'

'And you. I was sorry to hear about Jonathan. You might remember we were at Cambridge together. So hideously young to die. I felt I wanted to come and pay my respects.'

'That's very good of you,' she said. 'Do you have a drink? Let me get you one.'

Flick walked off to find a waitress with a tray of glasses. She had tried never to think again of that night in New York nearly twenty years ago. It was just a hazy memory now and she didn't want it to become any clearer. Henry's revelation had marked the beginning of the end of her love for Jonathan. The only good thing to come out of it was that, in her sick misery the following day, she had gone to find Rob. And that had been the start of their real friendship.

That's it, she told herself. *Concentrate on what was wonderful. The rest of it doesn't matter now. Henry Morfield did me a favour telling me about Jonathan's secret life. I owe him for that, really.*

It still felt unpleasant to remember it, especially today when she was trying to hold fast to the good things in her marriage to Jonathan, not its hollowness.

She would cope by refusing to let those memories in. There was no space for them right now.

Taking two glasses from a tray, she returned to Henry Morfield, who was examining some of the portraits on the drawing room wall.

'I say, a very nice Nattier you have there,' he said as she approached. He pointed at another portrait over the fireplace. 'And is that a Gainsborough?'

'It might be a copy. But you'd need to ask my brother

Brinsley all about that. This is his house, and he's been restoring it for years now.'

'It's in a marvellous state.'

'Thank you. It means a lot to us.'

She looked over to where her sister Prue was standing by the open French windows, her youngsters around her. Unlike Flick and Brinsley, Prue seemed to have found contentment in marriage. After her grand London wedding, she had gone to live in rural bliss not far from Caundle, raising a large family in a warm and comfortable home, devoting herself to her husband and children. Prue had become allergic to London and almost never went up to town, whereas Flick rarely left. As a result, they had only met at Christmases for years.

I need to spend more time with her, Flick thought suddenly. *If there is one thing this has taught me . . . life is brief. Family matters.*

She had been so touched by the bond between Etta and Mary, and how much they had comforted one another. They were with each other now, wandering around the garden, chatting easily.

I will make time to be with Prue more, she promised herself. *And Brin. I've neglected them horribly.*

Henry Morfield was talking to her, she realised. 'That's my boy, over there. Charlie.'

Flick looked over to where a good-looking young man was talking to another guest.

'He was growing up a bit too American for my liking, so I sent him to boarding school here. Now he's a curious transatlantic beast, going back and forth. His mother lives there.'

'You're divorced.'

'Darling, who isn't?' Then he looked repentant. 'I'm sorry. That was very bad taste. You've lost your husband.'

'It's fine. Really. I am technically a widow, but Jonathan and I hadn't lived together for some time by the end.'

'Oh.' He raised his brows again. 'I didn't realise.'

'I just mean . . . it's not quite how it might seem.' She felt awkward. 'Anyway, you have a very fine son. My stepson Samuel is over there. My girls are somewhere.'

Henry smiled at her. His eyes seemed to hold more of a twinkle in them. 'The next generation. Ready to take over and shunt us aside. Perhaps that means we can have a little time to ourselves now.'

'Yes.' She felt confused, as though she had somehow given him the wrong impression. 'Will you excuse me? I must talk to the vicar. Thank you again for coming, very nice to see you.'

'Nice to see you too,' Henry said, and bent forward to kiss her cheek swiftly. 'I hope we can catch up some time in London.'

'Oh . . . yes . . . perhaps. Well. Goodbye.'

'Goodbye.'

Flick could not shake off her inner discomfort after talking to Henry. It was his association with Jonathan's dishonesty that was causing it.

That must be it.

She went outside to have a cigarette and gaze over the gardens. She could see Mary and Etta sitting on the side of the clover-shaped pool. She had been beside it the night that Caius had arrived at her birthday party to whisk her away to a new and exciting life.

A lifetime ago now.

'Flick, there you are. I might have known you'd be smoking. I guess today is not the day to tell you to give it up.'

As though she had summoned him, Rob was walking towards her.

'Hello, darling,' she said, full of joy to see him.

He smiled, his eyes as warm as ever. 'You've been so brave today. And it was a beautiful service. I'm so glad I was here for it.'

'I was so very comforted to have you here. You know that.' She smiled back. 'I wish you could hug me.'

'Me too.' He sighed. 'Flick, this is terribly hard. For years, we've worked at holding this relationship of ours – this loving friendship – in the only place it can exist: in the space between your marriage and my life in New York. And now . . . Jonathan is gone. Today is about remembering and honouring him. So Mindy and I are leaving now. We've got a flight home tomorrow night and need to pack.'

'Of course, I understand. You must go. Thank you for coming.'

He took her hand. 'Come on, let's walk over here and be on our own for a moment.'

They walked together down the steps and out towards the wilderness garden, where she had asked Caius to run away with her all those years before. By an old oak tree, they stopped. Rob suddenly took her hands, and turned to her, gazing deep into her eyes. 'Flick . . . I know this is a crazy thing to do, and spectacularly bad timing. But I don't know when I'll see you again. This is our chance, can you see that? You're not married any more. We could maybe make a go of things. Couldn't we? Is this the chance we've been waiting for all our lives?'

She stared at him, astonished. 'But . . . Mindy! There's Mindy.'

'Yes, there is. But I can end that.'

'End it . . .?'

'Flick, I can keep it going when we're apart. Because you're not there. She is very nice and I love her on the level that works for us. But I guess that soon she'll start asking for marriage and kids and I'll have to remind her that I've been clear from the start that won't happen.'

'But why not? You should get married and have kids.'

He looked at her with such clarity and intensity that she had to look away. 'I only wanted them with you. And that was never an option.'

She was unable to return his gaze, filled with a sense of loss and missed opportunities, as well as guilt that she had deprived him of something fundamental. 'I'm so sorry. I made a terrible mistake. I should have gone home and broken off with Jonathan. But there was Mary. And then Etta. And—'

'You don't have to say it. I made my peace with it all a long time ago.' He looked wry. 'But it always goes the same way. In the end, I'll let Mindy go, like the others. And she'll find the guy she's meant to be with.'

'It's lonely for you.'

'It's my choice. I've told her about our friendship and how often we talk to each other. It will be her choice when she leaves. I've always been honest about what she can expect from me.'

'I feel so guilty,' Flick said wretchedly.

'We have a chance now, though,' Rob said quietly. 'We could be together. If you want that.'

She stood there, holding his hands, a tangle of emotions and longing inside her. She had wanted this very thing for so long, and here it was. Their chance. Then why did she feel awful? 'I think you should marry Mindy.'

'What?' He looked hurt. 'But why?'

'I'm terrible at marriage. I can't do it. I don't want to lose what we've got and if you became too close to me, you'd suffer too. This stupid curse of ours – it spoils the things that really matter.'

'You can't believe that rubbish, Flick! A curse? You wouldn't let that stand in our way, would you?' He sounded crosser than she'd ever heard him.

'It's a way of saying I'm no good for you. You deserve a happy ordinary marriage with someone like Mindy, not the black misery and damage that comes with me. And I can't give you children, Rob! I can't do that.'

'I don't care.'

'You say that now, but you might regret it and then hate me for taking away something you deserve in your life.'

Rob looked angry. 'This is madness. You really want me to leave now? You don't want this chance?'

'I'm doing it for your sake.'

He dropped her hands, his eyes hard. 'Don't say that. Don't blame me. You're doing it for your sake. I've been there for you, whenever you needed me, for years. You know that. I guess that when it comes down to it, you just don't love me enough. You might have to make some sacrifices of your own. Maybe come to New York. Maybe start a new life. And you don't want to. You just want me on tap like I've always been.'

'Yes,' Flick said suddenly. 'That's right.' She had the overwhelming feeling that she was doing the right thing in turning Rob down. She was sure with every fibre of her being that she wasn't worthy of what he was offering. He was right. She was selfish, she would put herself first and make his life a misery. 'You're right, Rob. Go home. Go back with Mindy. Enjoy your life. Have those kids you deserve, you'll be a wonderful father. We missed our chance. It wasn't meant to be. I'll always love you, but it wasn't meant to be.'

He gazed at her, hurt and misery all over his face. 'If that's what you want.'

'It is.' Her heart was telling her not to be so stupid and that if he walked out of her life now, she'd regret it for ever.

But I'm going to do the right thing. I'm going to let him go. I would only make him miserable and I love him too much for that.

'All right, Flick. Goodbye. I guess we'll speak again soon.'

He turned away and started walking rapidly back towards the house.

'Goodbye, darling. I love you truly. I really do.'

But she knew he wouldn't hear it. She gazed out over the wilderness gardens. In the far distance, she could see the towers of the belvedere, that ruined place that she had walked to day after day when she was trying to cope with her heartbreak over Caius.

Perhaps I'll walk there tomorrow.

She was filled by a sense of panic and was about to turn and run after him and tell him she'd changed her mind and please, don't leave. She would go with him anywhere. She could see him hurrying up the stone steps to go back inside and find Mindy.

Flick turned back to gaze over the garden.

Yes. I've decided. Tomorrow I will walk to the belvedere.

Chapter Twenty-Two

ETTA

1979

The funeral of her father at Caundle marked a new chapter for Etta.

She was devastated at her father's death, and had lived in a state of profound grief in the weeks between losing him and the funeral. After it, she was still sad, but something changed.

As soon as they arrived at her uncle's house, Etta had felt as though she had come home. Of course, she knew the house from many childhood holidays, and had watched it slowly evolve from the tatty place it had been into a house renewed. It wasn't lavish, but beautifully, softly comfortable. Everywhere she looked, there was something satisfying to see, from the freshly painted window frames to the roses climbing around the French windows. Rooms had somehow become more themselves, from the small sitting room with raspberry silk walls, hung with Brinsley's collection of Georgian silhouette portraits, to the dining room, which had lost its dark brown carpet and was now floored with broad boards of polished elm, while the marble fireplace was restored to a clean freshness.

Do I really belong here?

She'd always known that her mother had money, and she herself would have money one day, whatever was left to her by Granny and Mum. Yet, that didn't translate into endless luxury. It was true that Granny lived on a different level, and was always jetting off to glamorous places for parties and holidays. And her Carrington cousins, whom she knew more from the society pages in magazines and newspapers than in real life, lived a much glitzier life than hers. Etta's reality was the chaotic Kensington flats, and Mum's reluctance to go anywhere. True, she was spoiled to have a flat to live in of her own somewhere most people could never afford. But it wasn't the high life some people imagined.

Etta's life revolved around her job, her fairly ordinary social life, and looking after Mum, who had been in very low spirits ever since Dad's death, not surprisingly.

And yet, when she came to Caundle, she was aware of the spectacular luck she had being born into a family with a place like this.

I've heard so often about the family curse, how dreadful everything is. But what about what's wonderful and good?

When she and Mary wandered through the garden and sat on the edge of the clover-shaped pool, Etta dropped her fingers into its chilly waters.

'Do you still think about the family curse?' Etta said. 'You used to tell me that it wasn't true.'

Mary sighed. She had changed over the last few weeks. Some of the fight had gone out of her. 'Now I think it is.' She looked over at her sister. 'I reckon I'm cursed, anyway, even if you're not.'

'Why do you think that?' Etta said, dismayed.

'Cos look at me. I'm shit at fashion. I don't do anything but party. Mum and I hate each other. I didn't see my dad before he died because I was more interested in getting high. I managed to date my own stepfather . . .'

Etta looked at her big sister, pained by her sense of herself as a failure when, in Etta's eyes, she was so amazing. 'You've got so much, Mary, really. I don't think you're cursed.'

Mary shrugged. 'Let's meet again in twenty years. New Year's Eve, the Millenium, right here by this pool – if I live that long – and we'll see.'

Etta was relieved. At least Mary didn't intend to destroy herself. 'You're on. It's a deal.'

'You'll be fine, Etta,' Mary said, smiling at her.

'Will I?' Etta felt vaguely left out, as though her pain and problems were going to be glossed over and ignored. 'If you're cursed, I must be too.'

Mary shook her head. 'You've escaped, God knows how. I can just feel it.'

There was a pause and then Etta said, 'I'm glad Dad is here. Aren't you? I feel close to him.'

Mary nodded. 'Yeah. It's great here. I think it might be the only place where I feel safe.'

'I know what you mean. I feel that too.'

They stayed at Caundle for a few days, recovering from the trauma of the last few weeks. Uncle Brinsley was calm and welcoming, the house running on smooth and invisible wheels. Etta loved going down to breakfast in the beautiful panelled dining room with the spectacular carved fireplace. Laid out on the side was a delectable spread of fresh fruit, thick Greek yoghurt, croissants and, weirdly, honey cake. Pots of hot coffee quietly appeared in the hands of staff, along with fresh boiled eggs and buttered toast, and silver pans of bacon and mushroom and fried eggs.

Somehow, this was more luxurious than any of her grand-mother's lavish dinners of caviar and lobster and chocolate extravagances.

When it was time to go back to London, Etta felt she would miss the house very much. Part of her longed to stay.

'You're a bit weird,' Mary remarked when she said this, as they sat in the back of Mum's car. 'What girl your age wants to live in the country when they can be in London?'

Mary was right, she supposed. Although Etta loved London too. And she wanted to find the pathway into her future, whatever that was.

Uncle Brinsley had said to her, 'You know you can come back any time, Etta. I've reminded your mother that this place is her home too, and it's also yours. Anytime you want. Any time you want to visit your father. You don't have to ask. I hope you know that.'

She'd thanked him with tears in her eyes.

It was a comfort to know that Caundle was there when-ever she needed it.

*

380

Back in London, Etta began to make concerted efforts to find herself a job.

'Let me help you, darling,' Mum urged. She was still not herself, looking wan and lost a lot of the time, but she found comfort in working hard again. 'I've got lots of contacts. Do you want to work at the newspaper? I can do that for you. Or how about in film? I know lots of film people too, you might enjoy that.'

Etta felt guilty that she could so easily use these contacts when others could not, and decided that she would not do so. The only thing she asked her mother for was a list of likely film companies who might want a beginner to run errands and make tea. After that, she went around knocking on doors herself, and managed to get a position as a junior assistant on condition that she learned to type as quickly as possible.

'We usually require secretarial skills,' the woman hiring her said. 'But as you're available right away, then you can learn on the job.'

Etta felt a thrill of satisfaction as she walked away with all the forms she had to fill in before she started. There was no way that they had connected Etta Blair with Flick Templeton, the famous film reviewer, or the wealthy Carrington family. She was going to make it on her own.

Mum frowned at the letter in her hands.

'Oh goodness. I suppose I have to say yes.' She put it down, an odd expression on her face.

It was a Saturday morning and Etta was grazing on toast and marmalade and reading a magazine. She had moved upstairs with Mum full time ever since Mary, now in a bliss-fully happy relationship with an Australian barman called Scott, had moved her boyfriend into the ground-floor flat. Etta had not been able to relax with the atmosphere of ador-ation and the obviously intense sex life they were enjoying. She looked over at her mother. 'Yes to what?'

'Yes to this man, Henry Morfield.' Mum frowned. 'He's someone I knew once. I met him at a dinner party in New York before you were born – so a long time ago – and I haven't seen him again until Dad's funeral. He knew Dad at Cambridge, you see. Now he's invited us to the opera with him and his son. Apparently the boy wants some advice about writing for a career or something.' Mum sighed. 'I wish people wouldn't ask me for advice, I'm such a terrible role model and I really have no idea.'

'When are they coming?' Etta asked.

Mum picked up the letter again. 'Bloody hell. Tomorrow!' She checked the date on the envelope. 'It's taken an age to get here. I'll ring him and say all right. I suppose I have to.'

'You don't have to.'

Mum sighed again. 'No. I owe him a favour from a long time back. They can come. Seeing as they're practically here anyway. Will you come too, darling?'

Etta shrugged. 'Sure. If you want me to. I don't mind the opera, I suppose. I've never been.'

What do you wear to the opera? A ballgown? I'm not doing that.

Instead, Etta put on her favourite denim skirt which she

paired with a frilly white shirt and a long dark pink cardigan. She wound an Indian silk scarf from Kensington Market around her head and thought she looked pretty good.

Mum was waiting for her in the sitting room. She had changed out of her usual jeans and put on a black skirt to go with her black jumper, and dug out an old pair of high heels. She scraped back her hair and put on some lipstick. And yet, with her pearl and diamond drop earrings, she managed to look amazing. Etta felt very proud of her as they went to Covent Garden in a taxi, where they would meet the Morfields for an early supper before the opera.

Mum and Etta were already at their table when the Morfields arrived. Mum stood up to greet Henry in a friendly way, and said, 'This is Etta, my daughter.'

'Hi,' Etta said, getting up and holding out her hand, looking with interest at the arrivals. The older man, Henry Morfield, was a good-looking older man, with grey hair and dark eyes, deep-set over strong cheekbones. But it was the son who grabbed her attention. He was even better looking than his father, with dark hair curling over his shirt collar, dark blue eyes and a broad and generous physique.

'How do you do, Etta,' Henry said politely. He shook her hand. 'Flick, Etta, this is my son, Charlie.'

'Hey,' Charlie said. He had a smooth American accent that Etta thought was incredibly attractive. 'How are you doing?'

She felt herself blush. 'I'm fine, thank you. Gosh, you're American, I didn't expect that.'

Charlie smiled, showing regular white teeth. 'Dad sent me

to boarding school here to make me get rid of my accent. But somehow I've always held on to it. So I'm a kind of hybrid.'

'Oh, that's nice,' Etta said, trying to hide her pink cheeks by turning away, and then wondering how she could say something so anodyne and silly.

There was a general bustle as they all sat down, ordered drinks and scanned the menu. Polite conversation followed. Henry was funny, Etta thought. Acerbic and witty. He reminded her a little of her mother except that there was a kind of edge to him that made her wary. Charlie was, she thought, gorgeous. She had never been so struck by a boy. Not that he was a boy. He had to be at least six foot three inches tall, and he had that American college boy look that she had seen in films: fit, muscly, impossibly clean-cut. And he spoke well and intelligently, explaining to Flick that he had left Harvard with lots of experience of student journalism, had had an internship on the *Washington Post* and now wanted to try working in London.

'You don't need my help!' Mum exclaimed. 'You're far more qualified than I am! But I'll give you some pointers if I can.'

The supper passed off much more easily than Etta had expected, from her mother's initial reluctance, and both of the Morfield men were charming. Henry Morfield focused on Mum with intense interest and she seemed to perk up for the first time in ages. Etta wondered suddenly if he was after Mum. As soon as she thought that, it made a lot of sense. He was the right age, and clearly not married, and he seemed to like her a lot.

'Now,' Henry said, as the coffee was cleared away. 'We had better make tracks. The curtain goes up in fifteen minutes.'

'What's the opera?' Etta asked.

'*Madama Butterfly*. Have you seen it?'

Etta shook her head.

'You'll love it. Now – off we go, we don't want to be late.'

When they finally found their seats in the grandeur of the Royal Opera House, Etta was pleased to see that she was sitting next to Charlie.

The lights went down and the overture began and then Etta was lost in the story of love and betrayal. When the end came, she was horrified to find that she was in floods of uncontrollable tears.

'Hey!' Charlie said, concerned, as the lights came up. 'Oh my God, you're really upset.'

Etta couldn't speak. She was completely overcome by what she had seen and heard in a way she couldn't express. But it had blown her away. Charlie put an arm around her, and pulled a clean handkerchief out his pocket which he passed to her. 'Here. Take this. You need it.'

'Oh my, Etta!' Mum was half laughing at the sight of all the tears. 'I think you might be someone that opera speaks to. I'm afraid it just doesn't do it for me.'

'We need to get you a drink, Etta,' Henry said. 'Come on, we can go to the Garrick for a late one.'

Charlie took his arm away and they all made their way out of the opera house.

That was really odd.

When Charlie had put his arm around her, she had felt nothing at all. No spark. No chemistry.

Disappointing.

And yet, seeing Henry press his hand into the small of Mum's back as they went out among the crowds into Covent Garden, she felt a tiny bit relieved. There would be something complicated and strange about a situation where both of them were going out with a father and a son.

He's still really nice. I hope we can be proper friends.

Mum seemed to have taken a shine to the Morfields after their evening out. The bleak mood that she had been suffering from over the last few weeks got a little lighter, and she started to see Henry Morfield quite often. He always seemed to be ringing up, or popping over or suggesting something nice for them to do together. He usually had presents for her: plants for her window boxes. Books. Interesting objects. And lots of booze.

Mum would always open whatever he'd bought and then Henry would settle down and end up spending the evening there. Etta did not think he stayed the night, but he seemed to leave very late.

It was so weird to think about Mum having a relationship so soon after Dad had died. And yet maybe it was a good thing. Mum seemed alone in a way she hadn't before, even when Dad had been in hospital, and Henry was changing that a little. It was good for her to have a companion, especially one who so obviously admired her. And if it went somewhere, then that was most likely a good thing for Mum.

A healing thing. She was the kind of person who needed love, Etta thought.

Not like me. I'm independent, I'm not going to rely on anyone.

Her own grief did not have the skewering pain she'd expected. She was already used to Dad not being there. She'd felt worse when he first started being taken away to hospital, and when she had to witness him lost in delusion and fantasy. It had made her furious and desperate and then miserably horrified. That had felt like his death. So the grief now had a certain softness about it, as though she could accept it and hold it and learn to live with it. There was something comforting about Dad being at peace now, after those long struggles with the cosmic crisis he thought was coming.

As for romance for me . . . that's not going anywhere.

Her initial attraction to Charlie stubbornly refused to be reinvigorated. But that didn't matter. It was probably a good thing because it wasn't long before Charlie actually moved into the flat upstairs as Samuel's lodger when he managed to get a job on Mum's paper. He was just a lowly subeditor right now but he had been promised the chance of writing pieces as well. No byline of course, just small news items that he could cut his teeth on. But he seemed to love it.

Etta loved having him there. They continued to get on very well, maybe even because of the lack of chemistry between them. Etta had wondered if some of that might manifest if they spent enough time together. They certainly grew closer, spending evenings in watching telly while Samuel was out, and Mary was in domestic bliss downstairs with Scott.

'Are you guys ever going to get together?' Mary asked, and Etta shook her head.

'Nah. We get on brilliantly. But no.'

'You really do get on brilliantly. You laugh at the same things, you're always chatting away. He's gorgeous. It's a shame you don't fancy him.'

'I know,' Etta said with a sigh. 'But it's not there.'

'It might come. You know, a thunderbolt and you both see each other through new eyes and fall into bed and shag like mad.'

'Like you and Scott.'

'Yeah. You'd better believe it.' Mary made a funny growling sound.

Etta laughed.

'I've got some news myself.'

'Yes?' Etta's eyes went wide. Engagement to Scott the barman? Pregnancy?

'I'm going to Australia with Scott.'

'What? Oh my God. For good?'

'No, for a year.' Mary looked delighted. 'Isn't that great? I can't wait. Sunshine, beaches, barbies . . .'

'Big prawns. Beer. Snakes.'

'The first two are fine. Scott will save me from all the creepy crawlies.'

'I'm going to miss you!' Etta said, suddenly realising how far away Australia was.

'Of course you are. I'm the light of your life.' Mary giggled. 'Don't tell Mum. I'm going to tell her myself when I get the chance.'

'I don't know how she'll take it,' Etta said. 'She'll be so upset.'

'Yeah. I know.'

That afternoon, when Mum had come back from an advance screening of a new film and was scribbling on her notes at the kitchen table, Etta said lightly, 'Are you going out with Henry, Mum?'

Mum looked up. 'What? Oh no, darling. We're just friends.'

'Are you going to go out with him? I just wanted to say that Mary and I are fine with it, if you do. We don't think it's too soon after Dad, if you know what I mean.'

Mum smiled, her eyes filling with tears. 'Oh darlings. That's sweet of you. I'm glad you're okay with that. But you know . . . I don't think it's going to happen.'

'You should think about it,' Etta said. 'You two seem on the same wavelength.'

'Do we?'

Etta nodded. 'I mean, he's single and straight, clever and good-looking. You like the same stuff. You seem perfect for each other.'

Mum looked thoughtful and then frowned. 'Well, I think it's a bit like you and Charlie.'

Etta was surprised. 'What do you mean?'

'You're friends, aren't you? Not romantic.'

'No, not romantic.'

Mum picked up her pen again. 'Good.'

'Good? Why do you say that?'

Her mother shrugged. 'I don't know really. Charlie is

389

lovely but I don't really see you together. I think you need someone . . . else. That's all.'

'Oh. Well, luckily I agree. And so does Charlie.'

'I think that's how I feel about Henry. He's a good friend. But I can't see us together, that's all.'

'Do you think you'll ever marry again?' Etta said after a moment.

'To be honest, darling, no. I don't think marriage and I go very well together. But don't let that stop you. Now, I must get these notes down while the film is fresh in my mind . . .'

Etta went back to making tea, feeling the weight of her knowledge of Mary's departure lying heavy on her. This was going to disrupt Mum like anything. It was a shame that she wasn't in a relationship with Henry – she would need someone to lean on when her daughter left.

I suppose she will just have to lean on me.

Chapter Twenty-Three

FLICK

1980

Flick found the absence of Rob from her life one of the hardest things she had ever had to bear.

They had been intimately entwined with each other for so long: those transatlantic calls – her phone bill had been simply epic but she'd never cared about that – and the hours of talking. It had held her up in ways she had never quite understood until now.

But I had to set him free.

It had felt so counter-intuitive to say no when Rob had finally offered her something she had always longed for: his heart, just for her. The chance of a life together. The togetherness she craved. Why on earth had she turned him down?

She didn't know. All she knew was that it had felt right at the time. But afterwards, in the chill of loss, she regretted it. She missed him so much, it was a physical pain. She would lie in bed, moaning with it, longing for him to call her, fighting with her desire to call him. She didn't do it. It wasn't fair, considering that she had refused him and told him to marry

Mindy and have children with her. And the thought of that actually happening was exquisitely painful.

Why did I do it?

But there seemed no way to put it right.

The next blow was losing Mary, who had announced her departure for Australia with much excitement and happiness.

'That's wonderful news, darling!' Flick had said. They were sitting around the kitchen table after a Sunday lunch of roast chicken, the only thing Flick could really cook successfully. She forced herself to smile. 'I'm so happy for you!'

'Thanks, Mum.' Mary had smiled at her. The fissure between them had not been healed but it was now ignored. Mary was distant from her in some fundamental way and they had never talked about the situation with Caius and what had happened. Flick simply had to live in ignorance and hope that her worst fears weren't realised. She had apologised to Mary for not telling her the truth in the past, and although Mary had seemed to accept it, she never really came back to Flick in a meaningful way. Flick didn't feel forgiven.

And now she's going away. Leaving me. She might never come back.

Despite feeling desperate at Mary going halfway around the world, Flick put a brave face on it, and she and the girls and Scott had a happy conversation about all the adventures awaiting them in Oz. Mary wanted to take a camper van around the Continent but Scott was keen on sailing and was more drawn to sea voyages.

'A camper van is best, don't you think?' Flick asked, who hated the water. 'But of course you must do whatever you want.'

Etta chatted away as well, throwing in her opinions and being open about her envy of all the sea and sunshine that Mary was going to enjoy.

'You should come and visit,' Mary suggested, and Flick felt a stab of horror at the idea of both girls being so far away.

'We'll see,' Etta said, glancing at her mother. 'Maybe. In a bit.'

And Flick felt a little happier.

Henry had taken her for dinner at a French bistro near Cambridge Circus. These dates with him were a comfort to her, but every time she was reminded how unlike Rob he was. Henry couldn't read her mind in the way that Rob did. She was always having to explain how she felt, and somehow Henry often got the wrong end of the stick, or seemed not to care as much as she thought he might.

'I'm not looking forward to Mary going,' she said, as they ate their French onion soup. 'It's going to break my heart.'

'That's a bit extreme, isn't it? It's just an extended holiday. It will seem like she's hardly gone before she gets back.' Henry smiled at her.

She gazed back. 'I suppose so,' she said after a moment.

'Of course you're going to miss her,' he conceded. 'I suppose I'm used to not seeing Charlie for long periods. Perhaps I don't feel quite the same way.'

'Well . . . I don't know.'

'You do feel things very keenly, don't you?'

Flick didn't know what he meant. Was it possible to feel things more intensely than other people? She just felt what she felt, and assumed that everyone else experienced life in more or less the same way. But Henry was cool, rather removed, even while he was very friendly and more and more affectionate.

She wasn't sure how she felt about him. He was pleasant company. He was just right for her in many ways. Gloria was very keen on him, that was obvious. After all, she had thought him the ideal partner for Flick all those years before, and now she was thrilled that Flick seemed to be getting on so well with a man from the right bracket.

He's attractive. He's good company: intelligent, funny, educated . . .

But something made her keep her distance from him. That discomfort that she'd felt when she saw him at Jonathan's funeral still echoed inside her, even though she had grown quite fond of him over the last few months.

'Feel things keenly? I suppose so. I just don't like to think of Mary so far away, but I think that's normal . . .?'

'Of course it is.' Henry put out his hand and put it on her arm. 'I didn't mean anything else. You know I adore you exactly as you are, don't you, Flick?'

She smiled, uncertain, and nodded. Then quickly changed the subject.

Flick sobbed from the moment they got into the car for the airport.

Everyone else tried in vain to keep things cheerful, with

Mary talking excitedly about all the things they would do in Australia, and Scott reassuring Flick that she could visit any time, and that a year would go very fast. But Flick was inconsolable.

She had a great sense of horror that they were being parted without having properly made their peace. She was desperately afraid that it was too late. Life had seemed to be about missed chances lately. Was she missing another? And what if the worst happened and she never saw Mary again?

Those thoughts kept the tears flowing, though she tried to master them.

'Bye, Mum,' Mary said, giving her an enormous hug just before she disappeared through airport security, where they could not follow. 'Take care.'

'Oh darling!' Flick pulled her close, hugging her back. 'Darling, I'm going to miss you. Write to me, won't you?'

'Of course I will.'

Flick stared into Mary's face. 'You do forgive me, Mary . . . don't you?'

'Course,' Mary said, smiling. 'Ages ago. Don't worry about that.'

Flick wished that she could believe it. 'I love you.'

'Yep.' Mary let go of her and turned to Etta, giving her a tight hug too. 'Gonna miss ya,' she said in a silly voice.

'Going to miss you too,' Etta mumbled into her sister's denim jacket.

Mary let Etta go and took Scott's hand. 'Say goodbye to Granny for me! Bye, everyone!'

She sauntered through towards security and was gone.

Etta took Flick's hand. 'It's okay, Mum. It really is. I'm here.'

Flick nodded, full of love for her younger daughter. 'Thank you, darling. I know you are.'

'Let's go home. Airports are pretty depressing if you're not going anywhere!'

Flick stood on the small stepladder and reached up high onto the top of her wardrobe. The dust up there was thick and floated down in thick grey feathers, going up her nose and making it sting.

'What on earth have I got up here?' she wondered out loud.

She was not someone who relished tidying, everyone knew that, but now she was determined to do a clear-out. Brinsley had asked her if she would like to take on one of the cottages on the estate as her own.

'You know the house is always open to you,' Brin had said when they'd had lunch a few months ago. He was on a rare trip to London to see his dentist, staying with Gloria, who was finally beginning to slow down and take life at a more sedate pace. He and Flick had arranged to go for lunch at their favourite restaurant off Shaftesbury Avenue, and over the h'ors d'oeuvres he had suddenly talked of Caundle. 'But I think you need your own place. Somewhere you can settle in, make your own and use to write in. You said you were going to start a book, don't you remember?'

'Yes . . .' Flick cut a slice off the terrine on her plate and smeared it over a piece of bread. 'I've been planning some-thing for ages. I need to get started.'

'Then how about two fresh starts? You start your book and you get the cottage. I would like to see more of you, and now Mary has gone off, and Samuel has his own place . . . well, I know you have Etta but she'll be spreading her wings soon too. I don't like to think of you rattling around in that house in Kensington with the empty flats beneath you, all alone.'

'I'm not so alone,' Flick said. 'I somehow manage to have a lot of parties without really meaning to. I think there is some kind of conspiracy among my friends to instigate them secretly, like forest fires.'

Brinsley laughed. 'I like that. But they all go home at the end of the night.'

'Usually.'

'Then you're on your own.'

'There *is* still Etta, don't forget. And Charlie lives in the flat under mine. And there's Henry.'

'Ah yes, Henry. Your escort.'

'My walker.'

It was their joke that Henry was her regular companion in the manner of a royal personage who needed someone to be the plus one in her glamorous life, but would never dream of actually touching.

'Still nothing there?'

Flick shook her head. 'Not really. I think he wants more, but I'm not ready.'

'You mean, he's going to declare his love to you?'

'It feels like that. I'm a bit worried about it. Not sure what to say.'

'Are you sure he isn't a good prospect?' Brinsley asked. 'He seems perfect, if I'm honest. Even I can see that he's a handsome and charming man.'

'Yes, he is.' Flick thought about how Henry had slowly made himself indispensable to her. It reminded her sometimes of the way that Jonathan had made it his mission to look after her, when in fact it had been her looking after him – except it was more subtle in Henry's case. And Henry was sophisticated, witty and fun where Jonathan had been more wholesome in a way, with his cooking and gardening. She had found herself wondering lately if life with Henry might be something she would enjoy. And it had been a very long time since she had shared her bed with anyone. She was getting on, perhaps there would come a time when no one would want her any more and she might regret not taking the opportunities that had come along. Who didn't want to be held and caressed and kissed? It was a fundamental need, one that she had pushed away when Jonathan became ill and moved downstairs, and one that she had learned to live without until it was so familiar that she was almost afraid of something different.

Her physical connection with Caius had been so strong, and look how that had turned out.

But perhaps it was time to try again. And maybe now she would find out if physical connection and real affection was something that could grow just by doing it. A kind of act of will.

'But perhaps we will see,' Flick said to Brin and he smiled. 'I think you'd be happier. I'd like to see that.'

'What about you, Brin? Is anything happening in your love life?'

Brinsley laughed. 'No.'

'Can I ask something? Are you . . . gay?'

He shook his head. 'I think you would have known before now if I were. The truth is, I have had some brief relationships, but nothing serious. I lost my heart when I was young and it didn't work out. In fact, it never even got started.'

'Really?' Flick was amazed. 'Who was that?'

'Can you guess?'

'No! Who was it?'

'Beautiful Diana.'

'Diana!' Flick stared at him, seeing her brother look bashful for one of the first times. 'You were in love with her?'

'Of course. But she was Edmund's girl, so I never showed it. You can't think how happy I was when he got engaged to Marissa. But five seconds after that, she married Alfred.'

'Oh Brin! She should have married *you*. She only married Alfred to escape.'

'I know. It was hard to bear.' Brinsley shrugged. 'But I had no choice. And no one else has ever lived up to her – the most beautiful, clever, wonderful girl I ever met.'

'Brin . . . I'm sorry. Shall I ask her to visit?'

'Don't be silly. It's far too late. And I'm happy on my own.

Don't forget . . . you've got a cottage now. So you can come and visit me all the time.'

'Thank you, Brin. And thank you for the cottage. I think it sounds like a lovely idea.'

That was what had led Flick to start clearing out her flat.

She was going to make a fresh start, and work out what things she would take to furnish the cottage, and what things she would get rid of. The whole place would be aired and cleaned and then, she thought, redecorated. It would mark the end of her life with Jonathan, and a new stage.

The Flick who writes books and sees her family and maybe even has a partner.

She had more or less decided after her lunch with Brinsley that she would give Henry the chance that he had clearly been longing for. He had been hinting more and more broadly that he had feelings for her and wanted to move their relationship into something deeper. She had already had to do some judicious dodging of overlong goodnight hugs and kisses that were a little too intense to be simply those between friends.

She sighed. *If only I could feel with Henry the intensity of connection and the yearning I felt with Rob, then everything would be all right.*

She pulled down old boxes and bags from the top of her wardrobe, tossing them onto the nearby bed, which would need changing after the clouds of dust had settled on the linen. Finally, the top was clear and she climbed down to start examining what she had been hoarding for so long.

It appeared mostly to be old clothes and bags and the odds and ends that always seemed to accumulate: buttons, ribbons, odd socks and gloves, a squashed hat, and a quantity of old scarves. Flick made a pile of things to be thrown out, hard though that was, and of things she would keep.

She noticed a plastic bag that was crisp with age and opened it. Peering in, she saw that the contents were of beige fabric, and she put her hand in to pull them out. She found she was holding a raincoat, heavier and bigger than most of her coats, and she unfolded it slowly. It had stayed in remarkably good condition, she thought, with no rotting at all, though the lining looked a little frayed in places.

When did I ever have this raincoat? she thought in surprise. It was not immediately familiar.

Then, as she gazed at it, she began to feel a creeping sense that she did know this coat, and that it was connected in her mind with something unpleasant.

Standing stock still in her bedroom, she turned the raincoat around in her hands and a memory began to form in her mind. This was a man's raincoat. Too big for her. But it had covered her when she'd needed it.

When was that? When did I need it?

Then it hit her and she gasped with shock.

This was the raincoat that she had put on that morning in Henry's apartment. The morning after going to that club with him, she had woken alone in a bed, naked, her clothes on the floor beside her. The sheet beside her had been rumpled as though someone had been there at some point.

She had got up feeling ill, so very ill, and also afraid and worried that she had had sex.

Had I? she thought, astonished. She did not remember knowing this even at the time. She had not let that thought cross her mind. It was an encounter of which she had no memory at all.

Of course you did. And you told Rob about it the next day. While you were holding this raincoat. The voice in her mind sounded as clear as a siren.

Did I?

She realised she had not told him about waking up in a strange bed. She had told him about finding out the truth about Jonathan, and that was all.

Flick sank down on the bed, oblivious of what was on there, and held the raincoat against her. She had found the coat on the back of Henry's bedroom door and she had put it on, over her evening gown, which was all she had to wear from the night before.

She was shaking from head to foot. She and Henry must have had sex all those years ago. He had never referred to it again, probably out of a sense of decorum. But surely he remembered? Perhaps that was why he felt he could resume that kind of relationship with her.

How could I have forgotten?

She could remember now the sound of the shower, slipping out of the apartment and going back to her hotel, feeling grim. She had suppressed it but now it was clear in her mind.

Oh my God.

He had surely taken advantage of her? She had no memory

of anything after the club. It must have been obvious that she could not consent and yet he must have still gone ahead anyway. Or had she consented? Had she even asked him to?

It's too shaming that I can't remember!

Twenty years later, he had walked back into her life. And she had welcomed him.

She closed her eyes. The flood of memory brought everything from that time crashing back into her mind as though she had lived it all yesterday, and with the torrent of pictures came that crystal-clear voice, her own voice, slightly gravelly now after years of smoking. It was telling her the things that she had been shutting out of her mind for years and years.

I don't want to hear it!

She put her hands over her ears as though she could shut out the voice inside her head, but one word became louder and more insistent.

Etta.

There it was.

She could say it now. It had taken all this time and the feeling of a raincoat in her hands to let her say it.

I don't know who Etta's father is.

Flick stood up, feeling faint.

But I do know that it might be Henry.

PART FOUR

Chapter Twenty-Four
ETTA
1990

Burnout.

That's what her doctors and her therapist had called it.

'You've got burnout, Etta. You're going to have a breakdown.'

She wanted to say, 'You try working for a fucking megalomaniacal, highly demanding film producer. And even by New York standards, he is kind of impatient, so you can imagine what he's like. He wants the work done almost before he's told me what it is. And before I can get started, we have to race around the desk a couple of times while he tries to squeeze my tits and my arse or anything else he can get his dirty hands on. I have to keep him sweet and keep my job. Now add in a serious social life, at least half of which is work, so I have to do it. Parties, premieres, schmoozing, lunches, promotions . . . My life is awash with booze and seriously lacking in sleep. Now let's put the cherry on top of this ice-cream sundae and that's Mattie, my gorgeous actor boyfriend, who has the most appalling substance addiction problem, and who is either stoned, high or completely drunk nearly all the time, including on the recordings of his hit TV show which, thank God, he films in LA so I don't get too close to that situation. I know I should break up with him, but his melting eyes and fabulous body keep me addicted to him, while the drugs will always be his first love.'

Instead, she said, 'Yeah, I guess it's burnout. What should I do? Are there pills for that?'

In the end, the decision was made for her when Etta's boss finally got tired of the fact that she would neither massage him nor allow him to caress her, when there were a lot of girls who could do Etta's job and let him do everything he wanted on the floor of his office when the urge took him, which it did frequently.

'He fired me,' she said to Rob Gerstein over lunch in a restaurant near his office.

'Good.'

'Good?' She leaned towards Rob, indignant. 'Good? He fired me!'

'He's a pig, Etta,' Rob said, fixing her with a serious look while cutting up his steak. 'If Xeno Bridgewater's reputation has managed to get around the book world, then you can be sure he's pretty bad. If he's bad by film standards, he's appalling. I hated the fact that you worked for him so I'm glad you're fired and if you got away without serious harassment, then even better.'

Etta shrugged. 'He never really tried to force me. I think it's the English accent. He seemed to think I was some kind of minor royalty. Or too much of a lady. Something like that.'

'Thank Christ for that,' Rob said feelingly. 'But if he'd ever touched you . . . I would have personally helped you slap a giant harassment suit on him.'

'But he's so famous and successful, I couldn't do that.'

'And that's what lets guys like him get away with it.' Rob made an expression of distaste. 'So what are you going to do? Get another job?'

'I'm going to look about, I guess.' She had picked up the slightest twang of an American accent in the years that she'd been living here in Manhattan. She had a tiny shoebox of an apartment in midtown, which she'd decorated like a tiny English country house, with floral wallpapers, cosy chairs and flea market antiques. Not that she was in it terribly often.

'Maybe you could take a break?' suggested Rob.

As soon as she got her job in Manhattan, she had asked Mum for Rob's number so that she could get in touch. Mum had been uncharacteristically awkward around Rob.

'I don't know if you should trouble him,' she'd said, pink-faced. 'I'm sure he'd love to hear from you . . . but he might have a lot going on. He might be married by now.'

'You don't know?' Etta had asked, surprised. 'I thought you guys kept in close contact.'

'We've grown apart a little,' Mum said, looking away. 'I'll give you his number. And send him my love when you talk to him.'

Rob had been delighted to hear from her, and had immediately offered to show her around. He had been keeping an eye on her ever since. They had a regular weekly lunch when she regaled him with all her news and adventures and he listened, and laughed, or frowned and told her to be careful.

It was good to know he was looking out for her, and she had called him once or twice late at night to help her get home when she was lost and cold and had no money on her except a coin for a telephone call.

Sometimes they would talk about Flick or Rob would say, 'And so, how is your mother?'

Etta told him a bit about what she knew, and was surprised that he didn't seem to know any more than she told him. Weren't they in touch at all any more? Why not? Mum hadn't said anything about a falling-out, and Rob was wonderful to Etta, just as he'd always been. So Etta filled him in on the news instead.

She told him that Mum was still single after all this time. She had quite suddenly called off her relationship with Henry completely, and not long after had asked Charlie to move out as well. She said it was because she was selling up and, sure enough, she sold the Kensington house with its four crazy flats, buying one large, elegant Bloomsbury flat instead, so that she had a London base, and then had moved to live at Caundle practically full time.

Etta had felt a pang when she'd heard their old home was gone. But Samuel was married and had gone to live in Manchester where he did a doctorate and then became a professor. He was writing serious economics books now as well, following in his father's footsteps but with more dedication and acclaim. He had two children, and seemed busy and happy. Mary was still in Sydney, but not with Scott, who had exited the scene after a few months. She was now living in a community in central Sydney and, at weekends and for long

stretches, went to the community's farm up the coast, the
scene of retreat, meditation and, Etta suspected, some drug
taking.

Mary had been back to visit a few times, and it was obvious she was happy. Flick had been nervous that she was
following in Jonathan's footsteps towards the drug-induced
psychosis that had destroyed him, but Mary stayed anchored
in reality and appeared in control of herself.

Flick also feared Mary would never come home, and
would never find a path in life, but Etta felt that whatever
kept Mary happy and alive was a good thing. She had always
sensed a yearning for some kind of oblivion in her sister, and
as long as Mary had things and people to live for, she would
surely be okay. She found a freedom and contentment in Australia that she could not find here, that was plain.

And then Etta left for her once-in-a-lifetime chance to
work in New York. Considering how much film production
was in LA, this opportunity to work in New York was not
to be missed. Etta had been thoroughly excited when her boss
suggested she apply for the Girl Friday role at Bridgewater
Pictures. 'I don't want to lose you, but we're not big enough
to promote you. Working for Xeno would be an amazing
chance.' With a glowing reference from her boss and a thrilling trip to New York for an interview, Etta had bagged the
position but then worried about leaving Mum, who told her
not to be so stupid.

'I'm going home to Caundle,' she said simply. 'And I'm
going to be perfectly all right.'

Mum *had* been perfectly all right, just as she'd promised,

writing a book that had gone on to win her quite a few prizes. Etta had been thrilled for her. It was a much-deserved triumph that capped her career in writing and journalism – she had hung up her film reviewing boots now that she could not get easily to London cinemas.

Now Etta sat back in her chair at the restaurant and considered Rob's words. Take a break? She didn't know how to do that any more, after years of living at the skittering Manhattan pace.

'And,' Rob said sternly, 'what about this waste-of-space guy you're seeing? He's next on my list of things to be jettisoned.'

'Mattie? But I love him.' Etta's eyes went round. She had been as surprised as anyone when the biggest sitcom star in town wanted to go out with her. One catty girl at a party had suggested that it was Etta's closeness to her famous boss that was the lure. If you were the lead in a Bridgewater film, you were almost guaranteed an Oscar. And if you didn't get that, then fame and riches would have to do. She had told Rob about the suggestion that Mattie was using her, and he had looked cynical and said, 'Don't discount it, baby.'

Now he said, 'Does cute little Mattie know that you're fired from Bridgewater Pictures?'

'Not yet.'

'Why don't you tell him right away? Just so we can make sure that he is on the level and not in actual fact wanting to get close to Xeno.'

'Yeah, well, okay, I will,' Etta said tartly because she didn't want to think that of Mattie.

'Good. Then make me a promise. If Mattie dumps you, you'll stop looking for another job. You'll sublet your apartment if you don't want to give it up, and you'll go home and get some goddamned sleep. Stay with your mother. Go to that beautiful house in Dorset.' Rob shook his head. 'Sometimes I wonder if you girls know how lucky you are to have it.'

'It's Uncle Brinsley's.'

'You know what I mean.' Rob put down his knife and fork. 'Okay. Seriously. Do you promise, Etta? I'm worried about you.'

'If you want me to, I will,' she said heroically. 'But Mattie is not going to let me down.'

That was how Etta found herself on the flight to London only a couple of weeks later, waved off by Rob Gerstein and told sternly not to come back until she had recovered completely.

'Get some of that filthy stuff out of your system,' he'd advised.

'I don't take drugs!' she'd protested.

'Sure. I bet that creep Mattie made you do something with him. I am just glad the asshole decided to dump you.'

'I can tell. And it was actually very painful!'

But, Etta had to admit on the plane home, it wasn't that painful. In lots of ways it was a relief. Dating someone famous was like dating a crowd. There were always people around them, coming up to them, offering to do this or that or the other. The only times they were alone they were either in bed or Mattie was getting high or stoned. 'Don't want to get photographed doing *this*,' he would say, chopping out another line or sticking a pill under his tongue.

'Nope!' Etta would agree, thinking how amazing it was to be with a big star all on her own but also thinking that this was possibly the most boring way to spend time she could imagine. Later, if they went dancing, life would look up. If Mattie took MDMA, then there would be frantic dancing for hours, raving away in the clubs till dawn. That had been fun, although going straight to the LA office after a quick shower was not.

Commuting between LA and New York had also been draining.

Maybe that was partly why she was so completely exhausted. Mum had been so happy when she'd heard that Etta was coming home.

'You must come and stay with me at Caundle,' she said. 'This is just the place to recover. Home always is.'

Etta was shocked when she saw her mother waiting for her at the airport. She'd come back home a few times while in her New York phase, but she had never seen Mum looking quite so bird-like. As always, she had an air of Bohemian glamour in her black outfit, dark glasses and the fair-to-grey hair twisted up in a messy bun behind. She had a 1960s look, with a touch of the French intellectual, and the red lips of a film star.

Always effortless, Etta thought.

But Mum was thinner, that was obvious, and her skin paler. Her hands, too, were craggier, the knuckles larger as if she had bulked them up with all the typing she had done over the years.

Mum's eyes misted over when she saw Etta coming out of Arrivals with her luggage. 'Darling!' she yelled. 'Over here! I'm here!'

As though I might miss her! She's unmistakable and stands out like a beacon.

Etta went over and embraced her.

'You are too thin,' pronounced Mum, looking her up and down. 'But gorgeous. What has New York done to you?'

'You're the same,' rejoined Etta.

'Dreadful flattery. Come on. Someone is driving us home. I can't do that long motorway thing any more, I get too sleepy. Oh Etta, darling, it is so wonderful to see you!'

It took only a few minutes for Etta to feel as if she'd never left Britain. The cars were back on the right side of the road, the dear old lettering on the signs, the bushes and hedges the way they should be. She had not been homesick at all until now, when she was back, feeling tearful at how much she'd missed it all.

'Tell me all the news,' she said to her mother.

'Oooh. Well, now. It's all go at Caundle.' And Mum launched into a long talk about the state of the farm and the house and all the personalities involved, none of whom meant anything to Etta.

At last Etta said, 'Well, that's all fascinating. But how about the family?'

'Brinsley's much the same, but he's suffering from arthritis in his ankles. They were weak when he was a boy. Prue exactly the same, cousins all well; you will cross paths with them I expect. The lovely thing is the closeness, how everyone is in and out and connected. I never knew how comforting that could feel.'

'Oh lovely. That will be nice.'

'And look at you, so sophisticated.' Mum reached over, took her hand and squeezed it. 'You've blossomed into a beauty. I always knew you would.'

Etta felt a rush of pleasure at her mother's praise. She caught a tiny glimpse of herself in the rear-view mirror and she knew it was true. It had taken years but suddenly, she had grown into herself, and now she was a willowy brunette, long dark hair spilling over her shoulders, and her brown eyes liquid and enormous in her face. Those full lips were her greatest feature now, softening her strong nose and determined chin. 'Thanks, Mum.' She returned the squeeze.

'So . . . any boys?'

Etta thought of Mattie and the drugs and the all-nighters and the reckless squandering of the endless dollars that flowed towards him like lava from a volcano. 'No,' she said. 'I'm single again. And Rob was relieved, I can tell you! He didn't like my last boyfriend.'

'Well, I trust Rob,' Mum said quietly after a moment. 'So I'm glad you're single again. And he looked after you, didn't he? Rob, I mean.'

'Oh yeah, he was like a surrogate father to me.' Etta grinned.

'Good,' Mum said, but she seemed sad. 'And how is he

coping? Does he have anyone new since he broke up with Mindy?'

Etta had kept Mum abreast of what was happening with Rob, sensing they were not talking any more, for some reason. She had told her about Rob and Mindy breaking up, and then Mindy getting married only six months later. She shook her head. 'No. Mindy still goes round all the time to check on him, and he loves her kids. He's great with them. But he's pretty much on his own these days.'

'Oh,' Mum said, looking out of the window. 'That's what I thought.'

'Did you two fall out?' Etta said. 'You don't seem to have been in touch for years.'

'I suppose we did in a way.'

'But why?'

'It's hard to explain. I miss him, though.'

'Can't you make up? He's such a wonderful guy and you were always so close.' It occurred to her that the two of them were both alone, both single. It seemed crazy that they were no longer each other's best friends.

'I hope so. One day. It depends on Rob, really.'

'Oh.' Etta was puzzled. She hadn't got that impression at all while in Manhattan. 'I didn't realise.'

'It's just one of those things. But I'm so happy he's looked after you. I'm grateful to him for that.'

It was nearly three hours' drive back to Dorset and darkness was falling by the time they turned into the driveway at Caundle.

'I still can't get used to coming back here,' Mum said quietly. 'I wanted to leave it so much. I hoped I would never see it again. Now it feels the only true home I ever had.'

Etta watched as the house at the end of the drive grew bigger, its mullioned windows softened by the golden light behind them. She had a sudden thought. 'But I haven't asked you about Granny!'

'Ah, well, funny you should say that. I was just about to mention her. Granny is here. At Caundle.'

'What? Really?' Etta couldn't remember ever having seen her grandmother at Caundle. 'But why?'

'That's the curious thing,' Mum said, as the car took a turning just before the main house to head out towards the cottage. 'She says she's come back to Caundle to die.'

'What?' Etta was startled.

Mum gave her a look. 'I know. You can just imagine. She's making an enormous meal out of the whole thing. So I promised Brinsley that we would help him by moving into the main house for a while. We'll have tonight on our own and go back over tomorrow. It's rather a lot for him to handle on his own.'

'But why does Granny think she's dying?' asked Etta, dismayed. 'I didn't even know she was ill.'

'She isn't. There's a distinct whiff of performance about this whole thing. She's come down like a tragic actress to play her final and greatest role. Whether she actually dies or not is another matter.'

'Our family is bonkers,' Etta said, shaking her head.

'You can say that again. Welcome home, darling.'

*

The cottage was lovely, done in Mum's trademark style of faded rugs, lamps, pictures, books and mirrors, with flowers drooping in jugs and cushions everywhere, artfully disarranged and slightly chaotic and yet somehow a whole. Etta felt immediately at home, just as she had on her previous visits, delighted to have her own cosy room with a comfortable bed made up in soft linen, and full, double-lined chintz curtains at the little casement windows.

'I wish we were staying here,' she said, when they had reconvened in front of the wood stove that Mum kept burning even in summer as the cottage had thick walls and was often chilly. 'I don't really feel like going back to the big house.'

'I know.' Mum made a face. 'But needs must. Now, I've opened a bottle of wine and made some macaroni cheese. I know how you love it.'

'Oh, I do!' Etta said happily. 'I've come from the land of mac and cheese but it's nothing like what you make.'

'One of the few things I can make,' Mum said, smiling. 'Along with roast chicken.'

They sat down with trays on their laps by the fire, and Mum listened while Etta told her stories of her life in New York.

'Have you heard from Mary?' Etta asked at last.

'Not much lately. I'm sure she's fine.' Mum looked thoughtful as she ate a last forkful of macaroni. 'It's funny how things turn out. Mary seemed destined to burn bright and you seemed such a mouse. Now she's a hippy, probably for life, and you're a glamorous young thing in the film world.'

'Yes.' Etta speared a curl of pasta. 'Things never quite turn out as you expect.'

'Don't unpack,' Mum advised. 'We'll move up to the house tomorrow.'

'How long will we be there?'

'I suppose that depends on how long it will take Granny to die, darling. Everything hinges on that.'

Granny was lying in a vast four-poster bed in the main bedroom, which looked out over the parkland and woods around the front of the house. She was, of course, striking, although her purple hair was now a wig, concealing her real, thinning grey locks. Propped up by many pillows, she wore a pale green satin dressing gown, and was heavily made up including huge false eyelashes, despite her approaching demise.

'Darling Etta, you're here! My dying wish has come true.' Granny stretched her hands out towards her. 'If only Mary were here too. Still, I must be satisfied with what I can get. Come and kiss me!'

Etta advanced into the room. All her New York poise and sophistication deserted her in Granny's presence. She was back to being a gawky schoolgirl, the least interesting person in the family.

Brinsley had warned them when they arrived that Gloria was really going for it.

'She seems to want to win some sort of Oscar for best dramatic performance,' he said, rubbing his glasses on a small

lint cloth. 'But I can't yet tell exactly what she thinks is wrong with her.' He smiled at Etta. 'I'm so glad you could come back for all of this.'

'Happy to help,' Etta said, smiling back.

'Prue's arriving soon. She says she'll summon the children if it looks serious.'

Etta looked between her mother and uncle. 'So we all think that this is nonsense?'

Mum sighed. 'We just can't be sure, that's the problem. She seems convinced she's in her final days. I suppose that time will tell.'

'How are you, Granny?' Etta asked now, when she was free of the heavily perfumed embrace.

Granny grew misty-eyed. 'Darling, I am on the brink, I can see the eternal stretched out before me. I stand on the threshold. It is quite an experience, I can tell you. I wanted to be back where it all began, where my darling Philip and I set out on married life. Where our children were born. Caundle! The cradle of my life.' She looked pleased with this and said, 'The cradle of my life,' a few times in poetic tones.

'What's wrong with you?' Etta ventured. 'Do you feel awful?'

'What is wrong with me? Life! My time is drawing to a close, it's inevitable. It comes to us all, you know that.' Gloria sighed and lay back across her pillows, closing her eyes for a moment. 'Darling, will you ring the bell for my breakfast? It's late. And perhaps we can play cards later?'

'Yes, Granny, I'll go and find where your breakfast is now.'

*

Etta felt a little cheated. She had come home to recover and be looked after and instead, Gloria had slipped in just before her and was now sucking up all the compassion in the house, whether it was offered or not.

It would help if there was something actually wrong, she thought crossly, taking up her grandmother's evening gin, which there was no question she would give up.

'My last small pleasures,' Gloria would say mournfully. 'Easing my passage.'

Despite lying all day in her bed, Gloria's powerful personality dominated the house and everyone tiptoed around as if she were actually an invalid. It was clear, though, that her strength was fairly undiminished. Etta could see why Brinsley had wanted them to move in, as if to dilute Gloria's dominance. It meant that they could share the duties of answering her bell, despite the live-in nurse who glided about, delivering potions, pills and medicines, plumping her pillows and massaging her. Gloria still required devotion and attention from everyone in the house.

Etta was surprised to receive a message written on a card and delivered to her room by a maid.

Darling. You could spend a little more time with your dying grandmother. I know you're young, with your exciting life before you, and I'm just a dreary old woman on her very last legs . . . but, darling, a few more minutes a day? Is it too much to ask? Your loving granny x

She stared at it, astonished. She had spent two hours the previous afternoon with Granny, playing endless rounds of gin rummy. What did she mean? Etta felt hurt and guilty and amused at the same time.

At breakfast she found she was not the only one to have a card.

Mum was showing Aunt Prue hers, and laughing. 'She wants me to smarten up a bit when I visit her. "Could you make a tiny effort for your mama? After all, I shall soon require no effort at all, for eternity."'

The sisters laughed together, shaking their heads at their mother's incorrigibility.

Brinsley said, 'She's asked me if I can make the dawn chorus a little quieter, perhaps with the use of scarecrows or a boy to wave the birds away.'

Prue said, 'She's been rather nice to me. Sorry, everyone.'

'That's because you're a countess,' Mum reminded her. 'Mother loves that. You've got a pass.'

'True.' Prue shrugged. 'I'm not a grand countess, but what can I do? That's how it is.'

'You could go and sit with her in your gardening clothes with filthy nails and bird's nest hair, and she'd still say you look adorable.'

The sisters laughed again, while Brin shook his head, smiling wryly.

'I'm afraid my card this morning had something a little demanding on it.'

They all turned to look at Brinsley.

He went on: 'Mother wants a grand tour of the house and grounds, in order to bid farewell to it before she dies.'

'What?' Mum said, looking bemused.

Brinsley nodded. 'We have to wheel her around the whole place. All of us.'

'Is this going a bit far?' Prue said, frowning and laughing at the same time. 'I mean . . . really?'

Brinsley sighed. 'There's always a chance she is going to die. We can't refuse. The grand tour is this afternoon, and we're all up for it, I'm afraid.'

If Etta hadn't thought her family was eccentric before, she would have now as they processed Gloria around the house on a tour that seemed to last hours. Gloria looked astonishing in a feathered bed wrap, wig and full make-up, a cushion propped behind her in the wheelchair. Her nurse followed the procession carrying a glass of champagne, which Gloria would call for at various moments, in order to make a toast.

'To life!' she would announce, holding the glass high, apparently oblivious to the fact that she was the only person with a drink, then sipping the champagne and dabbing away tears.

She toasted rooms for their memories, or toasted absent friends who sprang to mind, or anyone or anything that occurred to her. The glass was frequently refilled.

The family followed behind in a procession, as two strong estate workers carried the chair up and down stairs when needed, and then finally out into the garden.

Etta was torn between amusement and a simmering anger

424

that they were all under so much control, forced to attend to Gloria's every need. Why didn't they just tell her what they really thought, and have done with it?

And yet, she understood why. Even as she resented trailing after Granny, she also knew that it was not too much to ask, to indulge an old woman who was really asking them to show how much they loved her, and asking them to understand that she knew her life was going to draw to a close before too long. She wanted their attention while she was still her old self, and to make an indelible last impression on their hearts and minds.

Don't forget me, she seemed to be saying. *This is my place and it always will be! I won't ever leave, not while you remember this.*

When Etta saw this, she couldn't help loving her spoiled grandmother, who had lived a life of vast wealth and great emptiness, and who was now afraid that perhaps she had concentrated on the wrong things and had missed what really mattered along the way. And she was too old to change now – still demanding that her wants be fulfilled instead of truly reaching out to connect and offer herself up to love others.

Etta watched her mother, staying close to Gloria the whole time, politely doing whatever was required. She knew that Mum had never received what she really wanted from Gloria: that unconditional love that gave itself because it wanted to.

It was no wonder, perhaps, that Mum had been so alone so much of her life, always trying to prove that she was strong and independent enough not to mind, or striving to win that approval, from men, from the world, or, at last, simply from her mother herself. But even her literary success had not brought Granny's praise.

'I have written several books myself,' Granny had said afterwards. 'I suspect you get your talent from me. Of course, I haven't had mine published but John Betjeman told me I had one of the great minds of the age. So perhaps I should think about sending them out to someone. You never know, *I* might win a prize!'

Etta's heart ached just remembering it. They had all laughed about it at the time, Mum more than anyone. But how could it not hurt?

She looked at her mother's slender frame as Mum walked behind Granny's wheelchair, obedient as a serving girl.

Mum wasn't perfect. But she tried her best with us. She's shown us more love than she ever got herself, and that's a big achievement.

They were in the garden now. Granny had directed that she be wheeled to the clover-shaped pool at the end of the path, but the going on the gravel path was so tough that the muscled workers had picked up the wheelchair and were carrying it carefully, trying to keep the occupant as comfortable and stable as possible.

Etta dropped behind, taking in the beautiful surroundings. Watching the little group proceeding down the path, she was seized by the thought that she must value the time she had with Mum now, here at Caundle. Who knew when everything might change? Not everyone was going to be able to do a farewell tour, like Gloria. Life would sweep her and Mum apart again soon. Etta had so much she wanted to do, after all. Everything lay ahead and she could hear adventure and experience calling her like a distant bell. She would answer its summons soon.

But first I'll talk to her. Really talk to her. Tell her how much I love her. That's all that matters, in the end.

She crunched after the others to hear Gloria toast the pool.

Gloria was lifting her glass. 'I declare the family curse is lifted!' she announced. 'It will die with me! You're all free of it at last.'

'I wonder how she's arranged that,' Mum said out of the corner of her mouth as Etta came up to join her. 'She's obviously in league with some big names in the underworld.'

Etta giggled. 'It's good news for us.'

'Good news for you, darling, and I'm very pleased about it. But I'm afraid it may have come just a little late for me.'

Etta took her mother's hand and put a kiss on her cheek. 'Don't be silly. It's never too late. I promise.'

Chapter Twenty-Five

FLICK

1990

After the farewell tour of the house and grounds, Gloria retired to her bed, demanded that the blinds be drawn and the curtains shut. She lay in the darkness with her eyes closed, waiting for death to come. But despite her best efforts, she remained stubbornly alive. After four days, she gave in, and arranged to go back to her house in London.

Flick and Etta laughed themselves silly about it, once they were back in the cottage and away from the stifling atmosphere that had gripped the main house while Gloria was there.

'You've got to admit, Granny is a character,' Etta said, wiping away tears of laughter after Flick had done one of her impressions of Granny toasting the dining room table.

'She is certainly that,' Flick agreed. 'I look positively pedestrian by comparison.'

'I wouldn't go that far,' Etta said, shooting her a cheeky look. 'You might not be up to Granny's standards but you've got a touch of the old eccentrics yourself.'

Flick had smiled back, relishing the way she and Etta could

talk and laugh together. She could never imagine doing this with Gloria. She didn't think Gloria had laughed at anything Flick had ever said in her life. *Perhaps I never said anything funny around her.*

But she knew that it wouldn't have mattered if she had. Gloria would have nicked the joke, or told her that her sense of humour came from Gloria herself. It was always like that.

I'm going to forgive her and I'm going to look forward. I'm going to spend all the time with Etta that I can.

She knew in her heart that she needed to do this.

Because one day soon, I'm going to ask Etta to forgive me.

Gloria had been gone for some weeks, and Flick and Etta were enjoying the lazy rhythm of their days as the year wore on, and the park began to look tired of summer and ready to begin its slow withdrawal into its winter sleep.

A letter arrived for Flick and, reading it over her morning coffee before she started her writing day, she let out a loud whoop of surprise and pleasure.

'What is it, Mum?' Etta looked up from reading the morning paper, her mug of coffee halfway to her lips. She looked as gorgeous as ever, her long dark hair in a messy bun, wearing an oversized white shirt and pink capri pants. The weather was still warm enough for summer clothes.

'It's my friend Diana!'

'Who?'

'I've told you about her. We were at school together. I haven't seen her for years. She's the one who had the very glamorous life in New York in the sixties while I was stuck in the country.'

'Oh, that's nice. How is she?'

'She seems very well. Her life has moved on quite a lot in the last few years. But excitingly, she's in the UK. And she's suggested coming to visit.'

'Great. When?'

'Soon. This weekend.'

'Do you want me to make tracks so you guys can hang out?'

'You're so American,' Flick said with a laugh. 'We can hang out with you here. I've got the other bedroom for her – we're not short on space. Besides, she'd love to see you again. You probably don't remember her.'

'Not really.'

Flick sat back in her chair, happy. 'What a lovely thing. I can't wait to see her.'

Time had done its work on Diana, as it had on them all, and yet she had managed to hold it at bay with some success. She was perfectly made up, her skin only lightly lined, her hair still very dark and beautifully styled. She was dressed in an elegant linen travelling suit and accompanied by a set of matching suitcases in chestnut leather.

'You look completely amazing,' Flick said, after their delighted reunion at the railway station, as she drove Diana back to Caundle.

'Money, darling Flick. That's what it takes,' Diana said.

'I've got money and I don't look like you!'

'Then you're not spending it the right way. Beauticians, dermatologists, facial surgeons – good ones who know what they're doing – treatments . . . you name it, I do it. It's quite normal in civilised countries. It's only in this godforsaken place that women let themselves go so badly.'

Flick laughed. 'Oh Diana, you're just the same! I can't wait to catch up on all your news.'

'And I want to know how my distinguished friend, prize-winning author and columnist, is doing too.' Diana smiled at her, dimples in her cheeks. 'You look a little too thin for my liking. Is Brinny looking after you?'

'You should see my fridge, stuffed with milk and yoghurt and cheese from our very own farm. He's making sure I'm well fed and getting plenty of calcium.'

'I'm glad to hear it.' Diana looked out of the window. 'Oh, it's glorious. There're a lot of things wrong with this country but the beautiful countryside is not one of them. It's like a song outside the window.'

'Yes. We're so lucky. There's nowhere like it.'

They drove straight to the cottage where Etta was waiting with tea. Diana exclaimed over Etta's grown-upness, and wanted to hear all about life in Manhattan, which she knew so well herself. They swapped the basics over their teacups, Diana explaining that her own daughter, Madeline, was working in a school in Switzerland.

'She's a lovely girl, you'd like her so much. You must meet,' Diana said to Etta. 'She's coped admirably with so many changes. When I married Hartley, she was very young, he was all she knew as a father really. Then, when Hartley and I divorced, I really wanted to leave the States for a while so I went back to live in Paris. There was another little marriage there, nothing really, and while we were there, Madeline was able to travel between her father and me more often. So she got to know Alfred and that side of her family too, which was very nice for her.'

'Paris sounds wonderful!' Etta said, impressed.

Flick listened as Diana described her luxurious life in France, made possible by the enormous payout she had from Hartley that gave her security for life. Or it would have done, if Diana had not had such expensive tastes.

Flick loved hearing the way Diana made such funny stories out of her marriages and love affairs, and the things that had happened to her along the way. But there must have been sadness. Diana let slip that there had been a car accident of some kind that had left her injured and in pain for a long while. 'But you'd never know now!' she said cheerfully. 'And then, when I had spent my divorce settlement, I discovered work.' She gave Flick a mischievous look. 'Rather later than you, darling. I could never see what you got out of it. And to my surprise, I liked it. Property was always my passion, and I found that I had an eye for finding interesting houses and making them beautiful. And before I knew it, I was a businesswoman like something out of *Dynasty* – shoulder pads and fancy cars and all the rest.'

Flick said, 'You always had that eye for style. I'm not surprised you found a way to make it pay.'

'It's a little harder than finding a rich man, but in some ways a lot more rewarding.'

'I'm glad to hear it,' Flick said. 'Do you hear that, Etta?'

Etta laughed. 'Don't worry. I don't intend to be supported by anyone but myself – and you, Mum.' She threw a cushion towards her mother. 'So don't write me out of the will, okay?'

'Your daughter is wonderful,' Diana said, when they were having drinks on their own in the garden later. They had reminisced over their time in Oxford, and talked of their breakups and losses, but also of their blessings.

'She is. She's a marvel. Mary is too. I'm just sorry she's not here to meet you.' Flick lit up a cigarette to smoke while she sipped on her glass of rosé. Diana looked reproachful.

'Oh Flick, honestly. I can't believe it. You know that habit will not only kill you, it is also terrible for your skin. Wrinkles, dryness . . . awful! Give it up, won't you?'

'I've cut right down,' Flick said. 'Just a few in the evening with a drink.' She smiled. 'Besides, it might be too late anyway.'

Diana frowned. 'What do you mean?'

'Oh, nothing. I've been having some pain lately, that's all.'

'Pain?'

'Just a regular pain, in my arms and legs. I can't shake off my tiredness too.'

Diana looked concerned. 'You are looking thin.'

'Yes, I have lost a bit of weight.' As she said it, Flick realised she had been thinking about this for a long time without realising it. She had noticed the persistent ache in her limbs, and dismissed it; she sat for long hours, after all. So she got a special cushion for her chair, which made things more comfortable but didn't make the pain go away. She got a new mattress in case that was the problem. She took baths in the evening to ease it away.

Sometimes it seemed to go away for a while. But then it always came back, a little worse than before.

'Have you seen a doctor?' asked Diana. 'I would have seen three by now, at least.'

'No. I ought to. I'd rather not know in some ways.'

'That is very silly, ostrich-like behaviour. If you *are* ill, you need to catch it fast. You know that, don't you?' Diana stretched out a hand and took Flick's. She looked down at the swollen knuckles as she felt them. 'Do you have arthritis?'

'Well, I thought I might. But then, again, it's just ageing. And it's my typing. You know how much I do. This is just a symptom of that. It hurts like billy-o sometimes. I put ice packs on my hands.'

'I see.' Diana looked more concerned. 'I want you to see someone, Flick. I have a doctor I know in London. We'll make an appointment. Promise you'll come with me?'

'All right, you martinet. Of course I will. A trip to London with you will be fun even if we do have to see a ghastly doctor.'

But secretly she was glad that Diana was ordering her about. She knew that she never would have done anything for herself, and would never have told Etta about her pains.

'You shouldn't be so stupid, you dear old thing,' Diana said now. 'And stop that awful habit right now!'

'Message received,' Flick replied, stubbing out her cigarette only half smoked.

*

Diana actually sat with Flick and made her call a doctor on Harley Street for an appointment to discuss the symptoms that were tiring her so much.

'Do you want me to come with you?' she asked when Flick had obediently got herself an appointment for the following week.

'No. I'll go alone. I have some other meetings and things I want to do while I'm in London.'

'Of course, darling. I might spend the day with Brinsley. He's asked my advice about parts of the house he's hoping to restore and redecorate.'

'Has he?' Flick had been wondering about Diana's presence now that she knew the secret of Brinsley's unrequited love for her friend. Was it possible that it might be rekindled? She could see that time had made Diana less brash and more sensitive, and her new skills and interests were perfectly in line with Brinsley's. He was managing a good-sized business, growing his dairy concerns, improving and caring for the house and everything around it. He seemed happy alone, surrounded by his dogs and the devoted staff and estate workers, but also seemed to appreciate Flick's presence, and, in his quiet way, had been delighted when Diana arrived to stay. Perhaps the time was right for them.

Is that how it works? That a missed opportunity can come back to you, and be more right the second time than the first?

That thought made her desperately sad. Had she made the wrong decision when it came to Rob? She still missed him profoundly, so happy to have crumbs of news about him from Etta. But she felt unable to be the one to break the silence between them. That, surely, was up to him?

'This is such a wonderful place, Flick,' Diana said now. 'You're unbelievably lucky to have the gorgeous house that Brinsley has made so comfortable. Not to mention this park and all the beauty of the countryside.'

'I know I'm lucky,' Flick said. 'And I'm glad you're here to share it with me.'

But privately she was wondering if her luck had started to run out.

The appointment with the Harley Street doctor was a brisk but thorough overhaul of her physical condition, and an interrogation about all her symptoms.

'You are somewhat underweight; we will keep an eye on that. I think you certainly need to cut back on drinking, and no more of that smoking nonsense.'

'I've stopped now,' she said quickly.

'Good. I'll take some bloods and then we'll have you back before too long for some more tests which I'll need to book. I'm going to give you some iron supplements in the meantime. I want you to concentrate on the basics: good food, sleep, gentle exercise. That's our starting point.'

Flick emerged from the practice, had a quick lunch at a cafe nearby and then walked to Covent Garden to do some shopping. She realised that she was walking past the Garrick, and stopped to look at the fine old building and the steps that led up to its front door. The last time she had been here was with Henry. He was a member and had often taken her into the club for a drink or dinner in the fine drawing rooms and dining rooms.

As she was standing there staring at the door to the club, she heard someone murmur, 'Excuse me,' as he went to go up the steps, and turned to find she was looking at Henry himself.

He was exactly the same, perhaps a little more lined, but still the elegant gentleman she remembered. Now he gaped at her for a moment before pulling himself together. 'Flick. I can't believe it. Fancy seeing you here.'

'Yes. How strange.' They stared at one another.

'How are you?'

'I'm all right. I hope you are too. Nice to see you, Henry.' She turned to go, feeling the strangeness of seeing him again like this.

'Wait, Flick.'

She turned to see him looking almost agonised. 'Please don't walk away like this. Come and have a cup of tea with me. I haven't seen you in so long. Please – as friends?'

She hesitated. Then she realised that she had walked here on purpose, half hoping to see Henry. And here he was. 'All right. I'd like that.'

He took her in and found them a sofa in a quiet corner where they could talk in peace. Flick asked after Charlie, who was doing well writing for a political magazine, and Henry asked after the girls, surprised to hear that Mary was still in Australia. 'And I told you she'd be back in no time!' he said ruefully. 'That shows what I know.'

'We can all make mistakes.'

'Yes, we can. And I feel I made a mistake with you and yet I don't know what it was.' He leaned towards her, his eyes earnest. He was wearing a blazer, shirt and tie and chino trousers, the ultimate smart older man with his iron-grey hair and mature good looks. Any woman would surely be proud to be his partner. 'One day we seemed to be getting on very well, building a relationship. And the next, you wanted nothing further to do with me. But why? Can you tell me?'

She looked away and considered. She wanted to tell him. She wanted some kind of answer. The time felt right in a way that it never had before, and she was finding her courage. 'I remembered something about our night in New York all those years ago.'

'Yes?' He frowned, looking bewildered. 'What?'

'Well, obviously you told me about Jonathan. And about his wife and son. It was a shock, a terrible shock.'

'I know that. You were overwhelmed. I felt very bad about it afterwards. I could have been kinder in the way I told you.'

'But afterwards.' She flushed slightly. 'After that.'

'After that? What do you mean?'

'After the club.'

'There was no after the club. Not for me, at least.'

Flick stared at him, uncomprehending. 'What?'

'My dear girl. You dumped me. Left me at the club. Jilted me for a better prospect.'

She gazed at him in growing bewilderment tinged with anxiety as his meaning sunk in. 'I didn't leave with you?'

'No, darling. You left with the piano player. You seemed

to know him, although you were frightfully drunk. He said he knew you, that he'd take you back to your hotel and you insisted. And off the two of you went.'

'What was his name?'

'I don't know.' Henry laughed dryly. 'It was a quarter of a century ago, at least! He was a piano player in some dive in New York who I met for about five minutes.' He frowned. 'Wait. I remember his name. It's just come back to me. Keys. You called him Keys. And he called you Pug. You seemed to know one another quite well, to say the least. So I decided not to intervene. I hope that was the right decision.'

The blood had drained from Flick's face and she felt faint and sick.

No.

'So what about your raincoat?' she asked weakly.

'What raincoat?' Henry looked puzzled. 'You left me in the club and went off with that chap. I don't remember any raincoat, I'm afraid.'

He had to be telling the truth. Why would he lie? How could he know about Keys and Pug if he hadn't been telling the truth? And he had clearly not connected Keys with Caius, who was unknown then in any case, and their marriage barely talked about.

So everything I thought I knew is wrong.

'We never slept together.'

'No, I'm sorry to say that we didn't. And when you came back into my life, I thought that might be put right. But you ended everything completely out of the blue.'

She could hardly hear him. *Henry can't be Etta's father.*

But, to her horror and amazement, there was another possibility.

I can't believe it. But could it be Caius? Oh my God.

She had never seen the man in the shower that morning. She had no idea whose apartment it was. She had simply assumed it was Henry's because he was the last person she remembered.

But it wasn't him. It was Caius.

Somehow Flick got through the tea with Henry and then hurried off, saying she had to catch a train home. He had wanted to make another date to see her, obviously hopeful that they could reconnect, but she put that off. She couldn't begin to think about such things.

How did I find myself in this position?

Flick wandered to the river and sat on the Embankment looking out over its waters, watching the barges and riverboats going by but hardly seeing them. Only recently had she been able to admit to herself that she didn't know who Etta's father was. Now it was worse than that.

When Henry had said the name Keys, she had recalled something from that night – unless she was imagining it. It was a familiar presence, whose body and scent and touch she knew and still longed for, like a drug she had long ago given up but remembered with pleasure.

Flick slumped, her head drooping, shoulders hunched.

How could she and Caius have met again in that way? And if they had, had he made love to her? Because it was possible that she had opened herself to him with the joy and

440

relief of reunion, recalling their deep physical intimacy and wanting to taste it again, one more time.

And the next night she had spent with Rob, their one and only night together. The bitter irony of it made her want to laugh and cry at the same time. The worst and best nights of her life, so close together.

And then she had come home to Jonathan, and forgiven him.

That meant that Etta could be the daughter of any of those three.

She hated herself for this.

It's too dreadful. How can I ever tell her? I don't know how! She'll hate me, and so she should! Poor, wonderful, beautiful Etta. What on earth am I going to do?

Perhaps it was easier and kinder on everyone if Etta went on believing she was Jonathan's daughter.

Flick hoped that she wasn't simply being kinder to herself. She hated that she could not trust her memory. But even if she knew exactly what had happened in New York, she still would not know who had fathered Etta. Etta had arrived a few weeks early, but that could simply have made her on time.

So they would never know.

And what about Rob?

More than ever, she longed for him. These memories brought back that night with him too. But how could she tell him the truth about what happened? She had not told him at the time that she thought she'd had sex with Henry the night before the one they spent together, she was just too ashamed.

441

She wanted her time with him, and all its bliss, to erase whatever had happened before, and it had. She had let herself forget.

When Etta went to New York, Flick had been comforted knowing Rob would watch over her. But that's when she realised that she was afraid of going anywhere near the truth that had lain unspoken between them all these years.

That there was a chance that Etta might be his daughter.

And, it seemed, as equal a chance that she could be Caius's daughter too.

Chapter Twenty-Six
ETTA
1990

Etta was beginning to think about what she might do. She was feeling rested and, as a result, itchy to do a bit more. The prospect of some travel was interesting her at the moment, and she had half decided to go and see Mary in Australia.

She was lying in her bed idly looking through travel magazines when there was a knock on her bedroom door and Mum put her head around. 'I'm going out for a stroll. Do you fancy coming with me?'

'Sure.' Etta closed her magazine. She would rather have continued lazing and dreaming about white beaches and blue oceans and the blazing sun, but Mum hadn't been doing all that much strolling lately, so she decided to join her. She pulled on a baggy cardigan and slipped on some plimsolls. 'You need to tell me all about London.'

They went out and into the late-afternoon sun. The clocks were about to change, and there was an autumnal chill to the air. Etta wondered if she should have brought her coat. Mum was well wrapped up in an old tweed coat, multicoloured scarf and beret. They chatted as they made their way out of the cottage garden, along the road and into the park in front of Caundle.

'I don't know if you've noticed, but Diana and your uncle . . .' Mum said as they walked along the perimeter of the park, staying close to the iron railings. On the other side, in the fields, herds of dairy cattle were munching on the last of the summer grass.

'I had noticed that.' Etta smiled at her. 'He's been quite bouncy since she arrived. But I'm not surprised he's bowled over.'

'Diana is amazing,' Mum agreed. 'Elegant, charming, intelligent . . . I think he's been a fan of hers since we were all in Oxford together. But Diana was going out with Edmund Carrington then.'

Etta nodded. She knew of her famous cousin, seen so rarely that he had a kind of mythical status for them. His children, her Carrington cousins, were often in the society magazines, their exploits followed by the tabloid press. 'And you like having her here too.'

'I do. But she's going to leave the cottage and move into the main house. Not *with* Brinsley. But sort of.'

'Ah. Fancy that!' Etta laughed. 'It's rather lovely. Now . . . what did you get up to in London?'

They walked on for a moment and then Mum said, 'I need to talk to you about that actually. You see, I've been having a bit of bone pain for a while now. Diana insisted I make an appointment with a doctor. I'll be honest. He phoned me yesterday and he says there's some cause for concern. So I'm going back for scans and a biopsy.'

'Biopsy?' Etta felt a chill of fear.

'Taking a sample to test. There will be X-rays. There's a new thing called an MRI, a sort of sophisticated X-ray, which can take more detailed scans and give more information about what's going on.'

'What are they looking for?' Etta asked, although she could already hear the word echoing through her skull. She felt stiff and scared.

'Cancer.' Mum put an arm around her shoulders. 'I know. It's horrible. It might not be that. It could be arthritis, though that is also a bad diagnosis. The doctor was very positive. But he told me that there is a possibility of bone cancer.'

'Oh my God,' Etta said in a small voice. 'I can't believe it.'

This wasn't supposed to happen. It was Granny who was doing the dying thing. Not Mum. Mum was still young. Etta felt frightened and strangely calm at the same time. It would be all right. Surely she would be okay?

Etta said, 'Is that why you've given up smoking? And what can they do if it is cancer?'

'They'll see if they can find where it is, I suppose. They'll treat it with chemo and radiation. There's not much else they can do, unless it's in a specific place. If it's in a bone and isolated, then they can consider amputation.'

Etta gasped. Two minutes ago, Mum had been fine. Now they might be going to amputate something? What if it were in her hands? Mum couldn't live without typing or writing.

They stopped walking and Mum wrapped her arms around her, holding her tight. A well of misery and fear opened in Etta's stomach. She felt her eyes burn.

Mum said, 'It's all early days. We don't know anything yet. I'm going to be around for a while in any case, don't you worry. But I'm going back to London before too long for the tests. I wanted you to be prepared.'

'Thank you for telling me,' Etta said, choked. 'But oh Mum. I can't bear it!'

'You can. We all have to bear it. And Diana knows. She's going to stay here to help me if I need it. She'll help you too.'

Etta took her mother's hand and squeezed it. 'I'm with you too. As long as you need me.'

'Thank you, my sweetheart. Let's not tell anyone else yet. Not Mary. Not until there's reason to worry. Okay?'

'Okay.' Etta had so many questions but the weight of her fear and sadness quietened them.

They turned and began to walk back the way they had come.

Mum did not object when Etta suggested she join her and Diana on the trip back to London the following week. They took enough things for a short stay in the London flat, just in case they decided to stay a few days. There was talk of galleries and museums but none at all of doctors, hospitals, tests and diagnoses until the night they arrived. Diana had gone out to see a friend, which Etta suspected might be a tactful ruse, and now Etta and Mum were alone in the Bloomsbury flat, with a view of the British Museum in all its Palladian magnificence.

'I wonder what these tests and things are going to show,' Mum said, pouring out a drink for each of them and handing a wine glass to Etta. 'At least we'll get some answers.'

Etta said, 'I can't think why you didn't mention the pains you were having earlier. You didn't say anything.'

'Pains are part of ageing,' Mum said with a shrug as she sat down. 'I didn't want to worry you. Or make a fuss.'

'You know how silly that is,' Etta said gently. It hurt her to see her mother sit down gingerly, knowing she must be feeling pain in her limbs. 'It isn't making a fuss.'

Mum looked up at last, her eyes sad. 'I'm sorry, darling. Let's hope it's nothing. I'm going into the private wing of the Marsden. They're wonderful there, I've heard.'

'It's a cancer hospital.'

'So they say!' Mum said wryly. 'Let's hope they throw me out for turning up under false pretences.'

'Oh Mum.' Etta's eyes filled with tears.

'Like I said, I didn't want to worry you. And I didn't want to think about it myself.'

Etta got up and went over to sit next to her mother, holding her hand and putting her head on her shoulder. 'I don't want you to be ill,' she whispered. 'But if you are, we'll get through it.'

'Of course we will, darling.' Mum smiled at her. 'I do love you, you know. Very, very much. I'm horribly proud of you.'

Etta's heart swelled and she knew it was true.

Mum was adamant that she didn't want Etta with her for the scans.

'There's no point in you wasting a morning hanging about in a waiting room.'

447

'But I could be with you!'

'Diana's coming, aren't you?' Mum looked over at her friend.

'Yes, I'm allowed to waste my morning,' Diana said with a laugh. 'Honestly, Etta, I'll look after her. We'll meet up afterwards for a nice lunch on the King's Road. I know a lovely Italian, the owner is quite the heartthrob. He'll be just the ticket after a dull morning being scanned.'

'All right,' Etta said, feeling a little redundant but also grateful she didn't have to go into the hospital. She had a feeling that the sight of Mum in there might be a bit much to cope with, even if it were only for tests. 'Maybe I'll go and see Granny.'

'She lives on,' Mum said with a laugh. 'Give her my love.'

'Shall I tell her?' Etta said.

'Why not? Let's hope it's a storm in a teacup, but even if it is, she will still hate me stealing her thunder, even for a morning.'

Diana shook her head. 'Then she hasn't changed a scrap.'

'She'll never change,' Mum said. 'I guarantee it.'

While Mum and Diana headed off to the Marsden, Etta phoned her grandmother's house and was told she could visit before lunch. She arrived to find Granny was still in bed.

'I'm so weak,' Granny said mournfully, although she looked in rude health, 'but grateful to be granted a little respite.'

Etta, sitting by her grandmother's lavish bedside, felt cross. Her anxiety about her mother was making her short-tempered, she could feel that, and she should try not to take it out on Granny. But that wasn't enough to stop her saying, 'I don't think you've got it that bad. You look blooming. And at least you're not being tested for cancer.'

Granny looked startled. 'No, I'm not. Why do you say that?'

Etta said nothing for a moment, and then thought that there was really nothing to lose in warning Granny. Mum had said it was all right to say something. If the prognosis were fine, then perhaps it might do Granny good to think about the possibility of someone else being unwell. Perhaps it might even make her a little kinder. 'It's Mum. She's being tested today at the Marsden.'

Granny did not react for a moment, and then said, 'Oh, I see. Oh, dear me.' She sighed. 'Well, the little fool's been smoking for years, what on earth did she expect? She's brought it on herself. If she's given herself cancer, she'll get no pity from me.'

Etta gaped at her grandmother, her mouth open at this brutal put-down. 'Granny, how could you?'

Her grandmother put her nose in the air. 'Don't get sticky and sentimental, Etta. I'm only speaking the truth. Perhaps I was a little harsh. If she's ill, of course I'll be sorry for her. But it's a bit much to go around crying victim over something self-inflicted.'

Etta looked away, full of sudden fury. How could her grandmother be so selfish and cold? But then . . . when had she not been? Why go on believing that she was capable of being warm and loving and sympathetic when she had never shown it before in her life? She had not been pretending. She couldn't be excused as somehow playing up to people for a joke. She was brutally honest about herself. But still, she must know how it looked. Couldn't she even try to look like a caring mother? 'Granny, I don't know how you can be so harsh. Poor Mum. She's always been good to you.'

'Good to me?' Gloria exclaimed. 'It's been me who's been good to *her*! Who do you think paid off her first husband, that horrid little piano player? Who do you think gave her a fortune which she was never grateful for? And then she had to pay off her second husband's first wife herself! She was a fool taking him on, he was obviously a bad lot.'

'That's my father you're talking about!' Etta said, properly furious now. She stood up. 'Why do you feel the need to take everyone down? You get so much love and attention from everyone and in return, you simply hand out insults. Can't you hear yourself?'

Gloria's eyes had turned cold and flinty. 'That's enough from *you*.'

'Mum's suffered so much. She's been alone so much of her life. She had to cope with Dad's illness. It nearly killed her.'

'Dad,' scoffed Granny. 'You mean, Jonathan.'

'Yes, my dad.'

'Oh, I don't think so, dear.'

The atmosphere turned still and icy. Etta stared at her

grandmother who looked defiantly back, her hands clasped on the cover over her front.

'What?' she whispered.

'You heard.'

'What are you saying?'

Gloria shifted with a touch of awkwardness but she was still defiant. 'Darling, you were born "early", but a good seven pounds in weight. You were no early baby. Your mother went to New York for a long trip and, as far as I could tell, came back pregnant. When she announced it, I could see by looking at her that she was further along than she said. I have no idea if she even knew it herself but *I* could see it. Clear as day! And when you were born . . . well, you don't look like Mary or Samuel, or Jonathan. Didn't you ever wonder?'

Etta knew that she had wondered. Maybe only once or twice, but she had wondered. It was obvious she was not the same as the others – but that didn't make her another man's child. Surely Mum would have told her if that was the case, when Dad died at the very least? And anyway, if she had wondered, that was her private secret. She would protect Mum and Dad to the ends of the earth. 'How dare you!' she said in a voice full of wrath. 'How dare you say such a thing!'

'You can't punish me for speaking the truth!' Granny said, still defiant but obviously quailing a little in front of Etta's anger. No matter, she was not going to back down. 'I don't say you're to blame, you're not. You're as loved as any of the others even if you're a cuckoo in the nest.'

Etta gasped, wounded to her core, and obviously showing it on her face.

'Not a cuckoo, that's wrong,' her grandmother said hastily. 'I meant something else.'

'I know what you meant.'

'Don't be so touchy, darling.'

'How dare you be like this, when Mum has been so good to you? You don't deserve her.'

'I suppose I should be grateful that she didn't drive me mad, like she did poor Jonathan,' Gloria said tartly.

In a second, Etta saw all of it vividly laid out: how Mum had been blamed and told off her whole life, in return for a desperate quest to win her mother's love. Her heart bled for her poor mother and all she had suffered, bearing the burden of having Gloria as a mother. She wanted to scream and shout and tell Gloria that she was a monster, a gorgon, who caused pain and misery wherever she went. But what was the point? She already knew it would achieve nothing, do nothing. She, Etta, would look like the cruel aggressive one, shouting at an old woman in her bed. She took a deep breath.

'I'm leaving now,' she said. 'We won't mention this again. But I want you to know that no matter whose daughter I am, I am definitely my mother's child. Your granddaughter. I'm proud of her, I love her and I forgive her if she made a mistake. She could have hated me and she's loved me, all my life. And that's the difference between you.'

Etta turned on her heel and walked out of the room. Her lip was trembling violently but she managed to hold it together until she was outside before falling into a fit of agonised tears.

So it's true. I'm not Jonathan's daughter. Mary's not my whole sister, Samuel's not my brother at all.

So who the hell am I?

Chapter Twenty-Seven
FLICK
1990

There was no point in worrying, Flick told herself.

The scans had been done – long, long minutes staying still inside a vast cylinder as the magnetic resonance had done its thing – and the very nasty biopsies taken. Now she simply had to wait for the results.

As long as she didn't have those results, then she was well. That was it as far as she was concerned. She tried not to notice Etta and Diana's obvious anxiety.

What would I do without them? she wondered.

They had met Etta for lunch after the tests, and Etta had been very distracted, and full of agitation. Flick had tried to calm her down by talking of other things, but Etta had not been able to relax. Flick was touched that she was obviously so nervous on her behalf. It was only later that she remembered Etta had been to see Gloria and reminded herself to ask her daughter how that had gone. She hoped Gloria hadn't rubbed Etta up the wrong way and added to the burden she already had.

They would have to wait a few days for the results. Diana

had some appointments and Etta had gone to see her old colleagues to sound out possible opportunities in the film world. Flick was on her own, and rather relishing it, drifting around her London flat and sorting things out.

There was always a pile of post to go through, as she was so rarely there these days. She really ought to sort out a redirection, she thought, but she had arranged for the most important things to be sent down to Caundle. As a result, she had mountains of junk mail: so many takeaway menus, she couldn't count them, and endless flyers and circulars. She usually picked them up in handfuls and put them straight in the bin. As they were sliding into the bin, she saw a familiar image, and reached down to grab the leaflet it was on. Hauling it out, she inspected it.

It was the same picture of Caius that had been used in that review piece all those years ago: an intense close-up of him playing the piano, eyes closed, head forward as though he was bending in to listen to the sounds he was conjuring out of the keyboard.

Oh my goodness. It's him. He can't still look like that.

She had not knowingly set eyes on him since the night of Prue's birthday party all those years ago, when he had booed her mother and then walked out. What would have happened if she had followed him, and chosen him instead of her family?

Well, I suspect pretty much the same. He's on his fifth wife. I don't think he would have remained faithful. He would have left one way or the other.

But, of course, she was wrong. She had seen him since that party, if Henry was right.

Flick stared at the picture on the flyer in her hand. There was a concert at the Halliday Hall tonight. Caius was appearing there.

She went through to the sitting room, holding the flyer and thinking. Sinking onto the sofa, she considered how long she had closed her mind to things. She had wiped the events of that night in New York from her mind. She had closed her imagination to the idea that she might have returned pregnant from the States. And, when she found the raincoat and confronted Henry . . . she had also closed her mind to the idea that it might have been Caius who had slept with her, not Henry.

I have to stop closing my mind. I might be dying. I may not have long to find out the answers I need. And Etta needs them too.

She stared for a while longer, and then suddenly got up and went through to her bedroom. She was going to prepare to go out.

The Halliday Hall was in a road behind Oxford Street, one of the many lined with late Victorian buildings and churches. The Hall looked undistinguished from the outside – a double-sized wooden door in a red-and-black brick facade – but inside it revealed a large auditorium, suitable for the finest musical recitals thanks to its wonderful acoustics.

Flick went up to the box office, where a bearded young man was busy with tickets and the telephone. When he was free, he confirmed that Caius Knolle was in the building, in his dressing room. With much pleading, Flick managed to persuade him to call the dressing room and ask if Flick could visit.

The young man was clearly astonished when he put the receiver down and said, 'He'll see you. I'll show you to his dressing room now.'

'Well, well. If it isn't the Little Girl Lost. So, are you found at last?'

Caius sat with his back to the mirror in his dressing room, a cigarette smouldering in the ashtray next to him. He was staring directly at Flick.

He doesn't look like the photograph any more. But I suppose I look different too.

'Hello, Caius.' She went forward and sat down on a chair opposite him. The lighting was kind to both of them, drenching their faces and erasing some of the wrinkles and hollows that time had wrought.

And that was one of the odd things about knowing someone when young. They never really thoroughly changed. That younger self was always visible, somehow more visible than the older person they now were.

And this was the man I loved so much. Madly. Passionately.

'Flick,' he said. He made no move to embrace her, and she was grateful for that. 'What's brought you here? I can't believe it's to hear me play.'

'You're right. I won't stay for your performance, though I'm sure it will be wonderful. I've come with a question, and I really need you to answer it for me.'

'Ah.' He stared at her. After a moment he said, 'You're still beautiful, Flick. I never thought I'd see you again.'

'Well, here I am.' She smiled. Despite the distance of years, they remained connected. Whatever it was that bound people to each other – love, experience – they were still bound and always would be. But, thank God, it no longer had the power to hurt her.

'And what's your question?' He was wearing his perform-ance clothes: white shirt, dark trousers. His hair was still thick, but almost completely white. His eyes were the same, though: dark and intense.

'Years ago I stayed the night at an apartment in New York. I was very drunk. Were you there?'

He continued to stare at her, fixing her with his dark eyes. 'New York?'

'In nineteen fifty-eight. You would remember. Please don't play games. Please just tell me.'

He smiled his infuriating half-smile. He was enjoying this, she could tell. He always loved to play with her at any oppor-tunity. 'Let me see now. Did I see you in New York in fifty-eight? I was there that year. And I had a small apartment at the time.'

Flick's heart beat faster. Was she going to discover the truth at last? Had she and Caius had a child, against all the odds, in the most impossible way? 'Yes?'

'And you came home with me that night.'

Her mouth went dry.

He went on. 'You were so young then. And so very drunk. So helpless and vulnerable. I loved you so much at that moment, my poor, helpless Little Girl Lost. I had missed you in a crazy way.'

'Missed me? You left without a word. I never saw or spoke to you again.'

'Ah, that was your mother's doing. She paid me off, you see. A very, very handsome sum, on one condition. I never saw you or spoke to you again. I was grateful to the old show-off in some ways. That money got my career started properly. But of course, it also meant I had to leave you high and dry. No farewells, no last night together. I assumed you hated me in any case. When I saw you in the bar in New York, I could hardly believe it. When you saw me . . . well . . .' He smiled at her darkly. 'You couldn't take your eyes off me. When I joined you, you fell into my arms. How could I resist you?'

'So what happened?' She could barely speak. She didn't know what she wanted the outcome to be. Which one was better?

'You were so happy to see me! That was nice. You asked me to take you home. So I did. To my little place.'

'What did you do?'

'I put you to bed in my room. I went off to make you some coffee. When I came back, you'd stripped off and passed out. I was worried you might be sick and choke, so I slept next to you. The next morning, I went to have a shower and when I came back, you'd gone. Now you really were my Little Girl Lost. And . . .' – he frowned – 'you took my raincoat! That was pretty bloody annoying. It rained all week. I had to buy another one.'

His raincoat. So it was true. Flick still felt confused. 'Then . . . you and I did not . . .'

'We did not make love,' Caius said, looking amused. 'Although you were flatteringly eager. But I don't like my women in that state. Even for old times' sake.'

'No sex.'

'No. But it's not too late, Flick, if that's what you want.'

She stood up. 'Thank you, Caius. And no to your kind offer. I'm afraid it is too late. Much too late.' She stared him straight in the face. 'Can I believe you?'

He stood up. His presence was still magnetic. She could see how the young Flick had been so entranced. But he was not to be trusted. A selfish and deceitful man. How could she trust him?

'Flick, I have nothing to gain by lying. I would never sleep with a woman in that state, I'm far too proud. And if I had, you would remember it. I guarantee. I'm an unforgettable lover.'

Flick began to laugh. He looked hurt.

'What's so funny?'

'You. I believe you. I do believe you are so vain that you simply can't imagine I wouldn't remember you making love to me. And that making love to someone practically comatose would hold no attraction for you. What is the point if they can't worship you, pay homage, make you feel wonderful about yourself? You didn't do anything.'

His eyes turned flinty. 'How many times? We did not. Now, much as I love your company, I'm afraid I must ask you to leave. I have a concert to prepare for.'

Flick walked slowly back to the flat, ignoring the crowds and taking the back streets so that she could think. She believed him. She had seen his need to win the power in the relationship. If he had thought it would benefit him, he might have claimed to have had sex with her. If he'd suspected for a moment that she wanted to know about Etta's parentage, he probably would have, just for fun.

But his vanity was stronger.

No sex with Caius. He could not be Etta's father.

Was she relieved or disappointed?

Looking into her heart, she knew she was glad. Perhaps it was no accident that Caius sounded so much like chaos. If he were Etta's father and he came into her life now, then it would cause chaos for her. A man married five times, famously unreliable, and utterly selfish. He had come close to her daughters when he had attempted to seduce Mary – she could only pray he had not succeeded. He could not take Etta as his own either.

It's a relief.

Yes. Caius would certainly have claimed Etta if he could, attempted to take some kind of ownership of her, to add to his collection of children by different partners and wives. That was the last thing Flick wanted.

There was something else playing on her mind.

I will have to tell her. No matter what my diagnosis is. She has to know. Before it's too late.

I just have to find the right time.

Diana and Etta were both with her in the consultant's rooms when he told them the results of her scans. They sat in front of his desk, with its little silver wall of family photographs between him and them. A nurse sat on a chair at the side of the room, her expression carefully neutral.

Etta held Flick's hand tightly, her face white and strained. Flick clutched on to her daughter, her rock, and waited, her heart thudding with nerves. She still felt that nothing was true as long as it wasn't spoken.

The consultant began to speak. He must have given news like this many times before; his sonorous voice was full of sympathy and kindness and easy to listen to as it told her the reality of what was happening to her, and what would most likely happen to her very soon.

Etta gasped, tightened her grip, and began to cry, reaching blindly for a tissue in her bag with her other hand, until the nurse gave her one from the box on the consultant's desk. Diana put her arm around her old friend and dropped her head lightly on her shoulder, before sitting up straight and firm and asking the consultant a range of sensible questions about treatment and time scales.

Flick could not take it in entirely. She rejected it, and yet also accepted it with a kind of calm stoicism.

I've lived a life. And now I know the answer to the question that all of us are born ignorant of. Perhaps not the time, or the exact date. But I know when death will come for me. And it is not so very far away.

Chapter Twenty-Eight
ETTA
1990

Take-off was always an intense experience: the sensation of the huge jet lifting off from the ground, forcing itself upwards by propulsion and aerodynamics, to do the impossible and take to the skies.

This time, Etta had not noticed it at all. She was hardly aware of anything outside her own thoughts and the constant, pressing sense of time running out.

The news about Mum had been worse than she'd been expecting. She had convinced herself it was not cancer but if it was, then it was bone cancer and it would be slow moving and treatable. A few weeks of ghastly chemotherapy and Mum would be better, recovering at Caundle where she was supposed to be.

But it wasn't that.

There was bone cancer, but it was secondary. The primary cancer was the dark tumour in Flick's lungs. They could not operate. They could try to shrink the tumours and growths in her bones with a round of chemotherapy and radiation.

But the outlook was not good. And in any scenario, time was most likely short.

Mum had been so very brave. She hadn't cried, not when Etta had wept there in the consultant's rooms, or later back at the flat. The only time she had looked grief-stricken was when they had turned into the driveway to see the old house sitting, warm, familiar and permanent, at the end of it.

'Dear old Caundle. I love it so,' she had said, her voice thick with tears. And then, finally, she had wept.

Perhaps Etta should have expected what Mum said next, but it was still a shock.

'No treatment,' Mum had said firmly. 'I don't want to spend my last months feeling like hell, hooked up to drips for hours every day, living in a hospital, especially if it can't cure me. It can only give me a bit more time and not much of that. What time I have left, I spend here at Caundle, where I'm happy and where life is beautiful.'

'You must get treatment, Mum!' Etta had said, desperate. There was no hope if she didn't. There was still the faintest chance that this would all go away if she at least did a round of chemo. 'Please, for me, for Mary!'

Mum was firm. 'I don't want it and there's no reason for it. Please try to understand it from my point of view.'

She had been adamant.

Mary made plans to fly back from Australia as soon as she could after Etta telephoned with the news, but she couldn't take immediate leave from her job as a teacher in a school in

Sydney. It would be at least a few weeks before she could return. Samuel, too, was summoned and he came down on his own to talk with Flick, hug and weep, and tell her how much she had meant to him in his life. He had his own mother but he and Flick had always been close, and she considered his children almost her own grandchildren.

While they were waiting for Mary to come back, they had to tell the people who also cared for Mum.

It had been awful breaking the news to members of the family, seeing the realisation and then shock and pain come into their faces. Prue had been sensible and practical, like Diana, but obviously holding back a flood of tears. Mum had told Uncle Brinsley herself, on a long walk in the garden. Etta had watched the brother and sister set off together, and then, under one of the oaks in the park, had seen the faraway figures embracing. When they came back, red-eyed, they were holding hands and somehow appeared serene in the face of Brinsley's obvious grief. Diana had been there to hug him, walking back with him to the house afterwards, clearly consoling him.

Granny had talked to Mum on the telephone, and immediately had moved into denial mode. Nothing was wrong with Flick. If there was, it could easily be cured by various homeopathic remedies, enemas and dietary changes. A flood of parcels and letters arrived, all with new solutions to the incurable. Mum took it in good heart, laughing over all the different ideas Granny had.

'There aren't enough hours in the day to do all this,' she said, opening yet another box of bottles and tubs. 'Even if I wanted to, and I don't. I suppose it's just her way of coping.'

Etta wished that her grandmother's way of coping had been to show love and support to Mum, perhaps to visit her and give her tender words and hugs. But Granny, being Granny, sent bouquets and bottles of champagne, as well her miracle cures, as though there was something to celebrate, even if the notes said things like: *A little something to hold the darkness at bay, darling!*

It was hardly the time to tell Mum about what Granny had said to her that day in the Chester Square house – saying out loud and brutally what Etta had wondered about for so long. She wanted to ask Mum for the truth, but it had to be done at the right time and that was hardly now, as she absorbed the reality of her cancer diagnosis.

But I want her to tell me before she dies. She must do that for me, surely? I can't really know who I am until I know who my father is.

Etta said, 'But Mum, have you told Rob?'

They were in the cosy cottage sitting room, Mum's feet lifted up on a stool as they were beginning to ache and this seemed to help a little. Mum went still, her gaze sliding away. Her pale skin pinkened over the tautness of her cheeks.

'No.'

'No? He's one of your oldest friends.'

'I can't tell him this,' Mum said simply. 'It's too hard. And I can't bear him to hear it over a telephone line. And the truth is that we haven't spoken for a long time. I don't know how

I'm going to do it. Or even if I should say anything at all.' She looked so sad. 'I miss him. But I don't know if I have the right to ask anything of him now.'

That was why Etta was now halfway across the Atlantic, on her way to tell one of Mum's oldest friends that she was dying.

She had told Mum she had an important meeting to go to, which was true, and Mum had assumed it was a job interview of some kind. She hadn't corrected her.

'Can I get you a drink?' asked the stewardess. She was a glossy blonde with kind eyes who checked on Etta frequently. 'Champagne?'

First-class perks. Like having a world-famous actress in the next row, wearing headphones with her face smeared in lotion, a cashmere shawl around her shoulders as she sipped on Perrier.

'Yes please, champagne would be lovely.'

When the flute of fizzing liquid was in front of her, Etta thought about the other reasons for this trip to New York.

Granny had said that Mum had come back from New York all those years ago pregnant. So it stood to reason that it was a possibility that Mum had met Etta's father in New York. And that was what she wanted to ask Rob.

Sipping her champagne, she made notes in her leather book of what to ask him. The only thing was how to balance the enormous things that they had to talk about. It was going to be hard. She had no idea how he would react to any of it.

*

468

New York was having one of those glorious autumns, with the sky endlessly blue and days crisp and warm. Etta had missed this crazy, bustling, noisy, energetic city and she felt the pleasure of renewing her acquaintance with it as the taxi drove her into the city. She was staying in a hotel in SoHo, a fashionable but cosy place. She wasn't drawn to the hotels that were like big glass boxes with their achingly trendy decor; she preferred a home-from-home sort of place.

After settling in, she checked her watch. Although it felt late in the evening to her, it was still only mid-morning here. Plenty of time to refresh herself before going to meet Rob for lunch. He had not seemed surprised that Etta was coming back on a trip but then she had spoken vaguely of work, meetings and friends so that he didn't get worried about anything.

A shower revived her, as did the walk from her hotel towards Rob's office. Gerstein & Gerstein had been bought out some years ago by a bigger talent and literary agency, and now Rob was a vice president of that company, significantly richer and with the luxury of choosing his own working hours and exactly what he wanted to do. But he deserved it, Etta thought, as she approached the modern skyscraper he now worked in. The sky was full of these towers, none of them as vast as the Twin Towers of the World Trade Centre, which dominated the others like two tall parents surrounded by their children. Rob's was not shabby, though, rising to at least a hundred floors. Etta took the lift to one of the upper levels and stepped out to see a glorious view of Manhattan through the glass walls of the hall. 'Wow!' she said, without meaning to.

'It sure is wow.'

She turned to see Rob, standing in the hall, smiling at her, his arms open.

'They told me you'd arrived,' he said, 'and I couldn't wait to say hi. Come here, Etta, give your old pal a hug!'

She beamed, delighted to see his warm, friendly face again. He was so familiar, with those twinkling dark eyes and broad smile, and she felt a rush of deep affection for him that took her almost by surprise. She strode to him and let him envelop her in a bear hug, which she returned as best she could, laughing at his strength.

'That's better!' he said, putting a hearty kiss on her cheek. 'It's so great to see you. And you look amazing! I knew you'd be better off without that actor asshole. Do you want to go out or come to my office first? You can take a look at the corner suite of a real vice president. It's a privilege accorded to few.'

Etta was glad her strain didn't show on her face. She had already decided that it would be better to tell him the news in private rather than wherever they had lunch.

'The problem with glass skyscrapers,' Rob was saying as he led her into his palatial office, 'is that the air con costs a fortune. I mean, a *fortune*.' He chatted on as they got settled, one on each end of the very fancy white leather sofa that ran along one entire wall, one of the two that weren't made of glass. Once they were seated facing each other, he looked at her, his eyes warm, his smile welcoming. 'Now. Come on. What do you want to tell me, huh?'

'How do you know I want to tell you something?' she said, hoping to put it off a while longer. She didn't want to see the realisation dawn and the face crumple, as she had so often lately.

'Ah, Etta. You want to tell me something. If you didn't, we'd be meeting for a straightforward lunch at our favourite place. So there's something. It's just a question of what it is.'

Her smile faded and she looked away. This was awful. Why had she taken this on herself? Then she thought of Mum and her sadness over the inexplicable estrangement from Rob. At least, it was inexplicable to Etta. 'I do have something to tell you, Rob. That's true.'

'It's about Flick, isn't it?'

Etta nodded slowly, knowing her eyes must be full of sadness.

'You don't have to say it. She's sick, isn't she?'

Etta bit her lip. 'How did you know?'

Rob's own smile had vanished and his dark eyes were full of abject sadness. He sighed. 'Oh Etta. I've always known things about Flick before she's even known them herself. Don't ask me why or how.' He drew in a shaky breath and said slowly, 'So . . . is it cancer?'

Etta's eyes filled with hot tears and she was overcome with the urge to sob. She couldn't speak. She bit her lip harder and nodded.

'Oh God.' He put his face in his hands and left it there for a long time. When he finally looked up, he was wet-eyed but controlled. He sighed heavily and said, 'How long has she got, Etta?'

'Maybe a year,' Etta said, her voice breaking on the words. 'But she won't have treatment.'

'Goddammit, Flick,' he said vehemently. 'Stubborn to the last. A year? Christ. She's still so young. She won't even see sixty.' He looked away again, overcome, but a moment later he had reached out a big hand to Etta and taken hers. 'You poor baby. You must be in agony. I'm so sorry, honey. I'm so sorry that your mom is dying.'

When he said it, in those tender tones of his, she felt the reality of it hit her with all its full finality and force, bringing with it a wave of grief, and she broke down in tears as he reached over to hug her tightly.

Later, when the tears had subsided and the shock receded a little, they went out onto the street, bought sandwiches, and strolled to a square where elderly men were playing bowls, and others chess at the little stone tables permanently marked up for a game. Etta and Rob sat down on a bench together to eat their sandwiches and breathe in the autumn air.

When they had finished eating, they got themselves takeaway coffee and walked on, talking of Flick and what would happen next.

'I've known that you two haven't really been in touch for a while now,' Etta said, almost shyly. 'And I couldn't help wondering why. You were always so close. But something changed when Dad died.'

'Yeah. I don't know how much to tell you, really. But something happened to drive us apart and I felt it was best to have some distance. Neither of us have crossed that divide during all this time. Both stupid and stubborn, I guess.'

'I think she misses you. A lot.'

'And I miss her.' He sighed. 'I've been a fool. I was hurt. And I've held on to that too long.'

'Mum can be stubborn too. But I know she really wishes she'd reached out to you. She said that she doesn't know if she can ask anything of you now, after so long.'

'Of course she can,' he said simply. 'And she always could. She tried to make a sacrifice for me and I think I took it in the wrong spirit. That's it.'

'You don't have to say more. But I know it would mean so much for you two to be reconciled.'

Rob sighed. 'I hear you. I want that too. There's not much time left and we've been so crazy to waste what we had.'

They walked on together, lost in thought until Etta broke the silence. She was thankful that they were walking, so that she didn't have to meet his eye as they talked. It was easier that way.

'There's something else I really want to ask you.'

'Uh-huh. Ask anything.'

'You met Mum in New York thirty-two years ago, right?'

'That's right.'

'And you know I'm nearly thirty-one, don't you?'

She sensed Rob tense a little when she said this but he nodded and said easily, 'Uh-huh.'

'So . . . My grandmother basically told me a little while

ago that my dad was not my real father, and she said that Mum came back from New York pregnant.'

Rob drew in a sharp breath. 'That was real nice of your grandmother.'

'Yeah. She's not an apple-pie-and-milk grandmother, I'm afraid.' Etta grinned. Then she became serious again. 'So . . . I can't ask Mum about it right now, it's not the time. Maybe Granny is wrong. But you see . . . I have a feeling I know who my father is.'

'You do?' Rob's voice sounded a little thick.

'Yes. And that's what I want to ask you. I know Mum tells you everything and you're her best friend besides Diana. So.' Etta took a deep breath. This was what everything had been building up to for all this time. She was desperate to hear his answer. 'Here's what I want to know. Is Henry Morfield my father?'

Rob stopped and looked at her, amazed. 'What?'

'I guess you don't know then?'

'Henry Morfield? How could he be your father? I know that name. He was the guy who told your mother about Samuel.' Rob told her how Flick had been unaware of the existence of Jonathan's first wife and his son until the dinner party at Diana's house all those years ago.

'I had no idea,' Etta said, eyes wide with astonishment. 'What a terrible thing to find out. How could Dad do that?'

'Good question. And Henry Morfield was the guy who told her. But that was all, as far as I know.'

'Okay. Nothing happened between them?'

Rob was still standing stock still on the pavement, staring

at her, as people walked around them, some muttering at the obstacle they were making. 'Not that I know of. And you think he might be your dad?'

'It makes sense, doesn't it? That they maybe had a one-night stand back then? And she got pregnant with me, just before she came home, back to Dad? I mean, Jonathan. Come on, let's keep walking.' She took his arm and they started strolling on, heading towards the river. She told him about what Jonathan had said to her in the garden of the hospital that last time she had seen him. 'So I think he knew all along too. Not who it was. But that I wasn't his. But Mum ended up reconnecting with Henry years later, as a friend, and I met him. They broke up in the end, before it got serious, I don't know why. But I've got the same colouring as Henry and his son, Charlie. *And* there was no chemistry between Charlie and me. Like, zero. Nada. And he's gorgeous. That might be because he's my brother. It could explain it.'

Rob listened as they walked along, regaining some of his composure. 'That's all good circumstantial evidence. But maybe Flick would have told you if Henry was your dad when they started seeing each other again. Because that would make sense.'

'Not if she wasn't sure about him. And she wasn't in the end, was she? So maybe she was protecting me until she was sure how it was going to go, so I didn't get needlessly hurt.'

'Uh-huh.'

'I guess you don't know then?' she said wistfully.

He put his warm hand on hers where it was sitting on his

475

arm as they walked along. 'Honey, I don't know anything for sure. And maybe your mom doesn't either. Maybe there won't be an answer. You have to prepare yourself for that, and just make your peace with being who you are, regardless of your parents.'

'Yeah. I guess so.' Etta took in a deep breath, savouring the autumn day and the atmosphere of the busy city. They reached the river and stood against a low wall, gazing down over its blue and khaki waters. She turned and stood with her back against the wall, almost sitting on it, clutching her coffee cup to get the last bit of warmth from it. She had planned this on the plane too but now she felt nervous. *Just say it*. 'There's something else.'

He smiled kindly at her. 'I'm all ears.'

'Well . . . I may never know who my father is but I realised something on the plane. You're the closest thing I have to a father now. You've known me all my life. You love my mum, even if you've been apart for a while. You've looked after me in a paternal way that means so much to me and I know I can rely on you. So . . . I would like to ask you if I can consider that *you're* my father. I mean, that you'll take that place in my life.' She smiled shyly. 'Would you? Because if I could choose any dad, I'd choose you.'

For the second time that day, Rob's eyes filled with tears and he looked away, muttering, 'Oh my God, Etta.'

'What? What?' She was anxious. 'Did I say something bad?'

'No. No. Etta, I have to tell you something. There is a chance that . . . that I could be your real dad.'

Her stomach plummeted and her mouth fell open. 'What?' she stammered.

'Yeah. Your mom and I kind of fell in love when we met. Kind of? We did. Proper thunderbolt stuff. And while she was here, a couple of things happened. She was really upset by that talk with Henry Morfield. She was devastated to find out that Jonathan had been hiding the existence of his first wife and Sam from her. She was broken by that. And in that moment of being estranged from him, and feeling betrayed and so sad . . . well . . . that's when something happened between the two of us.'

Etta listened, shocked, taking it all in. Why had it never occurred to her before that Mum and Rob had been lovers?

Because they are friends. Lifelong friends. He knew Dad. He stayed with us. I just never thought . . .

But as she thought this, she realised that it was not a surprise. Rob and Mum were obviously lovers. Lovers with different lives, different partners, on different continents. But their love was plain and always had been. The real surprise was that she hadn't seen it before.

'Have you and Mum ever talked about it?' Etta asked slowly.

'No. There are a couple of places we've never been. One was – clearly – what happened that night between us. And the other was you. And that you, born nine months after she returned from New York, with those brown eyes of yours . . . that you might be my daughter.'

'Oh my God.' She looked up at him, hardly knowing how to form her thoughts.

Rob grabbed her hand, concerned. 'Are you okay?'

'Yes, yes.' She turned to look out over the river again, taking in a deep breath and releasing it slowly before saying with a wry smile, 'It's quite the day for revelations, isn't it? I thought I was going to be the one delivering all the surprises.'

'I hope you're not upset.'

'No.'

'If you want, I can take a test. So we know for sure.'

She hesitated, then said, 'Can I think about it? You're the father I choose. That's good enough for me. But maybe a test is the right thing to do. To be sure.'

There was still a possibility that Henry might be her father. And yet, Etta knew in her heart that she loved Rob like a father and she always had. He was the father she wanted.

He took her hand and they walked back to the office together.

Chapter Twenty-Nine

FLICK

1990

Flick had not realised how much she had missed Mary until her elder daughter came running into the sitting room of the cottage, dropping her bags on the floor as she went, and threw herself into her waiting arms, sobbing. They stayed like that for a very long time.

Everything that had ever come between them was gone. They were mother and daughter, reunited.

It's all worth it, she thought. *For this.*

Flick sometimes thought that if this was dying, it was not so bad. At night, alone, she would weep, unable to bear the thought that she would have to leave them all, and that they would go on without her. But what could she do? That was her fate, her destiny. She had done what she could for them: brought her children into the world, loved as best she could in her messy, failing way. She had set them on their paths into their own lives, and she hoped that she had broken the cycle of her own pain. The damage stopped with her. They were loved, and they knew it.

And in the day, she herself felt surrounded by so much love and care that she could hardly believe she was worth it. Her family had gathered around her, to help ease her passage out of the world with all the comfort they could give her, telling her ceaselessly that she mattered, and that she was forgiven – had never really needed forgiveness, because she had tried her best.

Sometimes she dreamed of Jonathan. She had been down to his grave, to talk to him and to beg his forgiveness too, for whatever she had put him through and for all her failures.

But it was getting harder to move around, and the pain in her limbs was increasing. There was talk of palliative care, painkillers, a full-time nurse. Her lawyer visited so that she could make the arrangements for all those things that needed to be sorted out: property, money, possessions. All the things she would leave behind. She didn't care about them, but she wanted her family to be safe and secure. Of course they would be. She had had many worries in her life, but she had been spared having to worry where her next meal was coming from and how to put a roof over her family's heads. That had been a blessing. The money had been a curse, in some ways – *the family curse*, she thought, blackly amused – but also a safety net.

Flick could not pretend she was not afraid. She was frightened mostly of pain and what it might be like to suffer badly. Her consultant and nurse had assured her that she would be pain-free until the end. Already she was relying more on painkillers with the pain in her bones. Since she knew about the tumour in her chest, she had begun to feel pain there too.

So strange, as up until then, she'd been aware of nothing at all in her lungs. But she felt easier when she knew that everything would be done to keep pain at bay.

And then there was the fear of the moment itself. What would it be like? Would that hurt? Would it feel like being unclipped, or detached? Or just like falling asleep? And would the time come when she would wish to cease to exist? Surely not? Surely she would want to cling on to life and existence until the last minute, and would leave the world with the deepest and most elemental grief? She did not want to become the person who could leave it without regret.

She had never been so glad of Brinsley's wisdom and compassion. He came around and sat with her for hours, and they talked over anything and everything that occurred to her. He held her hand and passed her tissues when she wept. He comforted her, felt her pain, consoled her. Sometimes he told her that it was a privilege to have time to make peace with something that would happen to everyone eventually. There were people ripped too suddenly and too soon from life, and who never had the chance to say farewell. Flick had time to bring whatever she wanted to resolution.

'In theory,' Flick said. 'Although I don't think Mother is going to be part of that resolution.'

'You're probably right,' Brinsley agreed.

Gloria simply wouldn't consider coming to see Flick, and had asked that she didn't visit. 'I'm too old to be upset like that,' she'd said. 'Imagine having to see your dying daughter! It's really not fair on me.'

Instead, along with her usual collection of cures, she

had sent a flowery 'With Sympathy' card. Inside she had written:

Lots of luck, my darling. I hope it all goes as well as possible. I will see you on the other side! I'm sure it will be the most marvellous party! Love, Mama xxx

'It won't be so marvellous if she's singing there,' Flick said dryly. 'Imagine that for all eternity!'

Which made Brinsley laugh for half an hour.

Mary sat with her late into the night, and they talked into the early hours.

'I need to tell you something, Mum,' Mary said. She was still so girlish, with her long fair hair. She dressed in flares and flowery shirts and plimsolls, and looked like she did back in the days when she went to Armitage Hall all those years ago.

'Okay,' Flick said.

'I did something wrong. I punished you. I was angry and I wanted to get my own back on you.'

Flick felt a chill over her skin. When she had that confrontation with Caius, and he had told her that he had not made love to her, there had been one last question she wanted to ask him: what happened with Mary? But she hadn't been able to ask it, and had not even known how she might approach it. It was her great fear that he had seduced her daughter, but there was no way that she could trust him to tell her the truth. The moment that he suspected how much she hated the idea, he would prioritise manipulating her over telling her the truth, and he would enjoy causing her pain. But that wasn't Mary's fault. She had been a child, really, acting out of hurt. 'Do you mean about Caius Knolle?'

'Yes.' Mary looked away, sheepish.

'I want you to know that whatever happened, I forgive it. I mean, I don't forgive him, he should never have taken advantage of a girl your age. But I forgive you and I did right away. I owed you the apology, not the other way round.'

'No, Mum. You're wrong. It was my fault.'

'Oh Mary.' So something had happened. It broke her heart to think of Caius coming near her sweet daughter. 'It wasn't your fault.'

'You don't understand. Nothing happened. I mean, I did go for a drink with him, but as soon as we were alone, it felt all wrong. He was so much older than me, and not as attractive as I'd thought at all. It felt like going out with my dad. I said I wanted to go home and we went outside – that's when he tried to kiss me. But I pushed him off and told him he was a dirty old man. He seemed to like that more than anything. He laughed and let me go. Then he tracked me down to college and tried to ask me out.'

'I see . . . I think . . .'

'I wrote back and told him to sling his hook.'

'Did he know who you were?'

'I called myself Miffy Celesta. He didn't know I was your daughter. And he never touched me, not really.'

A wash of relief went over Flick. *Oh, thank goodness. My girl. He didn't touch her.*

'But I let you believe he had – to punish you for all my

own anger with you and Dad and all the rest. I mean, I was angry you'd lied to us by omission. But you didn't deserve that, and I've let you believe for all these years that maybe I'd slept with your ex-husband, when I never did. I'm sorry. I really regret it.'

Flick beckoned her into her arms for a hug. 'You don't need to be sorry. I'm just glad you were safe. He's not a good man. I couldn't bear to think of him having anything to do with you. You're so precious to me. You don't know how much.'

Mary nestled in to her mother's embrace. 'I'm just glad we got the chance to make it right, that's all.'

'Yes. Me too, darling. You've set my mind at rest after all this time, and I'm grateful.'

Etta came back from New York early one morning. It was a cold and grey November morning, with a sense of the world drawing towards the night of the year. Flick, lying awake, heard the car drawing up outside, and was filled with joy. She couldn't feel complete until Etta was safely home and now here she was.

She got out of bed as quickly as she could, gingerly putting her painful feet to the floor. Mary had brought her a pair of the most gloriously soft sheepskin slippers from Australia, and they were like walking on clouds, thank goodness. Nevertheless, she would need her first painkilling dose of the day.

Mary would be up by now. She was staying in the big house, where she could practise yoga, meditate and indulge in her other bizarre practices with plenty of room and without annoying anyone with her various chants and shouts. She could also cook her lentils and chickpeas and other strange food in the big kitchen without getting in anyone's way.

There would be a lovely reunion of the three of them later. And Samuel was bringing his family for Christmas. It was going to be a wonderful family time.

My last Christmas, most likely.

Hmm. She didn't want to think like that. She had decided to live every day as it came and not think too far into the future.

She pulled on the pale pink cashmere robe that was one of the better things to arrive from her mother. It was baby soft, and she craved soft things these days, to ease her bones. She went to the bathroom to freshen up, pulled a brush through her hair and prepared to welcome Etta home.

There were two voices in the sitting room, she realised as she came down the stairs. Etta's and another deeper one.

The taxi driver bringing in the luggage? she wondered as she opened the door. But she had surely heard the taxi leave a few minutes ago.

She stood in the doorway, looking into the room and unable to take in what she was seeing. Etta, of course. And a face so familiar it felt like she had known it intimately all her life. It was older now. The hair was thinner and grey, cut short to the skull. The face was broader, and carved with laughter lines, but the warm brown eyes and that broad, generous mouth were still the same.

'Rob,' she said in wonder.

He looked over and the distance and passage of time that

had come between them fell away. It was as if they had been apart for a few days. He might be older but he was Rob. Her Rob.

I thought I would be complete with my family. But I would never be complete without him.

He was smiling, holding open his arms, saying her name. A moment later she was in an embrace that made her want to laugh and cry at the same time.

'You're here,' she murmured.

'Of course. I was always going to come to you. You know that.'

Flick didn't even notice Etta slip quietly away.

The question really was why they had left it so late.

'We could have been together years ago,' Flick said, torn between the joy at having him with her, properly with her, at last, and the mourning for time lost. 'I sent you away when we could have had a decade together.'

'You can't think like that, honey,' Rob said, holding her tightly. 'I left. We both messed up. But we can put it right.'

'Rob . . . it's too late, I'm dying. You must know that.'

'I know you're sick. But I also know you're right here, with me right now.'

She closed her eyes and pressed in close to him as they sat together on the sofa.

This is everything. This is home. Why didn't I see years ago that this was how it was supposed to be? Why did I send him away when Jonathan died?

They talked for long hours about what had stopped them

taking the steps that would allow them to live as the couple they longed to be. Flick tried to explain the guilt of denying him a normal marriage with a normal person – 'There's no such thing, Flick, you idiot!' – and he tried to convey the stubborn hurt he'd felt. 'You were entitled,' she said. 'After all you'd done for me, and the years you'd waited – and I turned it all down for no reason at all.'

Rob tended to her every need, making her endless cups of tea ('I'm getting the hang of the way you curious British like to drink this stuff') and looking after her, keeping her pain free and comfortable, as they worked it out between them.

'Don't forget, it wasn't always so easy to hop across the ocean whenever you felt like it,' Rob said, sitting down next to her and tucking her cashmere blanket a little more tightly around her. 'Not like today. And we had our separate lives.'

'But it wasn't just timetables and airlines that stopped us doing what was best for us both,' Flick said, agonised. She was wrestling with the regret and the anger that came with the powerful sense of time wasted, and chances lost.

He took her hand. 'C'mon. You know it was more than that. If it had been what we both really wanted, then nothing would have stopped us. We chose. I did and you did. And if we did it all again, we would make the same choices. You have to remember that. There's no alternative life where we did something else.'

She clutched his hand tightly and gazed into his kind brown eyes. His brows were bushier now, with wiry grey hairs among the black, and he was lined and a little pouchy under the eyes. But to her, he was the most beautiful man in the world. She wanted to believe what he said with all her heart. 'Is that true?'

'Of course it is,' he answered. 'You know it too. You couldn't throw in your life, leave Jonathan when he was sick, uproot your kids, leave Samuel behind, and leave here – leave your home, this wonderful place – to share my New York life. And I couldn't leave my brother and our business and my home either. And you know what, if we had, we would probably have broken up years ago, instead of being free to continue loving each other in our own way, even when we were apart.'

She felt deeply comforted. Yes. They *had* had all these years together, and that was why he was sitting with her now, holding her hand, loving her in the days of sickness and telling her that now he would be with her till the very end.

It was getting close to Christmas and Flick was looking forward to it. They had got a tree for the cottage and Rob, Etta and Mary had decorated it according to Flick's instructions. She was not able to do much herself as she was now spending more time on the sofa. Her feet had become very painful and it was hard to stand for long, even with the industrial-strength painkillers that managed to numb her most of the time.

Etta had tactfully moved to the big house, so that Flick and Rob had their privacy, finally able to spend every hour together and finding that they were just as enmeshed together as they had been apart.

It's just so easy.

'Well, Mum, what do you think?' Etta said, standing back

from the tree after putting the star on the top, and letting Flick see the whole, sparkling, glittering, gaudy result.

'Glorious!' Flick pronounced. 'It's incredible! So beautiful!'

Why have I never seen how beautiful Christmas trees really are? It's like something out of a magical story!

Her eyes teared up, as they so often did now. The smallest things in life – that in the past had stressed her or she'd taken for granted – seemed precious and beautiful now. The sight of the tree along with the sound of carols playing on the CD player was almost too much to bear.

'Ah, Mum, you silly, sentimental old thing!' Mary said, sitting down next to her. She was careful not to hug her mother too tightly, knowing how tender she was these days. 'I tell you, it's great to have Christmas in the winter again. It was never quite the same, heading to the beach for a barbie on Christmas Day.'

'It's barbaric,' Etta said, laughing.

'It's the world gone mad,' Rob added. 'Things are as they should be here.'

'Exactly,' Flick said emphatically. 'This is where things work out.'

Christmas was beautiful. The entire family gathered at Caundle, including Samuel and his wife and children, and made the festivities something special. Flick loved seeing the excitement of the very young children, their eyes wide and sparkling at the huge tree in the hall, the piles of presents beneath it, and all the treats of the Christmas feast.

Diana had become a fixture at Caundle now, and it was a

delight to see how easily she and Brinsley had become a couple, and how natural it was that Diana could take charge of some of the burden of hosting a huge family Christmas. Her natural skill for hostessing, making every guest feel comfortable, came into its own. The house looked stunning, Christmassy to its core, and everything went smoothly.

The fact that it was probably Flick's last Christmas brought poignancy to every aspect. She was in a wheelchair now, and stayed in the main house for the duration, sleeping in a ground-floor room converted to a bedroom. Rob looked after her the entire time, keeping her comfortable and lifting her gently into her chair, or wherever she needed to be. He and the girls worked together to make sure Flick was always cared for. She was unutterably touched by their devotion, wondering what she had ever done to deserve it.

Whenever she was filled with desperate grief for the life she was leaving, she would remind herself of Rob's words, and concentrate on the fact that she was here, now, and needed to live this moment instead of mourning the last and fearing the next.

That helped her to feel the deepest joy she had ever known.

There was one last shadow in her life, and she had no idea how to banish it. She would think about it soon. Just not right now. Not yet.

The Christmas holidays passed. Exhausted, Flick concentrated on recovering as much strength as she could. She and Rob spent a quiet New Year together, with the girls going off for revels with friends. They didn't stay up until midnight, but toasted the coming year at eight p.m. instead.

'It's New Year somewhere in the world, after all,' Rob said, pouring out the champagne. He handed Flick her glass.

'True!'

They clinked glasses and welcomed in the new year.

'My last year,' Flick said.

'None of that talk,' Rob chided her softly. 'Actually, there's something I wanted to ask you . . .'

'Yes?'

To her surprise, Rob got up and then knelt on the floor on one knee. 'Flick Templeton, will you do me the greatest honour and marry me?'

She gaped at him, astonished. 'You crazy man, what are you doing? Marry you? Are you mad?' She burst out laughing.

'That is not the answer I was hoping for,' Rob said, but his eyes were twinkling.

'Oh darling. You know I adore you. But really . . . get married? Can you imagine me rolling up the aisle in a big white dress and a bouquet, like a dried-out Miss Haversham? I don't think so.'

Rob got up and sat beside her, taking her hand. 'It doesn't have to be like that.'

But Flick's mind was already racing over all the various aspects of their getting married. 'It would create a legal headache too!'

'Ah, well, that's the important thing.'

'I'd have to redo my will . . . and reassure the children about their inheritance.'

'I really don't think they would be concerned that I might take their inheritance.'

Flick was feeling anxious. 'But can you see, darling? It would create all sorts of issues.'

'My God, Flick, this wasn't supposed to stress you out! I thought it might make you happy.' He laughed, stroking her hand gently. 'Look, if you don't want to, we will just stay unmarried.'

Flick shook her head. 'I can't believe I'm saying no to getting married to you.'

Rob thought for a minute. 'You know,' he said, 'it doesn't have to be a legal ceremony. We don't have to do the full church and licence thing. What's the point? You're right, it would cause a whole raft of other issues. So . . . why don't we simply have a little ceremony, with just family, that is our own commitment to one another? Maybe the girls could officiate. We can do it here at Caundle and make it just what we want.'

Flick's heart swelled. 'Yes,' she whispered. 'That's it. That's what I want.' Her eyes filled with tears. 'Nothing huge and formal, just a way to mark what you mean to me.'

'And what you mean to me, darling Flick.' He kissed her. Their love was not about the heat of sex any more, but his kiss still filled her with the delicious potential of it, as well as with the strength of their bond. 'And if that's what you want, then that is what we will do.'

Chapter Thirty

ETTA

1991

It was funny what you could bear when you had to.

Etta had felt as though the world was ending when she realised that her mother was dying. And yet, the world had not ended. It kept turning. Things changed in line with the new reality. Thoughts about travelling and jobs were shunted into the future and she devoted herself instead to her mother.

While they could not live all day and every day in perfect contentment – and there was no getting around the fact that the pain and anxiety made Flick tetchy and difficult at times – Etta and her mother had rarely been in such harmony, and unafraid to express their affection for one another.

And Mary was a revelation. It had been so strange to see her sister again, after all these years. She was tanned now, obviously older, and with an Australian twang to her previously cut-glass accent, but her life clearly suited her. She was calmer and more balanced.

'You guys all think I'm so crazy with the things I do. I know you laugh at yoga and meditation and chanting and all the rest. And you think my diet is bizarre. But I'm telling you, it's the only way to live: at ease with your spirituality. Everyone is going to be doing this one day.'

'I can't see me ever eating lentil shepherd's pie or striking a yoga pose,' Brinsley said thoughtfully. 'But if I do, you'll be the first to know.'

Brinsley had blossomed now that he and Diana were together, and, having been a bit of a recluse, he now seemed to welcome having his family about him.

'This house is big enough for everyone. A place like this ought to have people in it,' he said.

'I agree!' Diana chimed in. 'A house is happier when it's full.'

Diana had gamely got rather into the yoga, getting herself a mat like Mary's, and learning to do her downward dogs. She still preferred her aerobics, done while watching a video, but she was doing her best to support Mary.

For Etta, it was wonderful to have Mary there to help care for their mother and to hug when the tears came and she considered the future without her. To have Rob as well was the icing on the cake.

'Have you talked to Mum about what we discussed?' she asked once, when they were in the cottage kitchen together, washing up after supper. 'In New York?'

Rob shook his head. 'Not yet. I'm waiting for the right time. It didn't feel right over Christmas. She is so incredibly sensitive right now, everything moves her to tears. I want to be completely sure before we talk about something like who your real father might be, and if we should find out or not.'

Etta could see that. There would only be one chance to get it right.

But what if Mum dies before we can talk about it? What then?

The consultant had said that there was a chance that Mum could have some kind of event – an infection or something – that could trigger a rapid decline. What if something happened that meant there was no time left to talk at all?

I don't think I can risk that.

Even though she had chosen Rob to be her father, part of her still longed to know the truth.

Who is my father? And who am I?

Etta walked slowly along the Notting Hill street, looking for the bright red front door in the baby-blue house. She knew which house was Henry Morfield's, having visited a few times when he and Flick were together.

Let's hope he's in.

The door was answered, but not by Henry.

'Charlie!' she exclaimed, surprised.

'Hi, Etta.' Charlie raised his eyebrows in surprise. 'What are you doing here?'

Charlie was just as good-looking as ever, she noticed. Despite their lack of chemistry, he was a hunk, with the American footballer shoulders, and preppy good looks. But now, he had matured, which had made him better looking, if anything.

'I just came to see if your father is in.'

'He's popped out to buy the papers. He'll be back soon. Come on in. Do you want some coffee?'

Charlie made her coffee in the bright kitchen at the back of the house, while he explained that he was lodging temporarily with his father after breaking up with his girlfriend.

'I'm sorry,' Etta said sympathetically. 'I hope it's not too tough.'

'Nah. I mean . . . yes. But it's the right thing for us. She and I weren't suited in the end. So I'm Dad's roomie for now. How about you, Etta? I read somewhere you were going out with Mattie Vaughn. That must have been exciting.'

Mattie Vaughn. Etta got a flash of her New York life and her wild experiences with poor, empty Mattie. That felt like another lifetime and another self. 'I'm single right now,' she said with a laugh. 'And not looking. I've got more important things on at the moment.'

'Oh?' Charlie asked. 'Like what?'

She was wondering how much to tell him when the front door opened and Henry came striding down the hall into the kitchen, a sheaf of newspapers under one arm. He stopped suddenly when he saw Etta, clearly shocked.

'Hello, Henry,' she said, smiling. 'I hope you don't mind my coming to see you. I've something I want to tell you, and something I want to ask you.'

'I see,' Henry said, coming over to kiss her hello. 'Well, I'm happy to help with either of those if I can. And it's lovely to see you, Etta. You look gorgeous. Will you come through to the sitting room?'

Leaving Charlie in the kitchen with the papers, they went through with coffee to the sitting room and Etta took her place on the blue-and-white sofa while Henry sat in an armchair.

'This isn't easy, so I'm just going to say it. First, I have to tell you something. Mum is dying – she has about six months, maybe a year at most.' She saw his expression. 'I know. It's awful. We are all devastated. She is coping with it, but as you can imagine, it's very hard for her.'

'Etta, I'm so sorry,' Henry said, solemn. He sighed. 'Poor Flick. It's so hard to imagine. She's so vibrant.'

'I know.' Etta felt it again: that spike of pain that was still so intense even after all this time. 'Thank you.'

'I'm glad you told me. I really appreciate it.'

'I'm sure you have a lot of questions and we can talk all that through. But first, there's something I want to ask you.'

'Oh yes. The second part of your mission. Ask away.'

'Right.' She fixed him with a steady gaze that hid the fact that her heart was beating faster and her palms growing clammy. 'Henry . . . is there any chance that you might be my father?'

She watched him carefully. His surprise and awkwardness was easy to see. Nonetheless, when he spoke his voice still sounded smooth and composed.

'Now, why would you think that?'

'Because my mother told me that she met you in New York thirty-two years ago. I was born nine months later. It didn't take a genius to work out that there's a possibility that I'm not Jonathan's daughter, and that I am possibly yours. Jonathan more or less told me before he died that he didn't consider himself my father.'

497

'I see.' Henry gazed at her thoughtfully. 'And I take it you haven't asked Flick about this?'

Etta shook her head.

'I'll be candid. She asked me about what happened between us herself, when I bumped into her last year. She seemed shocked when I told her that nothing had happened between us. But she's known since then that you can't be my daughter.'

'I see.' Etta blinked, trying to make sense of this.

Henry continued to look at her. She couldn't read what was going on in his mind. At last, he spoke. 'Nothing would give me more pleasure than finding out you are my daughter. But I'm afraid it's not possible.'

'Really?' Despite herself, Etta was shocked. She had somehow believed that she had a trio of fathers. Jonathan, her adopted father who had brought her up. Rob, her spiritual father who loved her like the father she wanted. And Henry, her biological father. And yet, he was saying it was impossible. 'Why?'

'Simply put, we didn't have sex. It's as brutal as that. I would have liked to but she didn't want to. She was very drunk that night. We were in a bar, and she left with another man. Perhaps she spent the night with him.'

'Who was he?'

'I don't know. He played the piano. She called him Keys. That's all I know. But leaving with him doesn't mean they had sex. I'm not your father so perhaps it was Jonathan after all.'

'Yes, perhaps it was.' She would not tell him about Rob.

'Do you want me to take a test?'

'No. I believe you. But I did want to ask you. Just in case.'

'I'm sorry it's not me. And I hope that's helped you.'

'Yes, it has.'

'I'm sorry you and Flick have not been able to talk about it. I hope you will. I think it would help you both. Now, will you stay to lunch with Charlie and me? There's so much I want to ask you.'

Etta thought for a second. 'Yes. I will, thank you. But there's one more favour I have to ask . . .'

When she returned to Caundle, Etta and Mary were invited for dinner at the cottage, where Rob and Flick announced that they were going to be married. Even when they'd explained that this was a commitment ceremony rather than legal marriage, there was still much excited squealing, especially when Flick explained that she wanted the girls to perform the ceremony.

'It's going to be in the drawing room in the house,' Flick said happily. 'In a few weeks. As soon as we can get everything organised. But you know what Diana is like. We'll only have to mention that we're going to do it and she'll have the flowers in hand the same morning.'

'Oh, it will be beautiful,' Mary said, dabbing at her eyes with a tissue. 'We're all going to be in pieces!'

'I'm so honoured to be asked to marry you both,' Etta said. This was wonderful news that filled her with joy. To balance the misery of Mum's illness and limited life, there was this last blessing to come. She gazed happily at Rob. Then she remembered that there was still a candidate for her biological father – the mysterious piano-playing man in New York. Only Mum knew the truth about that.

Flick had been right about Diana getting everything arranged as quickly as possible. It would be a February wedding.

'How about Valentine's Day?' Diana suggested. 'It seems appropriate.'

'Yes,' Flick agreed. 'I'm not one for St Valentine's Day usually but I'm prepared to make an exception.'

Etta and Mary worked together to write up a ceremony that would have the feel of a 'real' wedding.

'I've been to a load of humanist weddings,' Mary said wisely, 'and I know what to do.'

Etta had to rein in some of Mary's more out-there ideas, reminding her that Mum was actually quite a traditionalist despite her sometimes Bohemian ways. She wasn't going to want anything really unusual.

'We need someone to play the piano!' Mary announced.

'Well, I don't think it should be Caius Knolle,' Etta replied, 'if that's what you're thinking.' Then she went still. A piano player. Keys. Caius. *No. Surely not?*

Mary laughed and went pink. 'I was not thinking that. I was wondering if there was someone in the village who might do it.'

'We can get some names. And perhaps a harpist. There's nothing like a harpist at a wedding.'

*

Etta and Rob were out walking, both wrapped up against the bitter weather. They only managed twenty minutes before they dashed back into the big house and to the warmth of the library fire, where they could defrost.

'You're going to have to tell me all that again, honey,' Rob said, collapsing into a leather library chair. 'My ears were too cold to hear you.'

'I said that Henry Morfield is out of the picture. But that leaves the mysterious piano player, Jonathan, and you.'

'Any idea who the piano player might be?'

'I have a hunch. But there is no way on earth I'm going to ask him. None.'

'Could we just ask Flick?'

'It's so painful for her. I can see all the time that she longs to talk to me about it. But she just can't broach it. So if we can take the answers to her, then that's what we should do.'

'How will we do it?'

'Have you heard of DNA testing?'

'Of course. But it's only available in legal cases, isn't it? It's pretty complex as I understand it. Isn't it used to catch murderers?'

'And in paternity tests.'

'Ah.' Rob nodded slowly. 'I see.'

'And if we have a sample from you, and a sample from Jonathan – his hair or something, or even Mary's hair, or Sam's – then we should either get a result or no result, which will tell its own story.'

'I see your thinking.'

'I did some investigating and I've found a clinic in London who will do a DNA paternity test if we provide samples.'

'And cash.'

'And lots of cash.' Etta smiled at him. 'Would you do it?'

'Of course I will. Whatever they want, I will supply. Just give me the address and I'll be there.'

'Thanks, Rob. I'm going there for my test this week. So as soon as you can get there, they can start the testing.'

'Then I'll go as soon as I can.'

February was bitterly cold that year, and in its little valley, Caundle managed to get deep snow. Flick spent days in bed, keeping warm and getting her strength up for the ceremony. She sent Etta and Mary to London to choose her a dress. They fought their way through snow drifts to the station and took the train to town, spending a lovely day together picking out Mum's gown.

'This is very nice,' the assistant said as she wrapped up the ivory silk dress that they had chosen, and the ivory pashmina embroidered with dozens of silver bugle beads in a swirling pattern.

'It's our mother's wedding dress,' Mary said cheerfully.

'Oh?' The assistant raised her eyebrows. 'There's a story there then.'

'Yes,' Etta said. 'And it's a good one . . .'

'Sad and happy,' Mary added.

'Mostly happy?' the assistant asked as she taped the tissue paper shut. 'I hope so.'

'For now,' Etta said, 'and that's what we're concentrating on.'

She and Mary smiled at each other.

'I've got an appointment,' Etta announced. 'But it shouldn't take long. Shall we meet for lunch afterwards at Dickens and Jones?'

'Sure, if you like. Sounds mysterious, though. Any clues?'

'Nothing to reveal yet. It's a present I've got planned for Mum. You'll find out in good time.'

'Ooh. Exciting.' Mary grinned. 'Don't take too long, I'm starving.'

Etta headed off to the clinic in Harley Street, taking with her the sample of Dad's hair that she'd taken from his old hairbrush, still on the table in his dressing room at Caundle.

A letter came addressed to Etta, and inside was a note from Henry Morfield.

Dear Etta,
Thank you for coming to see me the other day.
I appreciated your visit. I'm glad I was able to clear up
a little more of the situation with your parentage. On
my own behalf, I'm sorry I'm not your father. I would
be immeasurably proud if you were my daughter. As it is,
I hope we do not lose touch. You and Flick and Mary
were very dear to me when I was lucky enough to be
part of your family for a while.

The enclosed letter is for Flick. I want to make my peace
with her in case I don't see her again. Just to tell her what
she meant to me and that I hope she forgives me for any
role I played in any troubles she has.

*Best wishes to you, Etta. I hope to see you again, and
so does Charlie.*
Love, Henry

Etta read it over, holding the second envelope addressed to
Flick that had been folded into her own.

Henry was not her father. She was glad. She was sure that
the letter would help Mum find her peace.

*And when I know the truth, that will be the final piece in
the jigsaw.*

Two weeks later, the snow had cleared, and the temporary
enforced isolation at Caundle Court was lifted. Rob had
driven into town and taken Mary with him. Etta knew her
mother would be alone, and had arranged to go over and
take care of her. The wedding was now only a week away.
Many of the people who had been with them for Christmas
were returning. There was an atmosphere of anticipation in
the house, where chairs and crockery were arriving for the
big day.

Etta let herself in the cottage and found Flick tucked up
on the sofa, reading a book.

In a way, you wouldn't know, she thought, as her mother
sat peacefully, her glasses on, looking quite normal. *But then
again, that could simply be a sign that I've got used to how
she looks now.*

It was not the old Flick who sat there so still. This one
looked older, greyer, thinner and more haggard with the
pain she was suffering. But when she looked up, her eyes

brightening at the sight of her daughter, a broad smile spread across her face. 'Darling! How lovely to see you.'

When they were settled with cups of tea, and had talked over the latest wedding arrangements, Etta knew that the time had come. She hesitated for just a moment and then began.

'Mum, I saw Henry Morfield the other day.'

Flick was startled. 'You did? But why?'

'I wanted to ask him a question. I asked it. And he answered.'

'What question?' There was a frightened look in Flick's eyes.

Etta felt moved by pity. Her mother was haunted by this, that was clear, and unable to find a way to remove the obstacle of it. *I should have raised this with her years ago, and drained the poison when I could.*

'I asked him if he was my father.'

'Then you know,' Mum whispered. Her eyes glistened with tears. 'When did you guess?'

'I think I've always known on some level that Jonathan was not my father,' Etta said softly.

'You must hate me,' Mum said wretchedly.

Etta leaned forward. 'No, Mum! Of course I don't! I know that you didn't plan what happened. You've always loved me no matter what.'

'I shut it out. I shut it all out. I told myself you were Jonathan's child, even though it was clear you weren't. I was afraid that this was why he treated you differently. Imperceptibly. But still differently. And I was afraid that was why he lost his mind.'

'Oh no. But—'

'I know it's unlikely. But I felt guilty. And I knew that in New York, I'd had sex. I thought it must be Henry Morfield because . . . well, shame, I suppose. I thought I had a drunken fling with him and getting pregnant was the only outcome. Later, only recently, I found out there was no drunken fling, not with him. But perhaps someone else.' Mum flushed again, her expression mortified. She whispered. 'I can't even talk about that. But I found out that it wasn't him either.'

'That left one person,' Etta said. She took the letter she had received that morning from her pocket. This was not from Henry Morfield – she would give that to Flick later – but from the Harley Street clinic, who had fast-tracked her results. She passed it to her mother who took it gingerly and scanned it, absorbing the contents. As she did, she went pink and then, by the end, her eyes were glistening. She put the letter on the blanket that covered her, and looked over at Etta, moved. 'So it is him.'

Etta nodded, smiling.

Mum let out a long, shaky breath. 'I've wanted to talk to you about it so much, I didn't want this secret between us before we're parted. And I didn't know how much I needed to be released from all this fear. Obviously I would change nothing. But I so wanted you to be born out of love.'

'And I was,' Etta said softly. 'Wasn't I?'

Mum began to weep. 'Yes. Thank God. You were.'

'Rob is my father.'

Mum nodded, pressing her lips together as tears flowed down her cheeks. 'Yes. You are Rob's daughter. You're ours.'

Etta felt unbearably moved. A sense of great peace came over her. They had said the words that needed to be said. There were no longer secrets between them.

Mum said in a broken voice, 'I thought I'd taken his chance of fatherhood away from him. And all along, he was a father. He is your father.'

'Good. I'm so happy.'

Mum opened her arms to her daughter, and Etta went into her embrace. They wept together, hugging for a very long time.

Chapter Thirty-One
FLICK
1991

The February weather continued bitterly cold but luckily it didn't prevent the people who mattered from getting to the wedding.

Flick stayed in the big house for the few days before, getting her strength up. The night before, they received a call from Gloria to say that there was deep snow in central London and there was no way she would be able to make it.

'I hope you're not too upset,' Diana said as they had supper in the small cosy dining room, a roaring fire keeping the cold at bay.

'I'm not at all,' Flick said. 'I will never be able to make my peace with Mother, she would never allow it. So I am finding peace *around* her instead. I expect nothing and that's what I will get. It's because she is a frightened old woman who can't bear facing her own mortality. And to be honest, do I really want another woman in a wheelchair stealing my limelight?'

Diana laughed. 'She would. Completely. She would certainly wear white.'

'She would feel compelled to tell me why all my weddings are so disappointing, and all the many ways the groom hasn't lived up to her high standards. Again.'

Diana shook her head. 'Oh Gloria.'

Flick shrugged. 'What can you do? You only get one mother.'

'Thank goodness there aren't too many like yours.' Diana laughed. 'So. Are you looking forward to tomorrow?'

'Of course. It's going to bring me my heart's desire,' Flick said simply. 'I'm going to be committed to Rob – although, in fact, we always were.'

'I wondered exactly what the story was.'

'It's a long, slow love story. It's taken us thirty years to be together.'

'To be married.'

'Well, actually we were always married.'

Diana looked bemused. 'I don't understand, darling. What do you mean?'

'We were joined together for life at the time we met. In Etta.'

Diana stared at her, and then realisation dawned and she said wonderingly, 'My goodness! So that's how it is! It explains so much!'

Flick nodded. 'She's our daughter. I hoped it was true and now I know for sure that it is.'

'Oh Flick. I'm so happy for you. What a marvellous wedding present.'

'And it was Etta herself who gave it to me.' Flick smiled. 'You know people joke that they could die happy if they had just one thing? Well, I can die happy now. I mean that. I don't want to go, but when I do, I'll feel complete.'

'That's wonderful.' Diana sounded choked.

Flick felt her own eyes moisten. 'If we manage to get through tomorrow without blubbing, it will be a miracle!'

A harpist played beautiful, rippling Handel to the small congregation who sat in the drawing room on their little gilt chairs.

Outside, Samuel bent down and lifted Flick out of her wheelchair. She felt his easy strength as she held her bouquet of winter roses, the other arm around Samuel's neck.

'You look beautiful,' he said, and kissed her cheek. 'Come on then, Flick. Let's get you married.'

As Sam carried her in, her family and friends turned their smiling faces to her. Dear Brinsley and Diana. Prue and her husband and family. And there was Edmund, his golden hair now white, but his blue eyes as bright as ever. Henry, smiling, with handsome Charlie. She was glad that he had written that letter. It had meant something to her. She was glad that nothing had ever happened between them, and now they could be friends. She had been able to invite him to be a part of her day. She could see old friends, dear colleagues. Not many, just those who had walked with her along the path and meant something to her. So many familiar faces.

And, at the end of the little aisle, her two dear daughters. *Mary. My beloved first-born girl.*

She had thought for years that she might lose Mary for ever. To drugs or to accident or to the fissure between them that stemmed from that horrible misunderstanding. But they had made their peace. Mary had found her own path and now she was a strong woman on her own terms, living the life she wanted. She would go back to Australia, Flick was sure, and continue to blossom in the sun. Who knew what waited for her? It would be good, though.

Etta. Darling Etta.

Dark where Mary was fair, soulful where Mary was spirited. But Etta was no slouch. She had character. She was learning to trust herself. She would need those things when Flick was no longer here to support her.

And what a support she has been to me. I could not ask for more. She brought me all the peace I needed. And I know she will always be cared for. Not just by my family, but also by that man. The one waiting for me with that smile on his face. He looks so handsome in that lovely suit, so strong and brave and true. And oh, what a smile! I want to see that smile and hear that voice when I travel into eternity.

Etta's father. How happy we were when we knew for sure.

My husband.

My true love.

Rob.

Epilogue

ETTA

1992

It was St Valentine's Day and Etta had bought a bunch of winter roses at the florist's on her way to the station that morning.

'Your boyfriend like flowers, does he?' asked the florist, thinking he was being funny.

'He does, actually, but they're not for him. They're for my mother.'

'Each to their own,' the florist said, clearly not wanting to ask more. People didn't give parents bouquets on Valentine's Day, and he evidently thought that Etta was a bit odd.

I don't owe you an explanation, Etta thought as she headed for the underground.

Charlie met her at Waterloo. He had been into the office very early so that he could take the rest of the day off for Etta. She had found a card and a beautiful little gift from him on the pillow beside her when she woke.

'Thank goodness it's not as cold as last year,' he said as they went to get the train. We might have had trouble getting there if it had been.'

'Nothing will be like last year,' Etta said. 'Do you remember?'

Charlie took her hand. 'It was a beautiful day. I'll never forget it.' He kissed her gently.

'I'm so glad you were there.'

They headed for their train and found their seats. Charlie bought them cups of coffee from the trolley buffet as it came through: horrible stuff but it did the trick. They both read as the train trundled out towards Dorset, Charlie checking copy and Etta reading a film script. She had not returned to New York but had found a job in an up-and-coming production company which she was enjoying very much. She and Charlie had idly talked about working in the US at some point but right now, they were happy as they were. Etta had inherited the Bloomsbury flat, and that was where they now lived together, in the kind of easy bliss Etta had always wanted.

Funny how I thought there was no chemistry between us. I could not have been more wrong about that!

When the train stopped at their station, Etta could see Uncle Brinsley on the platform, well wrapped up in a big tweed coat and an extravagantly long scarf, blinking owlishly as he looked out for Etta and Charlie, then waving when he saw them.

'The wanderers are home!' he called. 'Come on, wanderers, let's get you in the car! It's freezing out here.'

On the drive back to Caundle, Etta quickly filled her uncle in with all the news. Mary was back in Australia and had got herself a new job which she was very excited about. Etta's job was going very well. She and Charlie were planning a trip out to Australia sometime in the next year to travel, sightsee and spend some time with Mary.

'That all sounds excellent. Now, do you want to stop on the way?' Brinsley said as they turned into the driveway to Caundle. 'Or come back later? Diana's got a lovely lunch on the go, I expect it's nearly ready.'

'Let's stop now?' she said to Charlie. 'And then it's done?' Charlie nodded.

'Now, please, Uncle Brin. If that's okay with you.'

'Of course it is. And take your time. I'll be fine with the heating and the car radio.'

Instead of heading to the main house, he turned right and headed down to the little church that stood within its low walls in Caundle's grounds. At the gate, he pulled over so that Etta and Charlie could get out.

They walked hand in hand into the churchyard and over to where Flick lay, in her pretty plot. She was not beside Jonathan but she was not far away either. This was where she had wanted to be: home, at Caundle. Close to all those she knew and loved.

When they reached the grave, Etta said, 'Oh, they've finally put the gravestone up. That's good.'

The white marble headstone had plain lettering simply stating her mother's name and the dates of her birth and death. She had had four months of happiness with Rob, despite her worsening condition, before breathing her last in her own bed, in her cottage, with Mary and Etta beside her, and Rob holding her hand, telling her over and over that he loved her.

After she had gone, he had wept, and they had left him with her for a while to say his last words to her and hug her for the final time.

Rob came back and forth to Caundle now. He had needed to grieve and that meant travelling for him, and going back to the States. Etta had been afraid that he might not come back at all, now Mum was gone, but he had. And he said he always would. He would never leave Flick alone for too long. And he wanted to stay close to Etta too, of course.

Charlie, holding Etta's hand, said, 'I'm going to leave you for just a little bit. So you can be alone with her. I'll be over there. Just call me when you're ready.'

'Thanks, Charlie.' She smiled gratefully at him. He always seemed to know what she wanted.

As he strolled away, she turned back to her mother's grave, brimming with a bittersweet mixture of love and sorrow. She would never stop missing Mum, that was impossible. Even now, she sometimes woke with a start thinking she could hear her mother calling her before remembering with a sinking heart that she was no longer here. Mum kept popping up in dreams, though, which was a comfort. She often wanted to tell Etta jokes, as though she was having a real laugh in the afterlife with some like-minded souls and getting some great new material. Etta hoped so. It was a comfort to think of Mum at peace, out of pain, and laughing, as she had so loved to do.

She looked at the pale ivory winter roses. They were so delicate and pretty; the flowers that Mum had carried at her wedding a year ago.

Etta remembered it so clearly.

She and Mary had conducted the little service. Mum and Rob had read their vows to one another and exchanged rings. They had sung Mum's favourite hymn, 'Lord of All Hopefulness'. That had been hard to get through but they had stayed strong.

Then, when they were pronounced husband and wife, Rob had picked Mum up, her pashmina draping down behind her like a train, and carried her back down the aisle. He had been so obviously proud of his bride. Mum had laughed like a girl, waving her bouquet at everyone as she went.

People were crying. Etta was almost too choked to cry. Mary was clapping beside her and then everyone joined in. It had been beautiful.

And afterwards, in her speech to the room after the wedding breakfast, Mum said, 'A very clever journalist called Chase Dupone once wrote a piece about me in a magazine. He changed my life as a result, in all sorts of ways. He didn't mean to, but he did. That's the power of the written word, something I devoted my life to, like him. Inspired by him, in some ways, because he saw something in me worth noticing. He's dead now and the world is poorer for it. Because of him, I was once known – ridiculously – as the most miserable heiress in Britain. And now . . . well, I'm the happiest woman in the world. So I'd like to raise a toast to Chase, and all he brought about.'

They had toasted Chase Dupone.

'And I want to thank my beautiful family, who stuck by me through so much. Brinny and Prue and Diana and Sam. I love you all, especially my precious girls, Mary and Etta. I'm so deeply proud of you both. I know I was a curious sort of mother and thank you for loving me back despite it all. And of course, there's Rob. My touchstone. A man I am so proud to call my husband.' Mum had lifted her glass to the cheers in the room. 'To Rob!'

'Flick, you crazy girl.' Rob had pulled her tenderly into his arms and gently hugged her. He whispered something in her ear and she laughed, her thin face transformed with joy. Then he kissed her, her frail arms going around his neck, to more and louder cheers.

Etta had been so glad on the deepest level that Mum had found her peace at last.

Now, she put the bunch of flowers down below the headstone.

'Happy anniversary, Mum. Your wedding was the most glorious day. I'm glad you had your Rob for a while. We miss you. We love you. I love you. I wish I'd said it more often, but I know you know.' She blew a kiss to the headstone. 'I'll be back soon.'

Etta turned and waved to Charlie, who began to walk towards her.

'Come on, Etta,' he said when he reached her. He put his arm around her. 'Let's go home.'

'Yes.' She turned away from the church to see Caundle Court, magnificent against the frosty background of the park and woodland, smoke curling from its many chimneys. Uncle Brinsley's car was idling by the church, as he waited to take them there. It would be warm and welcoming inside. Diana would be waiting with lunch in the panelled dining room, the fires would be blazing, and Etta knew she would sense Mum there – as a young woman, terrorised by her outrageous mother, desperate to escape; as a wife and mother, trying to find a way to be a different kind of parent to her children; as an older single woman, accomplished in her work but bruised by life and loss, seeking peace and healing, and a home to belong to. And then, at last, reconciled to everything that had been, and was to come.

It's a place to be born, and a place to live and a place to die. It's my home too. And it always will be.

'Yes, come on,' she said to Charlie, whose nose was pink with cold. She leaned her head into his shoulder. 'I'm ready now. Let's go home.'

Acknowledgements

I would like to thank everyone at Pan Macmillan for their hard work, support and amazing input. Special thanks to Katie Loughnane, who is a dream editor. This story would be nowhere near as strong without her perceptive comments and sensitive insight, all delivered with so much kindness and efficiency. Thanks also to my copyeditor Lorraine Green, whose editing and encouragement is, as ever, invaluable. Thanks to Justyna Bielecka for her excellent proofreading. I would especially like to thank Lucy Hale, who has been a huge support over the last few years. And nothing could be done without the wonderful people in editorial, marketing, sales, publicity, production and design: Sanjana Samaddar, Maddie Thornham, Grace Rhodes, Stuart Dwyer, Chloe Davis, Holly Reed and Neil Lang. Thank you all for your brilliance, creativity and dedication.

I'm always hugely in debt to my wonderful agent, Lizzy Kremer, and everyone at David Higham, especially Orli Vogt-Vincent and Maddalena Cavaciuti. Thank you all so much for the amazing work you do for me, I am so grateful.

ACKNOWLEDGEMENTS

I have had so much support from my wonderful friends and fellow writers, from my local community, booksellers, festival goers and of course, my wonderful readers, whose encouragement means everything. Thank you all.

Thank you to my family – especially Barney and Tabby – and the friends who have held me up through all of this. I could not do any of it without you.